CHANGING PARTNERS

Vicky Martin

St. Martin's Press
New York

Also by Vicky Martin

The Windmill Years

Copyright © 1979 by Vicky Martin
All rights reserved. For information, write:
St. Martin's Press, Inc. 175 Fifth Ave., New York, N.Y. 10010
Manufactured in the United States of America

Library of Congress Cataloging in Publication Data

Martin, Vicky.
  Changing partners.

  I. Title.
PZ4.M38445Ch   1980   [PR6063.A7315]   823'.914
ISBN 0-312-12965-3   79-26743

FOR TOM

PART ONE

CHAPTER ONE

Clive Holden, late as usual, sprang up the flight of stairs towards his office, his shoulders still hunched against the rain which had been waiting outside the tube station. He pushed open the glass door and burst thankfully into the warmth of the reception area, shaking his big, wet head and taking off his raincoat as the familiar smell of the place, exaggerated after being shut up for the weekend, enveloped him. He walked down the corridor, passing his secretary's office and going into his own. He hung his raincoat and umbrella in the cupboard and leaned towards the mirror to smooth his hair. It was thick and dark and the rain had made it curl. The reflection was of a round, attractive face with big features, looking tired now, looking older than his twenty-eight years. His head ached mildly. Clive yawned and sat down in the leather armchair, making his ritual vow to drink less. Remembering small moments of the previous evening, he smiled and leaned forward to stab at the intercom button. 'Mary?'

There was a metallic acknowledgement.

'Oh, you're in. Pity. I hoped you'd be late. I feel like being nasty to someone!' He heard her laughter distorted by the machine. 'Bring me a coffee, love, and remind me about this morning.' He leaned back as he waited, turning his head to the tall windows which overlooked Conduit Street. A sudden burst of rain spattered them insultingly. This wet and miserable March day was typical of the whole winter of seventy two/seventy three, Clive thought, but the bleakness outside enhanced the comfort of this office. Clive had been articled to Bonnington's, a long-established firm of solicitors, for almost ten years. He was a partner now. He knew he was lucky to be with such a reputable firm and that from now on advancement would be slow but predictable, promising a secure but

1

reasonably successful future. Thousands of such Monday mornings, he thought, and headaches and making this effort to shape myself into a serious frame of mind for the week . . . He sighed and his mind wandered like a disobedient child. He thought of last night's party and laughed aloud.

Mary came in, a pretty, dark-haired girl with long legs. She put the cup of coffee and its quite unrelated saucer and a clean ashtray on Clive's desk and opened the diary. 'Two appointments this morning. At ten, a Mrs Caroline Boyd. Divorced. Wants a solicitor in London. Rachel Finch recommended you and I imagine they are much the same type.' She paused to let this observation sink in and Clive pulled the coffee towards him. Steam curled up invitingly. 'At eleven yet another girl for an interview.' Now her tone was reproving, implying that Clive had been deliberately rejecting the previous applicants because he didn't want Mary to leave. 'I left an hour between the two appointments because the Mrs Boyd types are always late and I'll go ahead and give the girl the standard test, shall I?'

'Yup.' He sipped the coffee and burnt his mouth. 'What was her letter like? Any hope?'

'Yes.' Mary took a sheet of paper from under the diary. 'She can spell and she's been working for a solicitor in Godalming for almost a year but she is rather young. Nineteen.'

Clive attempted the coffee again. His eyes slid down Mary's neat body. 'Why are you leaving? Don't get married. You'll be bored and miserable . . . all married women are miserable. What about the endless pathetic procession we have through here? How can you be such an optimist?' He touched her arm with one finger, watching her, head a little on one side, brown eyes narrowed. Had she been nearer he would have put an arm round her, expressing affection and familiarity.

Mary smiled, thinking that he could still make her feel it when she looked like that. She had worked for Clive for five years. She had watched him build up his circle of clients, using his considerable charm to advantage; she had liked him at the initial

2

interview and she liked him now but in the early weeks she had begun to take the constant attention quite seriously. She had been twenty-two then, experienced enough to recognize and appreciate Clive's considerable physical appeal but old enough, also, to see that his charm was brought out for every woman who came into the office. She had hesitated and the moment passed. They began to know each other too well. Now she knew Clive absolutely, his strengths and weaknesses; knew he had not advanced as quickly as he had hoped, that he was not quite solid enough to go to the top of this profession, that he never had quite enough money to live the kind of life he needed. More than once she had covered up for him when he bent the rules a little. He was a charming man, a lazy man, and he adapted his principles to suit the situation. He was often genuinely concerned for his clients and would exercise skill and stubborness on their behalf or he could lose interest.

'You're looking at me like God Almighty!' He imitated her Irish accent perfectly.

'Miss Henderson rang just before you came in, about the will, of course, and she wants you to go and see her when you can. Andrew is in court this morning with Mr Collins about the three endorsements and the deeds to Wilton Crescent have finally arrived, so we can get on with that.'

'Thrilling stuff indeed.'

'And on Friday afternoon John Hampton rang. You look as if you need a couple of aspirins.'

'Took some before I left. I expected to be disappointed. . . .'

'I wondered how long it would take you to hint! Happy Birthday.' She took a package from the large pocket of her cardigan.

Clive grinned and destroyed the tissue paper with his big hands, uncovering a box of small cigars. 'How did you guess that I've just given up smoking?'

'Like hell.'

He laughed. 'Thank you, Mary.'

As she left the room, closing the door behind her, he began to

3

organize himself, putting on the horn-rimmed glasses he used for reading and driving and giving an air of seriousness. He read the letter from the girl who signed herself Katherine Neale and liked the sound of her. He read the draft of Miss Henderson's will and then he thought about Caroline Boyd. Clive had handled too many divorces in the past year. He could picture this woman if she were one of Rachel's friends. Fairly tough. Thirties. Attractive. Bouncing back into it all, wanting to talk about herself, wanting attention and sympathy. Clive could be a very good listener. Expertly projecting the sympathy he quite genuinely felt at the time. He was extremely successful with women clients, with all women, attracting them without having to try very hard. They were drawn to his air of masculinity and the quite false impression he gave of being able to handle anything.

Clive anticipated the week ahead. His days would be filled with intimate slices of other people's lives, their struggles to buy houses or businesses, to side-step the less serious aspects of law-breaking, to uncouple their marriages and try not to damage their children. A strange profession, at times melancholy, at times fascinating, especially in court. But Clive was aware this morning that, in the ten years he had worked for Bonnington's, he had not lived up to his own expectations. He was a disappointment to the Clive who at eighteen had come here, flying his optimism and his academic success like a flag.

The telephone on his desk rang. 'John Hampton for you, Mr Holden.'

'Put him on. Morning, John.'

'Morning. Just wanted to say how pleased we are to have those two new clients. They've invested considerable sums of money . . . You should pick up a nice commission, Clive.'

'Glad to hear it.' Each time John Hampton rang Clive worried a little less. The investment consultancy firm seemed to be proving itself. Perhaps it wasn't such a gamble after all.

In her office Mary stared at Clive's door, her face serious. In some ways, she thought, she would be glad to go. For five years she had lived with the fear of disaster in the back of her mind.

Kate Neale was afraid of missing trains. She entered the carriage in a flustered rush, slammed the door and sat down, folding her jacket and putting her handbag on the seat beside her which was hideously patterned and slightly bristly to the touch. Then she sat back, embarrassed by her unnecessary panic, and examined the long carriage. It was almost empty. Rows of seats for two and three. At the far end some whispering schoolboys, exploding into bursts of guilty laughter; an elderly man with a briefcase on his lap sitting opposite Kate and trying not to fall asleep. She watched him for a few moments, fascinated by his closing eyelids, but nothing could divert her from her own nervousness. The eyelids opened. He looked at Kate and she felt obliged to give him a smile but only for an instant. She didn't want to talk. She turned her attention to the window as the train came to life beneath her and the station slid away.

The railway line curved out of the town, through the small industrial area and then through fields and a wet little village. A station flashed past too quickly for her to identify it and she swore softly and sat forward to be ready for the next. Although she had made this journey to London before and had asked the man at the ticket barrier, still she needed more reassurance that this was the right train. It infuriated her that she should be so anxious about this perfectly normal situation but her anxiety was a fact and had to be dealt with. It seemed that her friends handled their lives with far more confidence and skill. Or was it just that they hid their feelings better? David had said it was that, explaining them, explaining life, showing Kate herself, making her thoughtfulness, her nervousness, signs of an interesting depth. At the beginning that was, when she believed him without question. Later, when she knew him well enough to let the real Kate come out and speak, to reveal the wicked sense of humour and the cynicism which sat so uneasily on a nineteen-year-old, when she was angry and had bisected him like a

5

biology student, he had been scornful. 'It doesn't help, this end-less discussion of people, giving names to all feelings. You'll end up as a kind of life critic sitting on the edge, sniping and destroy-ing others and achieving nothing yourself!' His voice was clear in her head but David himself was gone from her life, taking the love and the argument, leaving her quite bewildered, only half adult, needing to break away from home but lacking the confi-dence.

The train slowed, vibrated, stopped, its electrical heartbeat suddenly dead. It was Three Bridges Station and Kate sat back with relief. Now, as long as the train was on time, she could find her way from Victoria to Conduit Street without too much worry.

'Let me come with you, Kate,' her mother had said, several times, demonstrating clearly that she had little faith in Kate's competence.

'I'd rather go alone. I'd feel stupid taking my mother to an interview.'

'Well, I could lurk outside and pretend I was nothing to do with you.'

They had both laughed, the same attractive sound, but Kate knew her mother was longing to be confided in and she had to make some excuse and leave the room, unable to talk but equally unable to watch her mother's anxious, unsatisfied curi-osity. If she had tried to explain why she wanted this job in London she would have had to talk about David and herself and it would have had to be a censored version which would not make sense. What could she say? 'For one autumn and one winter he delighted me, lifting me out of my uncomfortable, long-extended childhood, surprising me into feeling love for him, doubly intense because it came so late and because I had never let anyone get close before. And then, knowing that he was preparing to put me aside, I said it first! Now I am desperately trying to arm myself with a whole new life, thinking it won't hurt so much if I have a new job to absorb me, London all round me.'

Kate was an only child, born to Ben and Gabriel Neale after eight years of marriage, and three miscarriages. They were so alike, Kate and her mother, it was as if Gabriel had reproduced on her own. The same small-boned, boyish body, the same eyes, not large but brilliantly blue, jewel-like in an otherwise unremarkable face, the same mouse-brown English hair. Kate even stood as her mother did, very straight, back arched slightly as if to make the most of what little bosom she had, stood like the dancer she had once thought to be. From her father Kate had taken his shyness which concealed the sharp sense of humour, enchanting or cruel. She frequently lacked the courage to say the things which bubbled up in her mind when she was among strangers but at home she and Ben were a double act and too often Gabriel was their target.

'Do let me come with you, Kate' Gabriel had said again that morning, yearning to shield Kate, knowing the extent of her vulnerability.

David had said, 'Sooner or later you've got to get out. Your shell is damaging and unhealthy and the longer you stay at home the thicker it grows.'

'I'd much rather go alone.' Kate's tone had been apologetic. If she thought before she spoke she was kind, far too kind, wanting the world to be happy. 'It's not as if this is my first interview, is it? Or even my first job. I'd picture you hovering outside and it would make me nervous.' She had looked away from Gabriel's disappointment, promising to ring and report the result of the interview and her mother had been outwardly satisfied, lighting the first cigarette of her day and dropping pieces of bacon rind to her imploring dachshunds.

Two women got into Kate's carriage at Crawley with two small children. The women were young and plump, about Kate's age she guessed, and they studied Kate briefly with elaborately decorated eyes, noting her small, untouched face, her quiet clothes, before they lost interest. They took sweets and cigarettes from

7

their large plastic handbags and the children leaned forward and fidgeted and implored until the sweets were unwrapped and put into their mouths. Kate, disconcerted by their wide-eyed attention, re-read the letter from Bonnington's, opened her clean new A to Z map of London and decided to walk if the train wasn't late, up Buckingham Palace Road and half-way down the Mall and left into St James's Street. She closed the map and nervousness throbbed in her stomach as she watched the mysterious and constantly changing reflection of her own face in the train window, looked through it at the backs of terraced houses with their small, optimistic gardens and washing-lines. It began to rain. A soft sad drizzle. Umbrellas blossomed after Gatwick where the rain was heavier. Kate saw small parks and people with dogs, cars caught at level crossings, and she found it strange to watch people for a few moments and then move out of their lives for ever. How many people that she might be able to love would she pass in the street and never speak to?

'You can't keep every casual aquaintance in your life!' David had said disinterestedly when Kate tried to explain.

'I don't mean that. I don't want to know everyone. I'm just afraid I might not meet the people I need or meet them too late.'

'You get everything backwards. Life is deliberate. You meet and know the ones you need, the ones who appeal. Others you discard. Love isn't really planned in heaven, you know.'

'Don't be so bloody damning,' Kate had snapped. 'You refuse to take seriously any idea that I have. If it's your thought, because you're supposed to be such a clear thinker, then it's worthy of discussion!'

It had been like that for the past month, making her think that, even if David hadn't so abruptly removed himself from her life, they couldn't have gone on together. Why, then, was life without him so desolate?

South Croydon signal box slid by like an oval spaceship. The station had frivolous wooden trimmings; the rails made silver intersecting patterns and there were rain drops on the window

8

like angry insects; Battersea Power Station was an elephant on its back. Over the river and into Victoria and Kate stood up, pulled on her jacket, and walked with the other people up the platform to the barrier. Her ticket was warm from her hand. She moved with the crowd out of an opening into the street and she paused, surprised to have been delivered like this into the centre of London.

'Mrs Boyd is here,' Mary said and Clive was startled, so deeply involved had he been in the wording of the Mather contract. It was 10.15.

'Thank you, Mary.' He got up and came round to the front of his desk and he was in the centre of the room when Mary held the door open to allow a tall woman to enter. The impact of the woman's face made it necessary for Clive to look at her for a few moments before he spoke. In fact it was she who spoke first.

'I'm sorry I'm late. The traffic is terrible.' The voice belonged. It was gentle. She was dressed expensively but the effect was untidy as if she had hurried or the rain had flustered her. As he shook her hand Clive saw how very tall she was, her eyes above his.

'Please don't worry, Mrs Boyd. I know it's impossible to make precise appointments on a wet Monday morning.' He indicated the chair. 'Do sit down. Would you like some coffee?'

'Yes, I would. Thank you.' She sat in the chair which was positioned to face Clive's desk diagonally and she unbuttoned her cream raincoat, crossing her legs in their long leather boots. She pulled the silk scarf from round her neck and crumpled it carelessly on to her lap as Clive sat down in his chair and pressed the intercom switch and asked Mary for two coffees. He sat a little closer to his desk and looked at Caroline Boyd again. His first impression still held. Her face, with its large, even features, was quite beautiful in the sense Clive thought of the word. Not a modern face. A face full of secrets . . .

She opened her handbag and took out cigarettes, extending

9

the packet to Clive. 'Oh, you'll like him,' Rachel had said, and she had laughed. 'He manoeuvred me through the divorce quite expertly. Rather like a gynæcologist. But he's not all bedside manner. He's fun . . . Oh, you'll like him, Caroline.'

Clive shook his head at the cigarette packet. 'No, thank you. I've managed to get on to these small cigars.'

She had difficulty making her lighter work and Clive came round his desk and lit her cigarette for her. As he stood close to her for a few moments he could sense her nervous energy. She wore some light, expensive scent. He tried to guess her age. She was a woman rather than a girl but she was younger than he had expected her to be. His own age? A little older? She had the kind of dignified beauty which would not disappear with age but she did not use her looks at all. She seemed quite unconcerned with the impression she had made on Clive and yet, he guessed, she must realize it.

'Did you have to come far?'

'South Kensington.' Caroline sat back in her chair, inhaling smoke thankfully and making an effort to control the restless wanderings of her hands. She had detected Clive's interest and, although she gave no sign of response, it pleased her. Still quivering after a divorce which should have been amicable but had ended very bitterly, she found herself hoarding all admiration. She couldn't respond to it but she needed it anyway. 'I have been renting a flat for the last six months. I didn't think I would need a car, living in the centre of London as I do, but after this winter I think I was wrong. It's rained ever since I moved in last October.'

He smiled sympathetically. 'And this month has started out the worst of the lot.'

'Grey-water March. Wasteland of the year.' She smiled in return, settling down now. 'I can't remember who said it but it fits this year, doesn't it? In the country it wouldn't matter. There's always something new to see . . . In Hampshire now there would be daffodils and primroses.' She paused. 'Do you like London, Mr Holden?'

'I've never thought about it,' Clive said truthfully. 'I belong here so absolutely that it's never occurred to me to live anywhere else. I've been here all my life. I get panicky if exposed to a larger area of green than Hyde Park.'

She laughed politely, studying him and liking his face. He was not a tall man but he was powerfully built, his shoulders and body seeming too wide and strong for rather short legs. He projected a soothing air of being able to handle life, she thought.

Mary came in with a round tray. This time the cups and saucers matched and there were teaspoons, biscuits and sugar lumps. Caroline thanked her and stubbed out the cigarette. She stirred two lumps of sugar into her cup. Until this last year she had always felt she was rather too fat but a year of sleeping badly, of deep uncertainty and fear of the future had changed that.

'Well,' Clive said as Mary withdrew. 'how can I help you, Mrs Boyd? You need a solicitor in London, I gather?'

'Yes. I am divorced.' She thought how smoothly it came out now. Almost without feeling. 'My ex-husband made over a sum of money to me. I was going to invest it but I've hesitated because I couldn't decide where or how or even if I would stay in England. I have no advisors because I didn't want to be connected with any of the people Harry used. They were his personal friends. They have looked after his family for years. I find myself not only without a husband but somehow I've lost my doctor and dentist and bank manager too!' She smiled to lighten the words and took out another cigarette, This time the lighter worked. 'Now, at last, I know what I want. I've found a small antique shop down past World's End. I want to buy it and run it. I've talked to the owner. I used to know her quite well years ago when I was in the business. I should like to put all the money Harry gave me into this.' She finished quite firmly as if expecting Clive not to take the idea seriously.

'Do you have children, Mrs Boyd?'

'No.' The word was flat. She looked past Clive towards the tall, wet windows and she tucked a stray piece of fair hair back into the loose coil at the nape of her neck. It was her hair, escaping in wisps and curls round her forehead and ears which gave her the rather charming air of untidiness, Clive thought.

'I have almost nothing to show for my seven years of marriage,' she said softly and then smiled apologetically. 'Do forgive me . . . lately I find myself saying rather maudlin things. It's just that today is my birthday, Mr Holden, and thirty is rather a shock! I sat on the top of a bus coming here and realized that I am less sure of myself and what I want from life now than I was at twenty! That's not much to show for ten years, is it?'

'I know exactly how you feel. It's my birthday too. I did my thinking this morning on a tube, not a bus, but I reached much the same conclusion!'

There was a short silence and they registered the liking between them.

'It's actually your birthday today?' she said.

'Yes.'

It was an extraordinary piece of good luck, he thought, looking at her big, sweet mouth. He wanted to ask her to lunch. They shared a birthday. What could be more natural?

'Let's go over this idea, Mrs Boyd. Have you thought how long you intend to run the shop? It could pay you to operate as an individual. Or you could be a partner. If it's a company already, of course, you could buy it ready made . . . And have you discussed a price? There is great danger in this sort of venture of being under-capitalized and not allowing yourself enough money for living expenses. Is it the whole building you want to buy or merely the shop?'

'The whole building. It's on a corner, the shop front in the New Kings Road. A basement storeroom, a ground-floor showroom with a small workroom behind and two floors above where I can live.' She sat forward in her chair, becoming far more animated. 'The shop is very much one woman's personal taste at

12

the moment. I'd like to keep it that way. It doesn't carry enormously expensive things. Some pine. Some china. Some nice old glass. I won't tie up huge sums of money in stock but go for pretty and interesting things. I know a bit about English porcelain. The shop is a success now and I don't see why it shouldn't go on being so.'

'Where exactly is it in the Kings Road? I have a friend who's an estate agent. He could have a look and give us an opinion as to the price . . .'

'It's on the corner of Meadwell Street.'

Clive laughed. 'How extraordinary. Michael Redford, another friend, runs his business from the Fulham Road end of Meadwell Street. Now, did you say it was a company?'

'I'm not sure. What are the advantages?'

They talked for a further half hour. Caroline decided she liked him, his manner and his face and his smile and she was pleased to find herself reacting to a man even on this superficial level. She had developed a habit recently of watching herself, afraid that the cauterization of divorce might be permanent. Having loved Harry and then ceased to love him, having felt the love twist into near hatred and now a blank, it was hard to believe she would ever be able to go through the whole rigmarole again.

When the clock in Mary's office struck eleven they had discussed all they could. Clive was to ask Stephen Jones to value the property. Caroline had told him that her money was at present on deposit and could be redeemed at a month's notice, Clive had formed an opinion of a vulnerable woman who was nevertheless basically strong. She was self-possessed despite her unhappiness. She had smoked four cigarettes during the meeting, abandoning each one when it was half-smoked. As she stood up to leave, knotting the belt of her raincoat, Caroline was feeling considerably happier than she had felt for some time. Clive Holden had not dismissed the idea as absurd. She felt he would help, that she would get the shop, have a home again, work and interest and some direction in life. She held out her hand. 'Thank you, Mr Holden. I'll wait to hear from Mr Jones then.'

'Yes, and I'll ask him to get a move on.' He went with her to the door. 'There is one more thing, Mrs Boyd.' He hesitated, not wanting to sound smooth. 'I do like to get to know my clients right from the beginning. I find it helps in a lot of ways . . . and it's such a coincidence that we share a birthday. I wonder . . . could you possibly lunch with me today? I would make it later in the week but I know I won't be free.'

She was surprised; he saw it in her eyes, watched her try to make up her mind. She thought: Why the hell not? I like him. I can ring Jill . . .

'Thank you very much. As it happens I have a few things to look at this morning in this area. I could stay for lunch.' She looked round for a clock. 'It's quite early, isn't it?'

'Eleven-fifteen. Do you like fish?'

'Yes.'

'Could we meet at Bentley's in Swallow Street at one?'

'Yes, I know it.' She moved on towards the door and as she passed the second tall window she looked out, feeling some kind of last remark was necessary. 'Perhaps our birthday won't be so bad after all. The sun's shining!'

Clive watched her walk through Mary's office, and as she left Caroline glanced down at the girl who sat waiting in a chair by the door, hands in her lap, feet twisted round one another. A very young, thin girl who looked up at Caroline as she passed.

Mary went into Clive's office and closed the door. 'Well, a lovely surprise on a wet Monday morning she was! Is she nice with it? I hope not!'

'Fascinating. What an extraordinary variety of friends Rachel has.'

'The girl is here. Katherine Neale. She was early and I've given her a test and she's very good. Fast and accurate. She's shy but competent I should think. Shall I show her in?'

'Please, and afterwards I'd like to speak to Stephen Jones and

14

this contract seems okay if you want to get started on it.'

He was still thinking of Caroline when Mary ushered in the girl. Clive saw that she was small, built like a boy with long, slight limbs, her face a pale triangle. 'Do sit down, Miss Neale.'

'Thank you.' The voice was too deep for such a small girl and rather husky. She sat very straight in the chair, knees together, handbag on her lap, tucking her fine, straight hair behind her ears and watching Clive with very bright blue eyes. His mind wandered. He could still smell Caroline's scent.

'I see you have worked in a solicitor's office before, for a year. Was that your first job?'

'Yes, I went straight to Mr Boscombe after I finished at the secretarial college. Actually it's a very quiet little firm. Mostly wills and people buying houses and Mr Boscombe gets sleepy after lunch but I think I've picked up quite a lot.' She spoke very seriously, remembering what her father had said. 'You've got to put yourself across, Katy. This man doesn't know you at all. You'll have about ten minutes to hand him a good impression.'

'And what makes you want to work in London?'

She had been thinking what a strong face Clive had. This absurd question made her frown. She had to think before she could answer it politely. 'Well . . . I'm nineteen, Mr Holden. I would like to work in a much bigger firm with more people and more interest.' Perhaps it wasn't such a silly question. 'In fact, I haven't really thought about it. Everyone in the south wants to come to London. I want to make a future for myself. For eight years I trained to be a dancer and then discovered I wasn't quite good enough. I was fairly well educated and I'm quite intelligent but I'm not creative. I can't make things or cook or sew or grow things and I'm not pretty and I won't get married for years, if at all, so I want to get organized and be good at my job!' She stopped talking abruptly.

Clive leaned his arms on his desk, bent his head and smiled. 'Thank you very much. That's the most complete answer I've ever had!' In a few moments this girl had thrown him back to a

15

stage he had quite forgotten. 'Mary tells me your speeds are excellent and Mr Boscombe obviously worships you. We are a small, rather junior unit in a large partnership. I have an articled clerk, Andrew MacKenzie, and Mary at the moment. At times we are ridiculously busy.' She watched him with bright blue eyes, her face showing her every thought. He couldn't help contrasting this half-finished girl with the exquisite and self-contained woman who had just left. 'Do you think you could cope with pressure?'

'Yes.' She was wary now of letting the words run away with her, of making him smile again. 'I never get tired.'

Clive liked this unusual girl. He paused and wondered if he was being absurd to think of employing her. 'My secretary will need considerable tact at times . . .'

'We have had our moments at Boscombe and Barrow. There was a sensational divorce case about six months ago. The vicar's wife and the local vet.' Her eyes laughed but her face was solemn.

Clive laughed aloud, shortly, and sat back. He usually trusted his instincts about people simply because it was easier. He liked to take decisions quickly and he was also beginning to realize that if he didn't find a girl soon he would have to fall back on a temp when Mary left. 'I think you would suit me very well, Miss Neale. Mary is leaving on March the nineteenth. If you could come next Monday and work with her for a week I think it would help you a great deal.'

Kate couldn't believe he was saying it. He went on to speak of holidays and salary and a letter of employment but she didn't listen. She stood up when he did, trying unsuccessfully to hide her delight.

'Thank you very much, Mr Holden,' she said solemnly. 'Monday morning at nine o'clock?'

'Nine-fifteen,' Clive said, opening the door and holding out his hand. The hand she gave him was small and thin-fingered and he was careful not to shake it too hard. 'Goodbye, Miss

16

Neale. Shall I call you Katherine?'

She had signed her letter Katherine, intending to start any new job with the full and dignified version of her name but it sounded unreal.

'I'm usually called Kate.'

When she came into Conduit Street again the sky was blue and the sun was spread along the wet pavements and on the shining roofs of cars. Everything shone. Kate walked down into Bond Street, saying inside herself, 'I've got the job. I've got the bloody job. Just like that. And what a super man to work for.' She walked fast. All the people on the pavements were too slow for her. She wanted to buy something. Perhaps she should look for a flat? She remembered about ringing Gabriel and saw a telephone box in a side street which was empty.

Kate closed the door. She hunted in her bag for change and she pictured her mother, wondering, smoking, making cups of coffee which she wouldn't drink, followed everywhere by the pattering dachshunds. Gabriel would ring Ben and David's mother. David would hear the news . . . Kate lifted her chin, cheeks colouring a little. Would he care? Would he be pleased for her? He was so selfishly absorbed in his own life and plans. The village quivered with news of him but he always appeared to be bored with village news. To hell with him, Kate thought, unconvincingly.

She dialled and waited until Gabriel's voice came. 'Hello?'

'It's me. You won't believe this. . . .'

'You've got it. Darling, that's marvellous!' But the tone of voice contradicted her words. Fear touched Gabriel. Soon, in a month or a year, Kate would have gone.

'I'll come home on Daddy's train. I'd like to spend the after-noon wandering around now I'm here . . .' Kate talked until her money ran out. and as she put down the telephone she saw the woman who had passed her in Clive Holden's office. Through the glass, as she approached the telephone box, the woman looked unreal, disinterested in the shops she passed, unaware

17

that she attracted attention. She must be quite sure of her beauty, Kate thought wistfully, imagining her to be secure in a perfect cliché of a life with a good-looking husband and two or three pretty children.

Kate stepped out into the street and Caroline recognized her. They exchanged slight smiles, acknowledging the coincidence, and Caroline stepped into the booth and closed the door.

For a moment Caroline was filled with an intense longing to be as young as that, not to have started at all. She dialled, watching Kate move back towards Bond Street. The girl moved beautifully. Perhaps she was meeting someone? Someone she loved? Doing it all for the first time and, unlike Caroline, doing it right.

Jill's theatrical voice answered. 'Hello?'

'Jill, it's me, Caroline. Would you mind very much if we cancelled lunch today?'

CHAPTER TWO

Caroline was telling the truth when she said she intended to stay in Clive's area that morning. It was the antique shops which attracted her. She wanted to get her eye in again and although this area of London was selling far more expensive merchandise than Caroline would deal with, still she needed to look. After speaking to Jill she went back into Bond Street. The clothes shops did not interest her at all. Clothes bored her. A couple of times a year she forced herself to re-equip, always choosing good classical garments. Years ago she had decided that her type of face, her tall, big-boned body, needed simple clothes that did not shout for attention. Her bossier women friends constantly told her she looked dull. She ignored them. Even through the divorce, her confidence almost non-existent, she had trusted her own opinion of herself. She had to hold on to something.

She walked with her hands in her pockets, pausing to look in Agnew's window at a display of water colours and wondering why the hell she had allowed herself to be bullied into living here? Big cities made her uneasy. 'I could have looked for a little shop in some pretty country village. I could still do it. Build up its reputation . . . Instead, I have allowed myself to be persuaded, overpowered by well-meaning friends. Especially Rachel . . .'

'You must not let yourself rot away in some village! You can't opt out of life at thirty just because one marriage has failed. Come on, Caroline!' Rachel spoke from experience. Twice she had licked her wounds and bounded back aggressively. She was almost ten years older than Caroline, resilient and energetic. She had never liked Harry. 'You'll marry again, Caroline, but you must go where the men are!'

'Why should I re-marry?' Caroline had answered when she cared enough to argue. 'I loved Harry. It disintegrated. I regret

19

two things desperately. Not having a child and leaving the Manor. I loved that house, Rachel. I belonged there. I still dream about it. Why should I risk myself again?'

But she came to London, rented a flat, and found herself dragged into a world she had completely forgotten while in the safe, married cocoon. There was a level of hard, sexual activity here which she felt unable to cope with. She didn't want it. She was used to being alone because Harry was extremely ambitious and had travelled a lot. There was a flat in London where he spent two or three nights a week and Caroline had joined him in the winter but never enjoyed it. In London, the houses of all their friends were cluttered with school coats and toys and tricycles; there was the constant background noise of children's television programmes. All Caroline's contemporaries had their days sectioned by their children's needs. Fetching and carrying them, riding lessons, tea parties, dancing. In London, the lack of a child had hurt Caroline far more.

The endless experts she had consulted told her that the inability to have children must not be allowed to ruin her marriage. Test after test, at first Caroline alone and then she drew Harry into it. In the beginning, loving Caroline, wanting her to be happy, he allowed himself to be taken from one consulting room to another but he had no craving for a child. Harry's father had started an extremely successful plastics business, bought the Manor and six hundred acres of Hampshire and died when he was fifty-two, leaving Harry to cope. He was a very busy man. Tests revealed they both had inadequacies. He could only laugh for so long about the casual way they insulted his sperm count. He was Catholic, repelled at the thought of artificial insemination and unenthusiastic about adoption. 'I don't want just any child, Caroline.' Shortly after their sixth wedding anniversary when Caroline was talking of the fertility drug, there was a crisis. One of those horrific nights when words that have been fermenting for months, even years, are suddenly spoken, surprising and terrible because they are so thought out.

'I've had enough. You've got to be realistic. I'm not going to any more bloody experts and nor are you! You must accept we will probably never have children. There is so much else in our lives. If you take that drug you could well have not the one child you long for but a litter! Give up, Caroline!'

She had never been a fighter. It appalled her to have it spelt out like this but she didn't show it. She withdrew without telling him that her life was empty of anything that mattered. Sex had become an obsessive ritual for her as she still hoped desperately to conceive. Harry was constantly away from home and when he was with her the atmosphere between them was very strained. If he had the slightest reason to stay in London he began to do so. He had so many excuses he could use both to himself and to Caroline.

Caroline struggled to fill the void with friends and good works. She went to a great many auctions and bought too many paintings but the Manor was a huge house and its walls absorbed them all. And in the summer of nineteen seventy two while Caroline, in the country, grew vegetables and roses and ran stalls to raise money for the church and the Conservatives, in London and almost by accident, Harry found himself a girl to make love to who was not remotely interested in having a child. In October, through the kindness of so-called friends, Caroline found out. Despite the coldness between them she had been deeply shocked and hurt. There was no reason to struggle through a reconciliation which neither of them wanted. She had never been excited by her own beauty but she had always considered it a kind of insurance against hurt. Now even that had proved meaningless. She had some very bad months but the worst depression had passed and she was coming out the other side. When she made her way to meet Clive Holden for lunch Caroline felt happier than she had for many months.

Clive was a little early. He settled himself at a corner table and ordered a whisky and soda to try and kill the remains of last night's hangover. A man he knew slightly came over and talked to him. Clive had a large circle of friends, about half of whom were married. He was good value at any kind of party, an extrovert and an amusing man. He liked to spend money on himself and his friends and, like most of his circle, he spent too much. He lit one of the small cigars which Mary had given him and the discontent which had attacked him earlier that morning returned, a feeling that, at twenty-eight, there should be more in his life. Lately he felt himself running in the grooves of routine. He frowned and the strength of his face vanished. He rubbed his eyes. His father had had two children by the age of twenty-eight. His father, kind and anxious, always short of money, making absurd sacrifices to send Clive to the kind of school he considered essential and sending Clive's elder sister, who had a far better brain, to a small, uninspiring day school. Not that Clive wasn't grateful. His schooling had equipped him to live the only kind of life he considered worthwhile. A small law practice in a country town and a suburban life was not for him!

Caroline caused a slight stir by the door when she arrived, giving her raincoat to a waiter and looking round until she saw Clive. She was wearing a navy blue knitted dress, a silk shirt beneath it, and as Clive stood up to greet her, he noticed again the attractive untidiness about her.

'I'm not late, am I? Not twice in one morning? I'm afraid I never wear a watch.'

'You're not at all late. I was early.' He made it a compliment. 'Would you like something to drink? A whisky? Or a glass of wine?' he asked as they sat down. Clive had a very attractive habit of never taking anything for granted, however small. He did not assume she would drink merely because he had a drink in front of him.

'A glass of white wine, please.' She was already searching for her cigarettes. 'Damn things, always get to the bottom.' She found them and leant forward as Clive struck one of the book matches and held out the little flame.

'I think, as we are almost twins, we could call each other by Christian names, don't you?' he said.

'I should think so. But are we twins? How old are you?'

'Twenty-eight.'

'Twenty-eight!' Her eyes twinkled. 'That has a golden youthful ring to it. I suppose I was twenty-eight once!'

'Years ago, of course.'

'It feels like it.'

'It doesn't look like it.'

She smiled slightly and picked up the menu. Clive saw that she would shrink from any obvious approach. She began to interest him even more. He had always loved the first delicate stages of any relationship.

Caroline wanted only one course, she said, so Clive ordered two Dover soles, cooked with wine and grapes. He tried a couple of cautious questions about her past but it was obvious she did not want to talk about it so he steered the conversation back to the shop she hoped to buy, and she came to life, leaning forward, full of ideas. She talked about it almost as if it were a lifeline.

'I have no family in England at all. All my relatives are in South Africa. I came here at twenty-one, wanting to see England, and worked, met Harry and married. I was amazed by his enormous, entangled family. I have never belonged enough to have a relationship with them in my own right so you see I need to make roots. I need this shop.' She finished her fish and lit a cigarette. 'And you, Clive?'

'My parents live at Kew. Have done for years. My father is a solicitor as well. I've got an older married sister. I see far more of my friends than I do of my family, I'm afraid.'

'And you say you live in Pimlico?'

'Yes, Michael Redford, the friend I mentioned who runs his business from Meadwell Street, owns the house. I live there in the basement flat.'

They drank coffee and Clive watched her, fascinated by her lovely, rather gentle face, feeling the attraction strengthen,

23

wanting to make her laugh more often, wanting very much to see her again and know more about her. She was so different, with none of the typical London affectations. She was unpredictable and solemn.

'I suppose you're celebrating tonight?'

'Just a dinner party with friends. Rachel, actually. She is determined to find me a rich second husband!'

'Are you in London at the weekend? Perhaps we could have dinner on Saturday when we have both got over this birthday thing?'

He asked her so naturally it would have been hard to refuse even if she had wanted to. But she was silent for a moment, wondering if she really wanted to begin it all.

Her silence made him ask, 'Am I being pushing, Caroline?' He touched her arm which was resting on the table.

'No, of course not.' She said it too quickly, rather nervously.

'So you'll have dinner with me on Saturday?'

'Yes, I'd like to. But don't let me drink too much or I'll talk about myself incessantly and bore you!'

'I want to know about you. If you don't tell me I'll ask Rachel and get the dramatic version!'

She laughed at the truth of this and as the mood changed and the tension lessened she thought: Rachel is right. He is a very attractive man. But not just that. He could be a good friend, couldn't he, as well?

Clive attracted the waiter's attention and paid his bill. 'Can I get you a taxi, Caroline?'

'No thank you. I'll walk for a bit.'

He wrote down her telephone number and address, they put on their coats and went out into the narrow street. The sun shone as they said their goodbyes.

The flat which Caroline lived in was in a quiet square behind South Kensington tube station. It still felt strange when she let herself in. It was not her home and it never would be although

24

she had made it attractive. She walked out of her shoes, leaving them where they lay, and thought apathetically how untidy the room was with newspapers and a basket of shopping and piles of books with no shelf to stand them on and odd, discarded clothes. There were so many plants and flowers. She had tried, rather pathetically, to make a garden in the room. She had window boxes and geraniums and bowls of flowers everywhere.

Caroline went into the bedroom and sat down on the patchwork counterpane she had sewn through two winters of needing something to do. This room was full of her tapestries and cushions. She was clever with her hands and with colours. Perhaps, she thought, I could also run some kind of interior decoration business? Once I have the shop as a base . . . At once the vicious censor attacked. 'You have no training. London is crammed with bored women trying to be interior decorators. Amateurs. As you will be. Perhaps the shop will fail, horribly, defeated by your lack of experience?' What had she said to Clive? 'Years ago I was in the business! An exaggeration. She had worked for a couple of years in two antique shops but how much did she remember?

All the warmth which she had carried back from lunch with Clive evaporated to be replaced by the old desolation. The very freedom of her life terrified her. She had enough money, enough friends, enough good causes, to last an empty, childless lifetime. She began to shiver, wrapping long arms round her body, rocking herself gently. As she felt the misery grow too big she caught at herself firmly, controlled it, slipped into the old dream. Why not? With a home and a job, perhaps she could get a child? Caroline had discovered since her marriage ended that it was not Harry's child she had craved. It was her child. And it could happen, they had said. It was unlikely but not impossible.

And Clive? He was a nice man. An attractive man. She could not imagine herself loving anyone for a long time but it would be good merely to be close to someone again. She wandered about the room, restlessly, arms still hunched round her body, and when the telephone rang she sprang at it gratefully.

It was Rachel. 'I've been ringing for hours. Well . . ?'

Caroline sat down, laughing, resigned. 'You are impossible. Yes, I liked him. And that's all!'

Now, having committed herself to a whole day in London, Kate wondered what to do. She walked slowly down Bond Street and was drawn into Fenwick's by the bright, pretty clothes in the windows. She wandered through the departments, looking at other girls, contrasting them with herself and feeling dull. She picked out some clothes to try on, some trousers with deep turn-ups, a soft angora sweater, but Kate had no instinct about such things. She was happiest in jeans. She stood in the cramped little fitting room and stared at her reflection. So many years of dancing, training her body, studying the line and the movements minutely but ignoring what it was dressed in. 'You're far happier naked, aren't you?' David had laughed. It was difficult for her to stand far enough back to get a whole view of herself but she didn't want to step out and be revealed.

The curtain was abruptly twitched back by a sales girl. 'How are you getting on? Much too big, aren't they? You need an eight!' Kate waited. The girl came back. 'Try these.' There was admiration in her face. Kate had noticed before that her extreme thinness was considered an asset by almost all other girls. Here, in the outside world, the admiration was indiscriminate. The shape of arms and legs, the line of limbs did not matter as long as they were thin.

The difference was extraordinary. The smaller clothes fitted her narrow body closely, showing the shape of it, making her slightness something positive. She no longer looked as if she was wearing her big sister's clothes. She took them off carefully and bought them, knowing they would hang in her cupboard until she was quite used to them. Kate was nervous of new clothes. They made her feel obvious, as if she was trying too hard. She bought a knitted hat, too, and daringly wore it out of the shop

26

and, as always when she needed someone to show herself to, she thought of Alice. Her map open in one hand, large carrier bag in the other, Kate walked to the square where Alice worked, into the huge, glass-fronted estate agents. She made her way in and asked for Alice at the reception desk and they rang and told Kate she would be down at once.

Kate settled into an armchair. She loathed to be looked at herself but she loved watching other people—the hesitant and the confident and those determined hurried people who moved through this reception hall. A few of them glanced at her and she pretended to be absorbed in her map. The only time she had not minded being watched was when she was dancing. 'Eight years, from the first terrifying interview, living in one world.' Alice beside her, at class every morning, the familiar safety of the routine, the same music, the pain in the muscles; in the afternoon ordinary lessons, games, a more normal existence; always watching what you ate, always watched by others as you danced, admiring or jealous. It had never mattered being watched in that environment. And then, the gradual realization, and it was gradual, that she didn't have enough, that she would never be more than average as the weeding out began. The realization that to try desperately hard and sweat and struggle was not enough. Something more was needed. It could not be put in by work. Kate did not have it. Nor did Alice. At the end there was relief and regret and incredible freedom for her body, for her time. Feeling her body slip away from the rigid discipline. For one summer Kate was idle, hesitating at home, acting out the disappointment Gabriel expected. And because typing was the only other thing she could think of she spent a year at secretarial college and ended up with Mr Boscombe. Outward signs of a normal life, but inside she was unused. All the passion she had channelled into dancing was building up, searching for an outlet, until David came.

Alice came bounding down the stairs, a stone heavier than

27

when she and Kate had struggled, side by side, with grand *battements*, her hair a surprising mass of fuzzy curls. 'Like it?' She patted her head. 'Come on. There's a place opposite.' Darting through the traffic, pushing into a restaurant so crowded Kate would never have attempted it, finding a corner table with two empty seats. 'Okay if we sit here?' Making a space for Kate's shopping, lighting a cigarette. 'Well, how are you, Katy? What's been happening?'

'I've got myself a job with a very smart firm of solicitors in Conduit Street.'

'Marvellous. Now you must get a flat. I commuted for a while but it's hopeless. I go home at weekends now and eat and sleep and we all get on much better!' She looked up as a waitress appeared. 'Spaghetti Bolognaise and coffee, please.'

Kate had not seen a menu but looking up into the bored, middle-aged face she murmured, 'Same for me, please.'

Alice launched into a detailed account of her life of the past few months, of the lives of mutual friends, those who had stayed on and still danced and the very few who were really succeeding. If she closed her eyes, Kate could have been back at Greenhurst on a summer afternoon, lying on the grass after lunch, sucking the stalk of a daisy and listening to Alice while they waited for the afternoon work to begin. As if defending itself against being 'just' a ballet school, the pupils were worked extremely hard. There were school outings, there were performances. Kate could still feel under her fingers the hideous grey tunics, grotesque on the bosomy like Alice and cruelly undignified on skinny girls like herself.

'Did you hear that Miss Pearson died?' Kate interrupted.

'Really?' Alice was scornful. 'I never think of the place . . Except on the odd morning I stay in bed late. Then I remember how I loathed getting up for class.' She devoured spaghetti like a hungry bird. 'Do you still see David?' She blotted tomato sauce from her chin with an inadequate paper napkin.

'Not much.' The spaghetti kept sliding from Kate's fork and

28

she lacked the energy to subdue it. She hated food which fought back.

'Why not?'

How odd, Kate thought. All my life I have wanted a drama of my own in the sense Alice means it, to compete with. Now that it's real I don't want to tell her. I don't want her taking my sadness and passing it around at lunches like this. 'We just got tired of each other.' The sadness welled up, a lump in her throat.

'Did you sleep with him?'

At Christmas, Alice had asked the same question and then, feeling pathetically inexperienced and having no words to describe the autumn, the evenings with David in his room, in her room if her parents were out, touching each other, loving and loving but never actually having intercourse because Kate was a virgin and hesitant, always pulling away for a reason she could not sensibly put into words—just a need to wait, to be gradual, then Kate had lied with silence, giving Alice the impression that she and David were lovers. Why, now, with January and February, when she could have described the pride of having David as a lover, of owning his body for short periods of time, of absorbing him completely and lying with him in such intense joy and surprise, when she could have tried to describe the strength of her own responses, did she lie again?

'No.'

Alice had expected this. 'I've met an incredible man, Katy . . .'

Kate did not listen. Alice's voice made a background. She thought of David's bedroom with the afternoon shut out behind the heavy curtains and the room full of smoke and music from his cassette player. David's mouth, moving over her body. The sudden panic when his mother came home unexpectedly. The sleepy, laughing meals they had after love-making, desperately hungry, rifling his mother's kitchen to make sandwiches and mugs of coffee, kissing with their mouths full. Remembering the way he had of pulling her against him, half lifting her off the

29

ground with one arm, their faces still warm and hair wild . . . Everything inside Kate bunched tight into a spasm of pain and loss.

'He's a very attractive boy,' Gabriel had said, coming back from the Donaldsons' house-warming party. 'Well, man, I suppose. He's twenty-four. I've asked them all to lunch on Sunday. Do be here, Kate.' Gabriel was always struggling to keep Ben and Kate in the house, to fight the way they shrank from any social event she arranged. Kate had murmured non-committally and gone out but she had paused, listening, knowing there was more to come, feeling it was all right to listen when they spoke about her . . . 'He is just what Kate needs,' Gabriel said. 'Amusing and obviously intelligent. He works with computers.'

'Why does the word computer impress you and make you believe he is clever? A computer is a machine.'

'And he is committed enough to some girl in America not to be serious,' Gabriel plodded on. 'Ideal for a little while, to take Kate out and make her laugh. Responsible enough not to hurt her.'

Wrong. Wrong. All bloody wrong!

Alice said, 'God, I'd better go. I've been late so much recently. Here's my share of the bill!' She put some coins on the table. 'And if you do want a flat, I know some girls who are looking for someone. I could ring them . . . but why don't you? I know Judith's at home because she's got a terrible cold. You'll like her. And Venn.' Alice scribbled numbers on a scrap of paper from her bag. 'Let me know what happens.' She got to her feet, buttoning her jacket. 'Bye, Katy.'

Kate put out the cigarette which Alice had left smoking in the ashtray. The irritable waitress came back, slightly happier now the place was less crowded. 'Wanna pay, love?'

'Yes. But please could I have another coffee first?' Kate gave her a brief, sweet smile but she wasn't looking.

'Okay.' She scooped up the ashtray and the empty white

30

cups. Alice's was stained a vivid red on one side. She returned with a second cup of milky coffee for Kate. 'Pay at the desk, love.'

There was a telephone booth beside the cashier's desk. Kate stirred her coffee and wondered whether to ring the number Alice had given her. The thought of living in London was both appealing and frightening but she could at least look at the flat. It was just after two. Hours before she need think about the train. She made up her mind and drank the coffee quickly, finding coins for the telephone and buttoning her coat. Alice's scrap of paper she held tightly in her hand with the bill.

Judith Richardson lay on her stomach, arms folded under the pillow, eyes closed, in a warm, drowsy state between sleeping and waking. When Susie left at eight she had woken and then she must have slept again. The cough had kept her awake most of the night. She yawned enormously, rolling over and stretching and looking with disbelief at her small travelling clock. It was after two! It didn't really matter. This week was her own. She was between jobs.

The telephone rang and she swore quite amiably and got out of bed, her naked body flinching against the sudden cold of the room. Afternoon sunlight shone through the wet dormer windows and Judith picked up her dressing-gown from the armchair and went downstairs, two at a time, snatching at the receiver just as Kate was about to give up. 'Hello?'

Kate was not shy on the telephone. A year with Mr Boscombe had made her able to express herself. She explained who she was and why she was ringing.

'Yes, we will need someone else in about three weeks. We've advertised but we haven't liked any of them. You can come this afternoon but the flat's not looking its best!' That, Judith thought, was a massive understatement. Bloody Venn. Never doing anything unless forced. 'Where are you? Can you give me an hour? Okay. I'll see you at three.'

It was a big flat on two floors, roomy and shabby and cold in the winter. Judith went back into the small, chaotic kitchen and swore, loudly and efficiently, at Venn who had left at eleven. She filled a dented kettle and shook wholegrain cereal into a bowl, organizing her long hair with a complicated double flick of her head. She began to eat, wrapping her bare feet round the bar of the stool she sat on. Even in this dressing-gown, hair loose, face bare of make-up, Judith gave an impression of being older than her twenty years. She had had to care for herself for most of her life. She was the second daughter of a weak, bewildered woman who never managed to get the father of her children to marry her, who had taken them to her parents, to a flat as she changed jobs, back to her parents, into another man's house. Judith had hated school and the teachers hated her. She was a disruptive influence, they said. She left, thankfully, as soon as she could, with no qualifications and went to work in a supermarket in Dorchester, the town where she had grown up. Just after her sixteenth birthday, bored with her life in the little town, with her elder sister's endless marriage plans and her mother's criticism and the adoration of her current boy-friend, Judith took what little money she had managed to save, bought herself a smart grey suit, a suitcase and a ticket to London. She had arrived at Paddington at two in the afternoon, found a hostel where she could spend the night and began to think about jobs. The following morning she had put up her hair and enrolled herself at Angels, a rather smart agency which undertook to provide nannies, mothers' helps, cooks and all kinds of emergency domestic help. She lied about her age and her experience quite expertly.

By the time her first employer discovered she was sixteen, Judith had been running the house and looking after the two small children virtually single-handed for a month. The children adored her. She was kind but quite ruthless if they disobeyed her. She stayed for six months and earned a considerable amount of money; she watched her employer, the way she dressed, the way the house was organized, the way she spoke and expressions she used. In the past four years, Judith had seen the insides of many different houses and very many different lives. This, coupled with a basic common sense and toughness, gave her the air of maturity.

She made herself a mug of coffee when the kettle boiled and carried it upstairs, dressing in jeans and a striped football sweater, tying back her hair and beginning to cope efficiently with the room. She moved next door and cleaned the bathroom, pausing to go downstairs and put on some music. Beethoven flooded the flat. Judith had brought so little with her from her past. She had had to discover and create herself, surround herself with things that she liked. She never went home. The music she had discovered when she worked for a conductor and his family in Hampstead. It seemed all her life she had been needing the emotions that classical music aroused in her. She wrote a rude note and put it on Venn's bed. The music was solemn and she thought of the previous evening. He had been the brother of her employer before last, stalking her all the time she had been in the house, attractive, and money to spend but his attitude to women was furtive and immature. He had bored and depressed her and he was angry when she wouldn't sleep with him. The cold sarcasm with which she reacted to his bad manners had amazed him.

Judith was well aware of her attraction. It was far stronger than her appearance warranted. It had always been there, surprising her at first, part of her confidence now. She used it all the time, picking her men from all social levels, moving easily from type to type, taking life one job at a time, one man at a time. She was not promiscuous but if necessary she would use her attraction to get what she wanted. She had no other weapon. She had lost her virginity at fourteen and wondered what all the fuss was about. At seventeen she had been fond of a man for the first time but it hadn't lasted. Judith thought about the future a great deal, kept a book of accounts, kept a list of the things she wanted from life. She didn't know quite where she would be in ten years

33

but she was determined she would not still be looking after other people's children and cleaning their baths.

'What the hell do you want?' he had said last night, voice shrill with anger, as she moved expertly out of his reach.

'I don't know. A flat of my own. Enough money to travel and have a reasonable life. I've been nowhere. I want a car.' She had been talking to herself, not to him, her slanted eyes thoughtful. She prowled his room, her body short and strong, bosom too big for her size. Her face was very unusual. A big mouth and eyes that tilted at the outer corner. 'Whatever or whoever it is, I haven't found it yet!' He had followed her, putting his arms round her from behind, putting his mouth against her neck. She shook him off, annoyed that she had wasted time trying to explain herself, that she felt like making love but certainly not to him.

'I'm going now.' She picked up her coat. She coughed and her throat hurt. He had at least fed her and on the food she liked. 'Thank you for the meal.' She had let herself out of his smart little town house with its tubs of flowers and she had walked home, loving London, loving the crisp, cold night.

When the buzzer sounded Judith was cleaning the kitchen. She went into the hall and shouted into the speaker. 'Hello . . . push the front door hard when you hear the buzzer.'

She heard Kate's voice. 'Okay. I'm in.'

It was three tall floors up and Kate's carrier bag banged against her leg as she hurried. The stairs and landings were wide but there were no windows. Kate had pushed the light button at the bottom of the stairs and she knew from previous experience of her aunt's flat that the light only lasted long enough for a brisk climb up. The old or the slow had to finish the ascent in darkness, or grope for a light button on one of the landings. At the top she could see a lighted doorway, another flight of stairs and, as she got nearer, she heard music and a voice calling, 'Only one more flight. Don't give up.' The voice had traces of a soft West Country accent.

Judith stood at the top of the stairs. Kate saw an unusual face under a thick brown fringe. Strong, interesting face. 'I'm Judith Richardson.' They were level now and the same height but this girl was far more strongly built than Kate, short-legged, curved, a smile stretching her wide mouth and showing white teeth with a narrow gap at the front which Kate had heard was a lucky thing to have. 'I've got a bad cold so I'll try not to breathe on you. You're a friend of Alice's?'

'We were at school together.' Kate followed Judith into the kitchen, fascinated by her small, rounded bottom in the skin-tight jeans.

'Like some coffee? Or peppermint tea?'

'Coffee, please.'

Judith lit the gas under the kettle. 'This, as you see, is the kitchen. Bit small but all right. The worst thing is carrying the rubbish down to the basement.' She felt a sneeze coming and snatched a paper handkerchief from a box and sneezed twice, neatly, like a cat. 'Come on. I'll show you round while the kettle's boiling . . . This is the living-room.' Kate looked in, seeing some brown, rather sad armchairs, a table, a television, a bright rug, a white azalea and two huge windows with colourless and uneven curtains. 'Next door is Venn's room. She's a stewardess with British Airways and a lazy bitch but she brings back a lot of duty-free booze and cigarettes. You'll like her and she goes off for a week at a time quite frequently.'

She took Kate upstairs to the big attic bedroom with its dormer windows and slanted ceiling. Two beds at opposite sides and a worn, fitted carpet. This room was very tidy. 'My room and you'd be in here too. I work away a lot as well. I'm off on Monday to Scotland for a couple of months but I'll be back at odd weekends. The bathroom is next door.'

Kate tried to get a picture of the bedroom in her memory for later. Two chest-of-drawers, a bentwood hat-stand, a poster of yoga positions and an enormous wardrobe.

'There's masses of room for clothes. Susie and I have never

fought over space. I can hear the kettle . . . come down when you're ready.'

Kate walked to the windows and looked down on the quiet London square. At least Gabriel would approve the address. Some trees, still bare of leaves, but daffodils in the garden; wide pavements and parked cars and other houses, just as tall, and sky. She thought of her bedroom at the Old Vicarage. 'This is still a child's room,' David had teased her, looking at the shelf of glass animals and the posters and the teddy bear which Kate was quite indifferent to but Gabriel insisted on resurrecting each time he was hidden. That room was beautifully decorated but chosen by Gabriel. Somehow the bleakness of this big, cold room, was comforting. She could be anything she wanted in here. Above all, at times, she could be quite alone.

In the kitchen, Judith was sitting on one of the high stools, dissolving aspirin in a mug with the handle of a knife. Two cups of coffee stood by the kettle, steam curling upwards from them. She smiled. 'Have you had lunch?'

'Well, I had spaghetti with Alice but it was rather unpleasant and I didn't eat much.' Kate took one of the mugs of coffee.

'Like an Edam sandwich?'

The bread was brown and looked delicious. 'Yes, please.' She watched with fascination as Judith created sandwiches like a cookery demonstrator.

'What do you think of the place?'

'I like it,' Kate said truthfully.

For a moment Judith paused and studied her, guessing that she was young for her age, sensing shyness and individuality, guessing that Kate's personality would not conflict with her own. Her widely varied jobs, living with so many different people, had made her a shrewd judge of character. 'Do you have any horrible habits?'

'Not yet but I hope to acquire some!'

Judith laughed. 'One girl came to look round carrying her trumpet!'

36

Now they laughed together and Judith pushed the plate of sandwiches towards Kate. 'Susie goes to America on April the seventh, I think, but she's going home for two weeks first. She moves out of here in a couple of weeks so if you and Venn like the look of each other, you could move in on March the twenty-sixth. It's five pounds a week and we share gas and electricity and food according to how much we are here. It sounds complicated but it's worked all right so far.' She took a large bite of sandwich and grimaced. 'Can't taste a bloody thing!' Kate did not know it but she had just been chosen.

She stood up and consulted a large calendar which hung on the back of the kitchen door. 'Venn gets back Friday morning, I see. Could you come here Friday evening? About seven?'

'Yes.' Kate finished a second sandwich and wanted to talk, to give an impression of herself. 'How long have you lived here?'

'Two years.' Judith sat down. She talked easily. There was something extremely attractive about her, Kate thought, the voice, or the face or the combination of both. It was arranged that Kate would come on Friday, they exchanged smiles and Kate left, going down the endless stairs and thinking she would like Judith very much when she knew her. This time she reached the door with light to spare.

London was clean after another brief rainstorm and Kate's feet sounded sharply against the wet pavement. She walked slowly, wanting to see everything, along the Cromwell Road with its tall houses and hotels, thick traffic, grumbling buses, impatient black taxis. She turned down a side street with a flower stall and a newspaper stand with the papers and magazines protected by a polythene sheet. I can always ring. Say I've changed my mind. Say I don't want a flat after all. Kate thought of her home, meal cooked every night, Gabriel's gentle cross-examination, her father's gift of always making her laugh. But it wasn't enough. David had pushed his way in and shown her that.

A pathetic old mad woman, legs and body bandaged in many

37

layers of clothing, cursing insanely to herself as she tottered along the pavement, brushed against Kate. 'My God, you are so ridiculously sheltered here. You have no idea what it's like outside.'

Well, I will have. I'll live amongst all this, Kate thought and although the thought was amazing it was no longer frightening.

CHAPTER THREE

The remaining days of that week were extremely busy for Clive. His work tended to go in phases like this. It seemed that everything which had been building up gradually over the past few weeks suddenly chose this week to erupt. On Tuesday morning Joseph Hill rang. His eight-year-old daughter, who had been unconscious since being injured in a road accident eight months before, had died the previous week.

'We'll go ahead, then, with the damages claim against the car driver,' Clive said gently. 'There was no contributary negligence on her part . . . as I explained, you will bring this action as administrator of Karen's estate under the provisions of the Law Reform Act, 1934. How is Betty?'

'Oh, she's all right . . .' His voice was flat, tired. 'Thank you for coming to the funeral, Clive. Can I come and see you tomorrow? I shall be in your area and I want to get the whole ghastly thing over with.'

Clive consulted his diary. 'Yes. But make it the afternoon. I'm in court all morning.' He was in court on Wednesday too and on Thursday he drove to Essex to see Miss Henderson about her will. He found himself working at home in the evenings, the house silent round him, as Michael Redford had left for his annual skiing holiday. Clive hated silence. Leaving the office each evening he would stop for a drink and then go back to the quiet house, turning on the television, running a bath, creating noise. And all through the week, he thought of Caroline Boyd whenever there was a moment free. He found, despite the fact that they had met only once, he could picture her face quite clearly.

On Friday morning Stephen Jones rang to say that he had looked at the shop in Meadwell Steet . . . 'I liked it. Sound building, attractive proposition and a reasonable price! Provided your lady knows what she's about, Clive, she should do well with it. I should make an offer quickly!' It was bearing this good news and with a bunch of daffodils on the car seat beside him, that Clive drove to Caroline's flat on Saturday evening.

Caroline had been feeling rather nervous about the evening. The lunch seemed long ago. Perhaps she imagined the liking between them? Her week had been aimless. Twice she had caught a bus down World's End and wandered around the area of the shop, studying the opposition, pausing outside the window of the shop she wanted; both times on the way home she bought flowers, adding them to the mass that already festooned the flat. The daily ritual of tending to them all pleased her. She had planted tomato seeds and courgettes and dwarf French beans . . . She was being telephoned, constantly, by a cousin of Rachel's, a doctor, who wanted to take her out. She disliked him. He was very thin, nervous, intense and uncomfortable. She was running out of lies.

When the doorbell rang, Caroline jumped. She let Clive in and he handed her the daffodils. 'Thought they might remind you of the country and the spring . . .' And then he looked round the room which was more like a greenhouse and burst out laughing.

'It's like a bloody flower shop!'

'I know.' She took the flowers. 'But these are lovely.' She went into the kitchen to find a vase. 'What would you like to drink? I have most things.'

'Whisky?' Clive stared at the small, crowded room, the untidy heaps in the corners, the mass of plants; beautiful curtains, sofa covered in the same chintz, shoes on the floor. Touched and intrigued he said, 'I've got good news. Stephen thinks Meadwell Street's a very good bet.'

She appeared with two glasses, her face eager. 'Does he?'

'He thinks we should make an offer.' Cleverly Clive started the evening as a lawyer, discussing the shop, agreeing the amount Caroline should offer. 'First thing Monday morning I'll get on with it. Now, let's go and have something to eat.'

They went to a small restaurant near Caroline's flat. She found Clive easy to be with, enjoying his company as she had when they lunched together but he was more relaxed now. More amusing. The meal lasted until after eleven and when Clive stopped his car outside Caroline's flat and walked with her to the street door, taking her hands and kissing her mouth very lightly, it was easy for her to thank him. She had laughed more this evening than she had for months.

'I'll ring you on Monday and keep you informed . . . can I see you next week?'

'Any night. I'm not doing anything.' The tiredness and the affection she felt, the way she had enjoyed the evening, made her quite honest..

Kate found the first week at Bonnnington's a considerable strain. On Sunday night she hardly slept at all, convinced that she wouldn't be able to do the job, turning over and over in bed. When she finally fell asleep she slept so deeply she didn't hear her alarm and she leapt out of bed in panic when Gabriel came to wake her. 'It's all right, darling. It's only seven-fifteen.' Gabriel had cooked eggs and bacon and Kate forced it down.

'You've never cooked breakfast for me before . . .'

'It's your first morning. I'm going to cook something every morning . . .'

'Going to London doesn't use more calories than going to Godalming, does it?' Ben said.

Kate watched her mother's face, the way it closed when she thought she was being criticized. Kate tensed with pity.

She drove to the station with her father each morning that week, sat beside him on the train in a first-class carriage. In the office the days were a blur of activity. So difficult just learning all their names . . . James Williams, nearest office to Clive, a loud, intimidating young man. Secretary called Joan. Michael Paul, quieter and older, grandson of one of the founders. Andrew Mackenzie, Clive's clerk, tall, thin, worried and shyer than Kate. Five other secretaries. Two other clerks: Peter Powell and David Young Johnson at the far end of the corridor, dignified as God. This building was a rabbit warren, deceptive in size, of corridors and stairs and offices 'But this is far the best,' Mary said, and Kate thought she was probably right. It seemed much the most informal. Clive always arrived with a smile. Mary was extremely helpful, guiding Kate through that first impossible week, telling her all she could, lunching with her.

'I'll leave my number. If you get desperate, ring me, but you'll be fine, Kate. Clive's a nice man to work for. He does have another side and you'll have to cover up for him. Don't be taken in by all the attention; he flirts with everyone!'

'I can't imagine him getting ruffled,' Kate said, thinking that Clive was about as likely to be interested in her as in a pet hamster.

'He can. Once or twice he's been in trouble. He got out of it but it was quite a struggle. He's dedicated to himself and his own interest but isn't everyone? And he's such fun with it!'

'You mean he makes mistakes?'

'They all do, however cautious they are. But Clive, once or twice, has been involved with something rather dubious.' She said no more but she felt she had at least alerted Kate, sown the seeds.

Although Kate had met and liked Venn Tingley, and it was agreed she would move into the flat on March 26th, she still hadn't been able to mention it to Gabriel. She woke in the mornings, struggled to eat the breakfast Gabriel prepared, moved in a bewildered blur through the days, began buying an *Evening Standard* because everyone did, began to lose her fear of missing trains and learned to elbow her way into a non-smoker if she could on the return journey. In the station car park she would wait by her father's car. If he was going to be late,

Gabriel's battered Mini Clubman would come chugging into the car park, windows misted, the interior smelling of dogs and cigarettes. Gabriel would be hungry with questions which she disguised as conversation. She always asked, 'Are you going out tonight?' wanting to please Kate, insinuating that Kate went out a lot. Kate loathed the question. She never went out in the week. The evenings were empty and aimless without David and Kate knew that Gabriel missed him too. There had been affection between Gabriel and David, as if Gabriel had picked him for Kate. Some nights Gabriel could hardly keep the questions out of her mouth. 'Where is he?' she longed to ask. 'Why doesn't he come any more? Why are you so sad, Kate?'

At the end of that first week Kate told her mother about the flat, quite quickly, wrapping it all into a reason for sorting her bedroom. She was tired after the week in London and ruthless, giving Gabriel a great box of stuff to be given away, ice skates, books of children's poems, some rag dolls and posters and games. They were nothing to Kate now but for Gabriel they were full of memories and she struggled away with the large box to sort through again.

'David's home for the weekend,' she said, pausing in Kate's doorway. 'I saw his mother . . .'

Kate sat cross-legged, furious at the great leap of hope in her stomach, stirred to rage by her mother's casual tone. 'We're not seeing each other any more. Vanessa is coming back from America this month.' And I, she thought, have served my purpose . . . kept him ticking over! She was holding a notebook she had written in for years when things mattered. Sometimes every day for a week and then nothing for six months. She flicked through it both intrigued and scornful of her own past . . . 'Chosen to be Lilac Fairy instead of Myra! He said my arabesques were good. Good line . . .' 'Stayed a week with Alice. Went to three films three days running . . .' 'David is quite interesting. He seems to like me. God knows why.' In the doorway, Gabriel watched her bend her head, watched her slight body tighten and couldn't stop the words.

'Did you sleep with him, Kate?'

'Mothers aren't supposed to ask that, are they?'

'Probably not.'

'Well, I didn't,' Kate lied.

When Clive telephoned her on the Monday morning, Caroline was still in bed. 'Hello . . .'

'It's Clive Holden. I've just been speaking to the agents and I've put forward your offer. They should ring back later today . . . Will you have dinner with me on Wednesday?'

'Yes.' She sat up in bed, holding the telephone tightly. 'Ring me at once, Clive, won't you, when they ring you?'

'Of course.'

And they spoke so frequently over the next three days that his voice became familiar, the voice of a friend. The first offer was turned down. Clive, on her behalf, offered two thousand more. On Wednesday evening the owner was still considering the offer. Clive took Caroline to an Italian restaurant and she was completely at ease with him . . . 'This is delicious. Almost as good as my lasagne. Did I tell you I love cooking? I'll cook you a celebration meal if I get the shop, I don't get enough opportunity to cook now. My friends are all over-fed.'

'Next Tuesday? Whether you get the shop or not?'

'Okay.'

When he drove her home she stayed beside him in the car and he put his arm behind her, his fingers closing round her neck, moving his face towards hers. She accepted his mouth, enjoying it, the first unhurried touch of his gentle, skilful hands.

When he drew away, he said, 'You are quite unlike any woman I've known before. I think about you so much . . .' He stroked pieces of hair back from her forehead. 'Will you come to a dinner party with me on Friday? Old friends of mine.'

'Yes, I'd like to.'

On Friday they arrived as a definite pair. Caroline noticed the change in status and it pleased her but she did not analyse very much. She felt, instinctively, that the attention and affection which Clive gave her were exactly what she needed at this time. She enjoyed being with him. She found him very attractive. He made her laugh and when he spoke about his work he could be fascinating. She waited to hear about the shop, not daring to let her imagination run too much, telling herself that of course there were other places but she wanted this one so much. She had felt the appeal of it the first time she stepped inside. She felt she could belong there.

On Tuesday, when Clive drove Caroline to his flat in Pimlico, there had still been no definite answer about the increased offer.

'I rang again today,' Clive said. 'I told them that we must have an answer by the end of the week. I imagined this delay means that someone else is after it too . . .'

'Could I go up another thousand?'

'I don't see why you should. You've offered a good price.'

The house in Pimlico was tall and narrow, built on five floors of which Clive occupied the basement, in a street of similar small Georgian houses. Clive went down a flight of basement steps to unlock the front door, showing Caroline into a large L-shaped living-room. It was a dull room, Caroline thought, apart from two beautiful oil paintings which dominated the long wall. She admired them. 'Bribes,' Clive said. 'I once did a favour for a man,' and he laughed. There was a small bedroom and bathroom, a door to stairs which led up to the main house, double glass doors at the far end of the room which showed a neglected paved garden where cats prowled the high walls and weeds pushed up in cracks between the stones.

'How can you leave it like this?' Caroline said, opening the doors and shivering in the cold of the March evening. She looked up at the backs of all the houses which formed an oblong, at the tops of occasional trees she could see. 'Not a single flower pot. Not even a tub of weeds!'

Behind her, registering but still surprised by the strength of the feelings she gave him, Clive laughed. 'I'm sorry . . . but it isn't really my garden. It's Michael's. Is that any excuse?' He drew her inside again and poured her a drink.

'Doesn't he care? Where is he?'

'Skiing. In France.' Clive handed her a glass. 'I spent five or six Christmases skiing with him when we were at school but I never got anywhere near his standard. Oddly enough he's useless at all other sports. Every year he skis for two or three weeks and then goes to see his grandmother. She lives in Provence. His mother is French but she's lived in England ever since she married . . .' They were moving upstairs to the kitchen on the ground floor, a bright yellow room, so clean and bare it was obvious that very little cooking was done here. A two-doored hatchway opened into a dining-room.

'Let me see the rest of the house,' Caroline said. 'I love nosing into people's houses.'

She looked in the small square dining-room, went up the narrow stairs with their curving wooden banisters and red stair carpet into a living-room which occupied the whole of the first floor. Tall windows at either end. Velvet curtains. A room furnished comfortably and quietly, the feeling of it old-fashioned and rather comforting, filled with the ticking of clocks. Two more floors.

'This is Mike's bedroom and bathroom,' Clive explained, showing her a blue room, a bed with a mahogany bed-head, more clocks; above an attic spare room, furnished with left-over bits, with faded, cotton curtains. A very masculine house, she thought, intrigued by the man who owned it.

Caroline loved the actual processes of cooking, taking trouble to chop ingredients finely, using herbs, garlic, wine and inspiration to make each recipe her own. Tonight, wrapped in a big, striped apron which she found hanging behind the door, she made a first course of cooked white fish with shrimps and raw mushrooms. She was more relaxed with Clive that she had ever been, talking about her hopes for the shop. Clive sat and watched her pounding peppercorns, chopping parsley, watched the bend of her head, her expression as she concentrated, the way she occasionally looked up at him and smiled. He could have watched her for hours. It surprised him that, being as intensely attracted to her as he was, he felt so little impatience. He would wait until she approached him. She was a woman, not a young girl to be persuaded into bed.

'I like your house.'

'I wish it were mine!'

'Well, I mean this house you live in.'

'I do have a flat of my own but I let it. It's far nicer living here but I realized about four years ago that I must jump on the bandwagon and get a mortgage on something. My godfather died and left me some money, very shortly after Mike's dad died in fact. That was nineteen sixty-nine. It's odd how parallel things happen to us. He used his dad's money to start Mosaic and buy this place. I used what I had to get a flat and what was left I put into Mosaic with him.'

'You knew he would be successful?'

'He has always succeeded at anything he really wanted. He attacks so single-mindedly. He is an extraordinary man,' Clive said, pouring himself another drink and thinking back to the early days of Marketing Mosaic. 'It all started here. It was a year before he got Meadwell Street.'

'I've never seen so many clocks in one house. And what are those models on the shelves in the sitting-room upstairs?'

Clive smiled. 'The steam engines! He has a lathe in the basement shed under the road. Those engines are a hobby. I think at one time he was going to sell them in kit form but it didn't come off. Mosaic markets adult games, gimmicks, presents, and clocks. As you see, he has a fascination for clocks and time!'

'And all this is now run from Meadwell Street?'

'Yes. So if all goes well you should be neighbours. Some of the products he designed himself but he's found it far more profitable to handle other people's stuff. Especially since he got

47

Jenny. She's a fantastic saleswoman.' Clive paused, drank, thought for a moment. 'Mike is a difficult man to describe. You'll meet him when he gets back anyway . . . . I think, if I hadn't known him most of my life, I'd find him intolerable. He's so extreme, so self-contained. For four years he has worked bloody hard to get Mosaic going and now, when he's really beginning to make a name and make money and he's got this terrific girl virtually running things, he's tired of it. I know all the signs.' He let his eyes move down the line of her profile, the high forehead and straight nose. She filled him with the most complicated emotions and he crossed the room impulsively and kissed her. 'You need another drink.'

'Yes, but weaker this time, please.' Caroline lit the grill. 'And who is the girl in the photograph in his bedroom?'

'The faithful Susie!'

'His girl-friend?'

'Yes. For almost four years. Mike is one of the few people I know who seems, genuinely, not to need other people around. I hate being on my own. My own company bores me. I go to sleep or get drunk. But Mike is oblivious to other people half the time. She's convenient, poor girl. She has adored him for years and he alternates between affection and guilt, or so he says. I hope she gives up. I keep telling her that he'll end up in France. His grandmother has a vineyard which he will inherit in Provence.' Clive grinned. 'And I, I hope, will inherit Marketing Mosaic!'

'Could you do that and be a solicitor?'

'If it was successful enough, I'd rather just do that.'

Caroline took off the apron and carried the first course through to the dining-room. Clive opened a bottle of wine. He filled the glasses and they sat down and he took her hand and kissed it. 'It's lovely to have you here . . .'

She met his eyes and smiled but she said nothing. It was hard for Caroline to be a single woman again. She clung to the dignity of not responding, stayed on the edge. And yet she needed someone and she sensed that if she and Clive became lovers it would be a serious relationship. It could mean a lot. But did she want anyone yet? And she had no way of knowing whether or not Clive was serious Perhaps he gave the impression to all women that he could love them? In a way his very seriousness scared her.

After they had eaten they sat downstairs in Clive's living-room. They both held brandy glasses and the atmosphere made Caroline want to explain herself as honestly as she could. For the first time she wanted to talk about herself. Clive watched her so seriously and so sweetly.

'Rachel, who seems to know all about life, and told me the first thing I must do was buy some pretty new underclothes, tells me that divorced women either cavort in desperate circles, sleeping with every man who is willing just to reassure themselves that they still have what it takes or else, like me, they withdraw, need to rebuild on their own.' She sat up, leaning away from him. 'I want to make my own life. Before I was married I had a job, I was quite independent, but I've forgotten that time and how I felt. For seven years I was totally committed to Harry and obsessed with the idea of a child. I didn't notice how he gradually knocked all the secret corners off my life. "We don't want to go there or see them or listen to that!" And I let him do it. I was young and I loved him. He was almost ten years older than I. I gave in and narrowed myself to be the person he wanted.' She paused. 'There was a terrible night when it was all said, when I told him how he had thinned and flattened me and cured me of all my own ideas. My fault as much as his but it won't happen again!'

Clive sat forward to be level with her, turned her face and kissed her. For the first time she responded. When she drew away, he said, 'I'm in no hurry, Caroline. I think you must sense how I feel. I wish I had known you for much longer. It would make things easier to accept. But as I have years and years to spare, shall we just see what happens?'

'Yes . . .' She touched his face and then, needing to move,

stood up with a swift, nervous movement, separating herself from his warmth and his sympathy. She lit a cigarette and walked round the room. 'Will I get the shop, Clive? Have I enough money?'

'If she accepts this offer, and I think she will, you'll be all right. She seems a reasonable woman. If things go smoothly you could complete in five or six weeks. Luckily you've got a really pushy lawyer to hurry things along!'

She swung round, smiling. 'I'll have a party, to celebrate my opening!'

Clive came to stand by her. Without her shoes they were the same height. He kissed her, a light kiss, hands on her shoulders. 'That was a delicious meal. Will you do it again?'

'Of course. Next time at my flat.'

'And I've got tickets for *Godspell* next week. Have you seen it?'

'No. I'd love to.'

Deliberately he planned himself into her life. He had never approached a woman so carefully before. He drove her home, walked with her to the door, kissed her good night and drove slowly home. The open window of his car let in the night. It was still early. Crowds flowed out of the cinemas. People, cars. Energy and excitement pulsed through Clive. He repeated, cautiously, the thought which had occurred a couple of days ago. He loved Caroline. It was very unusual for him to bother to name his feelings but this time it was unique. After dozens of women, two he had quite seriously thought of marrying, for the first time in his adult life Clive Holden genuinely loved her. He thought of her through the day, too much, distractingly. She fascinated and enchanted him. He was even beginning to resent his nightly ritual drink on his way home. If he had spare time he wanted to be with her. The fact that she had attempted to explain herself to him tonight pleased him very much. It never occurred to him that, in time, she wouldn't respond. Her caution only increased her attraction. Clive had never failed with a woman he had really wanted. In fact, throughout his life, he had steadily achieved anything he set his heart on, using whatever means he thought necessary.

On the Monday morning of March twenty-sixth, Ben Neale helped Kate with her two large suitcases. She had packed towels and sheets, a picture she liked, a tapestry cushion and a lamp for by the bed. Gabriel had offered to drive up with the cases, with an armchair she didn't need, later in the day, wanting very much to see where Kate was going to live but Kate had gently refused. At Victoria, Ben helped her off the train, carried the cases to the taxi rank.

'You're dropping these off first?'

'Yes.'

'Goodbye, Katy. Have fun.' He kissed her forehead.

'I shall hate it I expect but I have to move out, don't I?'

'So they say. And you'll love it. Ring me and come and have lunch if you're lonely. See you Friday.'

She watched his tall figure move away. A taxi came and she gave the address in Queensgate Gardens and was too shy to ask the driver to help with the cases. She dragged them up the stairs on her own and was late into the office as a result and full of apologies.

'It's all right,' Clive said.

'I should have come up last night. I would have but I could tell my mother didn't want me to. She doesn't want me to move out and Sunday evenings are a bit of a ritual for her, Evensong and soup and talking . . .' She stopped suddenly, embarrassed because the words had run away with her.

'Where is the flat? Clive asked.

'Queensgate Gardens.'

'A rabbit warren of a place, littered with records and knickers and bottles of the most revolting drink? Stones Ginger wine and bitter lemon? Is it like that?'

Kate laughed, merrily, like a child. 'Exactly. The bathroom is festooned with wet tights. One of the girls, Judith, is very tidy but the other is awful. I shall love it. After my home where relays of daily women come in and tidy everything and arrange the untidy things in neat heaps, I shall love living in squalor!' She laughed again and then gave a small, shy shrug of her shoulders.

She had a most attractive laugh, Clive thought, liking it when she talked like this, so quickly, the words spilling out as if she could not stop them, the excitement she felt obvious. 'You must ask me in for a drink some evening! I'll bring the drink, though.'

'All right,' Kate smiled. 'I will.'

She disappeared briefly and came back carrying the coffee Clive had asked for, and her notebook, and she sat on the edge of the leather armchair which was too big for her, hair tucked behind one ear. She looked up expectantly. It pleased Clive that his instinct about her proved right. She was good at her job. She was conscientious and now that she had overcome the initial difficulties of finding her way around, efficient. She was beginning to look different, too, Clive noticed, dressing in a far younger, more fashionable way. The clothes were strange but they suited her boyish figure. She had no hips at all. She always sat or stood or moved her body with self-possession, despite her obvious shyness. 'You trained to be a dancer, did you, Kate?'

She had been sitting still under his scrutiny. 'Yes. Eight years. Everyone thinks it's a terrible disappointment to me not to have gone on but they're wrong. I used myself up. Far better to stop than go on to a second-rate career. I just felt aimless when I stopped.'

'Brothers and sisters?'

'Just me. Spoiled, sheltered only child.' She grinned suddenly in the disconcerting way she had, her face lighting.

'Is there a boy next door in Sussex?'

She shook her head and the soft hair came untucked from behind her ear. 'No. No one at all.'

'But there used to be?' Clive probed gently, leaning forward. 'That's why you came to London, wasn't it? New start?'

'Yes, there was someone.' She tried to talk lightly, to give the impression it was all long ago and done with. 'And he did live virtually next door.'

Clive smiled and wondered if she could still be a virgin. She was shy, certainly, but there was an undercurrent about her which intrigued. The telephone in her office rang and Kate went to answer it. Clive's mind wandered. He thought about the flat she described. He was always aroused by the female clutter that women took for granted. Like Caroline's flat, make-up, shoes and bags, underclothes . . . The telephone rang on his desk.

'It's the agent about the shop in Meadwell Street. Miss Jacobs has accepted Mrs Boyd's offer.'

'Marvellous. I'll speak to him and then you try and get Mrs Boyd, will you? Then the Mackfield Building Society, head office, and after that we'll do the letters!'

There was no time, in the day, to feel strange. Days were too short, the work frequently overflowing towards six o'clock and after. But the evenings in that flat, throughout the first week, Kate found very strange. Venn was there on Monday evening and then she left on a South American run. 'I'll be back Saturday.' Judith had left to work for a family in Scotland for two months and Kate was quite alone for the first time in her life.

When she first let herself in, she would wander around, just looking at it all, registering the emptiness, the stillness. Silence was quite new to her. After a while it made her uneasy to hear her own movements and she would put on some music that she liked, very loudly, and run a bath, lying in it with the door open, letting music in and steam out; then she would tour the flat, barefoot, face washed clean of make-up. She never bothered to cook. She ate bread and cheese or sultanas or fruit or Judith's muesli. Gabriel usually rang just before eight. On Thursday Kate rang Alice and went to see her. But on the whole, for the first time in her life, she had absolute command of herself and her time. No one attempted to cheer her up. She left her clothes where they fell. The smell of the flat, the dark mystery of its corners, the sound of its windows and hinges and floor-boards and water pipes, the telephone bell, the dust in the air, the heavy musty peace of it, became familiar. And there was time, at last, to mourn David.

When she first allowed herself to think about him without any reserve, imagining him here with her, making him say the things she wanted, it became so real it scared her. She rolled herself into a tight ball of pain, remembering tiny details of him, crying herself to sleep. But even as she cried she enjoyed the knowledge that there was no one to hide from, wash her face for. She was alone.

On the following Monday Venn returned, altering the atmosphere completely. She was a tall, pretty girl of twenty-four who hated to be bored, who laughed a lot. In a couple of hours she created chaos, littering the rooms with her belongings, constantly smoking the duty-free cigarettes she had brought back with her. She settled herself by the telephone and began to arrange a small party for that evening. Four men were asked and two other girls and Kate found herself swept into it all. They drank freely of Venn's duty-free gin and walked to a bistro where they stayed until midnight. The man Kate talked to most was small and fair-haired with a round, unappealing face. He walked back home with her and up all the stairs without being asked. He sat himself down on the sofa and reached for Kate.

'Shall I make you some coffee?' she said, sliding out of his reach, absurdly polite, knowing what he wanted and wishing she had stopped him coming here.

He shook his head and his eyes glittered and he caught at her hand, pulled her down to sit beside him. She stayed, docile for a moment, wondering how it would feel with someone else. He kissed her, banging his mouth against hers, pushing her hair about with his hand roughly and saying her name. She tried, opening her mouth for him, but she didn't like it. She didn't like his mouth or the smell or the feel of him. He began fondling her small breasts and Kate dragged herself away.

54

'Don't!'

'Why not?' he said, wheedling, as if he expected it, as if it were all part of the ritual. 'Come on . . .' She watched him approach again. She despised him.

'I don't know you and I don't want you and we've got no coffee.' She stood up, arms folded, voice flatly rude.

He looked amazed. She was such a little thing . . . 'Don't be silly, Katy.'

'My name is Kate. I'm tired. I wish you'd go!' Then, like a prompted child: 'Thank you for the meal . . .'

It was all too much trouble. He stood up, shrugged and left, slamming the door, leaving her in total silence. The flat felt menacing for the first time. The rough parody of love-making had scraped the top off the wound David had left. She couldn't sleep. She took out the old notebook she wrote in. There was a poem she'd written. She had shown this book to no one except David, handing him all her feelings, written down, waiting, wide open and as vulnerable as when she waited with her body.

'What does this mean? "The silent rainbows of the blind." It's beautiful, but what does it mean?'

'Nothing.'

She fell asleep in the armchair, book open in her lap, and woke cold and very stiff when she heard Venn in the room below. Kate had been dreaming of Clive, dreaming that she was curled on his lap.

Gabriel rang the next morning, early, her voice excited. 'David rang. He's been on a course for three weeks. He asked for your number. He asked all about you. I hope you don't mind. I gave it to him . . .'

Her heart lurched, beat in great marching thuds. 'Did he say why he wanted it? No, I don't mind. See you Friday.'

All that day she walked in a daze, buying sandwiches at lunch and taking them to Cavendish Square, sitting under a plane tree and pretending it wasn't cold. She found she had no appetite and fed the fat pigeons. She imagined so many different kinds of reconciliation, imagined them laughing over all this wasted time, and wasted love. She stayed far too long and the grass grew warm beneath her and the wind came and ruffled the pigeons. They had eaten all Kate's food and they wandered away and she realized how late it was, running back to the office, arriving breathless and almost colliding with Michael Paul. He frowned, disapprovingly, as she stammered apologies. Clive, watching from his office door, winked at her.

All that evening she hardly left the telephone, lying on her stomach on the floor, head on her folded arms, watching it as if it were a television. Once it rang for Judith. Twice for Venn. Once it was Gabriel. Each time she let it ring six rings, pretending she was busy. No more. Nothing the next night or the next. On Friday, going home in the crowded train, she thought: He never really meant to ring at all.

CHAPTER FOUR

The Wednesday afternoon flight from Marseilles was nearly an hour late when it landed at Heathrow. The Air France Boeing touched down rather heavily and Michael Redford sat forward in his seat and looked out of the oval window at a wet airport, the tarmac shining after a sudden violent rainstorm. As he watched, the sun came out, but he leaned back and sighed quietly, his mood bleak. He always felt like this when he came back from France . . . for eleven months of the year he pushed himself as hard as he could. When he allowed himself to stop it was so pleasant that he wondered why he lived his life as he did. For the past four weeks he had been completely happy. For three weeks he had skied obsessively. Three weeks at Val d'Isère with superb weather and perfect snow, the days spent stretching himself to his physical limits, the evenings peaceful, either dining with friends who came to the resort each year or eating alone. Michael Redford was a genuinely solitary man. He did not need other people. He could be charming if he wanted to but always underneath was a layer of reserve, almost of disdain. There were a lot of pretty girls at Val d'Isère but Michael had come for the skiing, to renew himself in the clean white light of the high mountains.

For the last four days of his holiday he did have company. His friend, Henri Bertrand, had driven to join him. On the Monday they went back to Jouvard together, the journey taking most of the day, and they had talked a great deal especially at the beginning when the chains on the wheels of the car and the twisting snowy roads made it necessary to travel so slowly. They spoke of Valerie de Jouvard, Michael's grandmother.

'She doesn't change much,' Henri said, 'although she has softened and aged these last two years but she is still a force to be reckoned with. She is nagging Gautier about the replanting.

Personally I hope they will wait until you come . . .'

'You're so sure that I will?'

Henri laughed. He was thirty-five, a quiet, kind man who had married a tough, very beautiful girl when he was a medical student in Paris. He had qualified and practised in a suburb for five years until his hopeless marriage finally collapsed and Colette removed herself and their daughter; then Henri amazed all his friends by abandoning medicine and moving south. He had bought an old cotton factory, twenty kilometres west of Jouvard, made up of a derelict house and some big stone outbuildings. When Henri took over it produced a small amount of traditional Provençal cotton. He began, at first rather cautiously, to introduce his own designs, flower designs he had been painting for years in the evenings, taking immense trouble over the detail and the colour; he had borrowed money and bought machinery. Ten modern knitting machines to make up imported American cotton yarn; he employed another designer, made his house habitable, began to make his French, hand-blocked cottons into pretty and saleable clothes.

'I think,' Henri said, 'it is important to make your living in a place where you want to live. You can't spend your whole life in London. I know you. Sooner or later you'll come and run Château de Jouvard.

Michael didn't answer but he remembered Henri's words as they neared their destination, as the landscape became familiar. He could have described each small field, every line of the mountains. Although he had never lived more than a few months at a time here, it was like coming home to turn on to the last narrow road with its tall earth banks, thick bamboo hedges, and then bend sharply left through iron gates to see the old house amongst its sprawling grey buildings. On one side and behind the neat vineyards, on the other the trees and lawn of the sheltered garden his grandmother had tended for so many years.

'Will you come in and see her?'

'No.' Henri stretched his back, aching after the long journey. He yawned. 'When do you go back to London?'

'On the Wednesday afternoon flight. Come and have dinner tomorrow. She always enjoys seeing you.'

She was standing in the hall, waiting for him, her head bent as she listened. 'Is that you, Michael?' He opened the doors and came in.

'Yes.' He came towards her, putting down his case and leaning his skiis against the wall. He put his arms round her and kissed her, seeing she had aged in the six months since his last visit.

When Michael's grandfather did, two years before, a part of Valerie had died with him. She had always been energetic and rather arrogant, given to strong opinions. As a young girl she had been large and plain. She had adored her attractive husband and she still could not accept his death. It was the first time he had ever let her down. Now she was gentler, older, still talking incessantly at times but her voice and manner demonstrated how lonely she was. During the time Michael spent with her at Jouvard, walking with her through every field, inspecting the machinery, tasting the wine, discussing the plans with Raoul Gautier, at times his grandmother would come to him and take his hand, holding it tightly; at other times she would walk apart from him, seeming to resent him. It was as if, having forced herself to get used to life on her own, his presence was an effort.

'The old are shut out, Michael,' she said one night at dinner. 'There is no place for us. It is as if the deterioration of our bodies were some kind of obscene failure not to be looked at and we are expected to accept uselessness as well.'

'But you have so much to do here.'

'Yes. We should be replanting, Michael . . . when are you going to come here and run things? We need your energy.'

'Do you want me to? Seriously?' They had been speaking in French for the past two days. The first evening Valerie insisted on English. It was her way of pointing out that Michael was not yet a Frenchman. Now she had relaxed, forgiven him, honoured him with her native tongue.

'I have always said I wanted you here, haven't I? Ever since you were a child. Marie-Claire, having married an Englishman, will never want to live here. Your mother does not want it. Anyway, it's yours as soon as I die, you know that. Sooner, if you want.' She picked up her wine glass, drinking slowly. 'We always said you would live here, didn't we? Even when you were a boy. Speaking of that, how is your friend Clive? Still charming people, wanting more out of life than he is prepared to put in? Still thinking his smile will get him anything he wants?'

Michael laughed. 'Why did you never like him?'

'Many reasons. But each time he came here with you, as you both grew up, I distrusted him more. Perhaps because he tried so hard to please me and I have always been a plain woman, suspicious of ladies' men!' She fitted a cigarette into a short green holder. 'When I die, will you come here, Michael, or will you sell it? Tell me the truth. It concerns me more than anything else. There have been Jouvards here since eighteen thirty-two.'

Michael would never have considered telling lies in order to make her happy. It would have been quite alien to his nature. 'Five years ago I would have said that I could not live here. But I have changed. I have made a success of this ridiculous company I run. God knows why people buy the stuff but they do. Now it bores me. I love this part of France, I love this place. I think it would fascinate me to run it. Yes. I want to come here very much.'

'When?'

'A year. Two at the most. I must give myself time to sell out advantageously, to round things off in England. There is one more clock, of my own design, I want to market. It has interested me for over a year. It is a large table clock.'

She listened as he described it, his voice and face alive with interest. 'Don't wait too long,' she said softly. 'And don't come just because you are sorry for me!' Her voice was harsh but her eyes implored him.

'You know me too well for that!'

Michael had intended to take the airport bus into London but the delay of his aeroplane had caused a build-up of passengers and when he finally cleared customs he was tired and impatient. He hailed a taxi and gave the Cambridge Street address. Spring had come to England since he had been away. He was not a particularly observant man, except about the detail of the idea which happened to be fascinating him at the time, but it was pleasant to see the blossom on the trees, the daffodils. He leaned back in his seat, anticipating the rest of the week . . . for the first time in a month he would have to wear reasonably respectable clothes, would have to cope with the accumulated disasters of the past four weeks, would have to pretend to care whether the Design Centre had approved the latest range of desk-top instruments and whether the post-Christmas lull had finally worn off. He thought of the endless succession of trade shows and groaned. Why the hell didn't he sell out, marry Susie, and go to France? Learn the business of making wine and change the whole direction of his life? Clive, he knew, would love to get his hands on Mosaic.

When the taxi stopped outside his narrow white house, Michael unloaded his skiis and boots, suitcase and plastic carrier bag of duty-free whisky on to the pavement and paid the driver. English money looked unfamiliar. He let himself in, leaning his skiis against the faded striped wallpaper in the hall, tossing down his suitcase and boots. The round ship's clock in the kitchen said just before five. He shrugged off his anorak, thought about making himself a cup of coffee and couldn't be bothered. He seemed to have been travelling all day and he was tired and felt dirty. And always, when he had nothing definite to do, he went upstairs for a bath.

The news that her offer was accepted, that barring disasters

Meadwell Street would be hers, had filled Caroline with excitement and energy. Clive seemed to think of everything, of life insurance, that she would need a car, to give notice in her present flat, to get hold of her money. She expected possession at the end of April and she held that day ahead of her, a goal, a beginning. And she and Clive slipped into a loose routine. There was definite affection between them, enjoyment of each other's company and a kind of pause. Clive thought, as she did, that once she had moved to Meadwell Street the relationship would deepen. He was content, knowing she enjoyed being with him, that she relaxed more each time she saw him, came to expect and enjoy the way he held her, touched her, kissed her; he did not press her to sleep with him. He sensed she was not ready.

About once a week Caroline cooked a meal at Cambridge Street. She enjoyed the planning and the shopping. This evening there would be four of them but as usual she had bought enough food for twice that number. She arrived at Cambridge Street at a quarter past five with a large cardboard box, fumbling with the unfamiliar key as the taxi behind her vibrated out of sight. She backed in the front door, arms full, and saw the skis as she pushed the door shut with her foot. An anorak was slung over a stool. She saw the unmistakable bags of duty-free alcohol on the kitchen table and was aware of the singing of hot water pipes. So he was back, the mysterious Michael Redford? She hesitated, wondering whether or not to call out and decided not to. Clive must have given keys to people before. She would wait until she heard Michael coming down.

Caroline made herself a pot of tea and tied the striped apron over her skirt. She put a lemon mousse which she had made earlier that morning into the fridge and turned on the transistor radio. Cheerful, repetitive music poured out. She preferred it now to the classical music she had listened to for years. She wanted to be distracted, even irritated. She did not want to think or feel too much.

The Finches were coming tonight. Caroline washed lettuce

and watercress; she made a salad dressing and chopped nuts for the mousse and sang with the radio. With her hair tied back, elated as she was by the thought of the shop, she looked far younger than her age.

'Hello.' He had heard her from the floor above. She jumped at the sound of his voice and swung round. She saw a tall man, narrowly built, very sunburnt, his dark hair damp from the bath and smoothed against his head. 'I'm sorry. Did I frighten you?'

'Yes . . . but you shouldn't have. I knew you were here. I saw the skis.' She wiped her hands down her apron. 'I'm Caroline Boyd.'

'Michael Redford.' He stood in the centre of the doorway making no effort to come in.

He was so unlike the mental image she had had of the man Clive described. 'How was the snow?'

'Very good for the first two weeks. Some of the best powder snow I remember. The third week it got a little slushy. Do you ski?'

'No.' He watched her so intently with his narrow, clever face that it made her feel shy. It surprised her. She was too old to be awkward with a stranger. She turned down the radio. 'Would you like some tea?'

'Tea?' He drew his eyebrows in and smiled. 'Now I know I'm back in England. I'll pour it. You go on with whatever it is you're cooking.' He came into the room and unhooked a mug from the dresser. 'I've never seen this teapot before. Is it mine?'

'I suppose so. I found it in the back of that cupboard.'

He poured the tea from a height as a child might for fun, as the Mad March Hare poured it. He sat on one of the stools. 'What's that?'

'It's a cold soup. And there is beef, salad and new potatoes, lemon mousse and a very nice bit of Brie. I hope you'll eat some later. There's far too much for four. I always cook too much.' She took small, snatched glances at him as she spoke.

'Oh, I don't want to push myself into your party. I didn't tell

63

Clive I'd be back today . . .'

'It's not a party. I love cooking and since I've lived alone I don't have enough opportunity. The Finches are coming tonight. Do you know them?'

'I don't think so but I never remember names.' He drank from the mug of tea. 'Funny, this isn't a bad drink . . . but I never make it. It reminds me of breakfast in small hotels.' He smiled the funny, closed-mouth smile.

'I'll bring you some really good tea to try one day . . . who buys this stuff? You or Clive?'

He shrugged. 'We have no system. I think that's why we've always got on quite amicably. No rules to break.' He was silent then, making no effort to continue the conversation. This silence was Michael's normal reaction when he felt unsure of himself. He would rather say nothing than something foolish but Caroline found it awkward and searched for something to say. It was very unusual for her to be ill at ease. The telephone rang, saving her the trouble of speaking, but he let it ring six or seven times before he moved into the hall to answer it. He walked slowly, rather gracefully, as if his body and his limbs were well put together.

Caroline began to clear the kitchen, waiting for him to return and wanting him to. She had imagined, or Clive had described, a clever, ordinary face. She had pictured a small man, probably with glasses, the lines of a frown on his forehead. Not this . . .? No words came to describe Michael Redford. She could hear his voice. She worked swiftly and the kitchen was immaculate, the only room Caroline ever kept tidy. She folded the apron.

He put down the telephone as she came into the hall. 'You're not going?'

'Yes. I've finished for the moment.'

'Have you got a car here?'

'No.'

'Then I'll drive you. It might rain.'

She was tying a scarf over her hair. She was disconcerted by his offer. 'Please don't bother.'

'But I'd like to. I always feel terrible the day I get back from a holiday. Restless and miserable. I'd much rather drive you home than sit here and anticipate all the disasters which are waiting for me at Mosaic.' He was searching a drawer in the hall table for keys, making a loud scrabbling noise. He pulled out a small bunch and turned back to her, wishing, as he had wished only occasionally before, that he had Clive's ability to talk interestingly to total strangers. But then, he thought, Clive likes people and I do not. But she is different, this lovely, solemn woman, so unexpectedly in my house.

Caroline smiled. 'Well, thank you. I live in South Kensington. Pelham Square.' She moved past him to the front door and the hall was so narrow that she brushed against him. She hesitated, looking up into his face, rather surprised at the sensation of being close to him.

'I rent a garage in Hugh Street,' Michael said, closing the door behind them. 'I hope the car will start. It hasn't been used for a month and it's temperamental at the best of times,' He led the way across the street, unlocked the first of a row of garages.

Caroline peered into the darkness. 'What is it?'

'An elderly Porsche. I hope the keys are in it.' He climbed in and opened the passenger door. 'I bought it in a weak moment because Susie liked it and I've been too lazy to change it for something smaller and more sensible. But I hate it and it hates me.'

Caroline's laughter was drowned as the engine started. The sound was exaggerated in the small garage. Michael backed the car slowly into the street. He fiddled with the radio and it crackled into life. 'Only thing that's any good is the radio!' He made the car surge forward and there was music as an excuse not to talk.

At a set of traffic lights Caroline looked at him at exactly the same moment he looked at her. They exchanged wary smiles.

'What do you do?' he asked. He had been searching for

65

something to say and thankfully seized on this least original of questions.

'Nothing yet but I'm in the process of buying an antique shop. It's very near where you are . . . the Kings Road end of Meadwell Street.'

'So I can come and buy from you?'

'Or I from you.'

'Perhaps we could meet in the middle and barter?'

She laughed and Michael overtook a motor bike so dangerously that she shut her eyes.

'I'm sorry. Did I frighten you? I'm afraid I drive rather badly.'

'I've never heard a man admit to that before.' It was still there, the feeling, enclosed in the car like this, the words just details.

'You're supposed to deny it!' They both laughed. 'You said you lived alone?'

'Yes.' She was ready to fend off questions. 'I'm divorced.'

He merely asked, 'Which number in Pelham Square?'

'Seventeen. Behind that yellow van.' The car stopped and she opened her door. 'Thank you very much. I hope you'll be there later, to eat some of the huge meal I've cooked.'

'I suppose so.' He leaned his forearms on the steering wheel. 'Do you have to go now? It's only six-thirty. Come and have a drink somewhere?'

She paused, very surprised, looking at him. 'I'd like to, Michael, but I can't. I have to change and Clive is picking me up at seven-thirty.' Her voice was quiet.

He gave her the funny closed-mouth smile. 'Well, I'll definitely see you later then.'

When Caroline let herself into her flat she went to the window and looked down at the square. His car was still there. She watched it for two or three minutes and then it suddenly moved away, making a red Mini brake sharply and hoot.

The telephone rang while Caroline was in the bath. She had

washed her hair under the shower and as she hurried to the telephone the heavy wet mass straggled down her back. She left a trail of wet prints. 'Hello?'

'Hullo, chef. It's Clive. I forgot to ask you what we are eating? What sort of wine?'

'Beef . . . anything red. In fact I've got some nice Burgundy here . . .

'Don't you dare. The least we can do is provide the wine. I say "we" but I mean Michael. I gather you've met and he seems keen to join us. And Susie will probably come too. Can we feed six?'

'Easily.' The knowledge that the girl was coming gave her a feeling of disappointment which she instantly stifled, angry with herself. No one in the world, married or unmarried, was totally unattached.

Caroline brushed her hair, dried it and thought as she had so many times since her divorce, that perhaps she should cut it. She looped it on top of her head with pins and combs and knelt on the stool by her dressing-table, to make up her face. Now that it mattered again she had begun to study her face more closely, seeing the fine lines beneath her eyes, each side of her mouth, the penalty of her smile. But it was still a young face, the skin smooth. It was easy to make her large eyes look even bigger with a little shadow on the heavy eyelids.

Caroline looked like her mother and her aunt. She had been a beautiful child and had grown into a beautiful woman. She had accepted her looks at an early age and they did not excite her. It pleased her that men sought her out and it was good to attract attention in a gathering but she knew her beauty was passive. Available girls would always claim far more attention. The fact that Harry, who had been so proud of the way she looked, had looked elsewhere only proved what she always suspected, that all beauty gave you was the opening.

She put on one of her long silky shirt-dresses, the magnificent string of pearls Harry had given her when they were engaged and some scent. She turned out the lights in her chaotic bedroom and drank a glass of wine while she waited for Clive.

Susie was a wisp of a girl, nipples pressing provocatively through a soft angora dress. Clive, who appeared to have known her as long as Michael, flirted with her kindly, attended to her while Michael ignored her and talked to Rachel and Ian Finch about skiing in France. There was about the evening, Caroline thought, an uncomfortable atmosphere as if there would be an argument later. She watched Michael make a sudden and guilty effort to talk to Susie. Two large drinks had made Caroline honest with herself. She returned Clive's frequent, intimate smiles and felt no excitement. She looked at Michael Redford, a man who would always look younger than his age, his long body the type which would always be lean. At this moment he looked bored, staring into his glass, listening to Susie. Caroline knew he was not concentrating on the conversation. He turned his head and met her eyes for the first time that evening and a wave of sympathy and interest passed between them.

It was after ten when they finally sat down. Caroline's meals were always late. They were loosened by the drinks they had had and the noise in the little candle-lit dining-room was enormous. Clive as usual dominated the conversation and Rachel was always ready to argue, her pointed face vividly made up, her red hair cut very short. Under the table her knee brushed Clive's leg frequently, reminding him. And they talked about money, the difficulties of making and keeping enough, of living life as they wanted to.

Michael finished his food long before the others. He always ate tremendously fast, disinterestedly, merely wanting to get the meal done. Now he circled the table, filling wine glasses, pausing at Caroline's shoulder.

'What I think is interesting,' he said, 'is the way some people's lives are settled at twenty, planned out and carried through in a straight predictable line, while others constantly change. You, Clive, have yours arranged. Caroline is about to start something quite new. So am I, I suppose.'

'Jouvard?' Clive asked.

'Yes.'

'So you haven't been wasting your time on your visit to Granny?'

Michael laughed. 'She still hates you too. I was glad to hear her sound vitriolic again. She's softened so much, Clive. She's more gentle and sadder.' He sat down.

'So you'll sell Mosaic?' Ian Finch asked.

'Yes. Quit while I'm ahead and go and learn about growing grapes. They were pruning when I was there and ploughing. March is a good month to see the plan of it all. They have to finish the first racking before the end of the month because of this mysterious sympathy between the wine and vines. A second fermentation is supposed to start when the sap in the vines rises and at Château de Jouvard they do everything the traditional way!' He was talking more to himself than the others and his face wore an expression both Clive and Susie knew well.

When the meal was over and coffee was finished Clive suggested they all go on and drink and dance. Rachel and Ian were eager.

'Would you mind if we didn't go?' Michael said to Susie.

'I didn't think we would.'

Michael said a rather stiff good night to Caroline. The house was suddenly quiet and Susie poured brandy into both their glasses. For four years she had waited for him, hoped for him. It was much too long. It hurt too much to go on loving a man who was happier on his own, who needed to be alone more than he needed to be with her.

'Susie . . .' He sat forward. This afternoon he had thought of marrying her. Now, a few hours later, he knew he never would. He wanted to tell her to find someone else who could be what she needed.

'I'd like to say it first.' She sat on the floor, facing him. 'I've

69

been thinking while you were away. I do it every year but this time I'm acting on it. I've moved out of the flat. I've been with my parents for a couple of weeks and on Friday I fly to Washington. I have an aunt and cousins there. I'm going to see as much of the States as I can until my money runs out and then I hope to work. I won't come back this year.'

He felt a sudden affection for her, for the dignity in her face. 'I don't know why things didn't . . .'

'I do,' she said softly. 'That's why I'm going. Funny, this is all coming out much more easily than I expected.' She moved across the floor, sat beside him. 'Did you know that Clive's new secretary has moved into my old flat? Buy me a drink for old times' sake, Michael. Wish me luck. And I hope you get her away from Clive if that's what you want.' She laughed at his expression. 'My love, you've watched her the whole evening. You've addressed every sentence to her. I admit she's beautiful but isn't she a little old for you?'

The remark was quite wasted on Michael. He was grateful to Susie for getting out of his life with so little protest and he took her to one of Clive's favourite nightclubs and they spent an hour drinking and dancing. He was never at ease in such places. He drove her home and kissed her goodbye, feeling a mixture of relief and sadness, resolving to send her a telegram and flowers on Friday but he forgot almost at once.

When he let himself into the house again it was just after two. Four clocks in the sitting-room chimed in succession. Clive was sitting on the long sofa, smoking a last cigar, waiting for Michael.

'How long have you known Caroline?'

'About a month. She wandered into my office on my birthday.'

'You didn't cope with the divorce then?'

'No. All done. No kids luckily. I think that was part of the trouble but she never talks about it. Michael, did you mean that about going to France?'

'Yes.'

'You know I'd like to own Mosaic wholly?'

'Yes. And there's no reason why I shouldn't sell out to you but I'd rather discuss it another time.' He smiled.

'Sure,' Clive said. 'Good night.' He stayed where he was to finish his cigar, to think about Marketing Mosaic and Caroline.

'But he's not at all what I imagined,' she had said of Michael. 'For some reason I imagined glasses. A boffin face. I pictured a plain man. He looks so young . . .'

'Twenty-seven,' Clive had answered. 'He's eight months younger than I am.'

'Very unusual eyes. Almost black.'

'Are you trying to make me jealous?' Clive had smiled. 'I've known Mike since we were eight and I can honestly say I've never noticed the colour of his eyes.'

'What an appallingly English male statement,' she had teased him. They had been sitting in Clive's car outside her flat and she had opened the door but had not asked him to come up. He came out to kiss her good night. The skin of her face was very white in the street light, her eyes larger and more secret than ever. He felt a sudden unbearable impatience for her. He had waited long enough.

'Caroline?'

She had kissed him lightly, quickly, as if she couldn't wait to escape and hurried into the hall.

CHAPTER FIVE

On Monday, April thirtieth, Caroline got possession of the shop in Meadwell Street. On May the first the signwriter painted 'Caroline Carter. Antiques.' in big white letters on a dark brown ground. She had decided to use her maiden name. She had bought a Peugeot estate car which she collected that morning and the sun shone all day. The paint dried quickly and cleanly.

On Wednesday, wearing the first pair of jeans she had owned for eight years, she supervised the unloading of her furniture. She ran happily from floor to floor, unpacking tea-chests, making cups of coffee; she came down to talk to the man who ran the shop immediately next door, a very smart double-fronted establishment. 'Hello . . . I thought I must introduce myself. I'm Brian Lessing.' He had come out of curiosity. He stayed to help. 'When will you re-open?'

'Well, it all needs re-decorating. Tomorrow the painters start in here and I haven't nearly enough stock yet although I took over some from Dorie. I shall have to do a lot of buying in the next few weeks but I hope to re-open by the end of May. I don't want to miss out on the tourists.'

'You must come down the road. We are like a pass-the-parcel game half the time, buying from one another. You must meet Fred and Amy Smith, opposite you. And Belinda Bell. She's next door to me.'

He smiled. He had beautiful white teeth and a lot of grey hair and Caroline guessed, quite rightly, that he was an unsuccessful actor.

'I haven't explored at all yet, but I will.' Her attention was demanded by one of the removal men, his arms full of her plants, his resigned face peering at her through the thick fronds of fern.

'Can you put them all in the garden at the back, please. I'll sort them out later.'

It seemed to take an absurdly long time to bring everything in, and to unpack the tea-chests. She had thought she had so little. Her bed was piled high with clothes. Four cases arrived which she had had in storage. At last, just after five, the van was empty. She gave the men a last cup of tea and a five-pound note and was thankfully left alone in the chaos. She poured herself a huge whisky and excitement and exhaustion mingled with the alcohol to make her light-headed. She walked from floor to floor, planning colours, things she would sell, a wonderful future; she went down to the damp stillness of the basement with its bare light bulbs and stone floors; she came up again and sat at the big pedestal desk which she had bought and stood at the back of the showroom. She touched the neat box files, the new blue books of blank invoices, the tray of biros. Like a child with a new doll's house, she thought, laughing at herself, shivering her shoulders in excitement.

She opened the glass door which led out to the wooden steps and the paved garden. It was surrounded by a wall of faded bricks and one tall plane tree grew at the far end, its lumpy roots pushing aside the paving stones which got in the way. There was a flower bed, almost empty, and all Caroline's plants and a lot of afternoon sunshine. She took off her shoes and sat on the top step, eyes closed, face turned up towards the sun, basking like a big cat. The sound of the Kings Road traffic was muffled. When she heard the bell it took a few seconds for her to register that it was the door of the shop. She got up reluctantly, to go and explain she had nothing to sell yet.

It was Michael Redford. He wore a fawn suit and a tie and he looked so different from the evening Caroline had met him at Cambridge Street that she hardly recognized him for a moment. He closed the door. He carried a tissue-wrapped bottle. She had not seen him for nearly three weeks but she had thought about him frequently.

'I thought you might want some refreshment.' He unwrapped the bottle of champagne. 'Would you like some now? It's cold.

73

Or you can keep it for later.'

The first surprise was becoming pleasure. 'What a lovely idea!' She thought how much she liked this intelligent face. 'But I don't know where any glasses are. Come up and we'll look.'

'You are exactly one minute's walk from Mosaic.' He followed her up the flight of stairs which led directly into the living-area. The back part of the room was divided off to form a kitchen and the square pine table and every surface was covered with china and glass and cooking utensils. Caroline found wine glasses on top of the fridge and held them out triumphantly as Michael opened the bottle. The cork hit the ceiling. He filled the glasses. 'To your success!'

'How did you know I was moving in today?'

'I asked Clive. I hope you don't mind my coming . . . I should have telephoned you but I loathe the telephone. I never manage to make myself understood. I tend to speak when the other person does . . . as on a long-distance call.'

'Of course I don't mind.' She leaned against the kitchen table. The quite definite attraction she felt made her uneasy and she concentrated with some effort, pushing back the pleasant cloudiness of the alcohol and trying to remember what they had talked about the last time . . . 'How did you find things at Marketing Mosaic?' she said at last.

'Not quite as bad as I expected.' He sat down on the sofa and she crossed the room and sat at the opposite end. There was nowhere else. Every other surface was covered with books or crockery or curtains. 'But I've had enough of it. Clive will tell you it is typical of me that I always lose interest when a problem is mastered but that's only partly true. I now realize that the end product of Mosaic is not what I want. The business is by no means completely organized . . . new problems come up every day but not the sort I want to deal with. I loved the design side. My father was an engineer and a designer . . . I should have done that. But unfortunately it's not that side which makes the money. It's marketing other people's stuff. They do all the hard work, get over all the problems and we cream off a percentage. I knew nothing about this business when I started. I imagine my personality is the exact opposite of a good salesman. Words never come easily to me. For four years I have worked bloody hard, spending days at trade shows in huge provincial hotels, forcing myself to become a salesman and to explain the products. We've got some good things now. Chess sets which were in the shopping page of the *Times* last week and in the Design Centre. At last I've got it going but I've also realized I don't want to be doing this in two years' time.' He sat with his long legs stretched straight out in front, the glass resting at an angle on his concave stomach.

'You're sure it isn't just the sudden sunshine?'

'No. The feeling has been building up for over a year. That's why I looked for someone like Jenny. I have one more project. This Sundial clock. I've always been fascinated by clocks especially by early clocks, and the enormous advance when someone discovered the mechanical clock. Before that, time was more rounded, less precise. Water clocks, portable sundials and fireclocks . . . The Sundial is merely a name for this clock I want to produce. It is a table clock. About twelve inches across the face. I want it to be a beautiful thing. To sit on a table. To be looked down at. Have you been to the British Museum? Have you seen the clocks there?'

She shook her head. 'What did you do before Mosaic?'

'School. University. I was reading the wrong subject and it bored me and I was sent down in nineteen sixty-five. I was advised to do accountancy and I was articled for four years but by the time I qualified I was bored with it. I already had the idea for Mosaic.' His voice altered. 'My father died, quite unexpectedly, and I used the money he left me to start the business. In the beginning I literally worked day and night . . . Luckily I'm quite happy on my own. I enjoy hard work. I don't like parties and I don't feel any great need to be liked.'

'You've known Clive for years?'

75

'We met at Prep school. Clive could always handle school. I hated it. I stammered very badly as a child and I wanted to learn what interested me, which was not necessarily what they taught. I couldn't hit a ball or run a hundred yards . . . Clive was always bailing me out. We went on to public school together and he thrived and I struggled. He could wriggle out of any corner, frequently towing me with him. We spent a lot of holidays in France, at Jouvard. Clive's career at school was exceptional. He used the system to his own advantage. He sailed close to the wind but never got caught . . . It was natural that, when I got a house in London, Clive would move in. I have very few friends, male or female. I hope he can take over Mosaic. I'd like to return the favour and it's his one chance of making money. Clive always needs money.'

'So you'll go to France to live?'

'Yes.'

'What makes you think that this time it will be different? Why will the vineyard absorb you more than anything else? You don't really know what it will be like, do you?' Harry's voice came into her head. 'You don't really know what it would be like to have a child. You imagine some dream baby, not a child that cries all night and is sick . . .' She shivered suddenly.

Michael turned his head towards her. 'I know it will absorb me because it is a continuation of all my interests. Time is there, vital, on a yearly scale . . . and the machinery . . . and a whole new way of life to learn. I don't usually talk so much. I'm sorry.' He sat up and refilled her glass. 'I hope I haven't bored you.'

'You know you haven't,' she said quietly.

'This is a nice place, Caroline. And you intend to make your own way in the world? Restore your self-respect?' His eyes were laughing. 'How long will that take?'

'I've no idea.' She disliked him laughing at her. It was not a game or a pose to be here.

Michael stood up and walked to the window which overlooked the Kings Road. 'I'm sorry I was away when Clive met you.'

She wasn't sure what he meant.

'Do you like the champagne?' he said after a moment.

'Of course. It's delicious.'

'As my future is to be in wine I've decided only to drink the best.' He put the half-empty bottle down. 'I must go. My sister had a baby yesterday. I have to go and see it. Can you think of some suitable comment?'

She laughed. 'I usually say, "What dear little ears" or "Isn't he like you!"' Caroline had visited so many new babies, trying not to let the jealousy and sadness show.

'It's a girl and quite hideous I'm told!'

'Then say she is beautiful. That she looks like her grand-mother!'

'Perhaps I'll say them all.' He smiled the straight smile she was coming to like so much. 'May I visit you again?'

'Of course.'

He went down the stairs very quickly and the bell on the shop door rang as he went out. Caroline sat down and sipped the champagne, eyes closed, admitting the strength of the at-traction now, and a curiosity to touch him. She wished she could have spent the evening alone. For the first time the thought of an evening with Clive did not appeal to her at all.

The baby was sleeping, wrapped in a white cellular blanket, black fluff on its head and its small face flickering with some dream or pain. Michael spent a restless half-hour pacing the hospital room, eating Marie-Claire's fruit, thinking how tired she looked. And when his mother, Suzanne Redford, put her head cautiously round the door and came in, arms full of flowers and presents, kissing Michael vaguely as she passed him, he murmured his goodbyes and escaped.

He found Clive in the kitchen at Cambridge Street, pour-ing himself a beer and looking tired.

'God, I've had a harrowing afternoon, Mike. I've been discussing Karen Hill . . . you remember? The little girl who was knocked down by that fellow in Wimbledon?'

'Yes.' Michael took a can of beer for himself. 'I've been to see Marie. Gave her your love. And I called in on Caroline . . .'

'Oh?' Clive looked surprised. It was most unlike Michael to call in on anyone he wasn't obliged to see. 'How has the move gone?'

'I didn't ask. She seemed all right. The place was chaos.' He went to the window and stared down into the empty garden. 'And talking of moves, we haven't discussed Mosaic again, have we? But I've vaguely mentioned my plans to Jenny and I'm sure she would stay. She's bloody good, Clive. Her judgement is so good. She has a knack of guessing what the retailers will go for and she almost seems to enjoy those awful trade shows. If she stayed on you'd only need to go in once or twice a week. Of course you'd need someone to do the accounts because I do them now but that's no problem!'

'So how do we arrive at a price?'

'God knows. I need capital to take to France, although I don't expect they'll let me take much at first, but I'm not out to screw you.'

'I can sell my flat. After that I shall have to raise a loan because you'll obviously be selling this place and I'll need somewhere to live. But it can be very small. In the end I might run Mosaic full time.' He was thinking aloud.

'Leave Bonnington's?' Michael said.

'Yes.'

'Well, I'll ask around, sound people out and try and come up with a price. I wouldn't go until next year, until the Sundial is launched.' He trod on the pedal of the small dustbin and dropped the empty beer can in with a satisfying thud.

Clive thought about Mosaic as he drove to see Caroline that evening, thought of both Caroline and Mosaic as long-term projects. At a set of traffic lights he was distracted by a blonde girl in a red sports car. Marriage, he thought, would be the end of all that potential. Clive had never been able to resist an invitation from a pretty girl but he now believed his feelings for Caroline were strong enough to change that. Just Caroline. It was a solemn thought but true. He wanted her above all other women. He couldn't remember when he had first realized it. Perhaps half-asleep? Perhaps watching her face and wanting her? The thought had been tiny at first but now it was firmly embedded. Marriage. Caroline. Mosaic.

He found her in a strange mood, elated and restless, showing him the building proudly, pulling him from floor to floor. She took the remaining champagne from the fridge and poured two glasses and when he took her hands, trying to still her, saying: 'I love to see you so happy,' and kissing her mouth, she stood very still. Chillingly still, like a child politely accepting an unwanted adult kiss. It hurt him. 'What is it, Caroline?' His voice was cold.

The last thing she wanted was any kind of analysis. She felt unreal. 'I'm sorry. I'm hungry and I've drunk too much . . . let's go and eat.' Again she took his hand, pulling at him uncharacteristically. Her calmness had always been part of her appeal.

'I thought,' Clive said, as they started to eat, 'that once you had moved it would be some kind of turning point.'

'Yes. Yes, it is.'

'For us? You and I?' He sat opposite her and the table was small. His big face was so serious, so close to hers.

'Give me time . . .' She sought to divert him. 'Tell me about Mosaic. Will you buy it? How will you do that? What is it worth?'

He saw through her strategy but he wanted to discuss it anyway. As he talked, if she closed her eyes there was singing in her ears and a swirling in her head. She hadn't been so drunk for years. She half-listened to Clive. They ate steaks and she drank more wine without noticing. She had to speak carefully now, the words wanting to run together. 'Clive, get me some coffee, please . . .' She laughed. 'I'm paralytic.' Her face was soft and sweet, the hair curling all round it. She leaned her arms on the table. 'I don't often get so drunk, do I?' She made her face rueful, catching her lip in her teeth and making him laugh.

She fell asleep in his car as they drove back. He woke her at Meadwell Street and she mumbled an apology as he put his arm round her to help her up the stairs. She was surprisingly light for such a tall woman. He took her up two flights to the bedroom and she lay on her bed crossways, yawning, laughing as he drew the curtains and turned on the lamp.

He sat down on the bed by her. He had looked forward to this evening for a long time, expecting it to change everything, expecting to make love to her; that afternoon as he sat and discussed the dead child's horrific injuries he had thought of Caroline as peace and sanity; he had plans to discuss with her, the weekend to arrange, things to tell her. That he would be away for the last two days of this week. He bent his head to kiss her face and her closed eyelids. He unbuttoned her shirt, opening it out, laying it each side of her like wings. He put his mouth against her neck and her collar bone and kissed the soft skin between her breasts where she always dabbed scent. She smelt warm and sweet. She wore a white lace bra with a pink rosebud in the centre, innocently contradicting the rounded breasts . . .

The violence with which she pushed him away and sat up amazed him. 'What the hell are you doing?' he said.

'Not like this! Not when I'm drunk. I don't want to drift into an affair. I want to mean it!' Her voice was harsh.

'I do mean it! I've meant it for weeks!' Clive was shouting. He was very hurt. 'How much time do you want, for Christ's sake? I'm not some bloody stranger you've picked up.' He stood staring down at her and many more furious things came into his head but he bit them back as he saw how her face closed up, how she crouched low against the bed as if threatened. His voice changed. 'Caroline . . .' He cared so much, far too much to use his skill to persuade her. 'I have to go away for a couple of days. I shall miss you. I miss you so much when I don't see you . . .' She said nothing. He moved closer to her and touched her shoulder and she shook his hand off and the hurt and fury poured into him again.

He had to take the anger away and he swung out of the room, slamming the door so violently the whole building shook. He ran down the two flights of stairs. He stopped by her desk and the rage was already muted, was disappointment. He took a sheet of paper and her pen and wrote: '*I love you. That's why I behave as I do . . . Come to the country with me this weekend? Two days is too long without you. Sleep well, my love.*

She came down the stairs a few minutes after he left, the anger having driven the effects of the alcohol away, padding down on her bare feet to apologize for her childishness but he was gone and she was relieved.

She telephoned Clive early the next morning to smooth things over. He was in a hurry, on his way to St. Pancras, and although he sounded quite normal she sensed that he was hurt. She said she could not come to Cambridge for the weekend, needing time. She agreed to dinner on Monday night.

All that day, all Friday and Saturday, as the painters worked in the showroom and then moved gradually upwards, Caroline tried to organize the living area of her house. The smell of paint was in every room. There were dust-sheets and newspapers and neat heaps in corners of their ladders and brushes and paint. On Sunday it was unexpectedly hot and the elation had worn off. She wished she had been with Clive in the country some-where. She anticipated a long, hot summer in London with misery . . . This solitary Sunday which she had planned so carefully, no painters, no people, just herself in her house, be-came an ordeal. At three-thirty she was lying on the sofa, win-dows wide open to encourage any breeze to come in, to let the smell of paint out, and picturing the Manor. The mowing would have started, the smell of newly-cut grass filling the downstairs rooms; the greenhouse would have been full of her trays of seedlings, her geraniums waiting patiently for the last threat of frost to disappear, her wallflowers growing leggy but still velvety and bright in stained-glass-windows colours along the beds at the front of the house. She made an angry sound and rolled on to her stomach, burying her head in the cushion. Her hair, tied back in one thick bunch, spread over her shoulders like a shawl.

The doorbell rang one long peal, startling her. She got up and looked out of the windows but could see nothing of the pavement below because of the jutting-out ledge which held the window boxes and supported the shop canopy. She searched unsuccessfully for her shoes, and then gave up and ran down the stairs, smoothing her hair like a swimmer, crossing the showroom and releasing the roller blind which covered the glass door. As it sprang up, it revealed Michael Redford.

'I thought of driving to the river. Henley or Marlow or Cookham. Will you come?'

She stood with her hands resting on the door as the pleasure which the first sight of him caused was registered. 'I'd love to. It's exactly what I want to do but I am too lazy to do it alone. Come in for a moment and I'll change.'

'I should have telephoned, I suppose, but I wanted to seem spontaneous. I was just driving by. I thought of you, you happened to be alone . . .'

She walked up the stairs ahead of him. 'You're thinking of Clive, aren't you? Clive and I are friends. No more than that. And he's away, this weekend, isn't he?' Her voice was light but she thought, uneasily, of his note. She thought: For an immoral society, a supposedly sophisticated society, we have some childish rules that are difficult to ignore . . .'

'You may not feel any obligation to Clive but let me tell you he has never behaved about any other woman the way he does with you. He takes you very, very seriously.' Michael stood at the window, looking at all her neatly planted window boxes. There

82

was something pathetic about them. He wanted to alter everything for her and he wondered why when he hardly knew her.

'I'll change.'

'Don't. You look lovely. As if you knew me very well and don't bother with the trimmings.'

'Well, I must at least wear shoes.'

'All right.' He walked about the room, making it seem small. When she came down again he said, 'This is pretty, this peachy colour. You're clever with colours. When I live at the Château, will you come and choose things for me? Curtains and colours? I'd like a room to be warm like this. You must meet Henri Bertrand, a friend of mine. He designs cottons. You'd have a lot in common.'

They drove slowly out of London. There was little traffic. 'A year ago,' Michael said, 'I would never have taken a day off like this, even on a Sunday!'

'I shall be like that,' Caroline said firmly and he laughed.

They drove to Marlow and walked by the river, seeing people lured out by the first hot weekend and reminded about summer. They watched boats and ducks, breathed the damp, ancient smell of the river and when it grew cooler they drove to a large hotel beside the river and sat at a wooden table on a veranda and watched the weir.

Michael leaned on the table, shirt sleeves rolled up to show smooth, brown fore-arms, his hands square and practical. He narrowed his eyes as he looked towards the red evening sun. He hated dark glasses, only wearing them if he had to, and there were lines by his eyes. He turned his narrow, interesting face to Caroline, his expression gentle. He took one of her hands. He wanted to tell her how she affected him but was unable to do so. He had never let women or the need for sex interfere with his life. He took what was available and appealing. He was not practised. The early stages bored him and rules annoyed him. But this was quite different. It surprised him to find how fettered he was by convention. He simply had not been with her enough to talk as intimately as he wanted to. The red light of the setting sun made her face and hair glow. Her eyes, he saw, were grey. 'Tell me about yourself. What you want.'

Caroline took cigarettes from her bag and lit one. 'I don't have many plans, Michael. At first, after the divorce, I was paralysed. Luckily I had friends, Rachel and others. Now I have the shop. I will cling to that and work at it. For the first time I will be a person in my own right. Harry was a very certain man. Reassuring in his attitudes. Living with him was easy when we were happy and when things began to go wrong at first he ignored it and then he laughed at me as if it were all some game I was playing, an act, because I didn't have enough to do. I thought I ran my own life because he was away so much, but I was wrong. I was safe in his organization even when he wasn't there. When I actually left him everything collapsed around me. I am proud of the way I have pulled myself together.'

'And when you are satisfied, what then?'

She laughed. 'You should have been the lawyer, not Clive.'

Michael sat straighter. He hated to be laughed at for being himself. 'I'm sorry. Am I cross-examining you?'

'Of course not . . . all I know is that I couldn't spend the rest of my life in London. I don't like cities. Perhaps in the end I'll go back to South Africa. My family are there.' She watched the ducks perform their comical bottom-waggling dives and the busy moorhens. Being with this man gave her a feeling of peace and pleasure which she loved but distrusted. 'What I want most is the thing I will never have. A child. I thought, before, it was Harry's child I wanted but it isn't. It's mine. My child.'

When he spoke again his voice was gentle. 'Shall we stay here and have dinner? Or would you like to go back to London?'

'I'd like to stay here. Are we dressed respectably enough?'

'I think so.' He looked at his watch. 'It's nearly eight. I'll go and arrange something.'

He pushed back his chair and Caroline watched him walk into the hotel, seeing again the way he moved. She attacked herself scathingly. What the hell am I doing, enjoying him so much? He is far too young for me. Another generation from Harry and his friends. Harry will be forty in two months. She imagined Rachel's voice. 'Darling, you're reacting quite predictably, swinging from one extreme to the other. It's only natural that after being married to Harry you should be attracted to someone young enough to be intense. Anyway, you never liked the old crowd, did you?'

Caroline slipped her arms into her blazer and shivered lightly. She looked up as Michael re-appeared, walking across the terrace towards her, and a sudden incomprehensible joy and optimism, which the sight of him and the thought of the evening ahead made her feel, was expressed in a smile she couldn't help. He came and stood behind her, his hands resting on her shoulders, and he bent down and lightly touched her hair with his cheek.

'All fixed.' He had knotted a scarf round his neck and put on a rather shapeless tweed jacket. 'I've changed, you see!' he said as Caroline stood up.

She laughed. 'I'd better do the same.'

'I'll be in the little bar at the bottom of the stairs.'

Caroline went upstairs to the ladies' cloakroom. She washed her hands and put on fresh lipstick and scent. She pulled out the combs and clips which held her hair back and brushed it, parting it in the middle and catching it above each temple. It hung halfway down her back, a deep gold, darker at the top. She studied her reflection critically and decided her face was not yet old enough to be aged by long hair. And then she forced herself to stop constantly censoring her happiness. Surely it was enough to be happy, no matter why? She came down the stairs, carrying her jacket, and found Michael in the bar. As she walked towards him she was self-conscious as she had not been for years, aware of each separate part of herself in a way which destroyed the normal smoothness of her movements.

Throughout the meal he talked a great deal, passionately

needing to make her understand about France, why he was going, moving his hands, driving his hair back from his forehead when it fell forward, pausing often and disconcertingly for her opinion. He filled her with optimism. He peeled the years from her. She could feel herself coming alive again. When she laughed it ran all through her. The woman she had thought she was, the cold and dignified shell she had clutched at to get her through the divorce and the subsequent months, lay in front of her, curiously empty, detached like Peter Pan's shadow.

'Did you realize how you affected me that first afternoon, Caroline? Did it show?'

'No . . . Did you realize how you surprised me?'

He shook his head. The meal had been delicious but they had hardly noticed it. They left just after ten and drove back to London and she asked him in. She gave him coffee and brandy and the mood between them was subtly altered by the change of surroundings but not spoilt. She was drawn to his intensity and his diffidence and the attraction between them seemed utterly unique, not a skill to be exercised or a practised thing. He took her face in his hands, looking at it closely for a few moments before he kissed her. 'It's not the way you look. That's lovely but it's far more than that . . .' Feelings she had totally forgotten began to affect her. Not felt for years and yet familiar, as if there hadn't been so much time in between without this intense excitement and curiosity. And they were both too old to waste such attraction.

He leaned back, arm along her shoulders, watching her. 'Can I stay, Caroline? It would seem strange to leave now.'

'Yes. It would.'

So many things she had thought she would have to explain to a lover . . . that she had not slept with anyone for over a year and that had been a ghastly desperate coupling with a near stranger which had frightened and repelled her. Before that Harry. Always trying to conceive. Before that she could hardly remember. But it was quite unnecessary to explain. They went upstairs. Caroline's room was warm, dim, lit only by light from the stairs. They moved together, standing close to one another at the end of the bed. So strong was the excitement that tore through her that she had to look away, to hide it, needing to wait, to be persuaded, wanting to be persuaded. She felt Michael's mouth on hers, at first delicately so that it seemed they were just mouths, small, delicious, unhurried kisses, his mouth investigating. They moved a little apart. She touched his face. His eyelids and his straight nose. She stroked the hair back from his forehead, felt the smooth skin of his neck, felt his heart beating, wondered how she had lived for so long without this? Although it had hardly begun. Anticipation made her quiver. Every part of her body trembled. She was not afraid for Michael. There was between them a marvellous confidence so that they were both free to dissolve into their own feelings, sure that the other was there too. An instinctive sureness. Now his mouth moved down and his lips were on her breasts and she touched and loved his dark head, heard her own small sounds of pleasure. She began to tremble again. They moved on to the bed. Michael smiled at her, asking her again with his eyes and his mouth if she wanted him. She answered with her own smile. He uncovered her body and his own and they touched one another as if neither had ever held a naked body before. She felt new. The beauty of his long narrow body was quite unexpected. She had not thought about it. When Michael finally entered her body it seemed to Caroline that she had waited her whole life for this and yet had not realized she was waiting. He said her name, over and over again, as her body rose up, sprang up, curling over and over her in waves that seemed never-ending.

'I've never felt like that before,' Michael said and he was so close to her that the words were spoken against her cheek. 'Never.'

'Nor have I.'

It took Caroline a long time to find sleep. Her body would not stop remembering. Beside her Michael breathed deeply, spread across the bed, forgetting her in his sleep. When she woke in the morning he was leaning on one elbow, looking down at her, smiling very slightly.

'Good morning,' he said. 'I still can't quite believe it.'

She felt very unsure of herself, waiting for the first reaction, expecting shyness, even regret. She half sat up, not looking at him fully. 'What time is it?'

'Half past eight.'

'My God! It's Monday morning . . . The painters . . .'

He stroked the side of her face, kissing her to silence the protests. 'Don't . . . don't rush. Please. Stay there. I'll make you some coffee . . . Can I telephone Jenny?'

'Of course.' She gave in to the happiness again, putting her arms round him, holding him for a moment before he got out of bed, watching his narrow, naked body. All the urgency to get up left her. She heard him in the bathroom, washing, humming some tune, and it was very nice to have someone else here. For the first time she realized how deeply she disliked the silence of living alone, the fact that all sound had to be deliberately created.

He reappeared with a towel tied round his waist, went down to the kitchen and came back a few minutes later with two mugs of coffee, toast and a jar of honey. One plate. A fish knife to spread with. He ran his fingers over his unshaven face. 'I suppose I must go and work. But I'll see you tonight, won't I?'

'Yes.'

He put the tray on the floor and leant towards her, putting his arms round her, rocking her slightly, feeling the warmth and shape of her body through the nightgown she had pulled on. Then he began to dress and Caroline went to the bathroom and washed the smudges of make-up from beneath her eyes and brushed the tangles from her hair. He came in to kiss her goodbye. She thought, as she watched him go down the stairs and heard his car start in the street outside, that she understood Rachel a little better now. She understood the desperate pursuit of love, or sexual attraction, however you cared to dignify it. In a life that was difficult and empty and sad it would lift you, transform everything. Then she wondered if, all along, it had been this feeling she had searched for and didn't like that thought nearly so much. She remembered saying bravely to Rachel, 'In the future I shall use love like a man does, as part of his life, along with work and friends. Not the whole!' Somehow, this morning, the words sounded unconvincing.

CHAPTER SIX

Kate was the first to arrive at Bonnington's on Monday morning. She had come to London on a late train the previous evening, having lied about being needed early on Monday, so restless was she to escape the house, to put the weekend and the atmosphere between her parents behind her. She unlocked the outer door and the rooms were quiet, and airless after the weekend. The flowers on her desk had died. Andrew Mackenzie came soon after she did. He was always early, always a frown between his eyes. He commuted each day from Welwyn Garden City. In the eight weeks Kate had worked at Bonningtons's she had only made him smile twice. She scared him, she knew, with her shyness and she tormented him with her jokes. It was a novelty for Kate to have someone fear her. 'Hello, Andrew. Heard the one about the game-keeper?'

'No.' He disappeared into the warren of passages which made up this place. Kate stared after him, chin in hand. The telephone rang and it was Caroline Boyd.

Clive, too, was earlier than usual, bounding up the stairs, ready to cope with the disasters which had built up over Thursday and Friday. 'Is Andrew in?' Kate looked pale, he thought. Rather miserable.

'Yes, but he's hiding because I started to tell him a joke.'

'You shock him.' Clive paused and smiled and had an urge to run his hand down her short, silky hair, touch the nape of her neck which was as slender as a child's. 'So what occurred while I was in Essex?'

'The money came from Arlington Road and I put it in the clients' account. Miss Henderson again. And Mr Mather, very upset about something we've omitted from the contract. I put him on to Mr Paul.'

'Christ!' Clive said.

'And I said you'd meet Mrs Mills outside the court at ten-thirty to introduce her to counsel. She's very worked up. Her husband keeps hanging round outside the house, trying to talk to the children. And Mrs Boyd rang to say she can't have dinner with you tonight. She is very sorry and will ring you tomorrow.'

'That Mills man is a real bastard,' Clive said but without venom because all the feeling in him was channelled into deadening disappointment. He had missed Caroline so much, through Friday and a boring dinner party on Saturday and a sleepy, over-fed Sunday. He had only accepted the invitation for the weekend because he had thought she would go with him. 'Bring me a coffee, would you, Kate?' He went into his office and sat down. He had wanted to see Caroline tonight, so much, to smooth away the anger of their last meeting.

Kate had studied Clive closely in the weeks she had worked with him. She had seen him displaying his old-fashioned good manners, watched him flirt gently, heard him ice-cold on the telephone, shouting once or twice behind the closed door of his office; watched him extricate himself when Michael Paul came after him for some oversight. She had stalled for him on the telephone, seen the way he juggled the women in his life now that Caroline had a very definite centre role. Once or twice he had caught her grinning at a beautifully fabricated lie and he had winked.

Basically a lazy man he did no more than he had to to get by but he was reasonably efficient and quite uncrushable. It was almost as if he enjoyed the last-minute panic, extricating himself by his coolness, by his personality. She came to understand Mary's warning. She realized that he had strongly recommended clients to invest with John Hampton long before that firm had proved itself. She suspected that, in some way or other, John made it very worth Clive's while. And once or twice she had seen him look as he had looked this morning when she told him about Caroline's message; his big face suddenly blank, all the merriment gone from his eyes and the colour from his voice.

The last time Kate had seen him with that expression she had, quite spontaneously, made him laugh. There was always something in Kate's mind, some succinct comment, waiting to be given sound. He had laughed with surprise and pleasure and the mood between them since was subtly altered.

This morning Kate had no laughter for him. In the little room which held a basin and the kettle and assorted cups and saucers she waited for the water to boil, sitting on a long-legged stool. Sun streamed in through the window. Summer soon. Already the wistaria which covered the Old Vicarage was lumpy with buds. 'In the summer,' she had once told David, 'I look better. I look quite nice when I'm brown.' The misery which had occupied her all weekend pounced now, taking advantage of her inactivity. It had started Friday night . . . She had seen the invitation on the dresser in the kitchen as soon as she came in. A white card with black lettering from David's parents. Kate was invited as well as Ben and Gabriel. She knew, although the card said nothing, that Vanessa must have arrived. This party was for them all to meet Vanessa. Kate had once seen a photograph. The face was thin, interesting, not pretty. Large eyes and a pointed chin. The face had superimposed itself on the white card. Kate knew that when she saw them together, saw David watching Vanessa with that peculiarly attentive way he had, concentrating the whole of himself on one person so that you almost forgot to breathe, it would really be over. No more pretended reconciliations, drawn in her mind in the dark. The words on the invitation were like a coded warning and she found, when she closed her eyes, that they were still engraved on the vulnerable lining of her brain.

'You don't have to go, darling,' her mother had said, touching Kate's arm stiffly because she longed to embrace her and drive the hurt away. 'Daddy and I will have to but you don't.'

'I'll think about it,' Kate had said and then laughed unhappily because she thought of little else.

Saturday night was Alice's twentieth birthday party. Gabriel drove Kate to Guildford to look for a dress, embarrassing Kate in the boutiques as she commented on the awful, deafening music, on the hideousness of the clothes. 'You're not that old. Why do you have to be like this?' Kate whispered, furiously.

Gabriel had relapsed into a miserable silence, the way she looked when Kate's father began one of his sarcastic attacks, waiting for it to be over. She hated the dress Kate eventually chose.

There was a discothèque run by two boys, carpets rolled back, cold food and wine and beer and Alice's parents nervously disappearing. Kate knew almost everyone but still it was agony to arrive alone, only the second party she had been to without David, no one she wanted to be with. She drank a lot of wine and talked so fast that the words merged in an unintelligible blur. The evening was endless. She loathed it. She had Gabriel's car but she felt she could not decently leave before midnight. It was like all parties had been before David and would be from now on.

'Was it fun?' Gabriel had asked at breakfast.

'Fun? Of course it wasn't fun. You've forgotten. You think a party is an entity in itself, enjoyable for its own sake. It isn't. A party is just a lot of people. A war. Trying to be with the person you want and avoiding those you dislike. I was so bored it was like a physical pain. Intolerable!' She paused for breath and looked at Gabriel and was ashamed.

'You enjoyed it then?' her father said, and Kate laughed reluctantly.

Water was bubbling out of the kettle and the little room was steamy. Kate said 'Shit' under her breath and turned it off. She made two coffees and mopped up the mess and thought miserably of the evening ahead, of going home on the tube, elbowing her way out at Gloucester Road, going into a silent flat because Venn was flying and Judith was with her Scottish family till the end of the month. She would have liked to have told David that, having fought her way out of the sticky net of her home life, as he had so eloquently called it, she now found her so-called freedom far more restricting in many ways. No car she could use in London. Fewer friends. Time taken up with boring routine jobs like washing and cleaning and shopping which left her mind free to churn. The churning pain which had been with her all week-end, through the party, on Sunday as she knelt at the altar rail and raised her hands for the communion wine and prayed until her body shuddered with effort, on the train this morning, here in this steamy little room, the churning pain was so strong. It was disappointment and misery and loss and sadness because she still wanted David and loved him and was desolate without him and he loved someone else.

'Vanessa's coming home early, Kate. She wrote to me. She says she misses me.' Watching her for her reaction. 'I haven't even mentioned you. I think she'd go mad. She's so highly strung.'

'I'm nervous too. I once panicked in an indoor swimming pool from the smell of chlorine and the strange sounds . . .'

'I can't stop her coming. It all went too far long before I met you.' His hands contradicted his words and Kate had turned on him like a small, wild animal, burrowing under his body with surprising strength, pulling his head towards her, willing her body to make him stay. And he responded, as always, constantly surprised by Kate in bed, by the forces which he had unleashed in her, proud of them both together, making love to her as he always did, cat and mouse, tormenting, 'Kitty, kitty, kitty . . . .' She had been so happy when he loved her. Tears formed in her eyes and burst over the lower lid and ran down her face. They were hot. She clenched her hands so tightly that they shook and there was a sound of pain and fury in her throat.

'Kate?'

She jumped violently as Clive looked in. 'Where the hell's my coffee?'

She smeared desperately at her cheeks and snatched up the cups so quickly that the coffee spilled into the saucers. 'Here it

94

is. I'm sorry. . . .'

'Why are you crying?' Clive said, in a different, gentler tone.

'It's nothing. It's just to inject a little drama into my life! I do it often. It's like yoga for the eyes!' she babbled, pouring the coffee back into the cups from the saucers and burning her fingers.

'You're not pregnant, are you?'

'Of course not! I'm not that bloody stupid!' she snapped. 'Oh God, I didn't mean to speak to you like that.'

'Not so much fun as you thought, living in London?' Clive said, even more gently.

'That's it. You're quite right. I get lonely. I might have known you'd guess. . . .' She held out the cup.

Clive folded his arms. 'Come on, Kate! Don't be so stupid. Tell me the truth. Perhaps I can help.'

She put the cups down. 'Oh, it's so pathetic. I came to London to forget someone. Instead I find I am alone so much here I think of him constantly. At lunch, when it's quiet here . . . I could go out with the other girls but I don't. My fault . . . and when I wake very early in the morning in the flat, that's the worst time. And some evenings too. She looked up at him and the tears had left her eyes very bright and soft. She gave Clive one of her swift, self-mocking smiles. 'Pathetic, isn't it? Sobbing my little heart out in the tea room?'

Clive put out his hand and touched her face, taking her chin between his fore-finger and thumb. 'You're so good at your job, Kate, I shall have to look after you. As Caroline has stood me up and I've booked a table at a restaurant I've wanted to try for months and as we both, apparently, hate being alone, you can come and have dinner with me tonight. Talk about the fellow if you want to . . . if not, we won't mention it. We'll just cheer each other up.'

'I couldn't,' Kate whispered, registering with amazement the enormous change in him. He had suddenly become human, someone to talk to, to want, someone who could cope with life, someone safe. 'I just couldn't look like the sort of person you take out to dinner.'

'Balls. Don't try and refuse. Look on it as overtime. I shall discuss Miss Henderson with you. Now, can we please get the letter done before I have to go to Court!'

Caroline's telephone rang constantly that morning and each time she answered it she felt guilty, certain it would be Clive, checking to see why she had cancelled, ready to catch her out in her lie about this evening. 'Later,' she kept telling herself, 'I will sit down and think this out like an adult and telephone and explain.' She was visited by Brian Lessing who was trying to buy a Victorian rocking horse which Caroline had stood in the window; the painters were in the bathroom, making it necessary to use the tiny, damp lavatory in the basement; an elderly American woman wandered in and seemed unable to understand that Caroline wasn't open for business. 'But I come here every year, Honey, it's my favourite shop . . .' And a runner arrived, a huge young man with a moustache and a Chesterfield tied on the roof rack of his van. Caroline bought it for thirty pounds and then regretted it. In every little space she thought of the previous evening and night and experienced a complicated blend of nervousness and disbelief and pure old-fashioned excitement. Just after midday when she answered the phone for the sixth time, it was Michael, and now that he had rung he had taken away the fear of humiliation.

'I've tried to get you four times. . . .' He sounded so different on the telephone, curt and uneasy.

'I'm a busy antique dealer now, you know,' she said gently, smiling into the telephone.

'I wondered whether you would like to come to a fair tonight? It has unpacked itself on Parsons Green. A friend of mine, whom I'd like you to meet, is coming here for a drink at about six. If you came here too I could show you round . . .'

'I'd love to see Mosaic. I'll be there about six-thirty.'

'Fine. Goodbye,' he said abruptly. She sat down, lit a cigarette and gave in to the happiness like someone stopping work to lie in the sun. Why shouldn't she enjoy his voice, the thought of seeing him, of making love to him? She was responsible to no one but herself. Caroline closed her eyes and tried to picture his face and wondered what the hell she had to wear that was suitable for a fair.

When Kate let herself into the flat that evening, Judith's music was drifting in muffled chords down the stairs and the smell of her musky bath oil permeated the air. It was extraordinary how Judith changed the flat, Kate thought, her presence revitalizing it, totally altering its character. Kate and Venn lived in it, were influenced by it, made sad and irritable by wet days, depressed by washing up, guilty about the stains where the bath-water had come through the ceiling, but Judith imprinted her personality on places, even on the weather. . .
'Hello.' She leaned over the banisters, her hair screwed into a tight bun. 'Surprise, surprise.'
'Have you got some time off?' Kate said, coming up the remaining stairs two at a time. 'I once danced to this. It was too difficult for me . . .'
'The man I work for had some important papers to go to his bank in London so I flew down with them this afternoon.' She held her arms out straight on either side and flapped them and grinned. 'Like some tea? I've just made it. Where's Venn?'
'She went yesterday, back on that South American rota. There's a card for you from Susie.' She took the mug Judith held out. 'Thanks. How is everything?'
Judith twisted her expressive mouth. 'Good money but dull. I'm bored. She's such a strange, weak woman. Her every sentence is a question. She seems to need my approval for everything and the baby cries constantly. It's been ill. And the husband is too young with too much money, amazed to find his pretty little wife has been softened and weakened and fattened

97

by this baby. The two-year-old is sweet but I can't wait to leave. The woman follows me like a puppy and the husband watches me and rubs up against me . . .' She studied Kate. 'You look smaller and thinner. Do you eat?'

'Now and again.' Kate sat on one of the stools and took the lid off the jar which held Judith's cereal. She dipped her hand in. 'I eat this stuff of yours. I'm an addict.' She paused for a moment while the Chopin record rippled to a conclusion . . . 'That was where I really got it wrong. I got further and further behind the music . . . A lot of men have rung for you. I tell them all you'll be home at the end of the month. Your mother rang. Venn knows all the details. She enters into long conversations with them all. She's in love with a married first officer at the moment.'

Judith held her mug with both hands and looked at Kate thoughtfully over the rim. 'What's the matter with you, Kate? The last time I saw you you were incoherent with excitement about living and working in London. Are you alone too much here?'

'God, no. I'm always, always out! Why tonight I'm having dinner with Clive, the man I work for . . .' She sighed and dropped her shoulders. 'And I shall bore him by trying too hard and I have nothing to wear that will look right. I shan't know how to be.' She thought: With David it was different. I never had to try. It was just there, like between Judith and me. Talking without thinking first, understanding when the other is being funny. 'Do you think I am one of those unfortunate people who make the best impression first and then are liked less and less when you know them more?'

'Well, you didn't impress me much the first time! I'd say you are improving!'

'Thanks!' Kate smiled and sipped the tea. 'I wish you were here more.'

'I'll be back in ten days and you'll soon come to hate me. Ask Venn.' She yawned. 'I shall be working in Notting Hill Gate, going in daily. Much better. I shall be able to organize a decent sex life.'

Kate listened in silent admiration. 'Perhaps I can find something for you to wear. I bought some pretty blue trousers last time I was here and a silky shirt that went with them. Might suit you . . .' They went upstairs as she was talking and she opened the big, ugly brown cupboard and sorted through the dimness inside, pulling out clothes. All Judith's clothes had a particular smell. Kate liked the smell. But the clothes were far too wide, hanging on her like dust sheets although she and Judith were much the same height. She stood in front of the long mirror, instinctively, after so many years of being taught how to stand, having her back slightly arched, holding her head, feet slightly apart, trying on everything. Nothing of Judith's looked right. Nothing of her own looked right. A lump of despair came into her throat. 'I can't go . . .' She had strewn the room with discarded clothes and she walked naked to the bathroom and turned on the taps. Water sprang out, steaming hot. 'I'll go like this. I'd like to go to bed with him, for experience.' Judith came in and sat on the closed lavatory. 'I shall be much better at thirty,' Kate said, testing the water with her toe and helping herself to Judith's bath oil.

'You're all right now,' Judith said, 'and you've got to go out! I've got someone coming to eat here! I must go out and get some food. I suppose I'd better change . . .' She stood up. 'I'm catching the eight o'clock flight back to Glasgow tomorrow morning.'

Kate wallowed in the water. She was still there ten minutes later when Judith returned in a navy trouser suit, hair pinned back demurely. But nothing could subdue the effect of her body or her face. 'Bye . . . you may be gone when I get back. Enjoy yourself, Kate. That's what I do. I think "to hell with him! I'm looking out for myself." Whoever I'm with, in bed or out, I put myself first. Get them to take me where I want, buy me what I want to eat, sleep with them if I'm in the mood and the way I want it. They love it!'

'It's all right if you look like you do . . . anyway, I don't believe you. There must be someone you are fond of.'

Judith shrugged. 'Haven't met anyone yet I'd change myself for. When I do I probably won't be able to!' She laughed. 'In five or six years, when I start to sag a bit, then I'll worry.' She called goodbye from the front door.

Kate dried herself, made up her face, put on the dress she had worn to Alice's party and paced the sitting-room restlessly because she was ready far too soon. She gulped at a warm gin and tonic. She'd forgotten to make any ice. She put on the Chopin record again and tried to remember the dance, running through, with her hands, the series of signs dancers use to memorize steps. She kicked off her platform shoes and hitched up her dress and took the much darned ballet shoes from a drawer in the hall. She had brought them just as a memento. But after five minutes her legs ached and she turned on the television while she waited nervously for Clive.

By the time Clive arrived home that evening he was regretting his impulsive invitation to Kate. It was just after seven and he poured himself a whisky and ran a bath. He dialled Caroline's number for the fourth time that day and there was no reply. She could have gone to the country to some sale or other. She had done that once before, disappearing for a couple of days. He wished that their last meeting had not ended so unsatisfactorily but he didn't see that he could have acted differently. He closed his eyes, knowing that the sight of her would lift him from whatever mood he was experiencing to look down on life benevolently. It occurred to Clive as he got out of the bath, towelled his solid body and dried his hair that, instead of merely thinking about marrying Caroline, he should ask her. He stood very still, anticipating her surprise and then her acceptance. He anticipated her body and his own quickened. He thought of living with her, getting to know the woman beneath the quiet façade. Previously when Clive thought of marriage he had been held back by all the things he would have to give up. Now, nothing on

100

the outside seemed worth a great deal.

Instead, he thought, and he smiled, I am taking my little secretary out and shall spend the evening listening to a series of first-love confessions! He pulled on a clean shirt, lifting his chin to fasten the neck button, moving his shoulders to settle the shirt comfortably. But Kate is an appealing girl . . . call it a good deed. He combed his damp hair and dialled Caroline's number once again before he left. There was still no reply.

Marketing Mosaic occupied premises on the ground floor of two houses which had been combined. One was on the corner of Meadwell Street. The other, with a shop front, in the Fulham Road. The name was painted in lettering which made Caroline wonder if her own choice had been too frilly. She opened the Fulham Road door and went into a white room, brown carpet, walls covered with photographs, a display table, glass cabinets, two desks with telephones.

'Caroline? We're in the office . . .' It was Michael's voice and she walked through an open door and came into a second room with harsh neon lighting and filing cabinets and a drawing board and more desks. Michael was sitting in a chair and he stood up as she entered. A slight man with a pleasant, tanned face and very short hair stood up also.

Michael kissed her cheek a little awkwardly. 'Caroline, this is Henri Bertrand. An old friend from Provence.'

He shook her hand. 'How are you, Caroline?' The English was perfect but the French accent made it very attractive.

'Would you like a glass of wine?' Michael asked her. 'Henri has brought me a few bottles to try . . .'

'To encourage him.' Henri said with a smile. 'I want him to give up this and run Jouvard.' He held out a plate on which were slices of garlic sausage. 'Try some of this.'

She took a piece. 'You live near Jouvard?' she asked.

'About twenty kilometres.'

'Henri is the friend I mentioned who runs the factory making, dying and designing cotton.

101

This interested Caroline and she relaxed. 'Are many of your designs traditional?'

'About half and half. In fact, probably more are my own now . . . and where we differ is that we make our cottons into clothes that are fashionable, not the usual table cloths and scarves. We have been very successful with long skirts and now I am here with some dresses and blouses to try and interest English buyers.'

The telephone in the showroom rang and Michael went to answer it. The Frenchman was silent. A shy man, Caroline thought, liking his face. 'Are you in England for long?' she asked.

'No. I have to go home tomorrow evening.' He held out a rather flattened packet of Gauloise. 'Do you smoke these?'

'I smoke anything! Constantly!' she said as she took one and leant forward for him to light it with a distinctively French coloured tube of a lighter.

'I'd like to stay longer. I love London. I was a student here in nineteen fifty-five. My God, that sounds a long time ago.' When he smiled his face was very kind. When he was serious, deep lines bracketed each side of his mouth. 'I must tell you I was only seventeen. I had a wonderful year and I learned English, which was the idea, and I lived with Michael's parents. We are distantly related by marriage. That was the year I discovered girls so I remember it with great affection.'

Caroline laughed. 'Are you coming to the fair, Henri?'

He made a gesture of exasperation, spreading his fingers and his hands. 'The fair! And Michael pretends that he works hard! I have to dine with three English buyers!' He poured some more wine into Caroline's glass. 'I hope you will come to France, perhaps later in the summer? I would enjoy showing you around my mill and factory and my studio . . . I am trying to buy a dyeing works in a mountain village quite near. They have such pure water.'

'Are you sure, Henri, that you won't meet us for dinner later?'

102

Michael said, coming back into the room.

'No, thank you. I am committed to my buyers tonight. I will telephone you tomorrow before I leave . . . any message for your grandmother?'

'It's good of you to visit her so often. Just give her my love!'

'I enjoy seeing her. And talking to Gautier. They were out with the stoves when I left, afraid of a frost. Up all night, protecting the vegetation. So many clear nights. And this week I think they are spraying . . . I took Françoise with me last time I went. My daughter,' he explained to Caroline. 'She and your grandmother got on very well!'

'Have a good evening, Henri.' Michael walked with him to the door.

'Thank you. Goodbye, Caroline.'

Michael closed the door behind Henri, locked it, pulled down the coffee-coloured blinds and then turned back to Caroline. There was a definite shyness between them. He came and took her hands. 'If I kiss you, will it help?'

'Yes.' She moved closer to him, lifting her face, loving the feel of his mouth and remembering the previous night as he touched her.

'Why the fair?' she asked when they moved apart.

'Because they fascinate me. Don't you enjoy them?'

'To be honest I find them rather frightening. Like circuses. Clowns have always scared me. All the glitter and the tinny music, the lights and the smiles as they take your money and that atmosphere when people are excited.'

'But you're looking at it from quite the wrong angle! You want to look at the machinery. Someone told me there's a Burrell Showman's engine there . . .'

'Well, why didn't you say so before?' she laughed. 'What the hell is that?'

'Come and see if we can find it.'

It was a warm, clean evening and the fair was spread over Parsons Green like a brightly coloured tablecloth. The movement and music and coloured lights grew more intense as they walked nearer. Smoke drifted from the hot-dog stands and it was very crowded. Michael and Caroline walked arm in arm past the roundabout where the gaping horses circled in their sedate dance. 'I had a roundabout horse in a shop I once worked in. It was beautiful. It went for a fortune.' Past swing-boats and side-shows, looking for the Burrell engine but not finding it. There were other traction engines, though, shuddering out power like tethered monsters. Michael's enthusiasm was irresistible. He pulled her from machine to machine, bought candy floss, won a coconut, stared, entranced, at the steam organ. It was after nine when they made their way into a bistro across the road and ate, looking across towards the green where the fair sparkled and revolved, more mysterious now it was quite dark.

They sat opposite one another and Michael asked her question after question, investigating, digging into her past life as no one had done for years. She realized that what Clive had said of him was true, that he concentrated on anything that interested him with such intensity he almost destroyed it. 'But why?' he asked and she tried to answer honestly. 'Why did you marry him? Why did you stop loving him? Why do you want a child so much?'

And he said of himself . . . 'I have only two real friends, Henri and Clive. I do not find it easy to be with other people. I frequently can't be bothered. They seem to me to live on such a shallow plain. They skim the surface . . .' There was no awareness of time, Caroline thought, as she listened, wondering at this insatiable curiosity they had about each other, wondering at the clumsiness of words when their bodies were already quite happily acquainted.

Michael leant over the table and put his hands each side of her face, moving his fingers along her cheekbones. 'Are you tired?'

'Yes. I am.'

'If I call in at Cambridge Street and get some stuff to shave with and a clean shirt, I could stay at Meadwell Street with you. If you want me to?'

'Of course I want you to!'

Neither of them mentioned Clive out loud but he was in both their thoughts and, as they neared the house, Caroline cringed at the idea of explanations.

'I'll stay in the car, Michael . . .' she said as they stopped outside Cambridge Street.

He nodded. 'I'll only be a few moments.'

Kate asked for whisky and ginger ale before dinner. She had no preference for any particular kind of drink but she thought sherry sounded feeble and gin and tonic dull. She studied the restaurant. It was self-conciously new and very expensive and at the red-clothed tables, reflected in the many maple-framed mirrors, were people who looked as if they would feature in magazines and gossip columns. She could not think of anything to say to Clive in such different surroundings, She snapped a breadstick into short pieces. 'I'm sorry I'm not saying much. I feel as if I don't know you. At work we have so much to discuss that I haven't time to feel shy. I never have to think of things to say except when you come in with a hangover.'

'Is that very often?'

'Not really. Once or twice a week.'

Clive smiled and thought of Caroline and then, with an effort, concentrated on Kate. 'Well, the same applies to me. You look quite different . . . what's the line I want?'

'Miss Jones, you're beautiful! But I should have glasses to take off!'

'Yes.' He chuckled. 'Seriously, you look super, Kate. Older. There aren't many women I take out I can say that to.'

'Judith offered to lend me something of hers. Her clothes are more exciting than mine but they don't fit although we're the same height.' She thought of David teasing, hands inside her

105

bra. 'Must be something in here. Yes. I think I've found one!' Her face set.

Clive watched the feelings flicker over her small face. 'You're looking the way you did this morning. Why were you crying, Kate? You don't seem the sort of girl . . .'

'That's the trouble. I'm not any sort of girl.'

A waiter hovered and they ordered snails and Chicken Kiev.

'We can breathe over each other in the office tomorrow,' Clive said. 'Now, you were telling me what sort of girl you were!' He grinned.

'You don't really want to hear me say it all.'

'Funnily enough, I do. As it is obviously upsetting you, talk about it.' His face was so kind and encouraging.

'Well, there wasn't anyone special before David. Just groups of friends. I missed so many years being at Greenhurst. In the holidays we tried to work, for experience, just chorus stuff.' She hesitated. In stillness her face was older, Clive thought. It was the constantly changing expressions which made her seem so absurdly young. Kate was thinking: I am going to talk about it because it has to come out first. It blocks all other subjects.

'His family moved into the village. Big excitement. New people! My mother met his mother doing the flowers in church. You're bound to talk if one is doing the font and the other the memorial. My mother is far too concerned with me. I am an un-satisfactory only child. She puts into me all the worry which should be spread over four children. She thought I needed a nice boy-friend for weekends. David's mother obviously thought I sounded suitably harmless so we were introduced, the way you push children together, hand on the back to nudge them forward. 'You two go and play.' She stopped and drank some of her whisky. 'You are very nice to talk to. I've heard so many people talk to you . . .' She thrust her hair fiercely behind her ear. 'I annoyed myself by liking him very much. He's a funny man like my father, amusing, saying things in a dry way that are funny or not depending on whether you are on the receiving end. He's clever. He was at St Andrews for four years. That's where he met Vanessa. He told me about her very early on. He is so careful. He works with computers now.' The snails came and they attacked them with long skewers. 'He told me that she was in America, working for a company which was designing high-speed printers for computers. They'd invented something called a daisy wheel and were going to be enormously successful and that he might go there too. Right from the beginning he planned the way out. He told me how nervous she was. It was easy for us to be together. At weekends his parents were often away. His house was so near mine. He had a car. I hadn't slept with anyone which surprised him. And all the time our nice mothers, especially mine, encouraging, seeing only the outside, like some gentle little memory of when they were young.' Her face hardened. 'Of course, they had no idea . . .'

'. . . that you slept with him,' Clive finished, using her euphemistic phrase.

'Yes. It was so incredible for me I thought it must be the same for him. I thought that I would never want anything else, that we would get married and after all I'd be a princess and not a frog. But Vanessa was real, not just some dreamed-up escape for him. She missed him. She decided to come home. And under this pathetic exterior I am like my father, destructive and vicious, and just because I loved David I didn't idolize him. When he started to put me aside I wanted to say it first. I told him what he was. I told him to get out of my life. He was amazed. Little Kate, adoring him, such a surprise in bed!' The empty plates were taken and the chicken came and after they had eaten for a while Kate said, 'The trouble is I love him so much. I tried to replace it with anger. I thought I'd come to London and grow up, work and love someone else in the end. But the anger has worn off and now it seems to hurt far more. Everything is terrible without him. He changed everything. He made it all so good.'

Listening to her, mental pictures flashed through Clive's

mind—Kate's narrow body in bed, the mothers she spoke of, the boy-friend. And it occurred to him that all the women he had ever wanted, however varied, had come from one basic type. City women, meeting him on a level, reading the expressions of his face, his intentions, responding as expected. Even Caroline belonged to the first group. But this small, sad girl, unsure of herself, talking so fast and so vividly, tense with feeling and flawed or gifted with her destructive humour, was utterly different.

He refilled her wine glass and delicately sought the right words to say.

'Could I have some pudding after this?' Kate said. 'I hate meals to end with meat.'

Clive burst out laughing, attracting the attention of neighbouring tables, leaning across and ruffling her hair in an entirely natural and affectionate gesture. 'Kate, I've got good news. You'll survive. You'll outgrow him and forget him!' He raised his hand slightly and caught the waiter's eyes. 'Can we see the menu, please?'

He sounded so convincing and Kate sat up straight and tried to believe him. She liked it when he touched her like that, so easily, as if they were quite familiar with one another. She liked being with him. She couldn't imagine any problem which Clive wouldn't be able to solve. She held the large menu and read each item. 'Marron Mont Blanc, please.'

'See what I mean?' Clive laughed again. 'Just coffee for me, please . . . No one who can eat Marron Mont Blanc, whatever it is, can be too heartbroken!' He took out his cigars. 'Will you mind if I smoke?'

'No. Not at all.' She folded her thin arms on the tablecloth, suddenly overwhelmed with gratitude for him. 'This is very kind of you. Do you want to talk about yourself now?'

He smiled , shook his head and felt genuine affection for her. He talked, instead, about Mosaic, because he wanted to think about it anyway and because Kate seemed interested. She asked intelligent questions.

At eleven-thirty they left the restaurant and Clive drove her home. She was rather glad he hadn't suggested going on any-where. She felt the evening had gone so unexpectedly well that it would be tempting fate to start on another more complicated phase. Clive stopped his red car and leaned towards her, touch-ing his lips to hers for a moment before coming to open her door. She tasted sweet. 'Good night, little Kate. See you tomorrow back at the grindstone!'

'Good night. And thank you.'

Caroline sat in Michael's car, slightly tucked down, looking up at the house, watching the light come on in the sitting-room, in his bedroom. She loved this feeling, this anticipation; she thought of waking in the morning with Michael, of a glorious unplanned weekend with him; she anticipated their love-making and had to fold her body inwards as the excitement hit her. She took a cigarette from her handbag and lit it and the light of the match was sharp in the darkness.

Clive, unable to find a space in Cambridge Street, had parked in Hugh Street. He was walking slowly. He saw the dim outline of a figure in the passenger seat of Michael's car shown up sud-denly by the striking match. He stiffened and then hurried for-ward, recognizing Caroline, bending and rapping on the window, his face lit with pleasure and surprise.

She jumped violently and wound down the window.

'Caroline . . .' He kissed her cheek through the open window. 'How lovely to see you. Where did you come from? Where did Michael find you?' He was opening the car door. 'Come on in.'

She climbed out, stiffly, her face changing from shock to an expression of wariness which surprised him. She looked absol-utely lovely, he thought, with her hair tied back in one thick bunch. She wore jeans and a checked shirt and he loved women in shirts. She made no move towards the front door.

'I wasn't waiting to see you, Clive.' The words were rushed

109

and awkward. 'Michael took me to a fair on Parsons Green and we had dinner.'

'A fair?' He smiled but he was beginning to be uneasy.

'On Parsons Green,' she repeated. 'Clive, I am sorry I didn't telephone you today. I was busy but also I didn't know what to say to you.' She stood very straight, her eyes moving to his and then away, smoking her cigarette nervously.

'You're not still angry about Wednesday night, are you?'

'Of course not. I was absurd . . .'

'In the end I took my secretary out.' Clive smiled. 'So you owe me tomorrow evening.'

'I can't tomorrow!' She looked fully into his face and realized the truth of what Michael had said, that Clive cared for her very much indeed. 'I didn't want to say it like this, in the street . . . I need time to think, Clive.'

'To think about what?' The coldness of his voice shocked her. He had never spoken to her with anything but affection. 'Well?' His tone was hard and bullying. 'What do you need to think about?'

She tried to back away from the scene she sensed as she had always tried to turn away from fights. 'Myself. How I feel.'

'I don't understand you. You must know that I love you, Caroline.' He spread his big hands in exasperation. 'What is all this?'

It was beginning to be like the last terrible night with Harry. She couldn't look at him any more. She longed for Michael to appear and yet dreaded the confrontation. 'I never meant you to love me. We are friends, not lovers!' She was trembling.

'That's balls and you know it! We are far more than friends. I feel more for you than I've ever felt for any woman. Look at me, please, Caroline. I'd marry you if that's what you wanted.'

She swung to face him now. 'I don't want that. I don't want marriage with you or anyone else! I really didn't know how much you felt about me . . .' She broke off as Michael came into the street, carrying a small hold-all. 'I want to go on seeing

110

Michael,' Caroline said in a desperate rush and opened the car door but Clive caught her arm.

Michael came down the few steps on to the pavement. He hesitated and then threw the hold-all into the back of the car. 'Look, Clive . . .'

'You bastard,' Clive said.

'It isn't anything Michael has done. I am responsible for myself! I am allowed to choose, you know! I am not some pathetic creature to be won, handed from man to man like a bloody prize! To be humoured and persuaded!' Neither of them looked at her. They looked at each other. Caroline got into the car and slammed the door.

'It only happened on Sunday, Clive. It surprised us both. Christ, you've been through this far more often than I have . . . I wish to God you didn't care about her so much but I understand exactly why you do.'

'It's so bloody ridiculous.' Clive almost laughed. 'I just can't believe it. There can't be two more unsuitable people in the whole of London. Surely you can see that? She needs and is always going to need the sort of attention and time you will never be able to give any woman . . .'

Michael walked slowly round to his side of the car and got in. The engine roared, drowning Clive's voice and the car moved slowly away from the kerb. Clive swore in a long soft sentence. He let himself into his flat and poured himself a brandy, sitting down, dropping his head into his hands for a moment as anger and pain thudded through him, and disbelief. Had she felt none of it then? She must have known how he felt. And Michael? They had always respected the other's women. He drank the brandy in swift gulps and felt in his pocket for his car keys. He was going out again because he couldn't tolerate this silence. He needed to get out and drink and think and plan. Because he was certainly not giving up!

111

CHAPTER SEVEN

Throughout May Michael lived with Caroline at Meadwell Street. He was not a man open to women. He was reserved and found it hard to express his feelings in words but he conveyed to Caroline that no woman in the past had affected him as she did. He always woke in the mornings long before she stirred. He had never slept well. The early morning was the time when he did most of his thinking, trying to imagine life at Jouvard, thinking constantly about the Sundial. As Caroline began to wake from her deep, childlike sleep, he would roll over and watch her, bending down to kiss her as her eyes opened and she put out her arms and pulled herself into his early morning warmth.

In the past there had been long stretches in Michael's life when women had not mattered. He had often been amused by Clive's elaborate manoeuvring to secure the woman he wanted, amused to listen to Clive's plans. Susie had been convenient and Michael had been fond of her but there was nothing in his life to compare with the weeks he spent with Caroline in the very female atmosphere of the few rooms above her shop, amongst all her flowers and the chaos of her life, the clothes and books, the piles of newspaper and magazines which she seemed unable to throw away. Those weeks were as intense for Michael as the first time, at eighteen, when, embarrassed by his virginity, he had met an Australian girl and found to his surprise she was eager to sleep with him. Those months with Helen, almost a decade ago had had this same intensity. He viewed every detail of Caroline's body as if through a magnifying glass, fascinated by the feel of her, by her movements. He seemed to carry the scent of her with him. Mosaic was deep in its early summer frenzy. Michael had produced a final, workable set of drawings for the Sundial but he was aware that his concentration was not good. As he stared at the intricate drawings or read Jenny's reports, his mind wandered and too often he left early and walked down the road to Caroline's shop, seeking her out in the showroom or the workroom. It made him feel guilty, the way he felt at first on holiday.

Caroline too felt that she had been flung back a decade. She was full of love and energy, driving through Sussex, Surrey and Kent, scouring London for the stock she wanted; she bought painted chest of drawers and stripped them down to the pine beneath and waxed them; she bought books of flower prints for framing and heavy brass fire dogs, Staffordshire figures and two white daisy bushes to stand on the pavement outside her shop. Her hands and nails were permanently stained from the gardening and the paint stripper which dissolved rubber gloves. She looked back incredulously on her life of only a few months before, and wondered how Michael and this intense happiness had come. She planned a re-opening party for May the twenty-first and sent out invitations, including Clive and writing a small note at the bottom asking him to come. She asked all the dealers she knew, her few real friends from the country and the set of people she had moved in, however uneasily for the past nine months. When she asked Michael who he wanted he wrote a list of six names. 'Six pretty girls,' he said.

She didn't see Clive after the evening of the fair. She had no reason to go to Cambridge Street and he had no legal queries for her. But on the Friday before her party Michael rang to say he was at Pimlico. 'I have to use the lathe. We're having trouble with the bezel on a thermometer we want to start manufacturing next week. I want to try and bore it out.'

'What's a bezel?'

'In this case a ring of metal which holds the body to the face. Could you bring the large folder of drawings I was looking at last night in bed? I think it's on the floor.'

She laughed at how quickly and uncomplainingly he had accepted her untidyness. 'I'll find it.' Last night he had sat up in bed, so deeply engrossed when Caroline had spoken to him and

113

touched him she had given up and fallen asleep against him.

She reached Cambridge Street just before seven and went down to the basement workroom under the road in what had once been the coal cellar. The neon light was bright in here, illuminating this cave, and heaps of silver swarf lay over the machining table and on the floor. Michael kissed her absentmindedly and took the drawings, stopping the machine and picking up calipers to measure the thickness of the metal. 'I'll be about half an hour. Go in and get yourself a drink. The door to Clive's bit is open. I came out that way.'

Caroline didn't want a drink but she had brought a list of guests for her party to check through, to count acceptances. She went through the door to Clive's flat just as he came down the stairs from the main house, a can of beer in his hand. He was loosening his tie. They were both disconcerted. Then he made a move to come forward and kiss her. 'I can still kiss you, can't I?' When he was close to her the scent and feel of her made him realize just how much he had missed her.

'Of course. I'm glad to see you, Clive. I wanted to ask you to come to the party. I feel I owe the shop to you, in some ways.'

He took off his jacket. 'Of course I'll come.' He had thought so much about the best way to behave and had resolved to be waiting, in the background, available and secure when Michael's attention wavered. 'I'm sorry if I said some things that night which hurt you. I was quite unprepared for what happened.'

'Please forget it. I should have telephoned you but I've always been a coward about such things. I put them on one side. Anyway, what could I have said?' She paused and smiled. She opened her bag and took out her cigarettes and sat down; As Clive watched her he registered love for her, sadness, anger at the waste.

'The shop is ready,' she said, returning to a subject which she felt was safe. 'I've got some marvellous stock. I'm sure I can make a success of it but I realize it won't happen overnight. I shall have to build it up gradually.'

'Can I get you a drink?'

'Yes, perhaps I would like one.'

'So the shop is a long-term project?'

'Yes.'

'And if Michael goes to France?'

She shrugged. 'I haven't thought that far ahead.' Clive knew she was lying, that she had thought about it and believed Michael would stay in England to be with her.

Clive was afraid for her. The most intense urgency filled him. He had to make her understand, to protect her. 'You won't move him, Caroline. I'm not saying this with an ulterior motive other than concern for you. I just want you to realize from the beginning that he will do as he wants!' He had poured her a whisky without asking, underlining their closeness in the past. He held the glass to her and sat down with his own. 'He'll go to France when he's ready, believe me,' he said more quietly.

She was jealous of Clive's superior knowledge of Michael and tried to hide it. 'It's all so much in the future,' she said coldly. She met Clive's eyes and looked abruptly away. She tried to tell herself he was merely making trouble but the thought was unconvincing. He watched her so gently.

'I miss you both,' he said.

A rush of affection for him made her sit forward and touch his arm. He put his hand over hers and stroked her fingers gently. 'I have to go out, Caroline. Some wretched cocktail party but they'll be hurt if I don't turn up. I'll see you on Monday.' He stood up and went into the bedroom to change and when he looked back she had a pen and was checking names off her list, a little surprised that he had not stayed to talk to her.

Kate had been feeling happier for the past couple of weeks. The dinner with Clive had given her something. The fact that she had enjoyed it, that there had been no horrific silences, that she had made him laugh and interested him pleased her very much. Perhaps, she thought, it won't only be David after all. Perhaps, sometime, another man will take me seriously. Even a man as desirable as Clive Holden. Because he seemed to her to represent everything that would make life easy. Confidence and humour and attraction and a definite place in the world. She did not expect him to take her out again, except in a similar spontaneous way, but she valued the memory of that one evening.

The flat was far more lively lately as Venn had changed schedule again and was at home for four days and away for three. And Judith was expected back at the weekend. Kate went to the hairdresser Alice used and had her hair cut into a pudding-basin style which suited her small face and straight hair. 'It's like an all-round fringe,' she described to Gabriel on the telephone, thinking back to her first years at Greenhurst when the only hair to have was dark and long and straight, scraped into the classical ballerina's bun. The sun had shone frequently throughout May and London was warming up and already bursting with tourists and shops full of pretty clothes. Kate wrote poems and kept the David thoughts well under control.

In this more confident mood, when Gabriel asked her nervously after several false starts, if Kate was coming to the Donaldsons' party, Kate said, 'Of course.'

Gabriel was lending glasses and an ice bucket and had made dozens of her cheese straws, as much her trade-mark in the village as the vicar's wife's flapjacks. She took them over on Saturday evening and reported when she came back that the party was to be in the garden, provided the weather stayed good. Kate could tell from her mother's manner that Vanessa had been there. Kate pictured the Sunday morning party. The whole village would be there in best dresses. A lot of children. David with Vanessa and herself with no one.

Ben was miserable the next morning when Gabriel made him put on a tie. He loathed to dress up at weekends. He sat and read the Sunday papers and Gabriel, who was always ready for everything far too early, kept easing the tight waist-length bra with one finger and patting her hair and wishing Kate would

116

hurry. When Kate came down, wearing white cotton dungarees a bright pink shirt and very high-heeled sandals, nails the same bright pink as the shirt, lips brighter so that her mouth completely dominated her face, Ben said, 'You look interesting.'

'Is that good or bad?'

'Now don't corner me, Katy. How do you want to look!'

'Coward.' She thought: He could always make me smile. If I was dying he would make it funny.

Once in the car what little bravado Kate had managed to gather vanished and she sat very quietly in the back and her face was pale behind the bright pink mouth. Ben parked in the village street. It was a cloudy morning but not cold and they walked on the brick path round to the side of the house, to the garden, where there was a trestle table covered with a white cloth and clusters of people on the newly-mown grass; children flitted and skirmished and fought over the swing on the walnut tree and Kate identified David's back and felt sick. She moved, with her parents, past the table and was given a drink. She saw Alice and took a cigarette she didn't want. She made herself talk. Outwardly, she must seem normal, she told herself. She disciplined her eyes. She would not look for Vanessa. But David's mother came up, kissing Kate and asking about London. Behind her was Vanessa and they were introduced. The face was not very like the photograph. It was more intelligent. A thin face. Very small white teeth. Very large eyes, giving the face the intensity, the nervousness he spoke of so reverently, hands with bitten nails. She wore a rather ordinary flowered cotton dress as if saying she did not need to be flamboyant in pink and white, to paint her lips and nails; her hair was black, half way down her back, thick ballerina's hair and she had a considerable bosom.

'You live in the village?' It was a careful, musical voice.

Kate nodded, rather surprised that Vanessa could speak and knowing David was there before she saw him. He leaned and kissed her cheek, all the sexuality blotted out, and she looked

117

into his face for the first time in nine weeks and her stomach twisted in agony. She had forgotten tiny details. The way he frowned when he listened, bending his head. The way he started sentences, 'Hey, listen, listen . . . .' His voice, full of expression. The way his eyes could laugh when his face was serious. He asked about her job. Kate answered as briefly as she could. She thought: The last time I saw you, you were naked and so was I. We were shouting and I was crying . . . Now we stand here, dressed up, absurd and talking about nothing. David's mother came back and swept him away.

Kate looked round helplessly and saw her father. He made a marvellous face, as if in torment, and she went across to him and her glass was refilled Alice came back and talked for fifteen minutes and Kate was only required to say 'yes' and 'no'.

'You look amazing, Katy.' Again she had felt him beside her before he spoke. His eyes were clouded and evasive and she knew he had drunk too much and she wanted to take him away somewhere and be quiet with him. She wanted to hear his heart beat, to burrow close to him. 'Missed me?' he said carelessly, reducing it all to a trivial level. Knowing it would enrage or hurt her.

'I missed you until I wanted to die, so don't ever joke about it. Whatever you felt, that you were passing the time or whatever, it mattered terribly to me!' She kept enough pride to leave it in the past.

All the laughter went from his face. The smile always made him wolfish. In seriousness, Kate thought, his face was beautiful. Now his eyes were complicated. 'I was going to come and see you. To talk. Then I thought: Why the hell should I? Let her ring me! I suppose your assessment of my character was partly right but I did go as far as getting your number in London.'

She began to hope then, eyes wide, hands clasped so tightly together they shook with the effort. 'You could still come. If you want to . . .'

Vanessa was there at his elbow, tucking a little hand through his arm, angling her body to his so that the large breasts touched him. Looking up possessively.

'Vanessa, this is Kate . . .'

'We've met,' they said together. Vanessa went on: 'Your mother wants you to get some more bottles from the cellar.' She smiled at Kate and showed the tiny white teeth. She moved David away and she didn't look in the least nervous to Kate. She looked competent and determined and utterly in control.

'For God's sake find me a quiet corner where I can get drunk!' It was her father. 'I detest these village parties. Lady Hope is crucifying the last vicar.' They went towards the low stone wall which ran along the edge of a paved terrace. 'Not such a good garden as ours. They work at it but it hasn't got the trees. Too flat!' They sat down and Ben lit a cigarette and coughed. 'Are you sad, Katy? You wanted him, did you?'

'Yes. And he wanted me for a bit which was more amazing.' She shrugged. 'Anyway . . .'

'Anyway . . .' He smiled. 'I think he's unconvincing. Rather a weak man but I suppose that's half his charm. I think you're too young to be so definite but it's difficult to choose the right age or the right person and difficult to stick with them.'

'You haven't been very happy, have you?' Kate said softly.

'Some of the time, like everyone else. I think we disappointed each other. Neither of us was what the other expected and we spent a long time pretending and so grew used to each other. Or was it too much effort to undo it all? Or perhaps it was you, like a little elf, smiling up at me, daring me to hurt you. Gabriel wanted a child so badly. She channelled her life into that.'

He had never spoken to her like this before, adult to adult. She felt a great rush of love for him and his sad, humorous resignation. 'And now?'

'Now? I expect we'll always be together, countering sarcasm with pretended stupidity; perhaps we enjoy it; who else would put up with me? And we have you to speculate about. But I do remember how it felt.'

119

'When?' she asked.

'Almost ten years ago. Again, far more seriously, three years ago.'

'We never knew.'

'Good.'

'Why is it so difficult?'

Ben shrugged. 'God knows.'

She took his hand. 'I think I'll just stay at home, with you, and dehydrate into an old maid.'

'I doubt it. There's too much feeling in you.'

'I'd like to go now. Would you?'

'I never wanted to come!' Ben stood up. 'I'll go and stand by your mother and fluster her until she has to leave!'

There was no chance for Kate to speak to David again. She said her insincere thankyous to his parents and looked across the garden to where David stood, Vanessa at his side. Kate was filled with a grand resignation. Vanessa had made her feel quite hopeless. When she walked out of the garden with her parents, although she certainly had not stopped loving him, she believed it was over. She had stopped hoping and that in itself brought some kind of relief.

The following evening, people began to come to Caroline's party at about seven, wandering up the street to the shop and through the ground-floor showroom to the garden. Caroline had bought herself a long dress of bright Indian cotton. It looked delicate and exotic. She had let her hair loose, caught at the temples with big combs each side of a middle parting. She looked happy and beautiful and her friends congratulated her, predicting success for the shop and looking curiously for Michael.

'He isn't here yet . . .'

Clive came at seven-thirty, steering his way expertly through the now crowded shop, where people shouted contentedly at one another and cigarette smoke lay in a fog. He went through to the garden and down the stairs to the table where Caroline stood, ladling drink from a flowered Victorian wash basin into glasses. She smiled at him, the noise and the people making her remote. She held out a glass and he took it.

'Did you ask all these strange people, Caroline?'

'Not all of them. I suppose they'll go when the drink runs out and it's good publicity, isn't it? Anyway, I'm loving it. It's so different from the discreet parties Harry and I gave, with men in white coats and trays of canapes.'

He couldn't talk to her for longer. Other people surged forward. Clive tasted the drink which he didn't much like and wondered if it would be rude to ask if there was whisky and decided it would. He stood and looked round the garden and his attention was caught by a girl at the far end. A small, strongly-built girl wearing black trousers and a long white lacy shirt. She had a very interesting face beneath a thick brown fringe and as he watched she laughed, wide mouth opening to show very white teeth with a gap at the front. Clive made his way towards her, paused several times to talk, and finally arrived in the far corner.

She was talking to three men, quite expertly. It was obvious she was in her element at parties. She looked at Clive and smiled. 'Hello. I'm Judith Richardson. This is Tom and Paul and Kevin.'

'Clive Holden.'

Her face changed. 'Well, you are not at all what I imagined.' She laughed. She loved such parties. She loved to investigate people, play with them if she could. So much potential.

'Why?' Clive said. 'Who do we both know?'

'I share a flat with Kate.' She tilted her glass and the last few drops ran into her mouth.

'Can I get you another drink?' Clive said.

'Not just yet.' Subtly she angled her body so that Clive was closer to her than the others, and she would be talking first to him. 'I thought you would be older. Kate is so in awe of you . . .'

'Is she?'

'Yes.' Judith was very skilled at silences, at making the other person feel they must speak.

Clive tried to remember what Kate had said about this girl . . . 'You look after children?'

'I look after people, too. Usually it's the mothers I am looking after. Women are often very helpless when they have small babies.' Her slanted eyes studied Clive quite openly, his face, his strong body, the conventional grey suit.

He felt he was being catagorized, subjected to some kind of test. 'What a responsibility. Did you train at all?'

'No. I began as a mother's help. I have read books on small babies because they interest me but it is mainly experience and common sense and a certain ruthlessness. Sometimes I stay too long, get too involved. Or rather, they get involved with me. I've been in Scotland for two months. That's a good length of job. After six months you are one of them however you try to remain apart.'

'Where in Scotland?'

'Near Perth. In a castle.'

'Very quiet?' Clive said.

'Not at all. In fact, the child I was looking after was kidnapped.'

Clive frowned. 'What happened?'

'They paid the ransom and got him back. It never got into the newspapers. They are very prominent people in a quiet way. Thank God I was in London the night it happened. I imagine they waited until I was out of the way.' She held out her glass in a small, square hand. 'Would you get me a drink now, please?'

'Of course.' He took the glass and their hands touched. Clive wove his way towards Caroline's table. The sun was setting and the little garden was very crowded. Michael, pausing at the top of the stairs, looked down and wondered at the adaptability of human beings that they could enjoy themselves in such a setting. It was the kind of party he most disliked. He made his way down the steps towards Caroline. She raised her head to kiss him. She was quite different, he thought, too animated, laughing too much. She was altered by the drink and the people. She gave him a jug. 'Could you go round with this, darling, and fill some glasses?' He took it and came to Clive, filling the glasses Clive held. They had hardly spoken to each other since the evening at Cambridge Street.

'How long will this go on?' he asked Clive.

Clive grinned. 'Hours.'

'I can't stand it!'

'I didn't think you'd come if you had half an excuse.'

'I have only just arrived. I've got a very, very good deal in the offing with an American company. Two of their buyers are coming tomorrow afternoon. I've been trying to make contact with them for months!' He hesitated. 'We should discuss Mosaic again some time.'

'Yes. Shall I ring you?'

Michael nodded. The friendliness between them was short-lived and he moved on, filling glasses, studied curiously by Caroline's friends. When the jug was empty he retreated indoors and upstairs to the first floor, sitting on the sofa and listening to the incredible roar of voices and laughter until the problem of the shape of the hands for the Sundial occupied his mind and he began sketching ideas on a small notepad.

When, after an hour, it was quieter, he went down again, trying to pretend he had been there all the time. Dinner was being talked of. It was nine-thirty. He went to find Caroline, putting his arm along her shoulder. More uninhibited than usual because of the party and the alcohol, she put her arms round his neck and kissed him.

When Clive saw them together, saw them touch each other, his whole body seemed to slow down. He hated it. He turned away. He had been talking to Judith for the last hour. He found her extremely attractive and interesting and tough. He had been about to ask her to have dinner with him but quite suddenly he wanted to get out, alone; he did not want anyone.

123

She saw the changed expression on his face. He made some excuse about being late and said goodbye, despite her raised eyebrows; he hardly looked at her before he went, crossing the garden, to thank Caroline, running up the steps and through the shop and into the street. Judith looked after him. Several other men moved in, now that Clive had gone. Dinner would not be a problem. But she was both surprised and a little disappointed. Judith had liked Clive Holden. His face and his manner, the hardness in his eyes and the impression he gave of being a man who liked women. It was some time since she had been so intrigued. She resolved to ask Kate about him. Then she turned her attention to Ian Finch who was beside her, smiling at him. The night was warm and she was hungry and life was good. 'How about dinner, Judith?' Ian Finch said. Rachel had flu.

'I'm sorry I was so late at the party, 'Michael said in the darkness. Caroline lay against him and she could hear his voice as the words were formed in his chest. 'I was speaking to my Americans. They're coming tomorrow afternoon. I think they'll take two or three hundred of that desk-top range if we can agree a price. It will be an enormous order. Just what we need.'

'I thought perhaps you wouldn't come at all,' Caroline said. 'I know you hate parties.' She laughed. 'It amused me to watch all my friends wondering who you were . . . and you weren't even there!'

'Would you have minded if I hadn't come?'

'Yes, but I would have understood. I love you now regardless of what you do.' It was the truth. She rolled over, curling her back against his stomach, and she slept but Michael lay awake for a long time, anticipating the meeting the following day, thinking of Clive and how best to hand over Mosaic. He felt as if he had only just closed his eyes when the telephone rang, shrilling through the darkness and silence of his sleep. He leaned over Caroline and found the receiver, expecting a wrong number. 'Hello?'

Caroline stirred, hid her face as Michael turned on the lamp, felt his body stiffen and heard the words he was saying. She knew something serious had happened.

'When do they think it was? And Gautier found her? Yes . . . You'll go tomorrow. Of course I'll come with you.' He changed the receiver to his other hand, sitting up more. The flex lay across Caroline's naked body. 'There is a flight at two, I think, on weekdays, to Marseilles. I'll ring you first thing in the morning.'

'My grandmother,' he said, leaning across Caroline to replace the telephone and pulling the bedclothes up to cover her. He swung his legs out of bed, sitting with his head bent, one hand thoughtfully stroking his forehead. 'She's had some sort of heart attack. Rather bad, they think. She's in hospital. Luckily the Gautiers were in the house that night. They were afraid of frost.'

'You're going to France tomorrow?'

'Yes. And I have these two American buyers coming at three and Jenny is in Belgium until Wednesday.' He pulled on his pyjama trousers and wandered the room.

'Can I do anything?' Caroline asked helplessly.

'I don't see how. You know nothing about it . . . but Clive could see them for me.' He turned, looking at Caroline with a strange expression. He thought: Illness and death. God, I will be so bad at it all. But there will be no one else to cope. My mother cannot manage alone.

'Do you want me to come to France with you?' Caroline said. She sat up in bed, wide awake, and she could hardly believe the casual way she was putting aside the first day of her shop as if it were some game she chose to play.

'How can you come, Caroline? Tomorrow is your first real day.'

'I know . . . I just said it.' They both used her shop as the excuse. But she knew he did not want her to come.

She pushed the hurt down. 'Come to bed, Michael. What can

125

you do now?'

'Nothing. But I certainly can't sleep . . . My mother must have rung Clive to get this number.' He sat heavily on the bed and began to dial.

'Clive? It's Mike. Yes. I'm sorry to disturb you again but I need your help tomorrow with Mosaic. I'm going to France in the early afternoon—Valerie has had a heart attack—and I have this meeting set up for three. I've been arranging it for months . . . Yes, the people I mentioned last night. They've seen samples and we've corresponded and they arrive in England tomorrow morning. I'm sure they are very seriously interested. It would be a very big order. Big commission for us.'

Clive lay in the darkness. The digital clock by his bed gave a dim greenish light. 'I could come to Mosaic early, about eight, but I'd have to leave at nine-thirty. We're briefing counsel in the Hill case. I could get back to Mosaic by three, though, if you can tell me enough about it in an hour and half tomorrow morning.'

'I'm sure I can. The figures are all written down. The price below which I can't do it is what matters. They'll beat you down as much as possible. But you'll probably deal with them far better than I could.'

'I'm sorry about the old lady, Mike. Really.'

'Thanks,' Michael said.

He slept very little for the rest of the night and at six-thirty he slid out of bed, trying not to wake Caroline. He put a few clothes into his small suitcase. Caroline lay spread over the bed, hair in a great cloak, hands tucked under her pillow. She woke when Michael opened the drawer near her and she sat up, getting out of bed and coming to kiss him.

'Let me get you some breakfast?'

'No, I really don't want anything. I'm sorry but I must go.'

'It's all right. I understand.'

'After nine, could you call Bulstead, the travel agents in the Brompton Road, and book two seats on the two o'clock, I think it is, flight to Marseilles? They know my name there. I always use them. I'll ring you later to check if it's all right.'

His unshaven face was rough when he kissed her. He ran down the stairs and the door to the street slammed after him. Caroline got back into bed. When he leaves now, he takes something out of this place, she thought. She looked round the untidy room. Michael had removed himself and his things as if they had had some terrible fight. She shivered. She thought of his grandmother and tried to feel pity. It was a bleak and clouded morning. Caroline turned on the radio and was irritated by it. As she turned it off she wondered how long Michael would be gone. The unexpected emptiness of the day, of the evening and night ahead, showed her just how deeply Michael had embedded himself in her life in a very short time.

Clive arrived at Mosaic at ten past eight, parking in Meadwell Street. He found Michael at his desk with two mugs of coffee and a lot of papers.

'Poor old girl.' Clive took one of the coffees. 'I couldn't stop thinking about her. Couldn't sleep.'

'Nor could I.'

'How bad is it?'

'They don't really know. My mother, of course, is in a complete panic. All this bloody guilt thing because she doesn't go to Jouvard enough. They've never really got on . . .' He rubbed his eyes. 'Well, here it is, Clive.' He spread out half a dozen black and white photographs. On a shiney red tray were pyramid-shaped black perspex objects. 'This is the Pharaoh range. You see, they are triangular instruments which can sit together like this or in any position you want on your desk. They're well designed. They have reliable movements. They're solid and they're fairly cheap and I can't sell the bloody things in England for some reason. I'm hoping these Americans will buy them for their Christmas gift market. They do a lot of this sending of Christmas presents with their company's name on them. These are particularly suitable for silk screen printing. I've had this one done with our name just to show them. We also have smart black cardboard boxes made up with polystyrene liners.'

'So it's clocks, barometers and thermometers?'

'Yes.'

'Price?'

'This is the vital sheet. I've got a good deal on the movements from Germany. I'll get hold of Jenny this morning to ask her to get back as quickly as she can and she can cope with any agreement. If she were here she'd cope with it all. She's done it before. These are the prices below which it is not economical . . .'

Just after nine-fifteen the telephone rang. Clive picked it up. It was Caroline. 'Could you tell Michael I've booked the seats. They will drop the tickets in to him at eleven.'

'Right . . . Michael, it's Caroline. Reservations are okay. Do you want to speak to her?'

He shook his head. 'Say I'll ring later. I must get these letters organized. You will be back by three, Clive?'

'Yes. In fact I'm glad to have this chance to feel out Mosaic.'

Michael looked serious. 'I suppose, if Grandmother dies, I shall have to go to Jouvard far sooner than I expected. Gautier runs the day to day stuff very well but he needs someone to deal with the money side.'

'Could you not commute back and forth for a time?'

'Perhaps.' He looked up as Penny, his secretary, came in. 'But I don't much like the idea. I hope it won't come to that . . .' He looked at Clive as if he would like to make some reference to their relationship to Caroline, but he changed his mind.

He never did ring Caroline back. He picked up his mother at twelve-thirty and it was not until he was sitting beside her on the plane, high over the English channel, that he remembered.

CHAPTER EIGHT

On Friday afternoon, when she had still heard nothing, Caroline telephoned Clive in his office, her voice stiff as she tried to hide the humiliation. 'It's Caroline. Have you heard any news?'

Clive felt a lot of things. Pleasure at the sound of her voice and pity for the embarrassment in it, fury at Michael and satisfaction at his own understanding of the man. 'A little. The old lady is still in hospital but not in any danger at the moment. They are trying to find a nurse to live in the Château with her. Michael's mother is going to stay for a while and . . .'

'Did he ring you?'

'Yes. On Monday night.'

'No message?' Caroline asked dully.

'Well, you know Michael . . .'

'Not really.'

All the explanations and excuses which came into Clive's head he pushed down. He was damned if he would make it easy for Michael. 'I think things are pretty tense over there.'

'Yes, of course.' Her tone changed. She felt selfish.

'The American thing went very well.' Clive changed the subject deliberately. 'They've ordered six hundred units initially and a possible four hundred more.'

'Good.'

'Are you busy? How about lunch today?'

'I really can't leave, Clive. There have been so many people in all week. It's been marvellous. And only half of them were friends. I shall have to go buying at the weekend.'

'I'll come down and see you when I can, in that case.'

'Yes, do.' She put the telephone down and tried very hard to remind herself that she had been married and divorced, had started again, that at thirty she should be harder. But she found instead that she was far more unsure of herself and vulnerable than she had ever been. She loved Michael with such panic and after five days she had exhausted all the reasons why he should not contact her. He had not been killed in a plane crash and his grandmother was not dead. She cringed, thinking of Clive making excuses. The truth was quite simple. Michael did not realize how much it mattered to her. He thought she could be put aside, with no curiosity or need of him, to wait patiently for his return. She even suspected he might be relieved to have time on his own, a little solitude, whereas to her the emptiness of evenings and nights, which she had learned to cope with before Michael, were now intolerable again.

On fine evenings Caroline stayed open till eight, pouring herself a glass of wine, smoking a cigarette. Saturday was very hot and the whole Kings Road became a party and the shop was busy all day. At seven Brian Lessing came in with a bottle of cold white wine. 'You need some help, Caroline. Someone to mind the shop in the day while you go out buying or delivering the small stuff. I know a girl who might do. Shall I ask her? Her name is Liz Moult.'

'Yes, please.'

When Brian finally left, at eight, and Caroline was about to close, Clive came in. 'I'm taking you out. No excuses accepted!' But she seemed quite happy to go with him. She was quiet and he saw the old restlessness back in her hands.

'When he comes back he will be amazed that you are hurt. If you are going to have any kind of permanent relationship you'll have to accept that he is no good at social details . . .'

'Damn you both! Bothering to talk to me and to explain to me what is happening is no social detail!' But her anger was short-lived and empty as her house and her bed were empty.

'What are you doing tomorrow?'

'Going buying. There's a village in Sussex I want to go to. They have two or three good pine shops there.'

'Can I come?'

She hesitated. Clive watched her closely. Her hesitation took all the spontaneity from her answer, showed him that she did not, whatever she had said, hold him on the simple level of friendship. 'I'd like some company,' she said at last.

'What time will you leave?'

'About ten . . . come for breakfast first.' She smiled at him, confused by her own motives, wondering if unconsciously she wanted to use Clive to punish Michael for his inattention. But it wasn't that, was it? Clive was a friend.

'Nine, then.' He left her outside the shop by the street door with a light kiss on her cheek. 'Sleep well, love,' he said, casually, perhaps demonstrating, she thought, that he would not be used in any kind of strategic game.

When Clive came the following morning she cooked him an enormous breakfast but ate little herself. She was quiet as they drove out of London and Clive was an uneasy passenger. Caroline drove well but slowly and after they stopped for petrol Clive asked if he could drive. She refused. They reached Balcombe at eleven o'clock and bought two small pine chests at the first shop and a set of chairs; at the second two American wall clocks and a blue china umbrella stand. They lunched in a pub, sat in the weak sun for a while and started back towards London at about three-thirty. Caroline was different now, pleased with her purchases. 'The man next door knows a girl who may come in three days a week. It would help me a lot. Not only can I get out buying but also she can help me in the workroom. Those stripped chairs go very well. Dining-room chairs are so expensive at the moment. Look, most of the skin is stripped off my fingers. I really think the shop will pay its way, Clive.'

'After a whole week, you're very confident.'

She smiled and was quiet for a while. When she spoke again, her voice was subdued. 'I nearly rang you, early this morning, for Michael's number. But he is so difficult on the phone.'

'The only telephone is in the office. They don't always hear it.'

He helped her to unload the car and came upstairs for a drink.

'Stay and I'll cook something,' she said.

They were quite easy together. Clive made her forget about Michael for short periods and when she remembered he watched as she hardened herself. Now, at last, Clive had stepped back far enough to be clever. When, towards the end of the meal, she began to talk he listened in silence.

'I don't understand why I am reacting so childishly. Why can't I be left for a week? I am behaving like Rachel and her friends in a way I have always despised, needing constant reassurance. I never wanted to feel love again the way I feel for Michael. I've thought about it so much. It's not that I'm so petulant that his silence makes me sulk. It's far worse. I don't want to love someone who will not give me what I need, not even realize what I need. Michael is, as you say, self-contained. I want him to need to ring me, need to hear my voice because things are difficult for him and it would help to talk to me. I can't bear to be put away, in a slot, as Harry put me away.'

The atmosphere had changed completely. Clive's voice had altered. It was hard and flat, all the lawyer in him coming out. 'Then stop it now, before you throw away everything you have just started here. Before you give all this up and go to France and find a way of life you don't understand with a man who can't be what you want. What is worse, the decision may be forced on you far too soon.'

Her eyes were enormous. The fact that every word he said was true started a numbing despair in her. She wanted to talk about Michael, as if words would bring him here. 'He is so young in some ways. You could be ten years older. So could I!'

'Just let things happen. Stay and make a success of your shop and enjoy the summer.'

She smiled. 'Simple as that?'

'Simple as that!'

Caroline stood up, gathering plates, bending to kiss Clive's cheek but he turned his face and it was his mouth that her lips touched. She had always enjoyed kissing him. She moved away.

132

Her body and its responses were so unpredictable. She moved into the little kitchen area and waited for Clive to come after her and wondered how she would react.

'I think I should go, love. I'm tired,' he said, surprising her. 'I'll ring you in the morning.'

She moved around the room when he had gone, carrying glasses, washing plates. The whole place was unusually tidy as she tended to do housework when her mind was preoccupied or she was unhappy. When she went to bed and closed her eyes the longing for Michael came, making all her earlier words to Clive meaningless.

The following morning a letter came. His writing was distinctive, very small, the lines close together. It began, *Dear Caroline,* and this brought a picture of him clearly into her mind. *I am sorry I didn't feel like writing before. And you know how I loathe the telephone. It paralyses me. I couldn't bear to have one of those stilted long-distance conversations with you. My grandmother is really very ill. Her heart has been damaged. We have found a nurse who seems honest and sympathetic and my mother will stay on here for a couple of weeks to see them both settled in. I have been trying to organize things so that I can come back to London but it is obvious that many things need doing here. The vines are just starting to flower and the weather is very good, warm and calm. I think you would like it here. I shall fly back on Wednesday, June sixth, and stay until the weekend and then come back here for another week. If you can manage it, I'd love you to meet me at Heathrow. If you can't, perhaps you would leave a message with Clive? I shall ring him Tuesday night. My flight is BE769 arriving at three thirty in the afternoon. I love you.*
Michael.

Caroline was at Heathrow far too early and she was acutely nervous. She wandered the glass-walled airport hall, looked at magazines and read the flight board; she had two cups of coffee and smoked constantly and his flight landed exactly on time. As she waited for him to clear customs and immigration, Caroline paced up and down, irritated at the attention she was attracting. And then the passengers began to appear. Brown holiday

133

people, the occasional business man, a family of Arabs, a party of school-children and Michael. The first sight of his face caused her a feeling of panicky shyness. He hurried towards her, putting down his suitcase, putting his arms round her. His narrow face was very brown and the touch of his body unleashed it all again.

They drove back towards London in Caroline's car. 'I've missed you so terribly,' she said.

'There is so much to do, Caroline . . .'

'I just couldn't understand your silence . . .'

'As soon as I have organized Mosaic, I shall go there permanently. I know that now. But I must get the Sundial under way. My last project to round things off.'

'I hate being away from you.'

'The house is in a deplorable state. You'll come with me, won't you, Caroline? You could do so much. My grandmother can't live very much longer. I don't know why it doesn't make me more sad. Perhaps because she has lessened so much over the past few years. We'll get married, shall we, when we go there permanently?'

She drove quite automatically, not concerned with the road or cars, her brain racing. 'Michael, I have the shop. I want to build it up.'

'Have a shop in St Remy. It's a nice little town. They have tourists.'

'You don't understand. It's not something to pass the time. I like the feeling that I support myself.'

'You don't support yourself! You have merely used the money your ex-husband gave you to invest in a shop instead of shares!'

She trembled with anger. 'I will not drop everything and go to France. I don't want to.'

He rubbed his face wearily. 'Well I can't stay in England more than a few months.'

'Why should I give up everything?'

134

'I thought you'd want to. I'm sorry. I misunderstood.'

She drove him to Mosaic and they both maintained the angry silence. Then Caroline drove down the road and parked beside her shop. Liz Moult had come in for the afternoon. She was seventeen, round-faced and keen. She sat knitting on the Chesterfield. 'I sold two glass candlesticks. Trade.'

Caroline checked the invoice book. 'Good.' She was tumbling inside.

It began to rain heavily and Liz went home and Caroline shut the shop. She had a bath and washed her hair and it was still damp when she heard the shop door. She stood at the top of the stairs as Michael came up.

He looked very tired, heavy with tiredness like a child, his face not yet old enough to become drawn. He put out his hands, standing on the stair below Caroline, and smoothed drops of water from her face. A great rush of love filled her. 'I've missed you so terribly. And you don't understand anything of how I feel.'

'What do you want from me, Caroline? I can't give you great flowery speeches. I thought of you. Sometimes I was too busy or too sad. I didn't ring because I hate the phone. I didn't write until I had something to say.'

Caroline poured him a whisky and he sat down. 'I want to marry you. I hate living without you. Is that good enough?'

Caroline poured herself a drink, stood away from him, tried to explain herself.

'When you weren't here I realized how much I loved you and I also realized that there is no basis for it. It is an instinct. We will never find it easy to be what the other needs. I don't really want to marry again. I didn't want to love you. Have you considered that it's most unlikely I shall ever have children? That I will constantly be asking for demonstrations of affection from you? That in many ways I could be far more than three years older than you are?' Michael stood up as she was speaking and came to her. He touched her face. And somehow they moved up

135

the second flight of stairs to the bedroom all the words forgotten, and made love with an almost telepathic understanding of what the other wanted. But afterwards nothing was solved.

She lay on top of Michael, her body all along his, her head sideways and her damp hair over them both. He stroked her shoulders and her back.

'Am I too heavy?'

'No. Stay there.'

'I was just trying to be sensible.'

'I know.'

'I won't come to France, just like that.'

'I won't stay here.'

She began to cry, very quietly, and he said, 'Don't, Caroline. Please. I'll go back on Friday. I must. But in a week I'll be back and then I'll stay until I have the Sundial launched and Mosaic sorted out. It will be several months. We'll work something out.'

Absolute despair filled her, despite what he said. She saw nothing ahead but decisions and either way one of them was going to give up too much. Perhaps it seemed extraordinary to Michael that her shop meant so much to her but it was a culmination of years of ambition, at first just vague outlines, just a strong desire to be a whole and self-sufficient woman, earning her living, using what skill she had. She must try and make him understand this because, in not taking the shop seriously, she felt he did not understand a very large part of her.

The two days that Michael spent in London were very unsatisfactory for Caroline. He was at Mosaic from eight in the morning until eight at night, talking with Jenny, one whole afternoon with Clive, planning the following months, laying down the programme of the Sundial. 'I'm going to tell them to go ahead with the bodies, Clive. I know it's more money than I've ever risked before but I want to see them in production. I really think they'll go. The commission from this American sale and the success of those acrylic photograph frames, and the paperweights, should carry us. But we'll need several new lines by the autumn, either ours or someone else's.'

Jenny sat on a desk, clicking her feet together. 'You're in danger of forgetting your own rule, Michael—not to have more capital tied up in your designs than in other people's. Never risk more than forty per cent, you told me that first day.'

'I made the bloody rule,' he snapped, knowing she was right. He leaned forward over the desk. 'How about some coffee, Pen?'

Michael's secretary slid out from behind her desk and the steady background rattle of her typewriter was silenced.

'How did it feel, Clive?'

'Very good. I had one or two awkward moments when they asked questions I couldn't answer but Penny helped out. They had made up their minds before they came, anyway.' Clive took a tin of cigars from his pocket, lit one and tapped his fingers on the tin. 'I could easily come in one afternoon a week if I organized myself. I'd like to do that. It will mean, if and when I take over, I shall know what I'm doing.'

Jenny stood up, opening the drawer of her desk and taking out her cigarettes. She was a very small square woman of Clive's age, brilliant at putting an idea or a product across. She was not attractive. She did not distract buyers, male or female, but gradually let her strong personality show. 'How long are you going to France for this time, Mike?'

'Only a week,' Michael said.

Michael and Caroline did not discuss France again but the subject hung between them like a black cloud. On Friday evening at nine Caroline drove him to Heathrow. There was heavy rain and the sound of the windscreen wipers with the hiss of the wheels made too much sound to talk comfortably.

In the airport bar they had a drink. 'Only a week,' Michael said. The flight was called and Caroline stood up and kissed him goodbye, awkward in front of so many people. As she watched him walk away, funnelled with the other passengers, taken out of her life, she felt as despairing as if he had gone for ever. She drove back to London with tears in her eyes.

The following evening Clive took her out, in his best mood, gentle and funny, his voice sympathetic and comforting as she talked . . . 'It's too sharp-edged, Clive. Nothing but unhappiness. He's too honest to pretend. Just marry me, he says, drop everything. Come to France . . .'

'Do all the men you know want to marry you?'

'Only the young ones.' She smiled for a moment. 'He says, as you do, wait and see, but I can't. I've made up my mind. I won't go. And he won't stay. So what is the point of prolonging it all? When he comes back I shall tell him.'

'And he won't listen. He'll arrive, unexpectedly on your door step, and you'll let him in and . . .'

'No! Not next time!'

Clive took her to a night club. It was dark, crowded, the music subdued and sensual; they drank double brandies and Caroline's glass seemed to be always empty. She drank without tasting, wanting the escape that alcohol could bring her, wanting to get away from her misery. Clive danced with her for a long time, holding her possessively, wanting her, and as the alcohol took hold Caroline was filled with a destructive wickedness. Why should she go on, letting Michael in again and again? Clive was right, wasn't he? He was always right . . . She moved her face. His skin was warm. The room and music moved as they moved. She wanted a positive break, didn't she? She sat down with Clive, talking a little unsteadily, lighting a cigarette, draining her glass. Clive kissed her and she was not thinking now, not analysing, just reacting. And his mouth was warm, hard.

He drove her back to Pimlico without asking if she wanted to come. She stumbled down the basement steps and laughed as he steadied her but it was not obvious quite how drunk she was. The room smelled nice, the thought vaguely, as Clive did, standing close to her in the semi-darkness.

'I want to make love to you. I have wanted you since I first saw you, Caroline.' She found herself walking with him, quite

138

docilely, into the bedroom, thinking: I wanted you too until Michael came . . . She sat down on his bed and then let herself lie back, waiting for him, because Michael was not here, would not be here, because she didn't want to love Michael so much. Clive touched her, stirring responses in her body and surprising her. She touched him in return and the brandy made her uninhibited and she felt him change. No one had ever made love to Caroline with such violence and it excited her and there was no stopping it. They became part of an irresistible pattern. 'I have wanted you for so long . . . so long . . .' he said and his strong body contorted and the depth of his feeling touched her and scared her. How strange, she thought, in an extraordinarily detached state of mind which the drink and the despair had caused, that Clive, who must have slept with so many women, cares so much whereas I, who have slept with only four men in my lifetime and do this knowing that it will change the direction of my life, feel nothing but affection. Even as she thought it the misery began to break through.

'Stay and sleep here, Caroline. I want to wake and find you here.' He needed to hold her so tightly that he was afraid of hurting her. She fell asleep quickly, breathing evenly. Clive slept too, but fitfully, waking with joy to register that she was there.

When Caroline woke in the morning and remembered she was utterly miserable but she tried to conceal it. Clive made her some coffee, sat on the end of the bed, leant forward to kiss her, wove a great web of plans which enclosed her. She was not awkward with him. She could look into his eyes and admit she had enjoyed him but she wanted to go home, to slide out of this possessiveness and think.

Yet she submitted, strangely docile, evening after evening, to Clive's organization throughout the following week, let him blot Michael from her mind, let a kind of love grow up between them. An appreciation and a friendship. Probably, Caroline thought sadly, a far more adult basis for a relationship than the way Michael and I felt for each other. Michael did not contact her. Clive relayed what news came. And on June the fifteenth, the day Michael had been expected home, Clive rang Caroline to say that Valerie de Jouvard had died the previous night.

It seemed to Caroline that it was an omen, a certainty that Michael would be living in France. She resigned herself to this. She began to work extremely hard, driving herself long distances, employing Liz for four full days a week now; deliberately creating an atmosphere of hurry and involvement in the daytime and in the evenings using Clive to forget with.

Michael had been working in the fields on the evening his grandmother died, with Raoul Gautier, tying the best shoots to the wires now that flowering had finished. It had been a good flowering, fourteen days, and Raoul was optimistic. At nine, his back aching, Michael went indoors. He went up to see Valerie, telling her how pleased Raoul was. She seemed tired but she smiled. Suzanne came to sit with her while the nurse ate. 'Your food is in the warming oven, Michael.' After he had eaten he read and went to bed and he slept but it seemed only moments before his mother came in, shaking him gently, tears on her face. The dawn was a faintly lighter stripe in the eastern sky, widening imperceptibly when Michael went to the window. 'She died in her sleep,' Suzanne said.

That day the Château was filled with subdued activity. The doctor and the undertaker, endless sympathetic callers from the village and messages of sympathy. Michael grieved more than he had expected. Knowing she was ill and tired and lonely, he had thought her death would be a relief but he found, now, that quiet though she had been in the last weeks, something vital had gone from the house. It was without a core. The family gathered five days later for the funeral and parallel with the sadness was an air of reunion. Many of them had not met for years.

'She was the last,' they said. 'The last of her generation . . . and you are coming here, Michael?' They drank the wine of Jouvard and said, 'Death in the country is never so bad, with

140

everything going on around you, continuing. With the vines to care for. Death in the city is a terrible thing.'

There was so much sorting, so many papers and letters and photographs and old-lady clothes; drawers of rouge and combs and hair-brushes and handkerchiefs. How could anyone have so many embroidered handkerchieves? Suzanne thought, resolving that when she was old she would sort out her own things ruthlessly so as not to inflict this sadness on Marie-Claire. As she sifted through the relics of her parents' lives, of her own childhood, she was sometimes moved to tears, sometimes remembering and laughing. Sometimes, unable to stand any more, she put on gloves and went out to work in the fields for a while: the days were hot now and she wore Valerie's old straw hat.

The tiny buds which had formed at the end of May, which had been watched with such anxiety through the vital two weeks of flowering, were now replaced by baby grapes. Michael found in Raoul Gautier an immense store of knowledge which the old man was happy to share. 'It has been done this way for generations.'

'But what have they discovered in the past few years? Surely there has been research, new methods, new ideas?' Michael said.

Raoul shrugged. 'We do not use them here.'

In the evenings Michael and his mother ate in the smaller of the three main downstairs rooms at a small round table. Raoul's wife, Yvette, prepared the meal. The silence was the strangest thing. No aeroplanes, no cars, no television, no radio except Suzanne's small transistor. Time was different here. There was one long pause between work and sleep in which Michael ate in his usual disinterested way and then studied the books of accounts.

The will had been read and there was not a great deal of money. What there was would be equally divided between Michael and Marie-Claire. Suzanne was to have all Valerie's jewellery to distribute as she wished. Michael knew he would need the money from the sale of Cambridge Street and Mosaic to undertake a programme of replanting and modernization.

He thought of Caroline frequently. He was afraid she would not come here. He was deliberately giving her time, and himself time. The way she had kissed him at the airport had had a chilling finality about it. When I go back at the end of June, Michael thought. I will ask her again to come. Once a week he telephoned Clive for news of Mosaic and Clive reported that he and Jenny were getting on well which was not exactly true. The weather in Provence was beautiful and Suzanne finished sorting her mother's things. Michael told Raoul he would be back in September for the harvest and at the beginning of July, he and Suzanne flew home.

The three weeks which Michael had spent in France had been the happiest of Clive's life. He adored everything about Caroline—the way she looked, her stillness, her laughter, her lovemaking, the way she was changing, buying herself long cotton skirts, leaving her hair loose. She wore sandals and her feet were brown with white lines where the straps of the sandals crossed. Once, quite by chance, an old friend of Harry's strayed into her shop and was amazed to see Caroline and the news was relayed back. Caroline laughed with Clive to think of the wires buzzing. She knew everyone in the street now and liked most of them, felt part of the community, felt that she belonged. Above all, she felt she was a professional.

Throughout June, Clive had become seriously involved with Mosaic. It had always appealed to him from the outside and from the inside he found it a small but fascinating company with good people working in it. His legal knowledge was extremely useful to them once or twice and although Clive was uneasy with Jenny Jacobs and could not like her, he respected her ability and knew he would have to learn to work with her. It was unusual for Clive to have difficulty with people. It came from both sides. He found her very definite, determined to have her own way and to back her own judgement. She found Clive too smooth. She felt he was unnecessary, that she could cope better on her own.

Clive talked a great deal to the one designer Michael employed, a quiet middle-aged man called Bill Carter, unmarried and totally involved in his work and his one hobby which was gliding. In his spare time and in the evenings, he designed gliders. One Tuesday, which had become Clive's regular day for visiting Mosaic, Bill told Clive that he had an idea for a product. It was after six and one by one the three secretaries left until Bill and Clive were alone. Clive opened the deep drawer in Michael's desk and got out a bottle of whisky.

'I wondered if you'd look at these drawings, Clive,' Bill said. 'If I could finance the thing myself, I would, but I just haven't got the capital. I hoped the company might take it on but I know Michael's committed to the Sundial and that's already well over cost . . .' He showed Clive drawings of a clock. 'This is the actual size. It is rounded at the base and weighted so that it stands at an angle, and rocks when you touch it. It will be good to touch and hold, it will spin and rock. I know what movements we can use. The expense would be tooling up for the body. It would have to be injection moulded plastic. They could be beautiful bright colours, scarlet and shiney bright green.'

'Could you make me a mock-up?' Clive asked.

'Sure.'

Two evenings later, when Clive called in again on his way to see Caroline, Bill Carter lifted a cardboard box on to the drawing-board. 'I've made up that rocking clock.'

'What rocking clock?' Jenny said, coming forward.

'It's an idea Bill has.' Clive put out his hands and picked up the object. He set it on Michael's desk and it rocked gently. It was shiney black. He pushed it and it spun. He picked it up and handed it to Jenny. 'I like it.'

'I was thinking,' Bill said, 'that we could do thermometers

and barometers, using the movements Michael uses for the Pharaoh range you sold to the States.'

'It's bloody ingenious,' Clive said. 'A marvellous thing to fiddle with at a business meeting. I'd love one on my desk!'

Bill grinned. 'I hoped you'd like it.'

Jenny was silent. She moved the clock from one hand to another. Her hands were very small, her round nails painted a dark red.

'I could get out some kind of costing,' Bill said. 'Then you and Jenny could work it out in more detail. The faces could be silk screened on glass discs. The weights could be lead. That's what I've used in this one.'

'It's the sort of thing the General Trading Company could sell,' Clive said. The smoke from his cigar spiralled towards the ceiling.

'It looks sinister,' Jenny said at last. 'It looks like a small bomb.'

'Is that good or bad?' Clive narrowed his eyes.

She put the clock down and faced them squarely. 'I'm sorry, Bill. I don't like it. I think that a machine to form the bodies will be enormously expensive, probably three or four thousand pounds, and that the whole idea is too risky for the company at the moment.'

'I don't agree,' Clive said coldly. Then he laughed. 'How can you reject it just like that?'

She shrugged. She folded her arms. 'It's just a feeling, I admit, but it seemed to me to be a contradiction in terms to have a scientific instrument in such an unsteady, jokey body. It doesn't add up.'

Clive put out the cigar. The room was silent. He sensed that this was the first of many such confrontations and he thought it essential that he was not defeated. 'Well, I think it's worth going into the costing and I'd like to see a mock-up in red. It would look quite different. Will you work out some figures, Bill?'

'Yes, of course.'

Jenny shrugged, her mouth a straight line of annoyance. She picked up her cardigan and bag and moved towards the door. 'Good night . . . see you tomorrow.' She walked down the street to where her car was parked and when she got in she sat for a few moments, thinking deeply, before she drove home.

CHAPTER NINE

The first weekend in July was extremely hot, as if summer had finally made up its mind to begin. Kate's parents were in their usual gardening frenzy. It was the one passion which Ben and Gabriel shared, the one subject on which he respected her judgement and did not constantly snipe at her opinions. The gardens at the Old Vicarage were lovely, laid out at the end of the last century with faded brick walls and a paved area by the house, tall beech hedges and low lavender hedges and lawns that sloped gently down to a small lake with willow trees and water-lilies. In May and June there were azaleas and rhododendrons and now roses and one long, brilliant border. Gabriel employed a full-time gardener, but she worked alongside him throughout the summer in a shapeless linen skirt, her arms a deep brown. Ben did all the mowing, constantly exchanging his machines for newer and better ones. After the tension of his week in the City and especially after business trips abroad with all the exhaustion of flying and airports and hotels, he could not wait for the peace and the beauty of this garden which Gabriel had developed.

She had changed so little, he thought, watching her on this hot Sunday. The first summer of their marriage she had knelt at the long border as she did now, totally absorbed. He remembered coming up behind her, kissing her neck, drawing her indoors to make love. The friction between them, so damaging now, had heightened the excitement through the first years.

Kate, in a new bikini, laid herself on one of the ancient sun beds, listening to her parents' voices, liking to hear them talk normally and remembering how, as a child, she had loved to hear them speak as if they were interested in one another. She listened also to the birds, to the occasional aeroplane, and the sun was so hot on her closed eyes that she raised her arm to

146

shade her face and drifted into a state of warmth and peace, thinking many things as her brain unwound towards sleep. Thinking of Clive and how happy and alive he seemed, how he had talked his way out of the mistake he had made in the Mather contract, how often John Hampton rang, how she was constantly asked to get Caroline on the telephone or Jenny Jacobs, whom she had not met; thinking of her own narrow life and of Judith and the way she had of making you do what she wanted, of imprinting her will, quite gently, on those around her. Judith made Kate go to parties with her, questioned her about Clive in great detail, talked about the Campden Square family with amusing sarcasm. 'The husband is much older, tormented with doubt about the wife, doesn't sleep well, diets constantly, watches me and never comes near me, has all his shirts hand-made.' Kate thought of how, on London summer evenings, she walked and got to know more and more, extending her territory, thinking of David far less.

There was a bee somewhere, buzzing and pausing, a slight breeze. Her arm smelled warm and clean and when David's voice said, 'I've brought you a cold drink,' she knew she must have fallen asleep and didn't bother to open her eyes. There was a sensation of a caress on her arm and the icy cold touch of a glass. She jerked her eyes open.

He was crouching beside her, browner than she had ever seen him. She had forgotten the way his eyebrows almost touched in the middle and the small scar on his chin.

'I'm home for the weekend. Thought I'd come and see how you all were.' He watched her with his blue, speckled eyes, circled with a navy blue ring, fair-lashed. 'I came through the kitchen so I brought you a drink.' He sat back on the warm stone. He was wearing a red T shirt and jeans which he had cut off into shorts. The shirt followed the concave line of his stomach. His coming here put Kate on top and they both knew it. 'Where are your parents? Have they killed each other yet?'

'Gardening,' Kate said and her heart was beating loudly

in her throat.

'You look nice. Brown. You once told me you looked good in the summer.' He drank from the glass and his eyes watched her over the rim, moved up and down her body.

Kate did not know what to do. It was all there, beating inside her, as if the feelings had been kept on another level of herself and just by coming here he had forced her down on to that level again. Most of her hoped that the miracle had happened, that Vanessa was tired of him or dead and that he had come back. She would retract all the things she had screamed at him on the night when she told him to go, get out of her life. They would start again . . . But one small part of her said, 'Don't let him see how you feel. You found the strength to send him away once but you'd never do it again.'

'How is the new job?'

'All right.'

'I'm doing a course in London for three weeks. Started last week. I'm staying with a friend. I'm driving up this evening if you want a lift.'

'Perhaps.'

'Is this your new image, this mature, taciturn Kate. One-syllable answers?'

'Perhaps has two syllables,' Kate said and there was a moment's silence before the smile came from both of them. She took the ice from the glass and crunched the cubes in her mouth. 'Where's Vanessa?'

'With her parents this weekend.'

Kate nodded. She watched David get up and fetch another of the faded sunbeds and put it beside hers and lie down, arms under his head, sometimes stroking his gymshoes-clad foot very lightly down her calf. He talked about the past few months, how hard he had been working, how he had been offered a job by the Californian firm which Vanessa had worked for. He talked about his mother's hay fever and the play at the village hall as if there were no gulf, no agony, as if he hadn't inflicted pain quite brutally, had never said, 'Well, I didn't ask you to love me, did I, you silly bitch? Your feelings are your own responsibility. You're too bloody clinging!'

Remembering this, Kate interrupted. 'I won't come to London with you. I've forgotten you now. There's someone else.'

'Well that's all the better. We can be friends, Katy. I often think of those afternoons . . .'

'Well, I don't.'

He sat up. 'Liar.'

Gabriel appeared, trailing her dogs, her face changing into a welcoming smile. 'David, how lovely to see you . . .' And then she remembered that perhaps she should not welcome him but Kate had never explained. He stayed for an hour and told them he would drive Kate to London, pick her up at ten, and then wandered towards his car. The sound of his Volkswagen, more than anything else, destroyed Kate's resolution.

The heat lasted into the evening. David was late as always and hooted outside as always. She kissed her parents and went out with the small hold-all and he leaned forward to open the door. The smell of the car was so familiar and the Rod Stewart tape he was playing, the way he made the gravel scatter under the wheels by accelerating too fast; windows open, Rod Stewart singing *Mr Tambourine Man*, warm air and a lot of stars as if the sky were a black paper with a million pinholes in it. David's hand, searching for hers when he didn't need to change gear. Little talking. Suddenly, 'I've missed you, Katy. I'm sorry I did it all so badly, about Vanessa. I was confused.'

'You and she still . . .?' Kate's heart beat in her throat again.

'I suppose,' he said, non-committally. Sunday night London was bright, crowded, full of traffic. The journey took an hour and at the end Kate directed him. He stopped outside the tall white house.

'Would you like to come up and see it?'

He turned to look at her, one hand gently tugging at a piece of

149

her hair, then his fingers on her throat where he could feel the speed of her pulse. 'I don't know, Kate.'

Now she knew it was her turn to approach. He had risked enough pride already. 'Please. I don't care what happens after-wards.'

She made him coffee in the little kitchen and in the sitting-room they talked. About how possessive Vanessa was, how vulnerable. 'She needs so much . . .' His hand moving on Kate's shoulder, her whole body contorting to try and stay still, his face close to hers, his mouth, sweetly teasing.

She took him to Venn's room, pretending it was hers. She had imagined the reconciliation and the love-making in incredible detail but had forgotten the joy of having his body, the way he gathered her into a tight ball. After the first rush of love she was cautious, drawing back, testing her feelings, trying not to get lost in it all. He sensed her detachment. He touched her expert-ly, knowing where and how much, watching her as she gave in and was lost in it all. The months she had waited dissolved into nothing and the hurt he had inflicted didn't count and all thoughts of forgetting him were pathetic. When they lay to-gether, relaxed after the love-making, tears ran slowly down her cheeks. He looked at his watch and spoke of going. He pulled the sheet over her. 'Don't get cold, Katy.' He was gracious in vic-tory. He was gentle, waiting for her to ask when the next time would be.

'It's better with me than her, is that it?'

'Yes.'

'But you want her?'

He sat down and stroked her hair. 'Perhaps not any more.'

'Shall I see you tomorrow? Why can't you stay tonight?' Her voice was casual, her eyes imploring.

'I am expected somewhere. We could have dinner tomorrow. I'll come here about eight.' He kissed her and went down the stairs and she went to the sitting-room window, heard his car chug away. She thought: He needs the adoration of us both. It's

150

our fault if we get hurt. We are not really considered. For the first time Vanessa was pitied and not hated. But Kate didn't want to be realistic. She wanted to pretend. She made Venn's bed and went upstairs, washed and went quietly into her own bedroom.

Judith was awake. 'Was that him? The one you are so crazy about?'

'Yes.'

'I hope it works out for you . . . My family are going on holiday tomorrow, Kate. Devon. Buckets and spades. They never make arrangements with any reasonable amount of notice. This was all decided last Friday. So I'll be gone for a couple of weeks.' Her accounts book was open on her lap, full of her neat black figures. 'When I get back, shall we have a party? We could ask your fellow and Venn's lot and Clive.'

'Yes, let's,' Kate said but hardly heard, climbing into bed, lying on her stomach, trying to believe the miracle.

She got up very early, had a bath and put on a summer dress she had bought the previous week. It was brightly coloured, the bodice ruched like a child's bathing suit. She said goodbye to Judith, who was packing. The street was already hot. When Clive came into the office at nine-thirty, Kate was singing Rod Stewart.

'What a surprising dress.' He looked at her bare brown legs, her feet in high-heeled sandals, bright pink toe nails. 'Come and sit in my office. You look so pretty and I've got so much work for you today. It's the Wilson contract. Final version. I've been thinking about it all weekend. It must be typed by tonight, I'm afraid.'

She was so happy, bubbling with life, tripping over her words. Her mood overflowed and touched Clive. She opened the windows to let in the summer and a sudden wind scattered Clive's papers and she knelt to gather them up, crawling under his desk, supple as a child. They worked all morning and at one Clive took her to the nearest pub and they sat outside on a low

151

stone wall, eating ham salads and drinking Pimms. He watched her eat all the fruit before she drank the liquid.

'Why so happy, Katy?'

'Oh well, he came back, the man I told you about. The one I was trying to forget.'

'And everything's marvellous?'

'Yes. I'm seeing him tonight.'

I am fond of her, Clive thought. In just a few months she has made me concerned about her. 'I hope he won't hurt you again. These on/off romances have a habit of forming a pattern.'

'I've thought about that. The thing is, it makes me so happy to see him, I shall just have to take the chance.' But her wide confident smile told Clive that she didn't think there was a risk, that she believed he was back for good.

All afternoon Kate typed the long and extremely complicated contract. At five-thirty Clive came through to her office.

'How's it going?'

'I've just about finished but I haven't read through . . .'

'I was going to offer you a lift home. I've got the car here. Can you check through it at home this evening.'

'Yes.'

'But for God's sake don't forget it. I shall want to read it myself and they're coming at ten tomorrow.' The memory of the Mather contract was in both their minds.

'I'm going out tonight. I could drop it through your letter box about eight or eight-thirty.'

'That's a good idea.' They walked to the small square where Bonnington's had five spaces reserved. Each time Kate thought of the evening she shivered with excitement. Clive took her to the door of her flat. 'Have a good evening . . . and don't forget to drop the contract off, will you?'

'Don't worry. And thank you . . .' She ran up all the stairs. She threw the contract on her bed, dancing into the bathroom, turning on taps, acting out a Ginger Rogers dance of joy.

She finished checking through the contract just before seven

152

and got into the bath and got out five minutes later when the telephone rang, snatching up the receiver, the water making dark stains round her feet. 'Hello.'

'Katy? It's me. Look, I'm terribly sorry but something's come up. It's to do with this course. There's a film and a lecture tonight and a dinner tomorrow.' He paused but she couldn't answer. She knew with absolute certainty that he was lying. 'I'm a bit stuck for the rest of the week because of Vanessa. I'll ring you. Okay?'

'Yes,' Kate whispered.

'I must go.' He made a couple of vague kissing noises down the line and it went dead. As it seemed to Kate that she died. Despair rose up in her, bigger and more terrifying than anything she had felt before and she wandered about the room, sobbing, breath coming oddly, and she was afraid. Afraid of being alone. Afraid of tonight and all the hours of the night because she could not bear the disappointment. She imagined him drifting in and out of her life at will. Once she had gathered up enough strength to put him out of her life. Had he brooded all this time? Nothing that came after could cancel out the agony. She thought: I can't go through all that forgetting again. I don't want to be alive if I can feel like this. The phrase, 'out of her misery, out of her misery', beat in her head.

The nearer Michael came to London the more real Caroline seemed. He sat next to his mother who looked out of the plane window in a sad silence, watching the familiar line of the English coast thousands of feet below. They were both rather surprised to find Heathrow enjoying such a beautiful afternoon. England had been so grey when they left. They shared a taxi to Marie-Claire's little house in Fulham where Suzanne was to spend a few days and Michael went on to Cambridge Street. The house was empty, the basement deserted. It was after six. Michael poured himself a glass of milk and went out to try and start his car. It took him ten frustrating minutes but he got it

153

going and drove to Meadwell Street. He was very tired which was unusual for Michael, and he had no plan for the evening. He had no idea how Caroline would receive him. On the seat beside. him was a large bottle of the scent she liked and one of Henri's beautiful cotton scarves which were almost big enough to wear as shawls. He found he had lost his mental image of Caroline's face. He parked outside his own premises, went in and looked round, felt regret that he would soon part with it and yet didn't want to become involved again in all its problems. He saw a prototype body of the Sundial and spent half an hour going through the drawings. And then he walked down towards the Kings Road and the door of her shop said 'Open' and Clive's car was parked outside. Michael went through the showroom and began to run up the stairs, wanting to reach the first floor before Caroline had to come down.

Clive was sprawled on the sofa, reading the *Evening News* and Caroline had been trying to get the ice cubes out of the ice-tray when she heard the bell. She was crossing the room when Michael's head appeared round the bend in the stairs. He came up the last six stairs in two huge strides and paused at the top. Both Clive and Caroline saw him at the same moment.

Michael stood still. No one spoke. He crossed the room towards Caroline. Always shy about kissing her in public he did not kiss her now, in this atmosphere, with Clive watching. Michael put the presents in her hands. 'I bought you these.'

Clive stood up. 'Why the hell didn't you say you were coming? I could have met you.'

'I wasn't sure until this morning that we were on the flight. It's so booked up in the summer.' He watched Caroline unwrapping the bottle of scent. She thanked him without looking up and began on the scarf, opening the paper, touching it, putting it carefully back into the paper again.

'It's very pretty. Thank you.'

'It's one of Henri's. He sent you his love.'

'Would you like a drink, Michael?' she asked, dully, automatically.

'Have you any beer?'

'Yes.' She turned back to the fridge and Michael sat in one of the armchairs, the atmosphere paralysed them all. It was Michael who broke the silence, quite uncharacteristically trying to gloss over the tension.

'I think I have organized things well enough for the moment. I didn't realize how much Gautier depended on my grandmother just being there. Although he has run things for years, he is lost without some kind of presence to sanction the decisions . . . and there isn't nearly as much money as I expected but enough to start modernization.' He took the beer that Caroline held out. 'How is Mosaic, Clive?'

'Absolutely fine.'

'And you still want to take over? These last few weeks haven't changed your mind?'

'Not at all.'

Michael nodded. 'I'm glad. I still feel so possessive about it I'd like to think it will go to a good home. I've been trying to arrive at a valuation. I shall want to put Cambridge Street on the market almost at once . . . Perhaps I could come to the office tomorrow and we could go through my preliminary ideas.'

'Yes, but it will have to be in the afternoon. I've got a meeting at ten, signing a big contract, and it's bound to grow into lunch.'

Michael nodded. He turned to look at Caroline who stood by the table, quite still, a cigarette in her hand. 'I'm sorry I didn't write! Yet again!' He tried to make a joke of it but her face was stiff and white. 'I'd love your help with the Château, Caroline. My mother hates it. I can't understand why as she grew up there but she says she hates the silence and the high ceilings. I love it. I feel that I belong. I'm going back in September permanently.'

Caroline drew smoke so deeply into her lungs that she felt quite faint. Or was it the unbearable tensions while she waited for someone to say something about the question they all had in

155

their minds, about Clive and herself. She took little quick glances at Michael and saw that his face was thinner, and browner and slightly older. She still had not allowed herself to name what she felt.

'Caroline and I were going out to dinner somewhere,' she heard Clive say. 'Why don't you come with us?' She stared at Clive, incredulously 'I think I should say it is "us",' Clive went on, his voice and his face, his whole manner, saying that he was determined to be adult and diplomatic. 'While you were away, Michael, things have altered.' He was such a wide figure against the window.

Michael said nothing. He drank the beer too quickly and some of it fizzed in his nose and he coughed as he stood up, reacting as he always did, removing himself from any awkwardness. 'In that case, I don't think I'll join you.' He looked at Caroline. Had he thought he had forgotten her face? How ridiculous. He looked into it, loving it. He put down his glass. He seldom analysed his feelings but now he recognized deep regret, a longing to touch her. But above all else he felt the desire to escape from such raw tension and he turned towards the stairs.

'Don't go.' The words seemed to be torn from her throat as she came across the room to him in an awkward rush and stood in front of him, put out her hands, taking hold of his arms, closing her eyes as she moved closer, shaking with the tears. 'Don't go yet. How can you just walk in and then go? Please . . .'

He bent his head, face touching her hair, and then pulled her so tightly against him that breathing was difficult, holding her for a long time and realizing how much he had missed her.

Such a combination of fury and pain possessed Clive that it seemed to close his throat and narrow his vision and he had to go, down the stairs and out into the street, trying to move faster than the explosive fury but it burst from him. 'Not again, Caroline . . . Not again!' His huge voice roared out and he slammed his clenched fists against the roof of his car and two women who were passing scuttled by like frightened rabbits. He laughed once but still he felt it would explode him, this sudden, terrible disappointment. He got into his car and drove very slowly, admiring his own control. He stopped at the first familiar pub and it was so early there were few people in the bar. The whisky did nothing: it could have been water. He knew he had lost Caroline and he was terribly hurt for himself and for her. He knew he would not love like this again in his lifetime. He knew he could have made her happy. The terrible waste of it all was the worst thing and the fear he felt for her. He knew Michael. He knew Caroline. He could have written down in detail the disaster of their lives together.

At some stage he realized he should eat and he remembered the contract and drove home pulling round himself the other parts of his life. It was not there. There was no message. Even through the restless despair he was surprised. Kate was absolutely reliable. He remembered how she had been that day, the infectious happiness. He remembered the lunch. And through all his own pain he was aware of concern and he looked in his diary for her number but it wasn't there. He went back out to his car and he drove to Queensgate Gardens. He parked and looked up, saw lights on the top two floors.

Clive went up the few steps and stabbed impatiently at Kate's bell. There was a London summer evening smell. He rang again. And again. The last time he kept his finger on the bell, the anger obvious in its ring, and at last there was Kate's voice.

'It's Clive. I've come for that bloody contract. Let me in!'

'I'm ill. Go away. I'll . . .'

'Like hell. Let me in. Now!' The buzzer sounded and the door swung inwards under his pressure and he went up the stairs very fast. He was out of breath at the top but he felt better as if some of the adrenalin had been used. The last door was open. He ran up the last flight of stairs.

She was wearing a cotton dressing-gown. She looked terrible. She was shaking, her thin arms wrapped round her body, her hands clenched into fists.

157

'Oh Katy . . .' he said, as if she was bleeding from some bad wound, helpless for the moment as he looked at her. 'What is it?'

He took her arm, steered her into the kitchen and sat her down. He lit the gas, put on the kettle, pushed her hair back from her forehead as if she were a child. He prised open her hands and all the white pills came out and he put them on a plate.

'Have you taken any?'

She shook her head. 'I used to like being alone. I used to think it would be such a luxury to be alone.'

He had never seen anyone shake so violently. He went to the next room and took a blanket from the bed. He found the empty bottle in there and came back, wrapping the blanket round her, patiently posting the pills back. They almost filled the bottle.

'It's not coming right,' she was saying. 'It never has with me. There's something wrong with me. I can't get close to people. I have no real friends. Just on the surface. Like my father. Wounding people, and myself. I was born like it. It's a deformity like any other but it takes so long to show.'

'This fellow's fucked you about, has he?'

'It's so quiet here,' she said, angrily.

The kettle screamed and Clive made tea, stirring in sugar. The little room was hot. He opened the window. 'Would you have taken those pills?'

'I don't know.'

He took her arm, leading her through to the sitting-room, sitting with her on the hideous sofa. He put an arm along her shoulders. She nestled against his body and he put the mug into her hands and she drank some of it. It helped him to be needed here. Clive leaned his head back, his voice tired. 'I think we might help each other out for a bit, Kate.'

'Has something happened to you, too?' She sounded more normal.

158

'Yes. Like you've I've been discarded. It's happened to me before but not with anyone I really cared for. Not like this.' It pleased him to describe the agony so carelessly.

Kate studied the side of his face. 'How extraordinary that Caroline doesn't love you.' She sipped the tea. 'She doesn't?'

'No, apparently not.' He brooded for a while, his hand moving gently and comfortingly against Kate's shoulder. 'How extraordinary that he doesn't love you, little Kate.'

After a while, Kate said, 'Why did you come? How did you know?'

'I came for the contract,' he said dryly.

'Oh God. I have read it.' She sat up. 'I'll get it . . .' She gave him the mug and stood up, lost in Venn's cotton dressing-gown, bare feet pathetic against the carpet, face a small pale triangle. 'I'm very muddled but I wouldn't really have taken those pills. I was just acting out my misery for myself. I couldn't bear the way I felt. I wanted to hurt myself physically . . . everything seemed far away but the misery which was huge. Is still huge. It isn't meant to be like this!'

'No,' Clive said, 'I don't think it is.' He stood up, towering over her and she made an instinctive move, putting her body against his warmth and his strength. After a few moments he gently pushed her back, very gently. 'Are you alone here all night?'

'Yes.'

'Get dressed then. You can come back with me . . . where's the contract? I'll read it while you're dressing.'

She turned and went to the table, picked it up. He began to read through Kate's immaculate typing, going to the bottom of the stairs and calling up, 'This is beautifully done, Kate. You make an art of it!'

She came down the stairs, wearing jeans and a striped shirt. 'They used to say that at the college. That I had a gift for spacing and arranging. I thought that was typical of my luck . . . other girls got piano playing or fascinating sex appeal or beauti-

159

ful tits and I got typing!' She laughed very shakily as Clive smiled and took the small hold-all she carried.

'That's your stuff for tomorrow?'

She nodded.

'Got your key?'

'Yes.'

They went down the endless stairs into the street and Clive's car. He turned on the radio. 'I'm hungry. Can you eat something?'

'I suppose so.'

They ate in the small bistro in Hugh Street and walked back to the house. Clive unlocked the front door and Kate made some coffee in the yellow kitchen. She felt quite unreal. She carried the tray down to Clive's sitting-room and he was pouring himself a brandy, his big face serious and tired. Kate's hands were not steady.

The coffee was warm in her throat and her stomach as the food had been. 'The food helped. I realized I hadn't eaten anything all day. I forget to eat when I'm excited.' She sat on the floor, leaning against the sofa. 'That was what caused it. I don't want you to think this means I've had some sort of nervous collapse. I refuse to suffer from anything so pathetic. I'm just so bloody miserable.' Her eyes filled with tears. 'Can I have one of those cigars?' She wiped away the tears angrily.

'If you like.' He gave her one and a glass of brandy. The smoke hurt her throat but it was at least a sensation, telling her she was alive and real, as when people pinch themselves after a very bad dream. Clive seemed to be lost in his own thoughts. Upstairs, several of Michael's clocks chimed eleven in succession.

Then Clive looked at Kate, sitting in a little heap, still very white. It was extremely hot, as if there was going to be a thunderstorm. He went to the garden doors and opened them but it was even hotter outside. Thunder rumbled, ready to burst. God, what an evening! he thought.

'Why doesn't it work out like you want?' Kate was standing beside him. 'He used to say, "Vanessa is so vulnerable. So shy." She told him that. She put all the words in his head. Really vulnerable people are inarticulate. They can't explain themselves because they don't understand themselves. If you can tell someone how you feel you aren't shy. Scared people, like me, just go away from places and parties and people. That's what I wanted tonight. I just wanted to go away.'

Clive made a big, weary effort to do the right thing, taking her upstairs to the spare attic bedroom, finding sheets, checking the bathroom cupboard in case there were pills. It was cold up there.

'Come down if you want me . . .'

She stood in the centre of the room. 'You're not really going to leave me here, are you?'

'For Christ's sake, Kate. I don't know what to do with you.'

'I want to be with you. Please,' she said stubbornly.

They trooped solemnly down again. Now he was tired and trying to hide the irritation. He turned off lights, washed, undressed, got into bed, trying not to think of Caroline, listening to Kate in the bathroom. She came into the bedroom in a striped cotton night shirt and he lifted the bedclothes for her and she hesitated and then got in, at first lying straight and stiff and then turning to him, holding him tightly, just needing another human being, a warm body. He put his arm under her shoulders and pulled her close. 'What a bloody strange evening . . . don't worry, Kate.' He put an affectionate kiss on her forehead. Thunder rumbled outside, complaining but not bursting into a storm.

They both slept surprisingly quickly but later, when the storm broke properly and lightning lit the room and the thunder woke them both, Kate put her hand on his face, finding his mouth, and he kissed her thin fingers. And Clive half lifted her small body, pulling her up to be level with him, looking at her face in the sudden brightness of lightning. They both wanted to make love, to use up some of the destructive sadness. But he

161

hesitated, conscious of her earlier mood, of her vulnerability. So Kate put her mouth on his, tucked her hands inside his pyjama jacket, so that he should understand what she wanted.

CHAPTER TEN

In the morning Kate woke before Clive but she lay very still, not wanting the day yet. There were so many conflicting things in her head. David and last night and the terrifying despair, Clive and the fact that he lay beside her, sprawled over the bed, leaving her a small edge. She remembered the love-making and shivered as she felt the excitement again. He had been so unlike David . . . She lay still, pretending sleep, and felt Clive stir. He got carefully out of bed, found his pyjama trousers and put them on. He went up to the kitchen, his head aching agonizingly. The whisky had been real after all. As was the pain when he thought of Caroline. Even thinking her name made him want to double over with the pain. And then tenderness when he thought of Kate. He stood with his bare feet on the tiled kitchen floor, wondering for a moment at the way they all seemed to affect each other's lives, like a series of carriages, shunted into one another, wondering if Michael's way was not better—to be separate and enough for himself.

Michael's clocks struck eight. Clive cursed them. He dissolved Disprin in orange juice and swallowed the mixture, shuddering. He heard the front door open. Michael came past, stopping, looking in, and for the first time in his life Clive felt genuine hatred.

'Why didn't you stay in France, you bastard?'

Michael rubbed his face wearily. 'Look, Clive, I know how you feel.'

'You don't know anything of how anyone feels. She's been married to one cold sod already. Why don't you leave her alone?' They had known each other for so long and neither of them had bothered to analyse the friendship for years. There had been so many good times, some marvellous holidays, good parties and a lot of laughter.

163

Michael retreated up the stairs, loathing any kind of scene. Clive would have had far more satisfaction in a violent argument. He made himself a mug of black coffee, a mug of white for Kate, and went downstairs to wake her. Her eyes were open. She lay with the sheet up under her chin and all the impatience in him vanished and was replaced by tenderness. Clive was a man who loved to be needed.

'Time to get up, Kate. We're leaving in ten minutes. We'll have to drive. The tube would kill me.' He sat on the bed, rubbing his fingers gently against her cheek. 'Funny the way things turn out, little Katherine!' He made all awkwardness unnecessary.

She got up, washing quickly, pulling on clothes, dodging in and out past Clive while he shaved, cleaning her teeth, brushing her hair, still unable to believe the previous night. At the door, as he paused to check that he had the contract and then glanced at her anxious face, Clive bent his head and kissed her. 'Will you be all right today?'

His kindness brought tears to her eyes. She nodded.

They sat in silence in his car listening to the Today programme on the radio and the morning traffic was heavy. The sun shone insolently like a child with its tongue stuck out. In the office sunlight streamed, unasked for and unappreciated, in the windows, lighting up Kate's Busy Lizzie.

The morning involved them. Clive spoke to Kate on the intercom. 'Could you ring Michael Redford at Mosaic and ask if he is still coming to see me this afternoon as arranged and if so what time? Make it after three. And book a table for five at *Midas*.' He read the Wilson contract slowly, making sure of every line. Kate brought him coffee. 'Mr Redford is coming at three-thirty.'

The Wilson contingent came, four men arriving, two and two. Kate showed them into Clive's office just before eleven. She had a lot of work to do and she was thankful. At one, giving her a smile as he left, Clive took the men to lunch and Kate went out to buy a sandwich but her stomach seemed to have closed up. The surprise she felt about herself and Clive was almost bigger than the sadness over David. She fed her sandwich to the pigeons and walked until two.

Clive returned only minutes before Michael Redford came in and Kate showed him into Clive's office.

Clive indicated an armchair. His face was blank. 'Well, have we looked after things all right while you've been away?' Last night was so real in his mind it was hard to sit and face Michael.

'Of course.' Michael wanted to talk about Caroline. He sat for a moment in miserable silence. 'I genuinely love her, Clive. I didn't mean to. I never thought of it . . . Christ, you know me. Women haven't meant a lot in my life. The first time, that weekend, when we met outside Cambridge Street, I should have said it then. How serious it was right from the beginning. I never believed in this kind of emotion before. I thought it absurd when written down in books or shown in films. But it was so strong. It still is. I'm not excusing myself. I made love to her knowing exactly how you felt . . .'

'Look,' Clive said, icily. 'Not now. I'm too angry. Too bloody angry. I don't want to start, do you understand. Just talk about Mosaic, about Cambridge Street. Let's discuss what we have to and not mention her.'

Michael shrugged, his long face tense and unhappy. 'Okay. I've told Stephen to come and measure up Cambridge Street and to put it on the market but I won't give vacant possession till you've found somewhere else.'

Clive shrugged. 'I could always move into my flat. I've already warned the girls they may have to go. Stephen reckons I should get about twenty-five thousand for it. I've been lucky at the way its value has increased. The area I suppose.'

Michael nodded, his face tense.

'While you were in France,' Clive went on, 'I've been through the Mosaic books. I've tried to estimate the assets and calculate future earnings. Of course a lot depends on Jenny staying. But reckoning that one would want at least as good a return from

165

Mosaic as if the capital were invested elsewhere, it still looks promising.'

'Yes. That's what I feel.'

'You realize the position over paying the dollar premium on any money you want to take to France.'

'Yes. I've been into that. You already own one fifth of Mosaic. I will have to pay the dollar premium initially on any sum over five thousand pounds. Therefore I thought, if we could agree a sum, you could pay me in two halves. The second amount treated as a loan to be repaid with interest on a given date.'

They discussed Mosaic until five, working out a rough plan of how to proceed. When it was done Michael stood up, running his hand wearily over his eyes. Clive stayed where he was, a forbidding figure in his large leather chair. Michael moved towards the door and Clive said, 'I'll get in touch as soon as I've something definite to report,' and Michael nodded, letting himself out in silence.

For a few moments Clive stayed in his chair and then he got up and put his head round Kate's door. 'Come on. We're leaving early, I need a drink.'

Kate piled the papers on her desk into a neat heap. 'Do you really want me to come, Clive? I'm quite all right now. I don't want you to feel you're obliged to . . .' She paused, lost for words.

'Maybe I want to,' he said gently. 'Now, come on.' She covered her typewriter, smiled and followed him. They went to a bar where Clive often stopped after work where they found several of his friends and stayed until 6.30. Clive's life, she thought, was made up of such soothing routines, of people who greeted him when he came in, barmen who knew him. He knew his way everywhere. She could not imagine him getting lost. They drove back to Cambridge Street and he talked all the way in his deep voice.

'This is my immediate plan, Kate. I shall work like hell to get my hands on Mosaic. Bonnington's frustrates me more and

166

more. I need a change. I shall find somewhere new to live, push this rocking clock despite that Jacobs bitch, win the Hill case and keep an eye on you for a bit, if you want me to.' And somehow, he thought, I will lose the melancholy which loving Caroline and liking Michael has inflicted on me.

Kate sat in silence.

Clive looked at her. 'I still can't quite understand the things that happened last night but I'd like at least part of it to happen again.'

She smiled at him, her face lighting. She dropped her hunched shoulders and was amazed at the calmness she felt. There was a total relaxation between them and although she reached again and again for shyness, she found none. 'What can I do in return?' she asked.

'Just make me laugh, Kate.'

Throughout July and August, Caroline and Michael lived at her shop and the future was not mentioned. She accepted that his presence was essential for her happiness at the moment and tried to live from day to day. When Michael hurt her it was never deliberate. He was always late for things she arranged, forgot promises, would hardly ever telephone her; when he was absorbed in Mosaic there was no other world and he was working extremely hard to get the Sundial in a saleable condition. If he saw that she was hurt he was bewildered. 'You know I love you—'

He made her feel shallow for minding that she was left alone when he had so much to do. He drove to Wandsworth where the Sundial bodies were being made, scoured the country for suitable hands; he rang France and had incessant letters from the French lawyers who were handling Valerie's will; he arranged the shipping of some paintings Marie-Claire and Suzanne wanted and booked advertising for the Sundial and forgot a dinner party Caroline was giving. He infuriated her because his attitude was that the things which concerned him were so much

167

more important than the trivial ingredients of her life! And yet he enchanted her, in bed and out, and she told herself that the feeling she had for him was so strong that it must be worth changing her life for.

Michael met Clive again to discuss Mosaic and Cambridge Street was advertised and Michael refused to come to Rachel's party because he was too busy. Nothing altered Caroline's feelings. Above all else, something quite unexpected, a secret and extraordinary hope, was beginning in her.

At the start of September they suddenly began to discuss the future constantly. Michael intended to go to Jouvard for the harvest. 'If only I could have one more year,' Caroline said, again and again. 'Survive through a winter!' These conversations were never resolved.

Rachel came to lunch in early September, bringing pâté and French bread and Brie. They ate in the garden and for once Caroline closed the shop for an hour. 'I need some peace!' She opened a bottle of Château de Jouvard.

'Is it all red?' Rachel asked.

'Yes. In that area. And quite good, Michael says. The local wines which are any good are marked VDQS like this. Vin Délimité de Qualité Supérieure.'

'How is your French?'

'Not good. I learned at school. Michael has bought me a Linguaphone course but I haven't played the tapes yet.'

'Ian and I thought we might take a holiday in France next summer,' Rachel said, crossing freckled legs. 'Will you be there?' Caroline didn't answer. 'So Clive may get another chance?'

'You're so bloody cynical. How do you think I could swing from one to another, backwards and forwards? I couldn't live like that.' She pushed the food away and lit a cigarette, looking out at her beautifully tended garden.

'So you will go to France?'

'I just don't know, Rachel.'

'You must be happy. You look lovely . . .' Rachel watched her carefully.

'I am. I adore him. I have grown fatter with contentment but I suppose I was almost too thin for a while.' She paused, half-wanting to mention the hope but terribly afraid that, if she gave it words, it would evaporate. Harry's resigned face came into her mind. 'Give up, Caroline.'

'Could you be pregnant?' Rachel said.

Caroline closed her eyes. 'I've never had regular periods. All those years and all those tests and all the hope. Just relax and forget about it and you might, perhaps, conceive, they said. It was impossible advice to take. Years and years. At first I used to rush off for a test the moment I missed a period. After four years I gave up going for tests. I went to the clinics. I had all sorts of minor operations. Once I missed three periods and I still wouldn't hope although, underneath, I was getting more and more excited. It was nothing. Loving Michael as I do, so ridiculously, with no logical reasons and the future such an undecided mess, I have been wholly preoccupied. And I've had the shop to absorb me and I can honestly say, for the first time in my life, I really haven't thought much about having a baby for some months.' She sat forward, drinking from the glass of wine. 'I've never used any form of contraception since I married Harry and I have always told any man I slept with that I can't have children. Quite definitely. I never wanted them to use anything because, if the miracle happened, I would love the child of anyone I cared about enough to sleep with.'

'Even the once-off, post-cocktail party get-together?'

'I only did that once. Before I was divorced. I thought at the time, life being what it is, I might have got pregnant.'

'Have you got a doctor in London?' Rachel asked.

Caroline laughed. 'Dozens of them. Specialists, all the people at the infertility clinic and one special friend.'

'Go and see him.'

'I can't. I've been through it so many times.'

169

'Just suppose,' Rachel said shrewdly, 'that at last, because you are so occupied with other things, you have conceived? You could lose it through carelessness.'

Caroline touched her lower lip thoughtfully.

'And you smoke far too much,' Rachel went on self-righteously, having given up herself six weeks before. 'Ring him now. Make an appointment. I'll come with you.'

'No. I must go on my own. I get peculiar when they tell me it's negative.'

'I suppose,' Rachel said, cutting off small pieces of Brie and putting them in her mouth, 'it would be Michael's child?'

'Of course,' Caroline snapped. 'If there is a child it was conceived since he came back. But there isn't. I'm not going to any more doctors to be pitied and soothed. Let's forget it.'

But she did ring, as Rachel had known she would, and she went to see him three days later on a radiant Thursday with a specimen and her hopes absolutely under control, repeating over and over in a monotone that it was a waste of time. For ten minutes she talked. He had become a friend before but seeing him again brought back all the years of empty hopes and all the heartbreak.

He examined her. He talked of a woman they both knew who had, at last, conceived. 'I gave up hope two years ago,' Caroline said.

'I'll telephone you later. Where will you be?'

She gave him the number, dressed and left. It was so hot and she had automatically dressed up to come to Harley Street. The tights felt strange and her feet disliked the smart shoes after months of sandals. She walked by a restaurant which had tables on the pavement under shady umbrellas and she sat down and ordered a glass of wine and a salad and then another glass of wine until the firm hold she had on her imagination was finally shaken loose. She sat and imagined that there was a child inside her, a curled-up embryo, vulnerable as Michael's grapes, tiny buds for arms and legs . . . She lit a cigarette, felt the sun on her

170

arms and her legs and willed her body to absorb the sun and its strength, whatever happened.

She got back to the shop at three and it was surprisingly cool. Liz was sitting cross-legged in the open doorway to the garden, drinking iced coffee. 'You've been a long time, Mrs Boyd. Brian came looking for you about the pine settle and a doctor rang and wants you to ring back.'

Caroline wandered through the showroom slowly, wanting someone to come in, wanting any reason to delay phoning the doctor. She could not make herself do it. She approached the telephone several times and then moved away because, whatever she had said, she was hoping now, desperately. She made herself sit down. She lit a cigarette. She knew the number by heart.

Liz was staring at her and trying not to, her round eyes moving back and forth. She was an optimistic girl, resilient and not usually curious about other people's lives.

Finally Caroline dialled. She held the receiver to her ear with both hands and waited. 'It's Mrs Boyd.' Waited again. It seemed an eternity but it was only a few moments until she heard his voice. The voice she had come to hate because, so often in the past, it had gently relaid bad news.

'Caroline? My dear, the test is positive.'

At first the room shook round her. She began to sob, very quietly, her shoulders shaking, head bending, the receiver slipping from her hands. She snatched it back. 'Say it again.'

'It's positive.'

Now tears poured down her cheeks.

'I'm so happy for you. Are you all right?'

'Yes. I'm all right.'

'Telephone me tomorrow and we'll make arrangements. We must hang on to it and it's early days yet.'

'I'll ring tomorrow.'

She put the telephone down and doubled up in the chair, her whole body shaking. Liz was hovering anxiously beside her.

171

'What is it? What's happened?'

'I'm all right.' She straightened, arched her head back, took some deep breaths. 'It's been so long. So long.' She let the tears stream down her face. Her body was limp like a dropped puppet. Liz stared and moved from one foot to another.

'Would you like some tea?'

'Yes, yes, I would.' Caroline wiped at the tears, looking up into the girl's face. 'Oh, don't look like that, Lizzy. I'm having a baby, that's all.' She stood up then, walked up and down the room, arms crossed round herself, the sobs still coming occasionally.

'Oh God,' Liz said.

'But I don't mind. I don't mind!' It was such an absurd understatement that she began to laugh. 'I've wanted a baby for eight years.' She went upstairs to wash her face. She took off the tights, the skirt and blouse and put on a loose cotton dress. Liz came up, concentrating on the tray of tea, and Caroline sat on her bed and drank it and ·didn't have a cigarette. Then she walked slowly up the road to Mosaic, thinking that London had never looked so pretty. She went into the front office and through to the back where Michael was speaking on the telephone, standing—as he always did when he had to use it— stiffly, holding the receiver with distaste.

Caroline went up to him and put her arms around him from the back, holding him very tightly, her face against him. He was amazed, turning, faltering in what he said, ending the conversation abruptly. The secretaries pretended not to notice.

'Caroline,' he said, 'what is it?'

The tears began to come again but she was laughing underneath them, taking his arm, her fingers gripping it rhythmically, shaking it, and he opened the side door and drew her out into the street and they stood on the pavement under a great ragged plane tree. Caroline leant against a parked car, shaking her head, her eyes immense.

'What is it?' he asked again.

172

'I'm going to have a baby.'

It took him a few moments to answer. 'But I thought you couldn't . . .'

'So did I. It's a miracle . . . well, not literally.' They both laughed, moving together. 'It's very early yet. Eight or nine weeks. They're not sure and I'm not but if I'm careful . . .'

He put his arms round her, suddenly realizing the full implications. 'Now you'll come with me to France, won't you? We'll get married. You'll come to Jouvard?'

'Yes. I'll come. But not until it's born, Michael. I must stay with the doctors I know. Don't ask me to risk it. Don't ask me that.'

'I won't . . .' His voice was thoughtful, very tender. 'Then I shall have to go backwards and forwards to France.'

'And you won't ring or write but I won't care.'

'I will. I'll make myself. Every night. Are you sure you want to come? Quite sure?'

'Yes.'

As he predicted, Clive had been extremely busy through the past two months, both by his own design and through circumstances at Bonnington's. The Hill case went to court at the beginning of September and that was the end of Clive's intense involvement in the difficult case. Miss Henderson died and, as Clive was chief executor, a new line of work opened up. There were two divorces and a mass of small cases.

Despite all this work, he missed both Michael and Caroline and he was disturbed by his feelings towards Michael, a jealousy which verged on hatred. When he thought of Caroline he felt only regret and sadness. He could never blame her for anything. He drafted out a document to show Michael concerning the hand-over of Mosaic but still no sum had been agreed. Clive stuck firmly to the plan he had laid down for himself. He saw himself controlling Mosaic, building it up, saw himself leaving Bonnington's for a brilliant commercial career. He spoke on the telephone to Michael quite frequently, to try and resolve Mosaic, but he had great difficulty keeping the coldness out of his voice.

Kate stayed in his life, surprising them both when they thought about it. She relied on him very much at the moment, staying the night with him if they had been out together, working with him every day. And although he couldn't understand why, when she was with Clive, she brought him peace. Clive loved her humour. She tried to live day by day, enjoying the way she felt with Clive, enjoying his concern and his kindness and proud of the way he wanted her in bed.

As she came to know Clive really well, Kate saw that his outward image of being able to handle anything was partly just an image but she was irresistibly drawn to his confidence. He seemed afraid of nothing. She thought he would be able to ignore her destructive qualities. She realized that it was very important to Clive how she looked and she began to buy even more strikingly modern clothes, using her extreme thinness to its best advantage. Clive teased her but he liked the attention her clothes attracted. He said it was the first time in his life he'd been out with a flat-chested girl. He treated Kate, as he treated all his women, with a consideration which she loved after David's rather childish cruelty, but there was also an intimacy between herself and Clive, left over from the night they first came together, which was always underneath.

Kate watched him change through those months of late summer, now that Caroline no longer held the centre position in his life. He was harder to outside people. There was a ruthlessness in his manner, his voice and in his mouth she had not seen before. He was impatient. He talked frequently to Kate about a great many things and she recognized it was because he needed company and because Michael had always been there in the past to listen. Now Kate was required to fill both roles. She alternated between moments of great confidence, talking back on any subject, and sudden retreats. She laughed at the way he

174

always listened to pop music, needing a background noise, knowing the words of the songs in the top ten and singing with them. She laughed at his laziness and admired his ability to overcome it.

Clive's friends teased him about Kate. 'What a bloody unlikely combination you are! You and that small, awkward funny, sharp-witted girl!'

In early September, Clive was sent the particulars of a flat in Bramsden Gardens, about five minutes' walk from where Kate lived. At lunch time he took Kate to see it. It was on the first floor and Kate bounced up the stairs.

'I wish I could understand what you want. Everything we look at is so different from the last thing.'

'I want to live in a convenient area in a flat which is cheap to run, not too noisy and, above all, I want to get it settled. I loathe all this trailing about. It's a bloody waste of time.'

'I never know what to say when we're shown round,' Kate said.

'Just admire the windows and cupboards.' Clive rang the bell.

They were shown round by a very pregnant girl who assumed they were married. She walked with a majestic roll, one hand supporting the small of her back. 'We're moving in two weeks. To Blackheath.'

'Lovely windows,' Kate said.

'Lovely cupboards,' Clive murmured and Kate began to giggle.

'The baby's due in three weeks.'

It had two large rooms, a small kitchen, a long narrow bathroom and a separate lavatory. It was attractively if rather amateurishly decorated and as the lease was short the premium was low. A cat twined itself round Clive's legs. The kitchen window sill was covered with half-dead pot plants and old brillo pads in saucers.

'I like it very much.' He gave the girl what Kate had come to

175

think of as his medium charming smile. 'Well?' he said to Kate in the car.

'Have you got any furniture?'

'You always answer one question with another. An irritating female habit. I have enough furniture, I think. My mother will probably produce a few bits and pieces. Did you like it?'

'It's all right. For a flat. But a flat is a flat. It's just temporary, not a real home. One day you'll need a house with a hall and a front door and rooms off each side and upstairs to bed. Why such a rush to find a place?'

'Because Michael has accepted an offer for Cambridge Street and I am just about to accept an offer for my flat!'

Clive sat up for a long time that evening, trying to decide on a figure to offer for Mosaic and eventually arrived at a sum of forty thousand pounds, twenty thousand now and the balance at a date to be decided on. The second amount of money did not concern him. He was confident that, once he had his hands on Mosaic, he would find it comparatively easy either to put that money aside out of profits or else to borrow it. What concerned him was raising enough money now to pay Michael and to secure the flat. He sat up late into the night, calculating, and decided he would just have enough. In an emergency he would go to John Hampton who seemed able to lay his hands on varying amounts of cash if not too many questions were asked and you were prepared to pay the enormous interest required. Or, more riskily, he could quietly 'borrow' some from the clients' account at Bonnington's as he had once, or twice before!

When Michael rang Clive the following morning Clive said, 'I was hoping you'd ring. I've found a flat and I should be able to move out of Cambridge Street in about four weeks. I've also made out a draft agreement about Mosaic if the money involved is acceptable to you. When do you actually go to France?'

'Something extraordinary has happened,' Michael said. 'But it has simplified everything in a way. Caroline is pregnant.'

176

The words made Clive feel very cold. They were final, destroying any last hope he might have permitted to nestle in a corner of his brain. If Michael had given Caroline a child, she would follow him to the ends of the earth and back.

'We're getting married next week. The fifteenth. She only found out yesterday . . . Caroline and I would be very pleased if you would come, Clive.'

Clive was silent.

'It's at Caxton Hall. At twelve. Just my mother and Marie-Claire and Tim and the Finches. God knows why Caroline wants them but she does. I've booked that private room upstairs at the White Tower afterwards for lunch. Then we'll fly to Jouvard for the harvest but we'll come back in October to settle the transfer of Mosaic and to launch the Sundial and sell Caroline's shop. She was going to stay here and sell it and come on when the baby was born but I've managed to change her mind.' Michael had never sounded so fluent and definite on the telephone before.

'She's having the baby in France?'

'Yes. I've convinced her that not all French doctors wear beads and feathers and have bare feet. Luckily this London gynaecologist she thinks is God has a colleague in Arles who will take her on.'

'And the shop, while you're in France?'

'It will close for two weeks and then Liz, the girl who works there, will re-open it. Caroline feels she must sell it as a going concern and I suppose she's right.' He sounded quite disinterested. 'At first she thought of getting someone in to run it but I've persuaded her that it's better to break all ties and start off realistically. If the shop hasn't sold by the time we finally go in October, I hoped we could give you power of attorney. Could you handle the sale and invest the money for her temporarily?'

'Of course.' Clive thought again that he had never heard Michael so businesslike. As if he were trying to round

177

everything off, settle old scores, heal the wounds. Oh, my poor Caroline, Clive thought. He will take your shop and all your hopes. Will a baby be enough?

'Will you come on the fifteenth?'

'Yes, I'll come. And later on this afternoon I'll come to Mosaic and we'll talk money.'

He got to Mosaic just before six and found Jenny enthusiastically describing the success of the acrylic salt and pepper and herb grinders. She waved black and white photographs and talked orders. 'This is the kind of product we need. No outlay. Easy to transport. Immediately attractive. Suited to all these new cookshops which are opening . . .'

Michael was leaning on his drawing board, depressed by the costs of the first fifty Sundials, idly sketching the shape of an aeroplane.

'The ultimate design challenge,' he said. 'Functional and beautiful, designed within strict natural limits . . .'

'This love affair with the shape of things has got to stop,' Jenny said crisply. 'Beauty is not what sells; it's the shape of bank notes I'm interested in. These cruets . . .'

'Are totally unnecessary for day to day life,' Michael interrupted.

'So are most of our successful ranges.'

'I know, I know!'

Bill Carter came forward. 'I've got some new costs out, Clive. I'm afraid Michael doesn't really like our rocking clocks either.' He took off his glasses and smiled, hesitatingly.

Michael shrugged. 'I could be wrong.'

Clive settled down to wait until the office cleared, whistling a Supremes record quietly to himself. Jenny was the last to go, calling good night, her brisk footsteps echoing through the outer office. Clive opened his briefcase and took out the agreement. He put on his glasses. Alone with Michael, the atmosphere between them was cold.

'Twenty thousand pounds when we sign, probably October.

178

Twenty thousand, plus interest of course, to be paid four years after your emigration, thereby avoiding any dollar premium. If France should relax her controls we could settle earlier. Are you satisfied with that?'

Michael read through. 'Yes. It's fair.'

'I could have the money by October.'

Michael opened a deep desk drawer and took out a bottle of whisky. 'Then let's drink to the hand-over . . . and I'll wait for the money if necessary, Clive. Don't take any risks!'

'Mind your own damn business,' Clive snapped.

'It'll be your damn business soon.' Michael smiled, but the atmosphere was not one of celebration or reconciliation. They could have been strangers, Clive thought, finishing his drink quickly and leaving Michael to play with his aeroplane design. 'I'll see you on the fifteenth.'

It was cold in the street, the wind chasing scraps of paper and a few prematurely fallen leaves over the pavements. Clive thrust his hands into his pockets as he walked down Meadwell Street. He pushed open the door to Caroline's shop and she was sitting at her desk, frowning over a pile of invoices. She turned as she heard him.

'Hello, Clive,' she said gently.

'I've come to congratulate you.'

'Thank you.'

'When is it due?'

'End of April they think. It's hard to tell exactly. Later perhaps they will date it more exactly.' She stood up, pushing her chair back, taller than Clive. He took her hands, stroking the long fingers. 'I tried so often to ring or write to you, to say how sorry I was for just throwing myself at Michael, just leaving you without a word. I wanted to explain that I cared for you very much in those weeks we were together.'

'As I recall, it was I who left.' He touched the insides of her wrists and found them limp and unresponsive.

'So it was.' She thought how attractive his face was, serious and kind and sad like this. She thought of the first time she had seen him, a mere six months ago. She would have liked to have kissed him but she didn't.

The knowledge of the baby was between them like a sheet of glass.

'You don't mind having the baby in France? Selling the shop?' Clive asked, releasing her hands and sitting on the edge of her desk. 'Has he been bullying you?'

'No, of course not. He just sweeps on with his plans . . . of course I wanted to stay here. I was terrified at first to think of going anywhere before it is born but they have all reassured me and also I began to think I must not put the baby above Michael. I want it so much, Clive. I cannot express what it means to me. It is so much more important than anything else that I must not shut Michael out. So I'll do as he wants.' She looked sadly round the shop. 'But it hurts to leave all this. My tiny stab at independence!' She smiled sadly at Clive. 'I always tell you things I can't tell other people and you've made me want a cigarette and I'm trying not to!' She lit one. 'Tell me about you. How are you?'

'Eagerly trying to get my hands on Mosaic. And I've found a new flat . . .'

'And someone new to love?' she couldn't resist asking.

'I don't know about that. Not in the sense I thought of the word with you. Someone I am very fond of. Someone unusual.'

'Bring her on the fifteenth. You will come, won't you?'

'Yes, but I'd rather come alone.'

She looked at him for a long time. 'Do you know, Clive, I'm rather afraid of this baby. Isn't that absurd? After all the years of wanting it, I'm afraid I won't know how to look after it. I'm going to try and get an English nanny for a bit when it's small.'

'Kate shares a flat with a girl who does that . . . Judith Richardson. She came to your party. Would you like me to ask Kate about her?'

'Yes. I'd like to meet her. I'd like to have something arranged

180

before I go.'

Clive nodded. 'And what do you want for a wedding present?'

'Just your good wishes,' she said simply. She looked so like she had that first afternoon, so lost, and he wanted her so much that he had to go, calling goodbye over his shoulder, taking the regret and the emptiness with him into the cold street.

The fifteenth was a mellow September day. Caroline wore a straw hat covered in daisies, a bright green suit, and in the restaurant afterwards there was noise and laughter. Michael was in a most unusual mood, intensely lively, demonstrative, taking Caroline's hands, kissing them; Clive saw an engagement ring of emeralds and diamonds which had come from Valerie de Jouvard, a narrow gold wedding ring; the lunch lasted until 3.30 and even then they lingered in the street. Clive could not bear to watch Caroline and Michael together, smiling at each other, or leaning to kiss each other. It gave him a twisting revulsion, a sense of dreadful waste.

When they were outside in the street, Caroline leaned across and kissed him. 'Be happy for me.'

'I am,' he lied, wondering whether the joy in her face was for Michael or the baby, wondering if she were marrying the man or merely the father of the child. As he watched them drive away he could not imagine ever losing this melancholy. He went back to the office and wandered in to find Kate. She looked up at him thoughtfully.

'What are you thinking?' Clive said.

'Whether we'll ever lay the ghosts? Whether people ever do.'

'I think they do. They forget and move on.'

She stood up and came to him, always a little uncertain, waiting for him to touch her first. 'You look so sad, Clive.'

'Well, I shouldn't. I'm intensely relieved. It's done with. She's gone. Tomorrow Michael and Caroline will go to France.'

'They'll be back in October?'

'Yes, but only to tidy up. If I am sad at all, it isn't for myself.

181

It's for Caroline.' He put an arm along Kate's shoulders. 'To-night, Katy, we'll go out somewhere and drink much too much and to hell with them all!'

CHAPTER ELEVEN

Through the autumn of nineteen seventy-three, Clive and Kate's lives were interlocked. They saw each other at work each day and Kate loved the secret knowledge of their relationship, loved the way Clive had of looking up at her when there were other people in the room, loved the swift, furtive touch of his hand. She was quite happy to be cared for, realizing that Clive was a possessive man. She could not forget the night it had all started and, however often she thought back, she could not see that she could have acted otherwise. Looking back over her life she saw that she had always been far too vulnerable to disappointment. Now she was determined to build up layers against the world, secure, for the moment, in the haven Clive provided.

She took an almost childish joy in staying at the new flat with him. She liked cooking breakfast, putting away his clothes in the long bedroom cupboard; she liked to see her own small, brilliantly coloured clothes hanging beside his, her small shoes beside his. Shrewdly, she realized he was a man dedicated to living what he considered a civilized life. It mattered to Clive that he had clean shirts, ice in his drink, good whisky, hot bath water, that his car responded when he put his foot down. It mattered that he be respected at Bonnington's, liked by his clients, that he could afford good food in fashionable restaurants. Seeing all this, Kate guessed that Caroline's rejection had hurt him far more than he showed and she tried hard to be what he wanted because it seemed so extraordinary that this second chance, this other man to love, should have come so unexpectedly into her life. Still the funny side of her kept bursting through, stopping Clive in his tracks and springing from him his big, deep laugh. Kate moved uneasily in his circle of friends but she tried hard with them.

'I think,' she said to Judith in the flat one evening, 'that David was just infatuation, that the way I feel for Clive is love.'

Judith didn't answer. She lay on the sitting-room floor, arms flung wide, in a position of total relaxation, eyes closed, face impassive. When she had returned from the sea, when she had found Kate's note . . . 'Staying at Cambridge Street this week with Clive!!' and the telephone number . . . she had experienced something close to fury. It surprised her. She had paced the flat, restlessly; how ridiculous, Clive and Kate! What an absurd couple! Judith hated to feel she had missed an opportunity. She had thought of Clive frequently, had been sure that the attraction was mutual. Could she have been wrong? This, too, unsettled her. By the time Kate returned to get clean clothes, and explained how it had all come about, Judith had calmed down. She was non-committal, skilfully undermining Kate's confidence whenever she could but very careful not to reveal her feelings. She liked Kate. She would have been pleased to find Kate happy with a man but as Judith wanted him, Kate must come second.

She sat up, twisting her legs into a lotus position, hands into flowers, resting on her knees.

'I just can't understand why he wants me,' Kate went on.

'Perhaps, as you are both getting over someone else, you are what the other needs for the moment.' Judith thought of the recklessness she had sensed in Clive, a slight cruelty, the way she had mentally put him in the back of her mind for later. 'I can't see you being happy together for any length of time.'

Kate stood up, hurt. These conversations were meant to be one way, the listener agreeing, matching enthusiasm, not damping. 'Why not?'

'Because he is a hard, pushing man and although your temporary helplessness appeals to him now . . .'

'Oh, shut up!' Kate said.

'I think you are like a tortoise without a shell. Like someone trying on various clothes to see if they suit . . .'

184

'You mean I'm talking myself into it all?'

'Why do you have to be so extreme? Enjoy him for the moment. You don't have to adore every man you go to bed with, do you?'

'Yes. It makes it all right if you love them!' Kate grinned. 'I've asked him to come home with me for the weekend, Judith. I took ages getting up my courage, wondering if he would feel cornered.'

Judith rolled forward, lay on her stomach. 'Kate, you are thinking on such a different wave-length from the way he does. He won't care if your parents like him, he won't feel cornered. He's not some twenty-year old boy, feeling he ought to do the right thing.'

'I hate you when you're superior!'

'I'm sorry.' She listened as Kate talked in swift flights of words and did not interrupt again.

Michael and Caroline arrived back in London in mid-October, very brown and seemingly very happy. They lived at Meadwell Street which was now being advertised for sale and Caroline could hardly bear to be there, trying desperately not to become too involved in the shop again. The party to introduce the Sundial to the world was held at Marketing Mosaic, the desks pushed back and covered with white cloths. In the showroom, on one low table, stood a single Sundial, beautifully machined, its solid brass body heavy, its face painted with the sun and curving outstretched rays, the lines of which the hands followed. It was to retail at £65. The press coverage had been good and it was greeted with enthusiasm.

Clive, when he was satisfied that the party was going well, found Caroline in a quiet corner, took her hands. 'Well, Mrs Redford?'

'I'm very happy, Clive. I had no idea Jouvard would be so lovely. My first reaction was overwhelming relief. I think I expected a huge place, like a film set, and I knew Michael would be watching my every reaction. I've never been to the South of France before. Harry liked skiing holidays. The sun made him go red . . .' She paused, remembering the impact of the scenery, the valleys between ridges of hills on the hour-and-a-half drive from Marseilles airport, the long autoroute and then smaller roads, between fields of olive and almond trees, broken up by their screens to ward off the mistral. At last the house itself, old and grey, settled into its surroundings, looking as tough as the countryside, a cobbled yard in front, its buildings and vine-yards, and the garden at one side which had so delighted her.

'And Michael gave you a complete tour at once?'

She laughed. 'Of course.' He had asked, so gently, if she were tired. She tried to tell Clive the first impression she had felt. 'Silence, I suppose, and coolness after the hot journey, and those ancient brocade curtains downstairs, all closed, chairs with tat-tered silk covers, the large flagged hall and the kitchen, looking as if Cinderella should have been crouched by that stove! So cool and dim indoors. I was filled with energy to transform it, make it lovely inside and I will. Isn't the view wonderful from the upstairs windows? And he took me everywhere, into the office to see the plan on the wall and through all the buildings, the first year chai with those great oak hogsheads of new wine, the hydraulic press, through all the fields, talking to everyone. And Madame Gautier in the kitchen, casually preparing to feed about twenty people who had come for the grape picking!' She laughed. She talked only of France.

She hardly looked pregnant, Kate thought, coming to stand by Clive rather uncertainly. She looked at Caroline and won-dered how anyone who had loved such a complete and beautiful woman could possibly be interested in herself. Kate thought Michael an uncomfortable man. If he liked me, if he talked to me, I would be flattered and fascinated but he won't, so I feel dismissed.

Liz Moult was there, ready, she said, to cope with the shop until it sold. Clive had been given power of attorney and was to invest the proceeds of the shop sale. Caroline and Judith had met and it was agreed that Judith would go to Jouvard in April. All the loose ends were being tied.

The final transaction between Michael and Clive regarding Mosaic took place on October thirtieth, the day before the Redfords left for France permanently. Clive handed over his cheque and he was filled with elation. Mosaic was his! And Michael and Caroline had really gone.

Now Clive went into Mosaic every Tuesday and many evenings he called in to talk to Jenny. They had given up trying to like one another and instead concentrated on working together. Some evenings, if Clive had taken his car to Bonnington's, Kate would come with him. She liked Mosaic. She liked the atmosphere and Bill Carter's drawing-board and Nancy, who had been Michael's secretary, and Pen. She liked the white walls and the big photographs and the displays of products. Above all, she liked the Sundial. It was a beautiful clock. It had a deep, dignified tick.

Jenny was not so sure about it. 'It's so bloody expensive, Clive. Okay, the initial orders aren't bad but they're not great either. I hope Michael hasn't left us with a white elephant.' About the rocking clocks, she had stopped commenting. Clive was quite determined they should be produced and as she disliked them intensely, she thought it better to say no more: she had registered her disapproval very strongly. Mosaic was in a pre-Christmas frenzy through November, struggling to despatch orders on time, and London was already wearing all the trimmings. The weekend at the Old Vicarage was put off again and again until eventually it was agreed that Clive would come for Christmas.

Clive was surprised by Kate's home, by the lovely old furniture, the glass they drank from; he commented frequently on the excellence of the wine, trying to engage Ben in a discussion about wine. Ben would not be drawn. Clive liked the old-fashioned ritual of Christmas here, church on Christmas morning when the whole village stared at him, a drink afterwards with people in the house next door, a Georgian house, typical of the whole of this pretty village. It had not occurred to him that Kate would come from such an obviously wealthy background; he was impressed by Ben although he found him extremely difficult. Clive made every effort to be charming, leaping to his feet to help Gabriel, amusing everyone if he could, talking constantly to Ben, and knowing, throughout, that he was being disliked.

It had never occurred to Kate that they wouldn't like him. She had worried about the atmosphere between her parents but never thought to find them united like this against Clive. She had brought him home so proudly and the hostility she felt after the first evening when they merely studied him politely, amazed her.

'What is it?' she hissed furiously at Gabriel in the kitchen on Christmas night. 'Why are you being like this?'

Gabriel looked haunted. 'What do you mean?' she stalled.

'You don't like him. I don't understand you . . . you threw David at me and, despite the fact that he hurt me so much, you still welcome him here. But Clive, who cares about me, who . . . can't you see how kind he is? How funny? He has the same kind of confidence as Daddy, not caring what the world thinks . . . making me laugh . . .'

The gin and the wine had freed Gabriel of her normal reserve. 'Don't look for a man like your father, Kate. I know you love him but you don't really see him . . . He sits on the sidelines, never getting close to anyone, tearing people down! I wanted David for you because I thought he was young and straightforward. Obviously I was wrong but this man is too old for you, too used. I hate the way he smiles, as if his smile has always got him what he wanted.'

'I thought you would adore him,' Kate said dully. 'I don't know why the hell I bother to try and please you. David was right. He said I was far too closed in.' She swung out, tears in her

188

eyes. She sought out her father.

'I see now you would automatically dislike any man I brought here.'

'That's not true, Katy.'

'Well, try then. Try and like him.' She felt the awful split. She wanted all the people she loved lined up on one side, liking each other.

'He is not what I want for you, that's all.' Ben said.

'I thought your parents were charming,' Clive said, as they drove back to London on Boxing Day. 'Individually charming and disastrous together.'

'They were trying to get on for your sake. You should hear them sometimes!' Kate said dully.

'Your mother, fluttering about, trying to get everything right . . .'

'Waiting for my father to pounce and then reacting with wide-eyed resignation, always hiding how he hurts her.' Kate reached into her handbag and took out some peppermints. She put one in her mouth and put her feet up knees bent, and sighed. Clive was always fascinated by the supple positions her body appeared to assume quite naturally. After four months he was still content to have Kate in his life. It had occurred to him more than once that, although he would never again experience love the way he had felt it for Caroline, in Kate, and quite by accident, he might have found the one woman he could love without feeling she was second best.

I care for this girl, he thought. I have used London for ten years. I have had enough. I could change now, settle now. Mosaic filled him with confidence and enthusiasm. And a new year was coming, a symbol of change.

'I was wondering, Kate, if, in a while, you would like to work at Mosaic instead of Bonnington's? Penny is leaving in the spring and I think you're wasted where you are . . .'

Kate sat upright, swallowing the sweet. 'Is this a way of

getting me out of your life?' She grinned.

'Quite the opposite. I hope to be at Mosaic more and more.' He looked at her and Kate's heart thumped.

'Nineteen seventy-four will be a year when a lot of things change, Kate.'

'Especially the date!' Clive didn't laugh. 'I've always thought Mosaic was interesting,' Kate went on. 'I could learn a lot about it, especially from Jenny.' Now that she sensed something was coming she was scared. Suddenly she felt she didn't know Clive very well.

'Are you coming back to the flat with me?'

'Well, it's warmer than Queensgate Gardens!' She was quiet, thinking of her home and the hurt her parents had caused her was fresh in her mind. She was angry with them. There was nothing at home for her now. She had tried on her own and failed miserably. To be safe was the thing. To be loved. Not everyone could be strong and independent. Some people needed to be part of a pair.

They went up the stairs to Clive's flat, through the front door with its stained-glass window panel, down the dark little hall to the bedroom. She knew Clive was restless here, that the flat in no way suited his image of himself. She was careful now, not to tease him too much about his love of the luxuries of life.

The bedroom was sparsely furnished. Kate opened her case and took off her clothes and dropped them over a chair, forgetting that Clive disliked her to undress herself. She pulled on a nightgown and washed and came back to bounce on the bed as Clive carefully folded his clothes over the chair. She bounced across to him, standing on the bed, putting her arms round his wide shoulders, her face against his hair. 'Any truth in the rumour you'll put up with me for another month or so?'

He turned and laughed, lifted her off the bed, looking into her face. 'If you make it worth my while! And don't keep me up too late. Work tomorrow! We must leave early. Have you put a note out for the milkman?'

He forgot nothing, she thought. He seemed to enjoy her vagueness about household things, watching her ineffectual attempts to organize the flat, even on a part-time basis, with affection. Only in the office was she efficient and competent.

He kissed her small nose. The words came out easily. He liked to take decisions fast. She was warm in his arms. 'Do you want to get married, Kate, next year some time, when things are more settled?'

She had guessed it was coming but to hear it in words was extraordinary. 'To you?'

'Well, I wasn't proposing on behalf of anyone else!'

She drew back a little, looking from his eyes down to his mouth, tucking her hair seriously behind her ears, then moving in close, safe when he held her, loving the smell of him, knowing how good it was in bed with him, seeing her life neatly laid out, precise as a calendar. 'All right.' She had no reason to refuse. No alternatives.

'Good,' Clive said and then laughed, thinking how he waited years and years to ask someone and had never pictured himself with a woman who answered as matter-of-factly as Kate. 'All right.'

At Rachel's New Year's Eve party word somehow got out and they were wrapped in congratulations and laughter and it was all so much fun, such a triumph to be the centre of attention. They sang *Auld Lang Syne* and no one went home till three. Alice was amazed and rather annoyed, Gabriel was silent and Ben said, 'You haven't been anywhere yet, Katy. Take your time.' Only Judith put into words what everyone really thought, her face quite calm, her voice casual, looking at Kate with her hard and slanted eyes. 'Has it ever occurred to you or to Clive that the way you feel about each other may not be delight? Is it just that the disappointment you both felt has worn off. That this is just a time of recovery for you both?'

'I've thought of it,' Kate said stiffly, 'but I don't care. No one is certain of anything!' She had meant to take time, as Ben said,

191

but Penny left Mosaic earlier than expected and exactly eleven months after she had come to Bonnington's, Kate left and went to Mosaic.

Clive had decided to stay with Bonnington's for at least another year because of the sudden and rather disturbing effect the Middle East war seemed to be having on prices. He thought it would be useful to have his Bonnington's salary. Mosaic would then not need to pay him for a year and the money saved through nineteen seventy-four could go towards repaying Michael. In February Caroline's shop finally sold. It had been closed for two months. The price was very good, far more than she had paid; Clive wrote and told her and invested the fifty thousand pounds. Then he pressed Kate to choose a date to get married. 'You live with me virtually all the time now. Why wait?' He was eager to have the loose ends neatly tied. Kate chose a Tuesday in April. Gabriel, seeing that there was nothing she could do to stop it and that if she was cold she would merely lose Kate, offered to buy them a house. At first Clive firmly turned down this incredibly generous offer but he was persuaded to change his mind. 'I knew he would,' Ben said dryly.

'He has a good job, Ben. He's been around enough to know what he wants. Perhaps he will make her happy.'

'As long as he doesn't make her actively unhappy!'

A house was found in Putney in a quiet street. A big red-brick building, ugly and solid with a garden at the back. Convenient for Mosaic. Convenient for the Kingston by-pass and the Old Vicarage. Kate was suddenly involved in a sea of plans, of bridesmaids and wedding presents, redecorating, choosing carpets. No time to think anything through properly. But it must be like this for everyone, she comforted herself, wandering through the tall empty rooms of the house in Rose Walk and wishing the ceilings weren't so high!

Clive brought her so many flowers. She longed to tell him that flowers depressed her. 'I feel obliged to arrange them, Judith, and I spend hours and they always fall over or look awful. I wish

192

you'd be here for the wedding.'

'It's your fault for choosing the time Caroline's baby is due. Anyway, I'm longing to go to France. I've been so restless this spring.' It was an unusual admission for Judith. 'I'm buying a car at last. It's a secondhand Renault but it's in good condition. I'm driving myself down. This is your present. You're going to need it!'

Kate unwrapped a large cookery book.

On Sunday, March twenty-fourth, there was a scathing attack on John Hampton's investment company in the business section of a prominent Sunday newspaper. Clive saw the headline and froze. He read the article twice and his heart began to beat very hard. It was extremely damaging. Such things would not have been printed without proof, he knew. It hinted of a fraud squad investigation. Clive reached for the telephone by his bed. As he expected John Hampton's number gave no reply. Clive finally contacted him late that evening.

'Why the hell didn't you warn me, Johnny?'

'How could I? And have everyone pull out? I had to protect my investors. And it's untrue. The whole thing is exaggerated. Anyway, you haven't done badly out of it so far!' His voice blustered on. 'They claim we take too high a percentage, that we recommend clients to invest with dubious people who make it worth our while. That's absurd. How could we keep getting results if we did that?'

'How long have you known this was brewing?' Clive asked, his voice dangerously quiet.

'I had no idea, Clive. Believe me . . .'

Clive laughed.

The storm broke the following morning. There was an emergency meeting with Michael Paul and five other partners. The telephone rang constantly with calls from anxious clients Clive had put in touch with Hampton and Edgar.

'Surely, Clive, you investigated the man thoroughly? I

193

remember you telling me you had known him for years, that he was brilliant . . .' Michael Paul's thin face was very serious. He had never liked Clive.

'It seems I was wrong,' Clive said shortly. He was not going to bluff it out, to crawl. He was going in a blaze of righteous anger.

'It's not the first time you've been wrong. That mistake over the Mather contract was extremely embarrassing!'

Strange to have it happen like this, Clive thought, with half his mind, standing back and watching himself resign eloquently, watching their mixed reactions. One thing to plan to move into another field. Quite another to have it thrust on him. They accepted his resignation rather thankfully.

'Why did you resign, Clive?' Kate asked. 'I thought you said you wanted to stay on for a time. What is the real reason?' She watched him with serious eyes.

'What does it matter, Kate? I would have left soon anyway.' He poured himself a strong Scotch.

'But please tell me what happened? I want to know.'

'Nothing happened.' He ruffled her hair and she shook his hand off angrily. 'Come on, we're going out to celebrate my coming to Mosaic full time.'

'I am an adult, Clive. I am capable of understanding why . . .'

'Just forget it!' he said coldly. 'If you want to help, talk about something else. I've had enough of Bonnington's!'

Her cheeks flamed like a child.

'Go and change, Katy. Where would you like to eat? Anywhere . . . we'll ring the Andersons. They're always good value.' He began to plan a small party.

Kate stood and watched him, head a little bent, body very still. She felt extremely hurt and disturbed, shut out. 'Am I just to be the clown then, the diversion? Kept in the dark? I won't be able to keep that up, will I?'

Clive came to her, picking her up, kissing her. 'Laugh, my love . . . come on. Go and change.' He put her down and sat down himself, taking a large drink from his glass, closing his eyes

194

for a moment, rubbing his face with his hand. Whatever he tried to pretend, to himself or Kate, the truth was disturbing. He would, far rather, have stayed at Bonnington's for a while. But he was not a man to brood over the inevitable. He sat forward, his face changing. He would turn it to his advantage! And damn those silly old men at Bonnington's with their censorous faces and grave manners! Kate stood in the doorway, watching him, seeing the different expressions move over his face. She knew she should go back into the room, try again, make him tell her. She knew she should start now, building herself up in his eyes, making herself worthy of joining a discussion. But she just did not know how.

CHAPTER TWELVE

Judith took five days to drive down to Provence, taking her time, getting to know the car, enjoying it. She relished the feeling that she was quite cut off, absolutely alone. She enjoyed having to find herself somewhere to stay each night, buying food, sometimes asking the way, all in very inadequate French. She stopped to visit places that she thought would interest her. Judith did not understand what it was to be nervous. New places excited her, increased her energy. Her extraordinary self-possession carried her. She drove down the autoroute, followed the Rhone, came to Avignon. She had lunch there, the fourth day, consulting her map under the old ramparts of the walled city, eating French bread and cheese and a huge peach; she left her car for a while and explored on foot, looking up in awe at the Pope's palace. Two boys played flutes in the dignified square and the sound was sweet and unreal. When she drove on again across the Vaucluse, past the endless little fields of fruit trees and vegetables, each guarded by its wind-breaking screens and trees to protect them from the Mistral she saw that already, at the beginning of April, they were picking strawberries and melons. She spent the night in a small village and early Friday morning drove south, following the detailed instructions in Caroline's letter, to Jouvard.

The sky was a clean, happy blue. A landscape of constant changes; a little church perched on a precipice as if demonstrating its faith in God; a long straight road flanked with symmetrical trees and bamboo and then she turned, as directed, on to a much narrower road and wound with it for a mile, rounded a sharp bend and saw the wrought iron gates. She turned through them, down a curved drive, and stopped before a lovely old grey house, smaller than she had expected, strong and shuttered with a lot of grey buildings on one side of it. In front a shady garden which extended round to one side; on the other side she saw the vineyards and a field of olive trees. The grass in front was very green and a sprinkler sprayed water in shimmering bursts.

Judith got out, stretching her body. Her legs were already brown, her feet brown in white sandals. She stood and looked up at the house, examining it as she always examined all houses before entering. Above the door the date eighteen thirty-two was engraved and on each side of the stone steps were clusters of large pots, filled with geranium, oleander and white daisies.

'It's a typical small château,' Caroline had written in her letter. 'Really just a farmhouse but built to look more important. The lay-out is quite traditional. It's a lovely house and now we have made two more bathrooms and changed the kitchen, it's quite easy to manage.'

Judith went through the double front doors, pushing them open, into a flagged hall. Heavy curtains hung at the windows, closed to keep out the heat, giving a rather mysterious air of peace. She paused, enjoying the coolness, changing the strap of her handbag to the other shoulder; a small, dark-haired woman appeared, her skin very wrinkled, smiling and speaking rapid French and Judith held out her hands . . . 'Please. A little more slowly . . .'

Yvette Gautier began again. Although she spoke more slowly, her Provençal accent made it extremely difficult for Judith to understand. 'The baby. . . ?' she picked out of the tangle of words and gestures. 'The baby has arrived too soon?'

'Yes.' The French woman smiled, took Judith outside to the car to get her luggage and then led her upstairs to a big white bedroom, the windows curtained with a pretty flowered cotton, a bright rug on the floor, crocheted bedspreads. All Caroline's influence, Judith guessed. The effect was very pretty and cool. She followed the older woman down again and found a cold lunch set out on a round table in a lovely room which opened on to a veranda. She poured herself a glass of wine and stood by the

197

open doors. It was only a few moments before she heard a car and footsteps across the hall and looked round to see Michael Redford.

'I'm sorry I wasn't here when you arrived. Has Madame Gautier explained?'

'She's tried to. The baby has arrived?'

'Yes. Caroline went into labour yesterday, quite unexpectedly. It's at least three weeks early but they are both fine!' He pushed at his hair wearily and poured himself a glass of wine. 'It was born two hours ago . . . A boy.' He sat down. The tension of the last twenty-four hours had temporarily driven away his normal reserve. 'Thank God it's over. I didn't expect anything so . . . so terrifying.'

'But Caroline has been well, all through?'

'Very well, I think.'

'And you're happy here?'

He frowned. 'Of course.' He studied Judith for a moment, wondering if he would dislike having her here. She had an interesting face. He had met her several times in London with Susie but they had seldom spoken. Michael helped himself from the plate of cold meat and then, realizing he was being rude, extended it to Judith.

She grinned. 'You don't have to bother about me. Pretend I've always been here. I think I'll just have cheese and salad anyway.'

'How is Clive? We had a wedding invitation. And Kate? And Mosaic?'

'Kate says she is very happy. She works at Mosaic now and likes that. Her parents are very unhappy but making the best of it. Kate being an only child, no one would be good enough . . .'

'I hardly know her,' Michael said vaguely and smiled. 'But then I hardly know anyone! And Mosaic? Clive sent me some Sundial cuttings.'

'I don't think it's selling very well. Even in the months since you left prices have risen enormously. Prices of everyday things I

198

mean. Perhaps the Sundial is too much of a luxury?'

'And Clive's rocking clocks?'

'To be launched later in the year, I think, despite tremendous opposition from the woman who works there . . .'

'Jenny.'

'Yes. Jenny is against them, Kate says.' Judith laughed. 'Kate is like a child speaking lines in a school play and Jenny is the witch. "She lacks the courage to take a risk," Kate says. And: "We took over at a very bad time."'

'I'm afraid that's true.' Michael heard Clive's voice. 'You always were a lucky bastard!'

'Did you know Clive had left Bonnington's?'

'No, I didn't. Why the hell has he done that?'

'I don't think Kate knows the whole of it.'

Michael frowned, eating in a fast, absent-minded way, forgetting Judith.

'When can I come and see the baby?' Judith asked.

'I shall go back tonight, about seven. They want her to stay in hospital at least a week. I hope you won't be bored.'

'Not at all.' Judith smiled. 'It will be a holiday.'

Caroline looked exhausted, face thinner, eyes huge, skin stretched tightly over the bones of her face. The first evening, when Michael was there, restlessly pacing the hot room, she said little but when Judith went alone the following afternoon she seemed eager to talk. She was holding the baby stiffly as if afraid she would hurt him. He was small and crumpled with black hair, eyes tightly closed, mouth moving experimentally.

'I longed for him so much and I felt well and calm but now he is here I am afraid and all the calm has gone. He is so small and floppy, as if the nappy and nightgown holds him together!' Her eyes glittered nervously. 'It's almost as if I have been asleep all the months we've been here, fussed over by Yvette and the doctors, moving slowly through the days, organizing the house. It's lovely, isn't it? Michael has been so busy. We have been out.

People ask us out of curiosity and I find it hard to relax with them. I love the country but I still feel as if I am on holiday . . . the garden is wonderful. Things grow incredibly . . .' She pulled herself more upright and grimaced with pain. 'I didn't expect anything so violent, Judith. I have wanted a baby for so long and yet I had never thought about the actual birth. I didn't expect so much blood I feel I have been torn open. But I am suddenly light, too, without him inside.' She laid the baby beside her and reached for a peach, peeling it delicately, disinterestedly.

'What is he called?' Judith asked, lifting the baby up.

'Charles.' Caroline pronounced it as the French would.

'Hello, Charlie.' Judith touched his tiny nose with the tip of a finger, handling him expertly.

'Tell me about Clive and Kate.'

'Well . . . they get married in two weeks. Kate explains herself a lot, using words like "secure" and "sensible". And the more she says, the less sense she makes . . .'

Caroline closed her eyes, suddenly very tired, feeling beaten with the joy and the pain. 'And Clive?' she said almost to herself. 'Why is he marrying Kate?'

'Because a lot has changed for him. Because she comes from a wealthy family,' Judith said, with a smile. She wandered the room, baby in her arms, and she thought: 'He is marrying Kate because, with you, he narrowed his horizons to one woman.'

'Do you know Kate well?' Caroline asked.

'Fairly well. I went to stay a weekend at her home in February. After that I understood her much better. Her parents are impossible.' She paused, remembering the atmosphere at the Old Vicarage. She had found Kate's father attractive, a sad and cruel man. She sensed that he could not tolerate pretension, would be unable to meet Clive on any level. Kate had said to Judith, 'Why is it that all the people I love hate each other? They are all separate and it seems impossible for me to change that. All my life I have been trying to get my father and mother in one room being nice to each other so that I could pretend it was all right. Now it seems it will be the same with Clive.'

'I think that Clive enjoys Kate's helplessness,' Judith said, seeing that Caroline wanted more. 'Perhaps they will be happy.' Her tone said she doubted it. Their eyes met. 'And you?' Judith said. 'Are you happy now?'

Caroline didn't answer for a few moments. She held out her arms for the baby. 'Now I will be,' she said.

Judith enjoyed her solitary week at Château de Jouvard. She began to communicate quite freely with Madame Gautier, struggling to understand the quite different accent here in Provence, dragging out of her memory the words she had learned at school; she was quite unworried if she sounded foolish. She kept trying and she picked up words very quickly. She used sign language if she were stuck and Michael if she was desperate. But she saw little of Michael. He left the house each morning before Judith came down to the huge kitchen, the heart of the house. Caroline had left the big black stove and the rows of copper saucepans but added new cupboards, a long tiled work surface, an electric stove and an enormous refrigerator. Garlic and salami hung from iron hooks. The old dairy had become a laundry room and there was a vast larder and a cellar; the wood store had been turned into a long white room where Yvette Gautier fed the extra workers who came for the grape harvest. At one side of the huge kitchen Caroline had put a sofa and a low table and a bookcase, as if she spent a lot of time in here, Judith thought.

Each morning she would find Yvette Gautier in the kitchen. There would be coffee, fresh bread and jam. She spent her mornings exploring St Remy and the surrounding area, stopping to sit on a swing seat outside a little café and drink a cold beer before she came home, watching the main street of the little town for a while. Lunch was invariably cold meats, fruit and cheese. Being almost vegetarian, she never ate the meat. She had brought her own supply of wholewheat cereal which

201

amused Michael. In the afternoons she lay beside the oblong swimming pool which was enclosed now by a trellis fence. Wistaria and honeysuckle rambled up the pillars of the veranda. This garden which Caroline had taken on so willingly was lovely and very secluded. The sky, most afternoons, was a smooth blue saucer.

'My grandmother built this pool when I was thirteen,' Michael said one afternoon, watching Judith as she lay in her small red bikini, registering the attraction of her almost naked body but unmoved by it. And one afternoon he took Judith round the working part of the château and when he explained everything, completely changed by his obvious enthusiasm, for the first time Judith saw his attraction. On the whole Michael left her alone and she was happy to be so, loving the solitude and only disturbed when she thought that, in a week, Clive would marry Kate.

Michael visited Caroline each evening. All through the day she longed for him to come, storing things to tell him; but he would pace the room so restlessly that after ten minutes she would be telling him to go, hating to watch him trying to think of things to say. In this very emotional mood, temporarily opened up by the baby's birth, she could have told him so much of her feelings of the last months. She wanted to touch him constantly. The sexless hood of pregnancy had fallen away. She wanted his mouth and his hands but she wanted them to be given willingly. Michael paced the room like a tiger. 'I'm sorry, Caroline. I want to see you and the baby but it seems such a waste of time, so much driving. When I'm here I forget all the things I wanted to say. When can you come home?' Always, the third time she suggested he go, he agreed, relief in his eyes. He could hurt her so much without realizing it, she thought, hating the silence of the hospital night when he had gone.

On a hot Saturday morning Michael brought Caroline and the baby home. The house was full of flowers. Judith took the baby upstairs and laid him in the crib Suzanne had slept in. Caroline, too, lay down on her bed and closed her eyes, repeating to herself the chant that was half a prayer. 'Now we will be all right. Now we will be all right.'

Henri Bertrand came that evening, having dinner with them on the veranda, smiling when he heard the cat-like sound of the new baby. Caroline was so pleased to see him. He had become a special friend. His English was so good she could talk to him without effort. Although she could now make herself understood very well in French, she found it very tiring to speak for a whole evening and always felt she was missing the subtle undertones. She could talk to Henri as she had once talked to Clive, confessing everything. He knew Michael so well.

Tonight Henri was full of enthusiasm, his quiet voice lit with excitement. 'I have been approached by the Mary May people . . .'

Michael looked blank but Caroline laughed. 'He wouldn't know, Henri, but of course I do! How wonderful. Do they want your cottons?'

'It's too early to say but I shall go to England in the autumn and see them. It's just an idea but we have similar set-ups, although they are far bigger. We both use cotton exclusively. Of course they also do wallpaper and curtain fabric which I don't. Yet.' He smiled.

'Mary May,' Michael repeated. 'Are they English?'

'Yes. Basically. But now they have shops all over England and have just opened in Paris and hope to open in Aix. I met their managing director last week.' Henri lit a Gauloise, his face wearing the expression Caroline now recognized; an expression of surprise at himself and his success. She liked him so much . . . she looked across to Judith, who spoke very little when in a group of people, and then dismissed the idea. Henri was far too gentle. There was a girl who came and went from his old, tiled house, a young American girl who had come to Jouvard to swim. Caroline had disliked her. She found so many of the English-speaking people who had settled in the area eccentric

203

and uncomfortable, their lives dedicated to loves and hates within their small community. Michael had nothing in common with them and they had tired of trying to understand him.

'Also,' Henri said with a smile, 'in my new role as tycoon I have produced some things I thought Clive might market for me through Mosaic. Some little purses made of cotton, a bigger bag. If they are ready, I will take some to England with me in the autumn.'

Just after ten, Caroline and Judith went up to attend to the baby. Caroline had stopped trying to feed him herself. He was too apathetic and slow and she was afraid of denying him the milk he needed. Judith had guessed from the start that the breast-feeding would not work. Caroline was too tense. Judith preferred bottles anyway. They were far more exact. He was a small baby and rather listless and it took a long time to coax the milk down but Caroline had unlimited patience. She allowed Judith to do the two o'clock in the morning feed simply because she realized the exhaustion in herself and knew she must use the time while Judith was here to recover.

Michael and Henri sat outside in the warm night, discussing the vines. 'They have such interesting ideas at Cavillion,' Michael said. 'I am determined to try some of these new vines they have developed but of course Gautier is suspicious. They tell me at the research centre that they have great difficulty getting any of the farmers to try new ideas. I have volunteered . . .'

'Your son is a fine little boy,' Henri said. 'But Caroline looks very tired . . .' He wanted to say, 'Give her more time, Michael, more attention,' but he could not bring himself to interfere. Once Caroline had said to him, sadly, 'I can never rely on Michael for anything. His presence, his laughter, his attention, even his love-making are always wonderful surprises, not any kind of safe routine.'

'What do you think of the nanny?' Michael asked.

'I am sure she is very competent but I dislike her. She is the same type of woman as Colette.' Henri refilled his brandy glass.

'I recognize them at once. They scare me!' He laughed. 'I know they are far stronger than I am!'

'I rather like her,' Michael said. 'She doesn't require me to make conversation and although she's virtually a vegetarian she doesn't fuss about it.' He smiled. 'She arrived with a bloody cardboard box full of cereal and nuts!' Michael, too, poured himself more brandy. He was silent, absorbing the night. There was a vast white moon. 'I love it here,' he said, quietly and irrelevantly. 'It encloses me more each month. I belong.'

'And Caroline?' Henri asked.

'What do you mean?'

'Does she love it here, too? Or is it strange for her? Lonely sometimes?'

'She hasn't said so,' Michael said stiffly.

A letter came from Clive while Judith was at Jouvard, thanking Michael and Caroline for the wedding present. He enclosed a statement of her invested money, congratulated her on the baby, mentioned the new house. It was a bleak note and Caroline did not write back. She felt that Clive was quite lost to her now, even as a friend.

In the end Judith stayed ten weeks. She came to love Jouvard, becoming interested in the day to day running of the house and the vineyard, watching the way the work intensified as the vines budded, as they watched anxiously for the frost, as they ploughed. She enjoyed shopping in St Remy. Her French improved and she explored. The baby, who had been very difficult, settled down more after six weeks and slept for longer stretches. And Judith had got to know Michael, as much as anyone ever did, and thought him a complicated man, so wrapped up in himself, needing time on his own and almost resenting the love he obviously felt for Caroline. Some afternoons when Caroline thought he was working, Judith had seen him walking by himself, just needing solitude. She understood Caroline very well, saw the unhappiness that Caroline was

205

hiding, the way she turned to the baby, pouring on to Charlie the love which Michael only needed half the time, talking to the baby constantly and building her life round each tiny new accomplishment.

'Charlie smiled today, Michael.'

'The flower buds are just about to form.'

'A real smile, not wind!'

'It's so calm at the moment, Gautier is worried. He senses bad weather.'

'He's looking at you, Michael . . .'

'I must remember to order the Bordeaux mixture!'

Judith watched them together and listened to them with a kind of fascinated pity. She saw that they loved each other and thought, as she had so frequently before, that love was not always a good basis for a marriage. She left at the beginning of June and Caroline was sad to see her go. She had enjoyed Judith's company. She had enjoyed having someone to talk to.

Kate and Clive were married on April the twentieth in Kate's village church with six bridesmaids and a tent in the garden of the Old Vicarage. The wedding was a culmination of several bewildering months for Kate. She was on a conveyor belt. She dismissed all doubts as childish. If they wouldn't go away, she hid them against Clive, in his bed, in his laughter, in the strength and confidence he emanated. She had decided she was an incomplete person, desperately needing his strength. Besides, she was so busy, there was no time to think. Her life was so full of the details of the wedding and there was no time to question the basic decision.

The garden was looking wonderful. Gabriel had lost half a stone worrying and Ben had retreated into a sarcastic corner. On the day, Clive was in his element, making a very funny speech, surrounded by his friends. Kate wore a lace dress, a neat white bonnet; the marquee roared and quivered until six when Clive and Kate changed and drove to London, spending the night in the Royal Lancaster Hotel and the following morning flying to Greece.

The honeymoon was a great success. Kate felt utterly lost, bewildered, unable to believe in any of it; she turned to Clive for everything and he responded, feeling himself to be all the things he most wanted to be for a woman. Also they both needed a holiday. Clive had two sets of friends they visited when they wanted company. He seemed to have friends everywhere, Kate thought. When they returned to London they moved into Rose Walk although the house was only half organized. Clive had had a good offer for his flat. On Monday morning they drove to work together and Kate tried to convince herself that this was how it would be from now on. She felt uncomfortably serious. She began to try and change herself into the person she imagined she should become.

A few days after Judith returned to London she came and had dinner with Clive and Kate at the new house, parking in the quiet street and looking up at the red brick house. Kate opened the front door, eagerly showing her round, the cellar and the bedrooms, the top floor.

'You sound unconvincing,' Judith said. 'Do you really like living here?'

Kate shrugged, deflated. 'I don't know yet. I like the fact that it's a real house, solid and strong, with a hall and a garden but I have never thought much about houses. I hate the wallpaper I've chosen in this hall. I meant it to look smart. Now I'd like to paint it white but Clive just laughs, tolerantly, and asked me to live with it for a bit!' She took Judith into the kitchen and poured her a glass of wine. 'People keep asking us to dinner. There are a thousand young married couples round here and they nearly all have small babies or are expecting and everyone knows everyone. They all have dogs and the same kind of pram and they are all pretty!'

Judith was laughing . . . 'And now you're one of them!'

'How could I ever be one of them? They give dinner parties

without being afraid! They all long for a drink when the baby's in bed and talk about their husbands and schools. Of course, they all love Clive. He's a great success at the dinner parties while I sit, speaking when I'm spoken to and watching the husband of the one Clive happens to be flirting with, wondering whether he ought to try something reciprocal with me! They all think, "What does that attractive man see in that pathetic little mouse?" So I wait for an opportunity and suddenly zap them with something really funny or sarcastic and Clive laughs, because they are too surprised to laugh, and he covers up for me! What are you doing?'

'I'm counting your complexes! Give me another drink and take a breath and something is boiling over!'

'Oh God!' Kate mopped at the stove. 'You know, Clive is quite extraordinary. He doesn't seem to mind the chaos. I can't understand why not. It makes me feel terrible. The more depressed I get over it, the nicer he is . . . Please don't talk about Caroline too much. I just can't stand the comparison!'

'Well, he married you!' Judith said.

'Only because she turned him down!'

Clive came in at 7.30, still brooding over a violent argument with Jenny. He came into the kitchen, kissing Kate, smiling hello to Judith as he took off his jacket and poured himself a whisky. He had temporarily forgotten how very attractive she was. She was very brown and she wore a simple white dress.

Clive pulled out a chair and sat down, lighting a cigar. 'How was Jouvard?'

'Hard work. A new baby always is.'

'And Michael?'

'Obsessed with his vines.'

'And Caroline?' he asked, his voice a little quieter, looking directly at her because he knew she knew it all.

'Caroline is more involved and delighted with her baby than any woman I have worked for. She used my experience and questioned me constantly in the beginning but once she felt

208

confident she would hardly let me touch him. I think she needed my company more than anything. I enjoyed being there. It was warm and very beautiful and interesting. I liked the fruit and the cheeses and the quiet. She asked about you both. So did Michael.'

Clive tilted his chair back on its hind legs. He had started the conversation but now he wanted to talk about something else. He looked at the piled-up dishes in the sink and Kate followed his eyes.

'It's awful. How do these working women with kids manage?'
Clive laughed.

He likes it, Judith thought. He likes her helplessness. It is different. She needs him now . . . What will happen when Kate grows up?

She left quite early, driving herself back to Queensgate Gardens. The lease expired in August and she wanted to look for somewhere smaller, to share with Venn, but somewhere which was her own. She had enough money now for the premium on a small flat. Almost enough for a mortgage deposit. She put a Mozart Concerto into the cassette player and shut her eyes as she listened, her strong body reminding her she had not made love for almost three months. There were several men she could have rung but she wanted to be alone. Tonight, looking at Clive Holden, she realized again that she had made a mistake in letting him slip through her fingers without more effort. She knew he felt the attraction too but he would do nothing about it. He was playing the role of new husband to the hilt. Judith stretched her arms, arched her back, her face catlike and cruel. She would wait.

PART TWO

CHAPTER THIRTEEN

Jenny Jacobs was always the first to arrive at Mosaic, first to unlock the door and send the blinds springing upwards. She loved this half an hour of peace before the others came, feeling Mosaic was really her own, thinking about her day, how to protect Mosaic from the damage Clive Holden was inflicting. She took off her coat and altered the day on the calendar, still hardly used to the new year. Icy February rain slapped the windows and she went into the little storeroom and put on the kettle. She washed some cups, wiped the draining board of the sink. She cared about every detail of the company. Jenny lived alone in a flat by Holland Park and Marketing Mosaic was her life. As month followed month, she became more and more afraid that Clive would cut Mosaic from under her, leave it in pieces, shrug his wide shoulders and smile in the way she hated, and move on. Although she never showed it, the violent arguments she had had with Clive throughout the past eighteen months had upset her greatly especially as she sensed that Clive was acting half the time, enjoying the anger, seeing himself as the man with the right ideas constantly harassed by this small, ugly woman.

Jenny walked back into the showroom and looked at the dozen rocking clocks set out in a semi-circle on a display table in the centre of the room. She twisted her mouth. She could not believe in them. The tool for their injection-moulded plastic bodies had cost £2000. 'Mouldy-looking, aren't they?' Kate had said, desperately, when Jenny and Clive last clashed over this. The final costing of the Sundial had been almost as much. There was no doubt that it was a beautiful piece of engineering, as all Michael's designs were, but it cost too much. It sold too slowly. Its golden face had smiled from a lot of glossy magazines but the orders only trickled in. Jenny looked down at the rocking clocks, touching one with her finger as if it were contaminated. Perhaps, she thought, these ugly little bombs will sell? But she didn't believe it.

'Mosaic is an unpredictable animal,' she had said to Kate. They talked so much now. They had got to know each other well in the ten months that Kate had been here and Jenny found Kate efficient and interested and sympathetic. She watched Kate, changing herself, trying to drag herself into seriousness; she watched Kate try to accept Clive's patronage.

'He will not discuss money with me, Jenny. He changes the subject. I've typed so many rude letters to people who owe us money. I want to know how bad it is!'

They had spent a whole lunchtime, when Clive was out, going through the books. 'There is too much money owing to us. We badly need some new products. The interest on our overdraft is far too high but at the moment we're scraping through.'

Kate had nodded. She frowned, trying to look serious until Jenny had laughed at her expression. However hard she tried, it was always Kate, erupting into laughter, some terrible pun, some lovely slanted comment, who relieved the tension and depression that so often stiffened the offices now.

Jenny made herself a cup of coffee and took biscuits from a dented tin.

'If Clive allows Mosaic to get out of control,' she had said to Kate, 'it will swallow far too much capital. We have enough good lines to cover costs at the moment but we haven't paid for the injection moulding tool. I've realized, through the eighteen months that Clive has been running things, just how much Michael with his obsessive, pushing fascination, put into it. Michael would work all night if necessary; he would drive anywhere to look for a better movement. As I will, for a good order. Clive is a brilliant salesman and a natural talker but he wants the buyers to come to him! He detests trade shows but they are the backbone of the trade. The inflation of seventy-four, and especially the devastating increase in wages, has destroyed a great many small companies but mere survival doesn't seem to

212

mean anything!' She had stood up, staring down at Kate, a frown between her brows. 'He sees Mosaic purely as an investment, Kate! He expected it to lay him a golden egg and it isn't going to.'

'Can't you tell him?' Kate had said.

'Jesus. Why do you think we shout at each other?'

Remembering the conversation, Jenny ate a third biscuit, taking small bites like a rabbit. This morning buyers and journalists were coming to look at the rocking clocks. Clive was confident, or outwardly so. Jenny was not.

Nancy and Tessa, the two secretaries, arrived just after nine. Bill Carter at ten past. Clive and Kate came at nine forty-five, only minutes before the first buyer arrived, and by ten the showroom was full. Kate was handing round coffee and Clive was dispensing a lot of smooth talk.

'We're very, very excited about them.'

'You're taking them to the trade fair at Torquay this week?'

'Yes, I'm leaving this afternoon.'

'He can't wait,' Kate said, and they all laughed, even Clive, after a first frown. No one enjoyed trade shows except Jenny but no one disliked them as much as Clive. They circled the rocking clocks warily. They spoke of market resistance to anything too unusual. They placed some small orders. By eleven, they were all gone. Just a lot of coffee cups. It was hardly the ecstatic reception Clive had anticipated.

Kate helped him to pack up the clocks, to load them into the back of his car. A small suitcase was on the back seat. He was to be away three nights. He stood by the car, put his arm round Kate, kissed her tenderly. 'Take care of yourself . . .' Every goodbye was a love scene if someone was watching, Kate thought and then hated herself.

'Enjoy the wet palm trees and the coloured lights.' She tucked her hands into her pockets. It was cold in the street. 'Will you ring me?'

'Yup. Probably tomorrow night.' The thought of three days

213

in Torquay filled him with alternate misery and elation. 'Don't get tired, will you?'

'Only at night.' She waved. She watched the red B.M.W. slice expertly into the traffic.

'I should like a baby, Clive,' she had said, last September.

'So soon?' He had smiled tolerantly. He so often smiled at her like that.

'Yes. Would you mind?'

'Not as long as it's mine.' He had ruffled her hair, holding her. 'But where would you put it? And could you cope? You can hardly manage yourself . . .' He had laughed.

'Of course I could cope! Everyone does!' So she stopped taking the pill. She wrote herself lists. Lists of when to clean which room in the house, lists of food for the larder, plans for the week, lists of lists. She bought note-books, books on babies, books on food and read no more than the first few pages. She studied her naked body and found she agreed with Clive. Where would she put it?

But a baby would make me belong, she thought. I would be part of them all. I could join in their conversations. I wouldn't sit on the edge, despising them and trying not to say something nasty. I would lose this terrible feeling that it is all temporary, that Clive is just being nice to me for a while. When Clive got back, she would know. She shivered.

'What are you doing, standing in the street?' Jenny said.

'Thinking.' She smiled and came in.

'A man has just rung. A Henri Bertrand. Friend of Michael's who was coming last November and didn't for some reason. He'll try and come in this evening. I wondered if you'd mind closing up? I'm going out.'

'I don't mind at all. I'm in no hurry to go home. I still don't like being on my own!'

'Who does?' Jenny said.

At 5.30, as Jenny went, Kate pulled down the blinds against the black London winter night and dusted the display stand where the one remaining rocking clock crouched like a black beetle. She poured herself a glass of sherry and sat down, wondering how long to wait for Henri Bertrand. It was extraordinary to have an empty evening ahead. Their lives were so busy, packed with over-lapping events. Always too many letters to write, rushing to catch the post, late for a party, late for a meeting, shopping to do, apologizing for a delivery that had gone astray, a telephone message that didn't get passed on; red demand bills, covering for Clive, long telephone conversations with Gabriel, one-way, Kate 'yes' and 'no'; arriving late for Sunday lunch with Clive's parents and Clive's father back on the same old topic—Clive's insanity at leaving Bonnington's; a short weekend at the Old Vicarage, with Clive so absurdly uneasy in the country, his clothes looking wrong, too smart, desperately waiting for the pub to open, marching down the street, ordering pints of beer for anyone he struck up a conversation with and all the time uneasy until he was back in London. Both Kate and Clive deliberately wore this air of intense activity.

If I had a baby, Kate thought now in this quiet room, coiling her body, thinking in a whisper, Clive would love it and I would, and my mother would and my father would, in the end, and we might all, one day, stand in a room and love it and be nice to each other! She rested her hand on her hollow stomach, trying to feel something.

She was dragged out of these most secret thoughts as the door opened and a man came in. A slight man, brown-haired, with a kind face. 'Is Clive Holden here?' he said, closing the door, putting down a suitcase.

'I'm afraid not.' Kate stood up and came towards him. 'Are you Michael's friend? Henri Bertrand?'

'Yes.' He held out his hand.

'I'm Kate Holden. You're a little late. We expected you last autumn!'

He smiled. 'I came then but these things weren't ready. Can I leave them now?'

'Of course. Can I see them?'

He opened the suitcase and took out a dozen different bags, all made from his distinctive flowered cottons, gathered on to gilt or wooden fastenings. Tiny, plastic-lined bags for make-up and larger sponge bags; handbags and a big shoulder bag which Kate picked out at once and tried on.

'This is lovely.'

'On you it looks like a sleeping bag! I knew it was too big!'

She laughed, turning to look at him, liking his face. 'Clive comes back on Friday. I'm sure he'll like them.'

'I hope so. I have signed an agreement with the Mary May people to sell my dresses, scarves and shirts but they very sensibly stick to certain limits and don't want these as yet.' He took cigarettes from the pocket of his jacket. 'Do you smoke?'

'Sometimes. Not now.' She put the big shoulder bag down rather reluctantly. 'Would you like a drink?'

'You're not in a hurry?'

'No. Clive is away. I was waiting for you, wasting time.' She led him through to the second room and opened the cupboard Clive had installed. 'We have everything.'

'Whisky?'

'Yes. Soda? Water? Ginger ale?'

'Ice?'

'Yes.' She poured him a drink and refilled the sherry glass, sitting on the edge of Clive's desk and putting an ashtray by Henri.

'This place feels peculiar without Michael.'

'None of us realized quite how much it was his. Or how much he put into it.' She was silent for a moment. 'How are Michael and Caroline?' she asked finally.

'She is delighted with the child. Her life revolves around him. You didn't know them well?'

'No.'

'She has found it difficult to settle in France. Her French is all right now but Michael hates parties. They know people but . . .'

216

Henri shrugged. 'Michael is fascinated by his vines. He has outraged all the traditionalists. I wish I had a fraction of his confidence. I worry about everything. I worry about worrying.'

'But you are very successful?'

'So I worry about how long it will last. Should I expand? Should I have bought a dyeing works? Have I enough money to carry through my expansion? What I really enjoy, Kate, is doing little flower paintings and then working them into a fabric design and choosing the colours. And I enjoy my house. The rest should be happening to someone else.' He paused. There was a silence. They smiled, registering the liking between them. His eyes were dark brown, she saw. 'This is delicious whisky.'

She sighed. 'I think we spend far too much on details like that but Clive goes mad when I say so. Especially as I don't drink whisky!'

'Are you having difficulty with Mosaic? The French newspapers insinuate that half the small companies in Britain are going broke!'

'Well, all today I wrote letters to people who owe us money. Everyone delays payment till the last possible moment. Luckily Clive, having been a solicitor, is good at threatening letters. They even frighten me while I'm typing them!' They both laughed. 'The rent and the telephone and electricity bills get bigger all the time,' Kate went on. 'But I don't really know how bad things are. We're still busy.'

Henri made no comment, thinking how attractively this small girl held her head, used her body and her face, liking the straight, smooth haircut and the husky voice. 'The last time I came here, Michael had just met Caroline,' he said, almost to himself.

'You know about all that? Michael and Caroline and Clive?'

'Yes. Caroline talks to me a great deal. She needs a friend. Michael is an impossible man in many ways. Sometimes I feel I must say something, but what? She has told me so much about herself and Michael and Clive and you. Don't leave yourself out!'

Kate shrugged. 'I was just incidental. I wasn't the cause of anything.'

Henri put out his cigarette and stood up, looking at Kate for a moment, head bent. 'If you are really doing nothing this evening, would you have dinner with me? I've been in London for five nights and I hate eating alone! I want to try a restaurant in Battersea which the Finches recommended. You probably know them? They came to Jouvard last year, after the harvest, and they liked the area so much they want to try and buy a farmhouse to renovate if they can. But I have talked right past the question.'

'I'd love to have dinner with you,' Kate said, and it was true.

As they moved back through the showroom to go out Henri touched the one remaining rocking clock. It spun and caught the light.

'Do you like it?' Kate asked.

'Not really.'

'They are such a risk. As the Sundial was. They have cost so much to produce.' She looked down at it. 'I don't know how much. Clive doesn't tell me. It's bad for a husband and wife to work together. You see all the defeats. You can't come home and pretend to each other.' She was embarrassed then, having said too much, and pushed her arms into her long tweed coat and turned out the lights. Kate's car was parked in Meadwell Street and she unlocked it and leaned over to open the passenger door. 'You won't mind if we go home first? I'd like to change.'

'How far is it? I'm a very nervous passenger.' He put out his hands and grasped the dashboard in mock terror as Kate started the car.

She turned and looked into his face. 'You're joking, aren't you?' She saw the smile, the deep lines which bracketed his mouth. She suddenly remembered the thoughts she had once

218

tried to explain to David, her fear of not meeting the people she would need at the right time, of meeting them too late.

The Finches were right. It was an attractive restaurant with very good food. Henri talked about his work, moving his hands, moving his expressive face. 'No one is more surprised than I by my success. I turned to this whole business out of despair when my marriage collapsed. I couldn't stand living in the city any more. I was never a good doctor. I took a gamble because I really didn't care very much and for some extraordinary reason it has all worked out for me. I hardly needed so much. I would be happy designing for someone else but you can't stop something like this. Now I have bought a stone dyeing works in the mountains, about forty kilometres away, a great stone building covered with ivy. They used to spin silk there. It is quite fascinating inside. Massive machinery and pipes and steam; all the time the sound of running water, wonderful pure mountain water. And the driers humming and machines folding and rolling and winding the fabric on to bolts.' He leaned forward, smiling. 'They have records of the secret ingredients to make the most subtle tints. At last I can translate on to cotton the colours I paint on the designs!'

'I'd love to see it,' Kate said. 'My father told me, when I said about marrying Clive, that I hadn't been anywhere. I thought he was mad. I wasn't brave enough anyway. Now that I have a bit more confidence and curiosity it's too late!'

'Why? You could come, with Clive, for a holiday.'

'I don't think he'd ever go to Jouvard. I don't think, even now, he could bear to see them together.'

Henri frowned. 'I'm sure that isn't true. He is married to you now. People forget.'

'But it still feels temporary to me,' she said quietly, finding the words came almost by themselves, had formed from thoughts she rarely allowed to surface. 'Nine months.' She spread her small, thin-fingered hands on the table, looking at

219

the rings. 'Clive has looked after me and I think we've been happy. Judith said I was like someone trying on various roles but that's too simple. I had to marry Clive, once he'd asked me. I had to burrow. I thought it would all simplify when we were married but it hasn't. Sometimes I feel like jumping up and down, screaming at him, "Tell me . . . tell me about things." I am protected.'

'How can he confide fears he may not even admit to himself? Clive puts on many different faces even to himself I imagine.'

Kate sighed. 'Is everybody's life a series of violent zig-zags? I struggled out of my mother's protective custody and lurched towards David and was pathetic and miserable when he lost interest and cowered against Clive . . .' She gave him one of her self-mocking smiles.

'I think you are much too critical of yourself, Kate.'

'Now I think that when I have a baby I will believe in it all and belong.'

'I wanted a child. Not Colette. At the time I believed it was because I loved her so much that I wanted us to have a baby. I had a mass of beautiful ideas. Now, looking back, I realize that I thought it would secure Colette. Instead it enraged her. She was afraid of getting fat, actually terrified of it. Afraid of the demands a baby would make. Luckily, Françoise passed through her mother's body without damaging it. Since we have been divorced Françoise spends the term time in Paris with her mother and an assortment of men I hate if I happen to meet them, and the holidays with me. I see how this division hurts her. I adore her but when I watch her trying to pull us together I wish she had never been born.'

Kate shivered, knowing exactly what he meant. 'But it can be just as bad having two parents live together for the child's sake, thinking they hide their unhappiness when in fact you see everything. Every pretence, every scene that waits until after bedtime. Nothing is worse than that. Better to live apart, give the child something positive to be sad about.' She raised her eyes to

220

Henri's face. 'I wish you hadn't told me. You've scared me. You've made me want to wait, to prove Clive and I together first.'

'I didn't mean to.' He took one of her hands. 'And why shouldn't you be all right, you and Clive?'

She didn't answer. She was aware of an extraordinary regret, so sad it could have brought tears to her eyes. 'Tell me more about Provence instead.'

He talked about his home, drawing pictures with words. The hours ran smoothly into one another and however lightly they tried to speak, seriousness kept edging in. There was such sympathy in him, Kate felt, and yet such lightness.

'Has there been no one since your divorce?'

'No one. Six lonely years!' His eyes laughed.

'No one you love but plenty of company?'

'Yes. But one gets tired of company which comes and goes. My own fault. I am scared.'

She looked round, surprised to see how empty the restaurant was, to realize how late it was. Henri paid the bill and they put on their coats and went out into the street. A cold wind flicked at them. He put an arm along her shoulders as they went to the car and Kate drove him back to the small hotel in the Cromwell Road where he was staying.

'You see . . . I am still cautious about spending money. I can't believe the success yet!' He turned his body to face her. 'I have enjoyed tonight very much, Kate.'

'So have I,' she said quietly.

He leaned across the car and touched her cheek with his lips. There was street light in the car. He took her hand, holding it for a moment, touching her fingers, and the intense sympathy between them was accepted and the regret that it could not be built on.

'We'll write to you. About the things you left . . .'

He nodded. 'Perhaps I'll see you later in the year?' And then his face changed, was almost impatient. He kissed her hand and got out of the car, standing with his collar turned up as he watched her drive away.

Kate drove home slowly, let herself into a silent house, clenched her hands and drove them into her stomach, realizing at last the enormity of the rules she had laid down for herself. That her body was no longer her own, to be given as she wished. That there could be a baby. That the years were now roughly planned. Clive, in control. Herself, following after. Even in bed, Clive was always in control, never the first to go sliding down into orgasm. She remembered David. Love-making with him had been far more equal, exciting each other, inexperienced as she was. There were times when it went wrong, when he came too soon, when she was quite detached, when he rolled towards her, 'Sorry, Kitty . . .' It never mattered. It was his presence that satisfied and there would always be tomorrow night.

God, I don't want this for ever, she thought, wandering the big silent house. 'What have I done?' Praying it was all a mistake and there was no child and there would be time to think, lying awake for a long time, thinking of the long, kind face, the gentle smile, the sympathy, wondering how much Clive really wanted her, wondering all the things she should have thought many months before.

The following morning Kate learned that she was pregnant.

On the morning of Clive's return a large order of the Pharaoh range was being packed for shipment to America and the back room was crowded with cardboard boxes. Everyone was helping, enclosing the pyramids in their polystyrene liners and black boxes, folding guarantees, labelling. Clive came in, putting down the boxes of samples he had taken.

'How was it?' Jenny asked, as Kate came forward and Clive kissed her cheek.

'Bloody tiring.'

'And the orders?' She knew she was cross-examining but she had to know.

'Not very good. They may be slow starters.' He sat down on the desk, his whole manner expressing unconcern. 'Sold half a dozen Sundials when I should have sold fifty but a lot of your photograph frames.' A mood of depression began to slow everyone up.

'How many rocking clocks?'

'About fifty.' They had hoped to sell four hundred.

The day was long, boring, tiring, no chance for Kate to tell him. He was silent in the car as they drove home, letting them into Rose Walk and going straight to the sitting-room, pouring a large drink, asking if Kate wanted one, sitting down heavily and dragging his tie loose.

'Did you like Henri's things?' Kate asked, hovering.

'Yes, at first glance. Has he gone back?'

'Yes, I said we'd write.'

'Did he say how Mike is? And Caroline?'

'He said they were well.'

'They don't like the rocking clocks,' Clive said suddenly.

'But it's so soon . . .'

'I should have had far bigger orders.'

'Jenny says we . . .'

'I don't give a damn what she says!'

Kate flushed, turning away to hide the hurt as she now tried to hide all her moods from him, hiding from Clive, as she tried to be adult and sensible, the very parts of herself he found most endearing.

'Let's go out,' he said suddenly, springing to his feet and going to the telephone. 'Anywhere you like, Katy.' There had been a girl in Torquay. 'Somewhere special.' A girl from a company which marketed leather goods. 'Regardless of cost!' Clive had slept with her all three nights. 'Smile, Katy! How about Dante's?' He had expected to feel guilt, or at least unease. He had felt nothing but intense enjoyment of her sexuality and her big, soft body. He had felt himself come alive again. Kate was watching him, small and pale and slightly desperate.

223

'I wish we could have a short holiday, Clive. I'd love to go and see Jouvard and Henri's place . . .' She stood so straight, he thought.

'We haven't the time or the money to spare.'

'My father said yesterday, on the telephone, that he'd love to give us a holiday.'

'I said we haven't time!' Taking things from Ben Neale humiliated Clive. From Gabriel it was acceptable. Taking from Ben underlined Clive's inability to provide for Kate as her father had. His voice was so hard and cold that Kate left the room, went upstairs for a bath.

They went to Dante's. Everyone was laughing, looking at each other. The restaurant was very hot and Kate tried to hide her weariness. She wasn't hungry enough to appreciate the very expensive food and only picked at the elaborate pudding Clive ordered for her, a kind of joke, remembering the first time. They met friends and went on to Annabelle's and stayed till three.

Kate sat, neatly holding a drink she didn't want, while the men each side of her discussed shipping across her. Apathetically she watched Clive dance with one of their blonde wives, a girl who angled her body against his, brushing him constantly. Kate's mind was absolutely clear, too tired for pretence. She wanted to go back and start again. She saw the future. The house. A child which would take away, temporarily, the one really enjoyable part of her life—working at Mosaic. Clive's head moved close to the blonde head. She could almost feel the tension. She knew he would laugh about the girl later in the car, make nothing of it. She saw a lifetime of looking the other way, of wondering when he would begin to respond.

When Clive came to sit down, hot and smiling, all Kate's tiredness became anger and she moved close to him and took his hand. 'Can we go home?'

'Are you tired, love?'

'Yes.'

He turned his head the other way. Kate imagined his expression of regret, perhaps his lips forming a slight kiss, as if they played a game, Clive and the blonde girl, way over her head. As the men discussed shipping. She closed her eyes and a wave of fury took her and made her dig her fingers into Clive's arm.

'I've been trying to tell you all day. We're going to have a baby.'

His head swung back her way. Amazement flickered in his face and disbelief and pride. 'Kate . . .' And then he was into the role he loved best, kissing her tenderly, ordering champagne, shouting . . . standing up, pulling Kate to her feet, then sitting her down carefully. 'I forgot you were finding out this week . . .' Kate met the blonde girl's eyes and gave her a prim smile. She leaned across. She wanted to say, 'Don't look so defeated. It's not the sort of trump card you can play very often!'

Gabriel was amazed, upset, driving to London at once to see how Kate looked. Clive's parents were quietly pleased and his sister rang to congratulate them with her two small children screaming in the background. Everyone at Mosaic was as pleased as if it were their own baby.

'I think,' Jenny said, 'we should run a line of rubber ducks for the autumn. When is it due, Kate?'

'July.'

By the end of the month it was obvious, a neat round lump. The rest of Kate's body did not change. She fastened her jeans with big safety pins and bought some loose shirts. She felt absolutely normal. It seemed that even in this she was to be denied the big change. Her narrow, tight muscled body contained the baby closely. She would not stop working, she said, until she had to.

In March she visited Judith in the new flat. It was in a smart little mews, on the first floor, four rooms over a large garage,

Judith had made it look exactly as she wanted, like a magazine illustration; nothing matching but everything going together; a lot of cushions; one or two striking modern paintings; some big lamps; a pine kitchen.

'It's fantastic,' Kate said. 'How can you afford all this?'

'I work,' Judith said. 'They pay me a lot. They give me things.' She was a little fatter, creamier, her face settled now. She wore little make-up but exaggerated her slanted eyes and she still had the heavy fringe, the thick silky hair. 'The last one gave me a fur coat.' She ran her hand lovingly along the back of the small velvet sofa. 'I sold it. I looked silly in it . . .'

'And that one who killed herself? She was one of yours, wasn't she?'

'Yes. It was inevitable really. She wasn't equipped for life. Pathetic. She tried once while I was there . . .'

Kate probed the story, full of curiosity. 'But why? Was she Eaton Square?'

'Yes, with the older husband. So possessive. Watching and watching her, waiting to catch her out . . .' Judith sat down, folded her arms behind her head.

'You must have known what she did. Did she have lovers?'

'One.' Judith laughed. 'I found them together quite by accident. I took the baby out for the day. I was taking him to the grandparents in Hampstead. I left his feeds in the fridge. I went back. You've never seen such guilty people. She thought I was her husband. Stupid girl. She loved her husband I think. People are so weak . . .'

'Was she afraid? That you would mention it?'

Judith turned her head slowly. 'Very afraid,' she said quietly. She changed the subject.

'You look all right now, Kate. You're organized, are you?'

'I don't know. They all expect me to be thrilled. My mother buys endless little white knitted things and nags me to re-decorate a bedroom for it and Clive's mother takes me to lunch once a week and everyone knows it will be a boy. And all the people

226

round us wait, smiling. How will I learn to mop faces and change nappies and gossip outside the nursery school? And learn to complain in that subtle way because I've been kept awake all night but I don't mind and my husband doesn't take any interest but I don't mind that either because it shows he's male and concerned with the real world, which is outside the home, but of course I, being a woman, know the real world is really where I am!'

'Give in,' Judith said.

'Why should I? I hate the gynaecologist. He is so pleased. Everyone is pleased. All the books are pleased. The gynaecologist congratulates me for not putting on much weight. I wish I could. I want to feel different. God, I hate his smooth, soothing manner.'

'You wanted it,' Judith said flatly.

'I know.'

Underneath everything, like a background noise, was the knowledge that Marketing Mosaic was sinking more and more deeply into difficulty. The rocking clocks did not sell. Everything was depressed. Interest rates climbed steadily. She knew these things because she filed the carbons of letters, not because Clive told her. As pregnancy exaggerated her character, she became more volatile, less inhibited, turning to Clive in the evenings. 'How are things? Please tell me.' She felt a primitive fear, a longing for security for the unborn baby. She hated the way Clive shuffled the bills into a heap, laughed, put them aside; she watched him on the telephone, saw that he still half enjoyed the crises, using his wits to get them out of corners, always managing, through his expertise as a salesman, to pull off a sale just before the month end when wages were due. They walked a precarious tightrope.

The summer was wet. Kate longed for a definite season, some division between autumn and spring, as she longed for definition in her life, but it did not come. There were some good days but not enough to build up into a genuine summer, not enough

227

to feel them round you, to be secure in the warmth. In the eighth month she stopped going in to Mosaic. She was uncomfortable now, ungainly and slow. The days were long and damp and dull and she had nothing to do but wait.

CHAPTER FOURTEEN

Kate's baby did not want to be born. 'It's not stupid,' Kate said. 'It knows it's better off in there!' In the end it took over her slight body completely making her grotesque, a stomach on legs. She was sleepy all the time but could not sleep well. Far too late to regret it or question it. It was Kate. Ten days after it should have arrived, just after Kate's twenty-second birthday, Clive drove her to hospital. It was a Wednesday evening. 'I don't want it to come tonight,' Kate said. 'Wednesday's child is full of woe!'

Clive went upstairs with her, as uneasy as she was, disliking the smell of the place and the feeling that everywhere, behind screens and closed doors, things were happening which you would not be told about. Kate held a bunch of rosebuds which Clive had bought her. He had also given her a beautiful night-gown of fine blue cotton and lace, and slippers because she never wore any. He watched her, his expression tender, and she tried very hard to respond but his attitude filled her with misery. She didn't want this loving concern. She wanted to be diverted, not treated like a mental patient. The fact that Clive was still buying her flowers and presents that she not only didn't want but that positively depressed her, underlined to Kate how little they understood each other.

A brisk nurse came in and told Clive to take away all Kate's valuable things. 'We lose a lot of stuff. We can't help it . . . don't keep more money than you need for newspapers, Mrs Holden.' Clive took away her gold chain and her cheque book and credit cards and she felt stripped for execution. Her teeth chattered. Clive stayed a little while, watching the television with her, then kissed her and left. Kate wandered round the room, opened the sliding door and looked at the lavatory and bidet and shower, went and sat in the hard armchair and looked out of the windows. Opposite her the lights of a tall building came on and went off in random patterns and on the television Shirley Bassey was singing, *Jesse, come home*, and the melody competed with the sounds of the traffic. The curtains were thin, a gesture against the night. Kate paced the room, tripping over the new nightgown, uneasy in it. It was made for a different type of woman. It would have suited Caroline, she thought.

She was afraid. She really didn't know what to expect. Her teeth chattered again and she rang Gabriel.

'They will induce in the morning. Judith says I must have an epidural. All the women she has worked for who have had them say they are wonderful. And you can still push . . .' What did it mean? Push how? She had been to classes but it was so unreal.

At 9.30 they offered her cocoa and a sleeping pill. She refused the pill, thinking of the night which had started it all, the night Clive found her with her hands full. She did want this baby, didn't she? Clive's baby? She couldn't sleep. She lay on her back, looking at the mound of her stomach, thinking of the unknown baby she had lived with for nine months. It kicked hard. Kate spread her fingers over her stomach, pulling up the nightgown, wanting to see through the skin, trying to make it feel wanted, apologizing to it for the way she had so disliked the pregnancy.

The telephone rang and it was Clive. 'Are you all right, love?'

'Yes. Will you come in the morning when things get started?'

'Yes.' Clive knew more about it than she did. He had come to the fathers' class. He had been a great success, asking questions, being funny . . .

They woke her at seven and dressed her in a white nightgown open all down the back. Nothing to eat or drink. They took her to a room with a lot of terrifying-looking equipment and sat her on a very high table on wheels and a woman anaesthetist came and chatted and then put an injection into Kate's spine. The feeling was indescribably horrible. Her legs went

230

mottled like uncooked sausages and the anaesthetist kept testing them with a pin for feeling and Kate could still feel. She apologized constantly, already it seemed, doing it wrong. She felt very faint. At last the anaesthetist was satisfied and the gynaecologist came with his jokes and his white bath hat to break the waters and Kate lay down legs apart, looking up at the ceiling with its big round light, looking sideways at the cylinders of oxygen and gas. She felt him and yet did not feel him. He chatted to Sister. Kate closed her eyes and wished it could all be different, that she could have gone away somewhere by herself and waited for the baby to start coming, to feel gradually the birth increase in strength. But here they talked across her as if she were deaf and joked about the wet summer.

Quite suddenly everything changed. She was aware that something was wrong. The routine atmosphere had vanished. There was an abrupt silence and they all drew a little nearer. She looked at the three faces and saw a very frightening seriousness. The Sister was mopping between her legs and then, to reassure her, they all smiled at once but Sister moved to a telephone and rang the operating theatre and the anaesthetist left the room and a nurse came in and she was running.

The gynaecologist came and stood by Kate's head. 'Something rather unusual has happened, Mrs Holden, but don't be alarmed . . . Nurse, will you please telephone Doctor Harrod and say I shall need him and take a blood sample for cross-matching . . . Instead of breaking the membranes as is normal, I have unfortunately cut into the placenta. This means it is below the baby and the baby cannot be born naturally. We will do a Caesarean and we'll do it quickly.' Her teeth chattered violently as she picked up the tension from him. She was terribly afraid. Afraid of dying. For herself and the baby, hardly considered before, now absolutely real. Afraid because of the obvious hurry. Hurried feet down the corridor, pushing through the swing doors, lifting her on to a trolley, asking her to sign a form and she couldn't spell Caesarean and she couldn't remember

231

Clive's telephone number but they smiled and said it didn't matter, they'd have it downstairs. They took blood from her arm and someone shaved between her legs but she felt nothing and they pushed her down the corridor, almost running now and into a lift, upwards and out and along another corridor, all seen crazily from flat on her back, and the fear was so big now it shook all through her. They were all so busy, so hurried . . .

'Now, Kate.' It was the woman anaesthetist, a sudden calm face, bending down, stilling the terror. 'Don't be afraid. We are hurrying because of the baby, because we have cut into the placenta and you are bleeding but in five minutes it will all be over and your baby will be delivered. I shall put an anaesthetic in the tube in your spine and you will sleep instantly.' She took Kate's hand and the comfort of the gesture, although she was a total stranger, was enormous. 'Don't be afraid.'

She lay so flat and they moved so fast around her. She looked up at their strange masked faces. No smiles. Just a few seconds when she thought, If I die now, God, I've done nothing . . . And then a shuddering in her ears and oblivion.

At first she was aware of a vibrating sound which gradually formed into words and made, 'She's awake now.' There was such pain in her stomach and she couldn't open her eyes because of the tiredness pressing down. Clive's voice came. 'Kate. It's a little girl.' And she made an enormous effort to take his hand and lay for an indeterminate length of time alternately aware of his voice or his hand or the pain or the violent shivering but not able to register more than one thing at a time.

When she woke properly she was back in the thin curtained room and she saw a large upturned bottle of blood and was surprised how dark it was. Dark red in the transparent tube which ran into her hand. Clive in a chair by the window reading a newspaper. She thought of sitting up but the whole of her lower stomach was a band of pain and she didn't want to move it. 'Clive.'

232

He got up, folding the newspaper, coming to stand by her, bending to kiss her. 'Hello . . . What do you mean by causing all this panic?'

'I'm sorry.'

He stroked her forehead with great tenderness. She looked so small and white. It seemed that fate intended Kate to reach out for him, again and again.

'Have you seen the baby?'

'Yes. She looks like you.'

'Poor little thing.'

'She's quite perfect.'

She was a small, pretty baby, untouched as all Caesarean babies are by the struggle to be born, merely lifted into the world, surprised out of the warm, wet darkness. Kate saw little of her for the first few days. She only wanted sleep but they kept coming and making her to move, making her get up despite the festoons of tubes connected to her body. They were so pleased when she tried. They were kind. It was like being a child again herself. She recovered quickly. She was young and strong. Outwardly everyone was delighted. She gave the baby her bottles, holding her warily and trying to feel the love they had so smugly predicted. But it was hard to believe this baby had come from her body. She had no memories of pain or birth. Just fear and oblivion and 'here-you-are, Kate. Baby.'

Kate found herself a celebrity now, having done something unexpected. Relays of visitors came, exhausting her after ten minutes. She was trapped in the bed while they circled her, talked at her, bursting with news for her; Gabriel and Ben, Clive's parents, Alice and Venn, the Finches and Judith. Flowers came every day. The tubes went away. They allowed her to bath, to wash her hair, and to be clean was one of the most wonderful sensations of her life. Gabriel said she had found a nurse to come and help and Kate was thankful, still alternately delighted and terrified by the baby.

'What are you calling her?' Judith said, sitting on the end of

233

Kate's bed and eating her grapes.

'Melanie Sarah.'

'So now it's happy ever after, back to Putney. Lovely baby, nice house, husband, everything settled?'

'I wish you could have come to look after it for a bit.'

'Perhaps I know you too well. Anyway, I'm off to Jouvard again. Haven't they told you? Caroline is pregnant again. Apparently it's rather touch and go and she's been told to rest a lot. So I'm going out to help. I'm looking forward to it.' She got off the bed and the door opened and Clive came in.

'Congratulations.' Judith looked up at him with her slanted eyes. 'Your daughter is lovely.' Her eyes moved over his face. 'I've got some books in the car for you, Kate . . .'

'I'll come and get them,' Clive said, going with her into the passage and following her down wide stairs, watching the way she moved, strongly, springing from the ground with each step. She would be lithe and strong. She unlocked her car.

'So you're off to Jouvard again?'

'Yes.'

'New car?'

'No, I bought it last year and it was secondhand then but I nurture it.' She opened the car door, leaned inside and brought out a bag of paperbacks. She held it against her body. She stood still.

'And you have a new flat?'

'Yes. One by one I'm working through my list of status symbols!'

'What's next?' He put an arm on the roof of her car, leaning on it. It seemed a lifetime since he had talked to a woman like this, slowed himself down.

She shrugged and held out the books and their hands touched. 'Look after Kate. It takes a while to get over a Caesarean . . . When I get back I'll come and see you.' She climbed into the car, shut the door and wound down the window. They both wanted to go on talking. She smiled up at Clive. 'I'll ring

Kate before I go,' she said and reversed slowly out of her parking space. She watched him in her mirror and, as always, was aware of intense regret. But she comforted herself by thinking she would probably get a second chance. She could not see Clive and Kate satisfying each other for more than a few polite years.

For the first six weeks Kate was protected, at first by the hospital and then the nurse. She rested as they told her to. She learned to bath her baby, mix feeds and establish routines. Melanie was a good baby, sleeping for long stretches, eating well. There was little excuse then. Kate told herself, for the misery. It came quite unexpectedly, dropping over her like a black hood. It was concerned with the baby and the casual way she and Clive had given it life, almost without thought; concerned with the blood and chaos of her body, with the helplessness of the baby and herself. What was she born for? To feel misery as Kate had felt it for David? To feel lost and hopeless like this? It seemed the most appalling cruelty to inflict life on such a perfect thing. Melanie learned to smile. She had creamy skin and thick dark hair like Clive's and his shaped eyes. The nurse was in her forties, kept the baby immaculate and fussed rather soothingly round Kate. The first time Kate went out in the street, walking to the Post Office in the Upper Richmond Road and feeling quite hollow with weakness, she was afraid. The cars scared her and she was afraid of falling down, collapsing in the street, so terrified that she sweated all the time and could not speak for a few moments when the woman behind the counter asked her what she wanted. She bought a stamp, the wrong sort, and went home, her knees trembling.

'Are you all right, Mrs Holden?' the nurse asked and Kate burst into tears.

They said she was still tired. Gabriel came to stay for a week after the nurse left and Kate tried very hard to give the impression that she was in control, even laughing sometimes, but inside she was channelled into one strong feeling. Fear. Of everything. The baby was just a part of it. She couldn't analyse the fear but it was concerned with not going away from the house in case the weakness attacked her and she collapsed. She couldn't mention it to Clive because it was inexplicable. She had always had it, underneath, in a small way, but now the underneath had taken over.

Jenny came to see her, bringing a large teddy bear and declining to hold the baby. 'I don't really like them but I'm sure she's lovely.' There was no reaction in Kate now, she thought. Whereas before she had been taut, responding and bouncing words back; now she hardly seemed to be listening. She absorbed sentences, like someone half asleep. Jenny stayed on to see Clive and drew him into his study.

'I can't sell them, Clive. I've tried bloody hard with those rocking clocks but they are like millstones round my neck. They are a constant stamp of failure in any collection I get together at any show. We shall become known as the people who market unsuccessful clocks. I think you should cut your losses. Scrap them and the Sundial. If Michael is still interested in it he can try and sell the bloody thing in France.'

'Like hell I'll scrap them!' Clive snapped. 'I'm paying interest on a five thousand pound overdraft for those damn things!'

'They won't sell! You can't make them sell!'

'I won't give up. I shall advertise them in a colour supplement. We'll try mail order.'

'They aren't suitable. They're too heavy.'

'You have never believed in them. You haven't given them a fair chance!'

'That's not true!' She stood up, her voice loud and furious.

'I'm sorry, Jenny.' He was suddenly aware of how much he needed her. 'I know that was unjust.' He gave her a slow smile.

Jenny was immune to all his smiles. 'So will you do as I ask, Clive? I will not take them to another show.'

'All right. But I will try advertising as a last resort.'

'It costs a bloody fortune, that colour supplement stuff.'

'I worry about the financial side, Jenny. That's my job.'

She let out her breath in a long sigh. 'Well, I don't want to go on working with you, Clive, if we are so absolutely divided on everything. It's too much of a strain.'

'Don't be dramatic, Jenny. You know you love working with Mosaic. It's virtually yours. I have put a lot of money into it. You can't begrudge me some ideas!'

She sat down, picked up the untouched drink which he had poured for her. 'All right. Try the advertising. But if it doesn't work, will you agree to throw out both lines?'

'Yes. I will.'

Kate, hovering, heard the voices grow calmer and opened the door. She looked like a small, pale child, face very thin. She held the baby. 'Do you want to stay to supper, Jenny?'

'No thanks. I must go.'

'That bloody woman,' Clive said. 'I wish to God I didn't need her!'

Now Kate was on her own, trying to make it work, trying to combat the terror which attacked immediately after Clive left in the morning. She began seeking out the people round her she had so scorned before, desperate to have someone with her or be with someone, afraid to be alone with the baby and not knowing why. She loathed the silence of the house. She was constantly on the telephone. She cried at the slightest thing.

Clive was bewildered. It was as if a quite different woman inhabited Kate's body. There was a small frown between her brows all the time. The house slipped through her helpless fingers.

Clive found Kate so difficult to talk to, let alone have a relationship with. There was no life in her, no response. Frequently she sat staring into space, twisting her fingers together. He tried not to think about it too much. He decided it would pass.

Rachel came, inviting herself to lunch, ready to mother Kate

237

and eager to look into Clive's life now. She brought the food. She tried not to show her amazement at the absolute chaos of the house. 'We've found ourselves a derelict farmhouse in Provence, Kate. A mas, they call it. It's a shell at the moment but it will be wonderful. Of course we'll have to wait until we can afford to renovate it but we can go and camp in the garden.' The idea of Rachel camping almost made Kate smile. 'It's about twenty minutes from Michael and Caroline, very isolated and surrounded by fields. The walls are solid stone, about two feet thick, and there's a well and a walled garden. More a walled jungle, in fact . . .'

Kate smiled politely. She felt now that she was only half with anyone. In the front of her mind were all the other things she should be doing and yet, when she had time, she finished nothing.

'And poor Caroline miscarried, which was sad, except that little Charlie is only one and they would have been so close; but she is unhappy about it. He's the most beautiful child, exactly like Caroline but rather strange. He sits very still. He is quite happy on his own, playing with bricks and things. He adores Caroline, of course.'

'Don't all small children adore their mothers?'

'I don't know, darling. I've never had any . . . I've never seen a child with such long eyelashes.'

Later she rang Clive. 'I'm worried about Kate.'

'Yes, so am I.'

'Take her to a doctor, Clive.'

'But she isn't ill!'

It was like living with a sponge, Clive thought. She was quite soft, ready to absorb everything and give nothing back; she cried so often and Clive had never been touched by this kind of helpless tears. The state of the house was no longer a joke. It maddened him and he tried to hide it but Kate hardly seemed to notice when he lost his temper. She felt as she felt, miserable and scared and concentrating desperately on getting from one day to

238

the next, building walls against the nameless, shapeless terror, cunningly bringing people into her life, arranging things so that she would not have to go out, ordering food from the one shop which delivered or relying on Gabriel.

On the day it all disintegrated nothing was different. Clive woke before Kate and made coffee and got dressed. The baby cried and Kate got up to fetch her and warmed the feed. Clive kissed Kate and left. Kate put the teet into the baby's mouth and then the terror pounced, no longer a shadowy fear but a total enveloping horror. She tried to keep the baby out of it. Her brain was going black, like a negative. She reached for the telephone and rang Judith, knowing at last there was something very wrong with her.

It seemed a long time before Judith came. Kate had put the baby carefully in the cot and she screamed and screamed. Judith came in the open front door, almost running, and took Kate's arm and led her upstairs. She looked anxiously in at the baby and picked it up. She asked for the number of Kate's doctor. It was just like the hospital all over again, events moving past Kate at great speed. Judith changed the baby, re-warmed the bottle, stuck it in the baby's mouth and rang Gabriel. Then she came to sit by Kate.

'Don't be so afraid, Kate. It's something to do with hormones. It's quite common. You're not going mad.'

The doctor came and gave Kate an injection and asked Judith if she would stay. She said she would. When Kate woke up, hours later, Clive was there.

He was pacing the bedroom. 'He says you are ill, Kate . . . I didn't realize . . .' He tried to make his voice gentle. 'You are depressed and it's quite common for women to feel like this after a baby but you have it rather badly. You must rest. Judith has said she will come here and help you. She was going to have a break after France but she'll come and live here until you can cope again. It will go away.' He stood by Kate and she took his hand, her small fingers gripping it rhythmically and

239

desperately. It occurred to Clive how much of his time Kate had always demanded. For quite obvious things, with Kate, needed unravelling, needed to be thought through. He sat down on the bed and looked at the white triangle of her face; whereas, in the beginning, it had intrigued him to be needed so much, to have to move so carefully, to care for her, to be rewarded by her sudden wicked laughter, he had always imagined her maturing into something bigger and braver. Now, it seemed, he had been wrong. He was married to a helpless child.

Kate watched the expressions on his face, felt the reluctance of his big hand, closed her eyes as she felt more tears coming.

Judith unpacked in the big spare room which overlooked the garden. The chest of drawers smelled nice. She folded her clothes neatly, hung dresses and trousers in the cupboard. On the dressing-table which Gabriel had given Kate, with its glass top and flowered skirts, kidney-shaped and reminding Judith of her mother's bedroom, she put her make-up, all the bottles labelled 'pure' and 'made without animal ingredients'. It was not that she cared about animals particularly. In fact she disliked them. She disliked them so much that she was revolted by the idea of smearing them on her face or eating them. She brushed her hair. The August sunshine came in this window. In the next-door garden children were playing, high-pitched laughter drifting upwards.

Judith went down the stairs, passing Kate's door and looking in. Kate slept, curled thankfully into sleep. The baby slept in the tiny third bedroom on this, the first floor. Upstairs were three more rooms. A big house. Judith liked it. She went into the kitchen, made herself coffee and began to prepare an evening meal, waiting for Clive to come back.

The baby was fed and would not need her again until the late feed . . . Judith chopped vegetables for a salad, made a Quiche, heard Kate stirring and went upstairs.

'I should be helping you . . .'

'Don't be stupid. You're paying me to work here. I'm not a

240

guest. Stay there. Don't get up. If you want to get well, let me do everything for a while. Are you hungry?'

'No.' Kate let her arms lie on the quilt, thin arms, palms turned upwards. She wanted to cry again.

'Stop it!' Judith said sharply. She looked at the tranquillizers on the bedside table and frowned her dislike of them. 'I can feel you, running round inside yourself!'

'Yes. I'm like a white mouse scuttling through my own brain.'

'Well, stop. Try and think more slowly. Think aloud. One thing at a time.'

Kate was hardly listening, so deeply involved was she in the panic.

'I said, think slowly. About now; about this room. Repeat to yourself how safe you are. I am here. I will look after Melanie and Clive and your house. You don't have to do anything. Think that.'

'I'll try,' Kate said.

When Judith went down she found Clive in the hall. She paused on the bottom step, thinking what an exceptionally attractive face he had, especially when it was serious, like this, thinking how strange it was to be here in his house.

'How is Kate?'

'Go up and see her.' It was an order, made to sound like a suggestion and he found himself obeying, going to sit with Kate but unable to stay still, wandering about the room, talking about the day. When she said she was tired he tried to hide his relief. He went down to the kitchen and asked Judith if she would like a drink.

'Have you a Dubonnet?'

'Are you serious?'

'Yes. I like it with ice and soda.'

'How extraordinary,' Clive smiled but he brought her what she wanted. 'Something smells good.'

'Vegetable soup, Quiche and salad. Do you mind if I don't cook meat too often?'

241

'Not really.' He sat down. 'It feels entirely different coming into the house tonight. I'm very grateful to you . . . I can't think why I didn't realize what was happening.'

Judith stirred the soup, her shoulders moving gently, sipping the drink. 'Perhaps you didn't want to. I don't suppose you'd have known how to cope on your own.'

'You're very damning.'

'I don't mean to be.' Her voice was colder than she intended because of the attraction she felt, because she knew he registered it too. He came and stood beside her, smiling down at her, starting the first light touches of a pass. She knew all the signs. She knew that he wanted her categorized, wanted to flirt up to a point to reassure himself. 'Kate is my friend,' she said primly and her eyes laughed at him and herself and the words.

But it grew, all evening. They watched each other and she put down any attempt on Clive's part to treat her as just a girl. She drank some of the wine he offered her. She made him real coffee, unearthing the beans from the back of the cupboard. Kate had drunk some soup and then slept again.

Judith watched the television, sitting beside Clive on the sofa, aware of sympathy in herself which she distrusted.

'Do all the husbands try and make you?' he said suddenly.

'Most of them but not so soon as you.'

'I'm sorry if I am obvious. I won't deny that I have found you extremely attractive for a long time.'

Judith looked at him. She smiled a little. There was something extremely appealing about him, she thought, the feeling that he could cope with things. It was, she realized, quite false but it was there. She pushed it away, always careful to stay on top. 'I must feed your daughter now. Shall I bring her down afterwards?'

'Do I have to keep up an elaborate pretence with you, as well as Kate?' he asked, tiredness making him honest.

'You're not very interested in the baby?'

'Should I be? It's not very interested in me. Later, when it is human, I'm sure I will feel more for it.'

'Then I'll say good night. What do you want me to do in the morning? Shall I cook some breakfast for you?'

Clive shook his head and the thick hair fell on to his forehead and he pushed it back. 'No. I can look after myself . . . I leave at eight. Good night, Judith.'

'Good night.'

It was all such a strange upside down way to begin it, Judith thought. Or not begin it. She had been in the house for three weeks. Kate was better, gradually coming alive, still sleeping a lot but coming down in the daytime, down to eat in the evenings, sometimes sounding almost natural, chattering, pausing, as she used to do. And Judith watched Clive, watched his marriage, came to feel at home in his house, put down any attempt of his to put her on a trivial level, remained aloof but could not deny the appeal she felt. She hid it absolutely. The necessity to hide it made her more aware of it, watching herself . . .

Long before she ever touched Clive she had watched him when he came home tired, rubbing his face wearily with big hands, pulling at his tie to loosen it as he poured a drink; he always looked clean and very male; she loved the smell of the lemony after-shave he used, his cotton shirts, his suits, his small cigars; she saw the disinterest with which he regarded the baby, the way he gathered himself up, making an effort, each time he was with Kate; she saw him shrink, hurt and angry and somehow cheated from the withdrawn shell of Kate; he was a man who liked to bring home flowers, to pay compliments, to be wanted in bed, especially now with such dragging anxiety through the day. If, in the short space of their marriage before the baby, they had been able to pretend that they were what the other needed now, Judith saw, it was impossible. As Kate recovered she changed; became herself but a new self; became what she had always meant to be under the panic. She could not be the kind of woman Clive wanted.

243

Judith would laugh with him, listen to him, drawing out of him the concerns of his day and keeping him at arm's length. But there were occasional, quite accidental times when they touched and the contact shocked them both. And she knew he was beginning to see through the absolute indifference, see it as a kind of unspoken 'Not now. Not here in this house.' She cooked for him and cared for his wife and his child and cleaned his house. She asked high wages and wrote down everything in her accounts book, each penny noted. She took his suits to be cleaned, pushed the baby in its pram, coaxed Kate back into the world. She kept her feelings as she always had, tightly bunched inside.

Kate lingered, reluctant to leave the safety of illness, terrified to try the world again and fail. She still slept a great deal, read books in great hungry sessions, watched television. The television was in the bedroom now and Kate tended to go upstairs after dinner, get into bed and watch it. She gave the baby the night feed. Clive came to bed so late. Sometimes Kate felt that she was a child again.

Clive watched Judith as he had once watched Caroline, fascinated by her efficiency. Everything was immaculate. Once the evening meal was cleared away she would do no more. She would sit with him in the rather unappealing sitting-room which Kate had painted bright yellow, and they drank wine and talked and the atmosphere between them was heavy, so that each word and movement had great significance. Clive talked to her as he had never talked to a woman before, sometimes almost hypnotized by her slanted eyes. He told her of Mosaic and all its problems with an air of bravado.

For the first time in her life, Judith confided something of herself in return. 'I had nothing. I dislike my family and they dislike me. I never go home. I had no qualifications. It is as if my life started when I came to London. I was reborn on the train! I was confident, even then, and I could pretend. And I knew I was attractive and I used it. God, how I used it, whenever I could! But

I've never loved anyone,' she said almost as an afterthought. 'Whatever that may mean. If I want someone I try to attract their attention. I've never been self-conscious or afraid of being put down. I usually succeed. Perhaps I've just chosen the wrong men.'

'Are there many? At the moment?'

'One I have known for five years, a friend, separated from his wife, in his fifties, chairman of a merchant bank. He makes lists of books for me to read. I use his education secondhand. I sleep with him sometimes. I talk to him a lot. Two or three other men about your age, they come and go. And I meet men at parties and where I work. Once there was a boy on a train, going to Scotland.' She laughed as she remembered. She looked straight at Clive so that he would know exactly what she was and that she was pleased with what she was.

'Kate is better now, isn't she?'

'Yes. I'm leaving on Friday.'

'Let me drive you home.'

'I have my car.'

'Doesn't it need servicing?'

'Yes, I think it does . . .'

It was a very wet Friday afternoon in late October when Judith left and Kate was sad to see her go. Through the past few weeks, as Kate returned to normality, she had enjoyed Judith's company. She stood on the porch and waved, made the baby wave and Clive carried Judith's cases. 'I shall be going in to Mosaic, Kate. Back about six.'

He got in to the car, slamming his door, starting the car and enclosing them. The tension of the past two months made the atmosphere between them now almost unbearable. They both knew that, very shortly, it would come into the open. Now. This afternoon. Just a question of who would say it first. Judith was surprised to find she was trembling slightly. The rain outside the car enclosed them in a shell of water fragments and hushed

245

sound. The traffic lights at Roehampton Lane caught them and Clive turned and curled his hand round the back of her neck, like a high, warm collar.

'Well?'

She smiled slowly, letting her big mouth express it all, 'Well?' she echoed, but as he leaned towards her she was already leaning forward to kiss him. They paused for a second before their mouths touched and a shock of joy shuddered through her. Someone behind hooted impatiently. 'Fuck off,' Clive said amiably.

When they reached the flat he carried her cases up the narrow stairs and they banged the walls at the awkward corner and he apologized. He put the cases down in the middle of the small living-room and then put his arms round her, very reticient for Clive. It was such a long time since he had cared so much, since he had felt attraction so urgent that nothing else mattered. So long since he had made love at all.

Judith took him through to the bedroom and drew the curtains. She waited until Clive stood behind her, turning slowly to face him. They made love with all the stored, unused feelings of the last months, surprised and delighted to find that the other met them absolutely. At last, in this rough, almost frighteningly intense love-making, Judith knew she had found what she wanted. She made herself look at this from the outside. 'How can you sleep with Kate's husband? When Kate has been ill? How despicable. Aren't there enough men in London for you that you must have this one?' But it didn't matter. It just didn't matter.

Clive read her thoughts. 'We're not breaking up anything,' he said, and this was the first time he had admitted it to himself and certainly the first time he had expressed it in words. 'Kate and I are not, and never will be, what the other needs.'

Judith rolled on to her stomach. 'Feeling about you as I do, I'm afraid I wouldn't care. I want you to realize this about me. I have always, and will always, put myself first.'

CHAPTER FIFTEEN

Through the autumn of that year, Kate treated herself with care, trying to enjoy her child, trying to belong in the set of people who lived around her. She understood them better now she had a baby. As freedom was so largely curtailed, as she could not work and was forced to narrow her world to the house and the child and Clive, she realized that it helped to talk about it, to know other women in a similar position. She no longer avoided them and laughed at them but she could not make any great friends. She could not let anyone very close. She tried to make the house look better, painting the kitchen vivid orange and wallpapering the bathroom. She tried to reclaim the garden from its invasion of nettles and fallen leaves. Gabriel came to London with all her gardening tools and there was between herself and Kate, for the first time, a kind of peace. Strangely enough, as with Ben, it was the garden that caused Kate to listen to her mother, to respect her knowledge.

Kate knew that Marketing Mosaic was in trouble. It was obvious from Clive's face and manner, from Jenny's voice on the telephone. A couple of times Kate put the carry-cot in the car and drove up to see them all. She was disturbed by the atmosphere, by a feeling of tension and an air of hopelessness. The windows were dirty, the desks untidy. Jenny herself looked tired and had lost some of her confidence. Clive was surprised to see Kate and not particularly welcoming. Now that she did not cling to him but had withdrawn, he was even more at a loss. Kate lived quietly in his house, caring for the baby, sleeping in his bed, responding with obvious effort when he approached her, which wasn't very often. They both knew they should discuss what was wrong but for the moment they could not mention it.

Clive still treated Kate with concern but there was no spark between them. He was not particularly interested in the baby who was sitting up now, enthralling Kate every day with some tiny new triumph. Kate bought a car seat and had it fitted to the Renault her father had given her for her birthday and at weekends she frequently drove to the Old Vicarage, finding the atmosphere there easier than the stiffness between herself and Clive. She kept expecting something to break, a reconciliation, some genuine feeling between Clive and herself but nothing happened. The weekends when Kate went away, Clive spent with Judith, feeling profound relief as some of the tension of the week slid from him, as he lost himself in her body and her mind.

In November a letter came from Henri, ostensibly addressed to Clive, announcing that he was coming to England the following week. It seemed so long ago that Kate had met him but on impulse she wrote and asked if he would like to stay at Rose Walk, not even knowing if the letter would arrive before he left. She was in need of a friend.

Henri arrived by taxi the following Friday evening with four suitcases, a bottle of brandy and a letter from Michael. He was standing on the doorstep smiling when Kate let him in, his solemn face lit by the wide, sweet smile. He kissed her cheek and frowned with distress. 'What has happened to you?' He saw how very thin she was. Her clothes quieter. 'You were ill?'

'Yes. I went temporarily mad after Melanie was born.'

'Oh—nothing serious then?' he said with a smile.

'No.' She laughed. She showed him upstairs to the spare room which she had painted a bright apple green. She watched him put down the cases on the bed, unzip them, hang a few things in the cupboard. He moved quickly, busily, his body slight and strong. Kate liked seeing him here, liked the fact that the months had done nothing to lessen the way she had felt before. Pleasure in his company.

'What are you thinking?'

'How nice it is to see you . . . wondering what is worrying you just now.'

'My drains,' Henri said, turning to her a face of mock tragedy. 'In nineteen fifty-nine they brought drainage to the village, which was amazing but, unfortunately, I am just out of the town and they still cannot connect me and the drains overflow and smell and we use so much water that the system I have installed is hopeless . . . Why are you laughing so much? I am tormented by drains!'

He crossed the room to her, smiling, putting his arms on her shoulders, his hands under the hair at the nape of her neck. 'I am so glad to see you laugh, Kate. What has happened to you, eh?'

She put her face against his. It was warm. He smelled different, of cigarettes, of rain on his coat, of France she imagined, although she had never been there. They stayed, quite still, for a time and when Kate finally moved back and opened her eyes his face was very serious. He kissed her mouth and it seemed that the whole of her body sprang forward towards him.

She moved away. 'You've confused me. Last time you did too.'

That night, Henri took Clive and Kate out to dinner, to the restaurant in Battersea he and Kate had been to in the spring.

'And your bags have sold like hot cakes,' Clive said. 'We can sell more. And the sun hats? Did you bring some?'

'Yes, I did. And Mary May has given me a massive order which we are struggling to fill. I have taken on ten more girls.'

Clive raised his hand, to attract the waiter and ask for more wine. 'I wish to God we were doing so well. I've just told one of the secretaries we can't afford her any more. It's down to myself and Jenny, Nancy and Bill Carter.'

'Things are bad?'

'Very bad indeed.' He hunched his shoulders, frowning, rubbing his forehead with his hand. Kate searched herself for compassion but she had lived with it for so long, was so used to the worry, it was hard to react now. She had watched Clive grow steadily more depressed and equally more flamboyant. He ordered the best of everything now.

'But why?' Kate had asked a few days ago.

'Because I refuse to be intimidated, ground down by this bloody government and the world. I will drink my whisky when I want it.'

'I don't understand you. You make things worse . . . You don't have to go on spending money like this.'

'It is nothing to do with you, Kate. The money is my affair.'

'Not when you manage it so badly,' Kate had snapped.

'You bitch! All I ask of you is a little support and sympathy!'

'You don't ask anything of me, that's the trouble.' It had been like looking at a stranger, the blank disinterested face of a stranger. 'Clive . . .'

'Yes?' he had said coldly.

'Nothing . . .'

'You have withdrawn the Sundial, I understand,' Henri was saying now.

'Yes. That has been a major part of our trouble, trying to get back some of the production costs.' Clive was tired of this meal, of this place, of the quiet Frenchman probing his failure. So many of his friends asked these questions, seeking out his difficulties, underlining that, in the eyes of the world, he had been mad not to stay at Bonnington's. 'I always knew it was a gamble,' he said quietly.

'How bad is it?' Henri asked.

'We have some steady lines that sell and will keep selling and Jenny went today to see some thing she's keen on but the whole world is so depressed. The interest on our loans are crippling us.'

The two men talked as if Kate wasn't there. She listened to Clive and was deeply hurt that he had never said any of this to her. They had coffee and brandy while they talked and Kate could have been at another table.

At eleven, Clive said, 'Come on. Let's go somewhere and have a drink.'

Kate touched his hand and he wanted to shake off her touch, hating the concern in her face. He wanted to forget Mosaic, he wanted diversion not sympathy. He closed his eyes and imagined Judith here, her thigh against his, her hand on his, all her attention on him, her body hinting of the love-making to come. The violence with which she had come into his life, the strength of the hold she had over him in just a few months, amazed him. And yet it saved him, the one good thing about his life at the moment. Her strength, her hypnotic, snake-like eyes, the enjoyment and pride she drew from his body.

Henri looked at the two faces. 'Clive, I am rather tired after the flight. Would you mind if I didn't join you?'

Kate said, 'I don't want to go anywhere, really. I told the baby-sitter I'd be back before twelve. I'll go home with Henri.'

'All right. There is someone I want to talk to who will probably be at Tramps but I won't be very late.' They all knew the words were meaningless. 'You take the car, Kate. I'll get a cab. That was a delicious dinner, Henri. Many thanks. See you tomorrow.' He bent and kissed Kate's cheek, never forgetting the outward signs, she thought bitterly, however meaningless they were.

'More coffee?' Henri said when Clive had gone, when the air settled round them, when they unconsciously moved closer.

'Yes, please.' She sat and looked at this man she hardly knew and yet would have stayed with for hours, happy to be with him. How was it possible to feel like this?

'I don't really want to start talking about it,' he said gently.

'Clive and me?' She shook her head. 'I wouldn't know where to begin. I don't think about it. All I know is that it gets colder and colder.'

'I tell myself if I keep out of it all for a while it will be better for you . . .'

She laughed. 'Let us fight it out on our own, you mean? Whose fault is it?'

'Who does he go and see?'

Kate frowned. 'A woman, you mean? Is there a woman?'

'I imagine so.'

'Oh God.' She put her hands over her face, unconsciously copying Clive's gesture. She had learned so many things from him. 'I'm afraid that I will say too much if I try and talk about it. I can see through him, all the time, all the acts. I see every pretence and I cringe. It's not fair. Why have I got all this sarcasm in my head all the time? And the quieter and colder I become the more flamboyant Clive is. I'm not even helpless now.'

Henri took her hand, opening it up, looking into the palm, kissing it. 'A lot of people get it wrong the first time, Kate.'

'So soon?'

The waiter refilled their coffee cups and they sat, quite engrossed in one another, talking their way into the night.

Clive hailed a taxi and went over Battersea Bridge, up the embankment towards Judith's flat, knowing that tonight he had been clumsy and obvious but too tired to care. He needed to see her, he rang the bell in long impatient peals; she raised the window, looked out and smiled, coming barefoot down the stairs to let him in, holding him, laughing with him, kissing him until they paused for breath. 'I shouldn't stay long,' he said. 'Quite suddenly I couldn't stand the politeness, that bloody Frenchman and his questions, his successes. Kate's concerned face. I had to come here. You keep me sane!'

'I hoped you'd come. Even one night without you is a waste now . . .'

'Next month, mid-December,' he said as he lay along the sofa, his head in her lap, 'I'm going to France to see Michael and Henri and some man in Paris about this loan. Just a few days. Will you come with me? Stay in a hotel . . . Perhaps I'll have to be one night with Michael. No more.'

'I finish this job on the ninth. I could come.'

'We'll go on the fourteenth. I've promised the Finches I'll look

252

at their derelict *mas* for them too . . .' Judith massaged his shoulders with strong fingers. She wore a lot of gold rings, gold chains round her neck. When she moved she made small sounds like little bells. A heavy gold bracelet swung against Clive's cheek and he caught at her wrist. 'Where did you get that?'

'She gave it to me. I've always wanted a plain gold bracelet.' Judith held out her arm, turned it slightly. 'It's lovely, isn't it?'

'It must have cost a bloody fortune!'

'It did. She never liked it.'

'Why do they give you so many things?' He looked up at her. She stroked his forehead. She wanted him. More and more. As she had never before wanted a man. 'Not all of them. Just the ones who become dependent. I find I can quite often make them do what I want. Suggest things, frighten them a little.' She laughed. 'And remember I only work for very rich people.' She stroked his thick hair, dark and strong. He lay still, watching her. They let the excitement build gradually. After the love-making, she would encourage him to talk, delicately, drawing from him every detail of Mosaic and its problems, storing this knowledge.

In the kitchen at Rose Walk Kate paid the baby-sitter, thanked her and the girl left. It was 12.30. Henri said, 'No more coffee, no brandy, just sleep.' Kate nodded and turned out the kitchen lights, linked to him by a temporary enchantment, as if there were no barriers, as if the future was open and free. They started up the stairs and outside the spare-room door they paused.

'Kiss me good night,' Kate said and he moved towards her, arm round her shoulders, smiling at her.

The baby cried suddenly, a raw burst of sound in the silent house, some bad dream erupting from her and Kate went at once, without thinking, into the small bedroom, looked into the cot and reached down for the baby. She was a warm, damp weight in Kate's arms and against her shoulder, body quivering with sobs, face silky and wet. Kate murmured soothing noises and laid the baby on the bed, unfastening the sleeping suit to change the nappy. Melanie laughed now, stirring the air with fat starfish hands, looking towards the door where Henri stood, a dark shadow against the light of the hall. His face was gentle. 'Good night, you two,' he said.

Kate didn't look up. Tears formed in her eyes and she blinked, bent and kissed the baby's round, warm stomach. Melanie laughed delightedly.

Clive came in quietly, just before three, sliding into bed, sleeping almost at once, but the night was far too short. He always got up at seven, made his own coffee, left at eight. Each morning it was harder, more of an effort of will. Sometimes he sat in his car, wanting to put off just for a few moments the inevitable misery of the day. He was being battered down with such agonizing slowness. Sometimes he drove to a shopping area and looked for Mosaic goods to reassure himself but eventually, every morning, more or less on time, he parked in Meadwell Street and went in, shaking off the depression, smiling, flirting with Nancy. 'You look lovely today.'

'Thank you.'

'Morning, Jenny.'

'Good morning.' She was so wary now, always afraid that one day they wouldn't be able to save the violent arguments for the evening when they were alone. 'I've got the orders back from the *Sunday Times* advertisement for the rocking clocks.'

'And?'

'Disappointing. I was wondering if you want to cancel the second full page in January.'

'No, I don't.' Sometimes he wondered whose side she was on, this neat, cold woman, spelling out the failures word by word. 'I thought we might add several more lines. A whole page of products. I'm sorry I didn't think of it in time for Christmas.'

'What other products?' Jenny asked carefully.

'I don't know . . . perhaps some of Henri's things. He's

coming in at lunch time anyway.'

Bill came forward, hovering, waiting for an opening. 'Clive,' he said, 'I've got something to show you.'

With an effort Clive tried to show interest.

'I was thinking what else we could do with the basic shape of the rocking clock, bearing in mind the expense of the tool, and I hit on the idea of taking two bodies, joining them by some kind of bright bezel, still weighting one end, and screening a face on the other. As a kid's toy. They might look quite nice . . .' He held out a page of drawings. 'We'd need a good name for them.'

'But we're not in the toy business,' Jenny said crisply. 'It's very specialized.'

'Why aren't we in the kids' toy business? We do adult toys. It's the useless stuff that sells best.'

'All our outlets are to gift shops . . .'

'These could go through gift shops and they look as if they could be cheap. I love the face.' Jenny's expression made him furious. 'Could you make me some mock-ups, Bill?'

'Yes.'

Jenny took a packet of cigarettes from the pocket of her cardigan, lit one, sat down and shrugged. 'You're amazing, Clive. I'll give you that! Here we are, absolutely at the bottom and you're calmly branching out in a completely new field. And who's doing the Manchester Trade Fair tomorrow?'

He looked into her tired face. 'I suppose it's my turn. In fact, it will be a relief to get away from the dramas here for a few days. We're not broke yet, Jenny.' He smiled but neither of them believed the optimism he pretended.

For three days of that week, through dull November weather and with London wearily trotting out the Christmas cliché in all the shops, Kate and Henri saw each other every moment they could. Clive rang once from some huge hotel and Kate felt that he was on the moon, so remote did he sound. The outward pattern of her days was quite normal, all tied up with Melanie and the house, but in the mornings there was Henri at breakfast, hair damp from the shower, clean-shaven, a very tidy man, quite silent at breakfast and cringing from Kate's youthful bouncing. He grimaced as she spooned boiled egg into Melanie, into herself. 'Oh God, how can you eat that now?' He hid himself in a mug of coffee.

'Surely you should eat breakfast, Henri?' she teased. 'Don't you worry about your energy levels through the morning?'

'That is one of the few things I don't worry about. My years of being a doctor taught me to disregard all fashions in eating.' He put a second spoonful of sugar in his cup. 'Was that pompous?'

'Awful.' She put the spoon into Melanie's hopeful mouth. There was no fear with Henri. She was not afraid of hurting him. She would never want to hurt him.

'I love the way you look in the mornings,' Henri said. 'Just as you look in the evening. You wake up looking like yourself, not some crumpled morning version.'

'Where are you going today?' She changed the subject, not because she disliked what he said but because she was not ready.

'To Wales. By train. I will come back tomorrow night.'

Kate nodded, bending her head, thinking how she hated to waste one evening. One whole evening of feelings she had no names for. Pleasure in his company? Feeling like a woman again and not a mental patient?

'Can we go out to dinner tomorrow? Will Clive be home?'

'He comes back on Friday. I'd love to go out but there is a cocktail party I should go to first. Will you come?'

Henri stood behind her chair, bending and kissing the top of her head, and she pushed back her chair suddenly, making him step back. 'Don't do that. Don't put me in some far-off, affectionate category. Don't pat my head and kiss me like that!' She put her arms out stiffly, hands at the back of his head, moving her mouth to touch his. He kissed her for a long time. She felt unreal, as if she hadn't breathed enough.

'You don't have to prove anything to me, Kate,' he said softly. 'But it is not simple, is it?' He went towards the door. 'Shall I telephone you tonight?'

'Yes, please.'

And when he did and she was alone in her house apart from the sleeping baby they talked happily for half an hour about nothing much and when Kate finally went to bed she imagined herself with him and wondered whether, according to God's rules or whoever it was who judged when the world didn't yet realize what was happening, it was just as bad to be unfaithful in your mind.

There was such peace between them through those strange innocent days. She began to know about him, picturing his life, his child, his ex-wife . . . 'She has someone much more suitable now. More money, more confidence, enough energy to live in the permanent battleground she creates and thrives on.'

'And you?' Kate said, leaning against him on the sofa with the television an excuse, talking to itself. 'Do you have someone?'

'There is someone who comes and goes. She belongs to the set of people who so disturb Caroline.' He laughed. 'Poor Caroline. One minute she is with the old French families, friends of Michael's grandmother, people he has known all his life but not well. The next she is with the strange exiles who build their villas round about, rather eccentric people but fascinating if you can leave them at will. You must come to Provence, Kate.'

'Clive is going in December, to see Michael, to talk about the loan but only for a few days. I don't want to go.'

'Why not?'

'I'm not quite ready yet to go that far away. I can drive quite happily now. I have occasional attacks of terror but I can cope with them. Once you overcome one, there is that victory to look back to. But I have only just got there. And I have only just come to know Melanie.'

There were so many questions between them about the future

but as there were no possible answers he left them unspoken. The following afternoon Kate took him to Heathrow. The sun shone. They parked the car and she went into the terminal building with him and watched him check in his cases and pay his excess baggage, watched from a distance and saw him as a slight man, smooth-haired, with such a sympathetic face, turning to look for her, finding her and smiling slowly. He bought her a small flower print of a lily-of-the-valley in one of the airport shops.

He bought two coffees and they sat at a round metal table, stained with the rings of countless other coffees, surrounded by the peculiar atmosphere of waiting, of having nothing to say that meant anything. 'I shall be busy this winter. I have the new designs to finish. I shall spend Christmas with my parents who are old and lonely. Then perhaps go skiing with Michael in January . . .'

'The months go so quickly when you speak them. But they are all made of days. Day after day. What shall I do?' It was the first time she had asked him.

'Perhaps talk to Clive? Try and work it out.'

'Do you want me to?'

'No. But I don't want you bouncing again into another relationship you haven't thought about.' Suddenly he sat back, 'God, I am doing just what you asked me not to. Treating you so carefully, like a child almost. I should like you to come with me now. Back to where I live and be with me.'

For a moment she let herself go with the idea, loving it. Henri stopped it.

'Next year, Kate, when Melanie is a year old, when you are more sure of what you want, perhaps have had a chance to work again, not to be so isolated. Perhaps things will be better for Clive. If not . . .'

'If not, I'll come and visit you.'

'Yes.'

Then his flight was called and he went and all the words

seemed so vague without him. Such hollow plans. So many months. She drove back to London with tears on her cheeks wondering if, yet again, she was just letting things happen, drifting until the problem solved itself.

She preferred the house now when Clive wasn't there. It was extraordinary how the days built into weeks, each one lived through quite normally and nothing resolved. The bills kept coming in. Clive had a box file on his desk and sometimes Kate took some bills, electricity or telephone, down to Gabriel and asked her to pay them. Gabriel always did, without a word, happy to be wanted.

In December Clive left for France to re-negotiate with Henri for the new year, to stay a night with Michael and talk about the loan. He was curious about his feelings for Caroline now he had Judith beside him. They stayed two nights in a hotel in Paris where Clive ostensibly talked with the manufacturers of some leather goods.

'Will you be bored while I'm with Yves Pernet?' he asked her.

'No. In fact I have a friend to meet for lunch?'

'Oh?' Clive was tying his tie. He stopped, looking over his shoulder. 'Who?'

'An old boy friend. He lives here now.' She smiled, her face wearing its expression of satisfaction. 'Just lunch.'

'I shall be back about three.'

'Then so shall I.'

Clive's meeting did not go very well. However confident he appeared and as his despair intensified he became more and more sure, full of plans, acknowledging difficulties, yes, but explaining the confidence he had in the future, his plans for the next twelve months, somehow he didn't quite carry it off. There was an air of unreality, a desperation about him. He smoked more. He drank a lot. Or perhaps it was just that Yves Pernet too was suffering from world circumstances and was cautious. He agreed to ship a small trial amount of his

259

products to England. They had an Armagnac and Clive left the restaurant at three, strolling down the wide, cold Paris street, watching the cars play games with each other, watching the women. He let himself into his hotel room and lay on the bed, wanting Judith to come back. She returned at about four and Clive hid all his jealous questions. She came to kiss him.

The following morning they left early and drove down the autoroute towards Avignon and the Château de Jouvard. They booked Judith into a small hotel in Avignon and then went on to see the Finches' house. Clive was curious about it and Judith insisted on coming. Ian's instructions were efficient and they found it quite easily. It was at the end of a long bumpy road with a high grass-covered ridge in the middle, between fields, quite isolated. It had a large stone barn. Clive parked the car in the yard and found the key, hidden where Ian had said, on a ledge in the single storey stone lean-to on one side of the house. He stood and looked up at the solid, desolate building, its shutters hanging brokenly beside some windows. The whole place looked as if it had not been lived in for years. Judith was pushing a side door open and stepped into a small walled garden, overgrown but warm. She came back to the yard. Clive had unlocked the heavy wooden door and she followed him into a large, stone-floored room. It was dark because the ground-floor shutters were closed and Judith went to the single window, pulled the windows inwards and pushed the shutters outwards. The light showed the large, empty room, high-ceilinged, with a staircase and a doorway. There were two more downstairs rooms, in one a stone sink, an old stove, and a lone piece of furniture—a kind of wooden dresser along one wall.

'No electricity,' Clive said. 'No telephone. No heating . . . It will cost them a fortune. No wonder they are leaving it alone this year.'

'But it will be beautiful in the end.' Judith started warily up the stairs and found herself in a huge room which took up the whole of the second floor. More stairs up to two more rooms.

She looked out of a tiny window at the top. She could not see another house at all. The fields were neglected. The roof seemed sound. She leaned out and waved to Clive who disliked empty, derelict buildings and was outside in the yard again.

'Come and look at the well . . .'

She found him winding the handle and eventually a bucket appeared full of icy water. Clive tasted it. 'This well must be seventy or eighty feet deep . . .'

Judith dropped a small pebble down into the circle of darkness. It seemed a long time before they heard the splash.

'I wish I had thought to bring a sleeping bag and a camping stove,' Judith said. 'I could have stayed here.'

'Alone? Out here?'

'Yes. There is something about total isolation which appeals to me very much.'

'You are a strange girl,' Clive said.

She laughed and reached into the car, bringing out bread, *saucisson* and cheese, a plastic bottle of Vin Ordinaire. They ate in the walled garden and a wintry sun came out obligingly. At three, sleepy from the food and wine, Clive drove her back to Avignon and took her into the hotel.

'Can you stay? An hour?' She closed the curtains, coming towards him slowly, wanting to imprint herself on him before he saw Caroline.

Two years, Caroline thought. She had been wondering about her feelings for some weeks, wondering if there would be anything left. All day she had waited, almost nervously. When she heard the car she went to the upstairs hall window and saw it turn between the gates. Suddenly she was eager and ran down the stairs, Charlie in her arms, then paused in the hall before she moved towards the double doors. She opened them and watched Clive come up the steps. At the first glance he seemed the same but close to him she noticed subtle changes. His thick hair was greying a little; his body seemed thicker; his eyes were

261

wary. He came into this hall he had stood in so often as a child and kissed her cheek, looked at the little boy. The child hid his face shyly against Caroline.

'Hello, Clive.'

She led him into the smallest of the three large downstairs rooms. It was quite changed since Clive had last seen it, with long curtains, looped back by thick cord ties, a new rug on the floor, the walls a pale green.

'This looks lovely.'

'Yes. I enjoyed the house. I enjoyed changing it but I have done it very gradually, thinking a lot about each thing. I have plenty of time.' She put the child down on the sofa and he sat quite still, watching Clive with huge grey eyes, like Caroline's. His hair was dark and straight. 'Will you have a drink?'

'Please.'

'Still whisky?'

'Yes.' Now he allowed himself to look at her properly, seeing her face was still solemn, and she still had her air of dishevelment. 'You haven't started a shop then, in St Remy?'

'No. Perhaps when Charlie is older. They start school very young in France, you know. They can go all day at three years old . . . But perhaps I shall keep him till he's four.' She handed Clive a glass of whisky and sat down by the child, her arm encircling him protectively, giving him a little smile. He smiled back. 'He is so quiet. He makes no attempt to speak. Michael says I am stupid to worry, that he is confused by the two languages. Henri says that very few children of nineteen months have more than a few words. But I wish he would say, *"Maman"*.' She stroked his hair. He leaned against her, playing with the buttons on her dress. 'Suzanne tells me that Michael was very late with his talking. How is your baby? Melanie? Have you any photographs?'

'No, I'm afraid I haven't but she is fine. Too small to do anything interesting.'

'And Kate is all right now? Rachel told me she suffered from

262

very bad depression.'

'Yes, she did. But now she's better. It's changed her though.' He didn't elaborate. He lit a cigar, testing himself now for reaction to Caroline. He registered that her face still delighted him, her voice and her movements attracted him, but the old desperation had gone, the old longing, the feeling that when she went out of his life part of him went with her. So time did help? Or was it Judith, so strongly stamped into his life now? 'How is Michael?'

'Very well. Working absurdly hard. He is organizing some great co-operative experiment. The harvest was very good this year. The local farmers are beginning to lose their suspicion of his ideas.' She was drinking whisky too. 'He said he would be back at seven. I asked him particularly to be early but you know Michael and his sense of time, or lack of it . . .' She could not quite keep the bitterness out of her voice.

'Yes.'

'I should go and put Charlie to bed now. I'll be about half an hour. Help yourself to another drink, Clive.'

'Can't I come up and talk to you?'

She was standing, lifting the child, and she frowned for a moment with surprise. She had forgotten what it was to have someone want to be with her, talk to her through the boring routine events of the day. She smiled. 'Of course you can . . . do you spend time with Kate when she baths the baby? How lovely. They are so sweet all wet and bare and then clean in their pyjamas. I am always telling Michael he should watch Charlie in the bath but he is never here in time.' She led the way up the wide stairs and Clive carried his case. 'You are in that spare room, Clive. I have changed that too. I have made a bathroom in part of the huge linen cupboard. I shall be with Charlie in the bathroom at the end of the passage.' She went down and turned on the taps, and Charlie held on to the edge of the bath and bounced and watched the water, making small squeaks of joy. Caroline undressed him. He beat the surface of the water with

263

the palms of his hands, making delighted sounds, laughing as water splashed on to his face, making his long eyelashes spikey, making him shake his head. Caroline knelt and watched him. She never grew tired of watching him. The miscarriage had underlined the miracle that was this child. He played with a sponge, with a duck.

Clive came in, sitting on the white wicker chair and watching her.

'How is Mosaic?' she asked.

'Not too good.'

'I'm sorry. And my shop? Do you ever go past? How does it look?'

'Quite different. They have painted it red. They have a lot of leather chairs and huge china pots. Rather contrived. Not the sort of stuff I'd want to live with.' He watched as she lifted the child, wrapped him in a towel, played hide and seek with him. She got up, grimacing because her legs had been beneath her for so long, carrying Charlie to the bedroom and putting on a nappy, pyjamas, tucking him into a large cot. He lay down and made kissing noises. Caroline wound up a musical roundabout which hung from a string above the cot and kissed him once again.

'Now, I will change, quickly, and come down,' she said.

Clive sat in a big soft chair, liking this pretty room, liking the whisky, thinking of Judith and wondering what she was doing. And he heard the front door open followed by quick footsteps and Michael came in, unchanged by the two years except that his skin was a deep brown, his hair a little shaggier.

'Hello, Clive.' He held out his hand and Clive stood up and shook it. 'I'm glad to see you.' He turned to the low table where the bottles of alcohol stood, pouring himself a glass of wine. 'How's your drink?'

'I helped myself.'

'Good. How long have you been here?'

'About an hour. I went to see the Finches' house this afternoon.'

'I think they're insane,' Michael said flatly, sitting down, letting his long body relax. 'God, what a day! It gets worse, Clive. I was determined, the first year, to work with Gautier and the other men, to find out everything about it. Fascinating. Now I go backwards and forwards to Cavillion and bring back new ideas and try to persuade them to experiment. But we've done well. Very well.' He sat up. 'I gather things are not so good with Mosaic. Jenny wrote to me and said you'd scrapped the Sundial.'

'Yes. We had to.'

'I'm sorry about that. Very sorry. And your rocking clocks?'

'No good. It's the small stuff that sells. The cheaper stuff. And Henri's goods are very successful.'

'Henri the tycoon.' Michael smiled. 'No one is more surprised than Henri himself. He stayed with you recently, I understand?'

'Yes.' Clive sat forward. 'We might as well discuss the money now, Michael. About your letter . . .'

'Yes. Although I agreed to wait until nineteen seventy-seven, I wondered if it is possible to settle part of it now? I want new machinery, Clive. I want stainless steel fermenting vats. You can control the temperature so much more precisely. I want a new bottling machine.'

'I owe you twenty-five thousand pounds,' Clive said slowly. 'We've got some good new lines and Jenny is optimistic, thinks things will pick up in the spring. I've been looking at some excellent leather stuff in Paris and we're doing much more mail order now. But I won't deny things are extremely difficult.'

Michael knew Clive would use the guilt he was still expected to feel about Caroline, knew Clive would use every pressure. Clive had always taken whatever he could, all the way through; lived in Michael's house without paying rent on the pretext of free legal advice which, to give him his due, had occasionally been very useful; stayed so many holidays here at Jouvard. But I

265

asked him, Michael countered. And I wanted him to have Mosaic, knew he wanted it, sensed perhaps that it was time to get out. It was convenient, selling to Clive. Oh, but he knows all this.

'What about Caroline's money?' Clive said. 'She has almost sixty thousand pounds now. I've taken it out of shares as the market is so odd and it's on deposit, earning massive interest.'

'That's her money,' Michael said. 'I won't use that. Could you let me have ten thousand pounds soon?'

'By "soon" do you mean tomorrow?'

'No. Next May or June.'

Clive nodded. He had no idea where he would raise it from.

'Tell me what lines you are selling now?' The old interest stirred in Michael. 'What about the pyramids?'

'Still good. The sales are okay. It's the bloody wages, insurance, telephone, postage, electricity . . .' They talked and the constraint between them seemed diluted by the years.

When Caroline came in, wearing one of Henri's long cotton dresses, her hair loose, looking quite lovely but rather strained, both men looked up and the same thought was in all three of their minds. If the situation arose again, now, would any of them care so much?

Caroline made herself a strong drink. Nearly every evening, especially after Charlie was in bed, waiting here for Michael, she drank enough to blunt her feelings. Through the day she was totally absorbed by the child. She came and kissed Michael, more to display the act to Clive than because it was habit. She sat down. Michael smiled at her for a moment before carrying on. She had strange images in her head sometimes. That she was a big bird, flying aimlessly round Jouvard. Clive was so funny through dinner, making her laugh, taking her out of herself.

'I've tried to persuade Caroline to start a shop here. St Remy has a lot of tourists in the summer but she won't . . .' Michael said.

'How can I? Charlie needs me . . .'

'Next summer he will be two and a half . . . You can't channel your whole life into him, Caroline. He will grow up.'

She stood up, fetched the cheese, sliding out of the conversation. Impossible to explain to Michael how she felt, needing the child's love, answering to every demand.

In bed that night she reached for Michael and he put his arms round her, responding, loving her. And when they lay still afterwards and he kissed her he felt tears on her face.

'What is it, Caroline?'

'The same old thing. That I don't see you enough. That I don't understand enough. That you are a stranger in Charlie's life, that you come and go as you want, without considering us, that you enjoy being alone. It still hurts me.'

'I don't want to hurt you. I can't help how I am.'

'I know.' She gave in, as she always did, lacking the courage to do more than hint, lying very still with all the words inside her. She should have said them. 'Why don't you put us first? Charlie and I? Why is your ambition, your compulsion to work, so vital? Why do you think yourself almost out of the world?' She never said it. Afraid of what he would answer perhaps, of the youth he had, afraid of the truth. She believed now that, in those intense summer months of nineteen seventy-three, Michael had treated her as if she were his current fascination, pouring into her all the attention of which he was capable. She believed she had since been replaced by Jouvard.

CHAPTER SIXTEEN

The one Sundial which Clive still kept at Marketing Mosaic struck once for half-past five with its dignified chime. The offices were deserted. Only Clive, sitting very still, the sheets of paper in front of him on the desk covered with figures in Jenny's neat hand. Bank statements, his own scrawled calculations, a colour supplement open at a whole page advertisment of his . . . his glance wandered to the opposite page, to the face of a beautiful girl advertising make-up. He finished his drink and put the glass down, pushing the spectacles on top of his head as he rubbed his eyes.

This defeat was so absurd. It should have worked. The little company had had so much promise. It still had good sales but could not earn enough to carry the failure of the two very different clocks, to cope with the overheads, to meet the debts.

Clive stood up and slowly crossed the room and accidentally he brushed the display table where the rocking clocks stood and they all moved and nodded and mocked him like a group of chattering old women and a surge of fury made him sweep them to the floor. They smashed, the noise violent, but still a couple rocked and he kicked at them and two of them slammed into the far wall. He was breathing fast and his pulse hammered but he felt better. He poured himself a second drink, his feet crunching over some broken glass.

The cold and absolute realization of failure which had preceded the fury had touched him a few minutes before when he finished speaking to Michael. It came back now. With it came weariness. Strange, he thought, how all that fierce ambition has narrowed to a mere craving for survival. Now I want Judith and a quiet life. He thought back to the dignified boredom of Bonnington's and it seemed another lifetime. He had been another man. He still wore a brave face and his so-called friends watched him with fascination. Some had been made redundant, some struggled on and some, like John Hampton, had bounced up again. Most of them watched and waited and Clive had a frightening sense of the disaster just out of sight. One morning he would wake and it would happen. He would look bankruptcy in the face. Perhaps it would be a relief? An end to the waiting and the fear that had grown all through the early months of 1976 as he tried, hopelessly, to find a backer, raise another loan. Clive looked towards the windows. It was early June and the weather was ridiculously hot. The temperature had been in the eighties for over a week. London throbbed with heat and people and tension.

Clive wandered about the back office, looking at a set of Beanies which Bill had made up from the bodies of rocking clocks. He hated them but he was conscious of Bill's loyalty and grateful for it. And for Jenny. Because they were still trying. Even now Jenny was taking the Beanies somewhere, still gathering orders. 'God, what a mess!' Clive said aloud. There was Kate, waiting quietly for the failure of their marriage to be expressed in words and occasionally still trying to interest Clive in the baby. But Clive looked at Kate and Melanie now across an enormous gulf. Kate had grown into a secretive woman. She could not be what Clive wanted and he could not touch her. She waited as Clive waited and Judith waited.

Judith loved him. He knew that. There was such strength in her. She pushed at him more and more. 'When will you tell her? When? What is the point of going on with her? It's no good for Kate either. I want you all the time.'

A few minutes earlier, Clive had dialled Michael in France guessing that he would still be in the office at Jouvard despite the hour's time difference. He had guessed right. Michael answered. 'Hello?'

'It's Clive. How are you, Mike?'

Michael never answered such questions. 'Clive?' he repeated.

Clive went straight to the point. 'I thought we should discuss the repayment. It's June.'

'I wrote to you yesterday, funnily enough. Caroline suggested that you bring Kate and stay for a week. Bring your child if you want.'

Clive had paused, surprised. 'I can easily arrange the transfer of the money without coming in person.'

'But we'd like you to come.' Clive heard the unspoken effort at reconciliation. 'And there are a few other things you could bring too. Caroline's pearls are still in the bank and my mother has a few papers. That's if you feel like coming . . .'

'I'll talk it over with Kate and ring you later in the week,' But he had no desire to go at all. He imagined a stilted week with Kate. A week without Judith . . .

As he thought of her he heard the outer door open, looked up and watched her cross the showroom. She was not afraid of discovery now. She wanted it. But she was frustrated by Mosaic's problems. She loathed to see Clive bowed down. She paused by the heap of broken clocks.

'I see you've been re-designing.' She touched one with her foot.

Clive laughed. 'It made me feel better.'

'That's how you should be. Angry!' She came to him, squeezing his arms. 'You must never give up, Clive.'

He sighed. 'I've just been speaking to Michael. I shall be repaying the ten thousand at the end of the month. I wish to God that was all I owed him.'

'How much is it, altogether?'

'A lot.'

'I'm not Kate,' she snapped. 'Tell me how much!'

'Twenty-five thousand, two hundred and three pounds and ten pence!' His voice was cold.

'Where will you get so much money?'

'God knows. I have some remaining money from the sale of my flat which is invested; I have a second mortgage on Rose Walk; I've sold the two ship paintings for a surprising amount

270

but by the time I've paid Mike ten thousand there will be almost nothing left to help Mosaic limp through to the end of the year.' He put an arm round her and kissed her. 'Let's go out and have a drink. I have to have dinner with the Finches later.'

'Can we have a drink here? I'd like to talk.'

'This place depresses me.'

'Please . . . I want to talk about Kate.'

'I can only handle one disaster at a time, Judith!'

'Leaving Kate is not a disaster!'

'I know that.' He stood by her, dropping his head on to her shoulder. 'Judith, I cannot walk in the door and say, "Kate, I'm leaving." Much as I want to be with you I can't just walk out.'

'Why don't you take her away for a few days? Tell her then.'

He looked up. 'Michael asked us to stay with them for a week . . . At the end of the month. I could take the money in person. I dismissed the idea . . .'

Judith looked thoughtful. 'Is Caroline's money still invested here?'

'What?' He frowned. 'Yes, it is. Nearly sixty thousand pounds.' He watched her closely, wondering if she thought he would be robbing Peter to pay Paul. Robbing Caroline to pay Michael. She was wearing her strange, satisfied smile, her slanted eyes dreamy.

'It's such a pity you have to repay Michael,' she said quietly, pouring more whisky into Clive's glass and pouring a smaller drink for herself. 'After all, you inherited so many problems with the Sundial. Why can't you make him wait indefinitely?'

'How?'

'Don't you know something about him? Or about Caroline?'

He was silent for a moment. 'You really mean it, don't you?'

'Yes, I do. It's no crime to survive. In a hundred years who the hell will care how ethical you were?'

Clive shrugged, hardly taking her seriously. 'I may be unlucky but I'm no criminal.'

'I wish you would show me the figures, Clive. I'd like to

271

understand exactly how the money is tied up between you and Caroline and Michael.'

'In one great incestuous triangle. I owned one fifth of Mosaic. I paid Michael for two more fifths. I owed him twenty thousand pounds for the remainder initially and over the years it has become roughly twenty-five. We agreed to final settlement in September or October seventy-seven, exactly four years after his emigration, to avoid the payment of the dollar premium. But in December he asked for ten thousand pounds to be paid earlier. When that is done I shall still owe him fifteen thousand, two hundred and three pounds . . .'

'And ten pence.'

'I made up the ten pence!'

'And Caroline's money for the sale of her shop is quite separate.'

'Yes, it's on deposit.'

'Easily realizable?'

'Yes.'

'And if she needed it suddenly?'

'The same rules apply to her as to Michael. She has to wait out her four years or pay the dollar premium.'

'Or put it in a suitcase?'

'Yes. People do that too.'

'I've read that in special circumstances the Bank of England will allow money to be transferred freely . . . in the case of severe illness in the family or something.'

'Yes, they can do that.'

Judith moved farther back from him. She sat on the edge of a desk. 'I've had an idea for some time, Clive. For over a year, in fact. Ever since I realized how much you need money, to get you through this time, to get you to me. Money for Mosaic and for a divorce. It's ideal if you are there, with Kate, in France. An attempt at reconciliation. How nice. Afterwards the strain will bring out the truth.'

'What are you talking about?' Clive said, moving towards her

272

but she put up her hands to keep him back.

'I'm talking about Charlie. I'm going to take Charlie for a few days until they pay me a large sum of money and then I shall give him back. He will be perfectly safe with me. He likes me.'

Clive threw back his head and laughed.

'I shall take him to the Finchs' house,' Judith went on. 'I shall take food and camping things. I have already told my employer I'm taking a few weeks off. I've told her I'm going to drive around France. My lover, who is married, is trying for a reconciliation with his wife. I'm very upset. I love Provence. It will allow me to think. I need a break. She likes it when I talk to her. I shall pour my heart out to her.'

'You can't be serious, Judith!' He laughed again, trying to divert her. Her words seemed ridiculous and utterly unreal. He wondered if she were joking.

'I shall take my tape recorder. Unfortunately we have to do the dramatic demand bit. There is never a way round that.'

'Oh, so you've done this before, then?' Clive teased.

'No, of course not! But I've thought about it. It's a marvellous crime because people nearly always exclude the police, especially where a child is involved. Especially a man like Michael, withdrawn and stubborn and clever, hating the telephone. It all fits so neatly, the way they are, the way the child is.'

'How would you take the child?' Clive asked coldly.

She ignored his tone. 'I should leave my car outside the gates and walk into the garden and pick him up. He plays outside on his own all the time. I know all about him . . .'

'And if someone sees you?'

'I shall say I've come to see Caroline. Or that I found him too far from the house, in the road in fact. I know the routines so well. You and Kate will want to visit something and will take Caroline out for the morning and just let me know when.'

'No,' Clive said. 'It's ridiculous. Let's go and have a drink.'

'I'm serious, Clive.'

'So am I. I absolutely refuse to have anything to do with it!'

273

She straightened with anger, her eyes narrowed. 'Does that include taking Kate to France? Do you refuse to do that? Take her and tell her? It's an ideal opportunity!'

Clive stared at her. He sighed.

'Ring Kate. Please. At least tell her about the holiday. Let her think about it, Clive.' Her voice had changed. She moved close to him, put her mouth against his, turning the 'please' into a kiss.

'All right. But I will have nothing to do with the other idea. You understand that?' He picked up the telephone.

Kate stood at her bedroom window, elbows on the sill, looking out at the garden. She liked to lean here. She liked the clean cotton smell of the curtains and the children's voices drifting up from the garden. The late afternoon sun pressed down and Melanie, naked except for a sunbonnet, crawled round the paddling pool and the sunbathing au pair girl, chased in a joyful circle by Robert, who was two and lived next door. Karen lay like a sleeping Gulliver, sunbathing stubbornly despite the noise, her solid body inadequately clothed in a small bikini, her extended arms revealing the unshaven armpits which so fascinated Melanie. An aeroplane moved ponderously and deafeningly across the clean blue sky, sliding down to Heathrow.

Kate left the window. She crossed the big bedroom and lay on the bed, arms folded under her head, legs and feet bare and brown. Such an un-English summer, surprising and scorching them all, contributing to the restless unhappiness which was growing in her. In one hand she held Henri's latest letter, folded small. She brought her arms down and opened the letter again . . . Through the autumn and winter she had been dormant, building herself again, recovering. But now the scar on her stomach was just a faint white smile, almost hidden by the pubic hair; now she was not afraid and she had looked for Clive again and found he was no longer there. A strange, preoccupied man lived in the house with her. The atmosphere between them was agonizingly polite and Kate knew it could not go on.

The telephone pulled her out of her thoughts and she rolled over and lifted the receiver, lying now in Clive's half of the bed, seeing the dust on the table and on his thick pile of *Penthouse* magazines.

'Hello, Kate. Everything okay?' Clive's deep, very English voice.

'Fine. You must be hot at Mosaic . . .'

'Yes, it's almost unbearable. I'm going to stop for a swim on the way home. What time are the Finches expecting us?'

'About eight-thirty.'

'Right. The main reason I rang is that I've been speaking to Michael.'

'Is he over here?'

'No, I rang him about something and he asked, as he always does, when we will go and stay with them and he suggested the end of the month. I could get off for a week then.'

'You said we'd go?' Instinctively Kate was bunching herself up. A series of complicated thoughts swept through her mind.

'I said I'd ask you. If we go for eight days there's a cheap way of flying with a car thrown in . . . he said how much Caroline would enjoy seeing you. She misses the company of her women friends a lot, even now.'

But I hardly know her, Kate thought and asked herself the silent question: And Henri? and Is this some attempt, at last, from Clive to mend us? She was shivering despite the heat.

'What about Melanie?' she said carefully.

'Well, it's certainly not worth taking her. It would be too hot.'

'Judith?' Kate interrupted. 'She might come . . .'

Clive hesitated. It was not a long pause but the telephone emphasized such spaces and it was obvious to Kate that for some reason she had disconcerted him. Since they had moved so far apart she noticed everything about him, the most minute details of his behaviour.

'I never thought of Judith,' he said. 'She's bound to be working. I'm sure my parents or yours could cope, with Karen's help. So, to be fair to the girl, we should wait till the end of the current term of English classes.'

'Can we afford it?' Kate asked and instantly regretted it. She knew they could not. Their life style was altering in steady stages as were the lives of most of their friends, but Clive refused to acknowledge it or even discuss it. 'I won't insult my friends with cheap wine if they come to dinner. I'd rather not have them!'

'Of course we can't afford it,' he said coldly, 'but it won't stop us going.'

She flushed at his tone. 'Do you want to go, Clive?'

He paused again. He avoided the question. 'I'll be back about eight. The Finches will fill you with enthusiasm about Provence tonight and go on and on about their farmhouse. . . .'

'Yes. I remember the vivid way you described the smell of damp and the peeling walls and the wasps' nest and the bottomless well. It sounded irresistible!'

Clive laughed. As he put the phone down he thought that she would always be able to spring laughter from him unexpectedly, when there was nothing else left between them, with her sense of the ridiculous. When her illness had temporarily dried up that sense of humour, he had missed the laughter without realizing what was missing, obsessed with Judith but still aware that some sharp, sweet edge was missing from his life. He thought now, rather sadly, that when Kate was gone from his life she would take that sharp sweetness for ever.

Judith had watched him speaking to Kate. She knew he was an emotional man, a man who loved women. Wasted on Kate, she thought. A man who was soft underneath. It was one of the reasons she loved him so much, the contradictions of the man. The brave face, the despair inside, the mastery in bed and failure in the world. Even now, after nearly a year, it surprised her that she had let one man take control of her happiness. Clive was

276

the only man she had ever cared enough about to be unsure of. The first human being she had ever genuinely loved. The first explosion of passion between them had changed into a deep and powerful relationship. She believed that she alone knew the fears which lay beneath his reckless attack on the world. She was prepared to organize both their lives if she could. And despite his expression when he spoke to Kate she was not afraid to send them to France together. She knew they would never be reconciled.

'Must you go out tonight, Clive?' She stood against him.

'Yes. But I'll be with you tomorrow.'

'What was the name of the Frenchman who stayed in your house last autumn? Michael's friend?' Judith asked as they moved towards the door.

'Henri Bertrand.'

'Yes, that's right. I met him several times at Jouvard. Dull man but Caroline liked him. So did Kate, you said.' Judith smiled. 'I hope they meet again this time.'

When she put down the telephone Kate's thoughts were moving slowly. It was the trick she had learned from Judith to counteract the panic which could still pounce. Kate moved away from the bed, automatically smoothing the covers. She worked hard in her house now. It was neat and clean and blank. The way she felt. She was utterly changed from the frightened girl Clive had once loved. That girl was dead but who was alive in her place?

At last she let herself think of Henri. He wrote frequently, long, rambling letters, full of his triumphs and worries, letters exactly like the way he spoke. Kate had kept them all. She had no idea what Henri would mean to her but she needed him to think about now that she and Clive were quite separate, living together and yet not living together as they waited. Kate lacked the courage or the desperation for a confrontation even now. She and Clive still went out together, two or three times a week, dining with couples outwardly like themselves . . .

It's an endless circle, she had written to Henri. *All the people here are about the same age and from the same background with one or two or three children and dogs; they meet too often and drink too much and after the first few years they begin to seek their stimulation by loving or imagining themselves to love the husbands and wives of others in the circle though they're all so alike I can't see why they bother! We all talk and reassure or attack each other round polished dining-room tables and everyone's children cause the same problems and everyone is suddenly short of money and some go to church but most do not. The couples who love each other must go home laughing. It must be a good life if you share it with someone who cares about you and satisfies. Unfortunately many of them, like Clive and me, can't seem to give each other very much.*

She sat down on the bed again, opening out the last letter. *Come to France, Kate, and see me.*

When Melanie was in bed, Kate ran herself a bath and poured in some of the exotic bath oil which Gabriel had given her. The water lapped the back of her neck and the ends of her hair and Henri's voice came into her head. 'My house is so quiet, Kate, especially at night.' Would he have changed? Would the sympathy between them still be there? Would it all still be there? At last she let herself imagine a week at Jouvard, let her thoughts drift tantalizingly round the edges of excitment, thinking at first of little things; of waking in the morning without a small insistent voice calling; swimming and lying in the sun. Kate loved the sun. Already this unusual summer had made her very brown. She thought of how David had once made her feel, of how Clive had affected her a lifetime ago. And at last she thought of Henri and that extraordinary, innocent week last autumn and how, after the first shy day, she had felt for him. The clock struck once for seven thirty and the water was almost cold. Kate got out and wrapped herself in a towel and padded to the cupboard to find something light and cool to wear. She had a sense of drawing herself together, a feeling that things were about to be resolved. She tried to imagine herself and Clive moving back together and the idea was sadly impossible. She

278

had never really let Clive in. She thought of their marriage as one of the large photographs the popular Sunday papers sometimes printed of a lion with a rabbit between its paws under the headline *Just good friends*. But I am more vole than rabbit, she thought, and laughed. And Henri? She only knew that she wanted to see him again very much.

'But you knew Caroline long before Michael did, didn't you, Clive?' Rachel Finch said that evening. They were eating in the garden and although it was almost ten it was very warm. The stored heat of the day and the scents of the garden made it hard to believe this was England. Light from the house spread patterns on the paving stones and touched Rachel's bare brown back and Clive's hair. A thousand moths attacked the lantern.

'Yes,' Clive said but let the subject die. Kate had noticed, long ago, that he spoke of Caroline as little as possible.

'But Michael is such an intense and uncomfortable man,' Carol George was saying.

'Exactly what I always thought,' Rachel laughed. 'How extraordinary to choose Michael and not Clive!'

'I always comfort myself by thinking of it as a straight cash deal,' Clive said dryly and there was delighted laughter. 'Anyway, I'd met Kate by then.' He smiled across the table, drawing Kate in as he always had. Everyone smiled at her and she went on eating, sensing the cruelty in Rachel's smile.

They are all Clive's people, not mine, she thought. They have never let me in. They have always made me feel too young and dull and unworthy of Clive. They are insultingly surprised when I make them laugh. And when Clive and I separate they will blame me for not keeping him and they will be satisfied. She was suddenly so sick of it all she could hardly swallow her mouthful of food. She had noticed in herself recently the return of the old anger . . .

'So you're going to Jouvard?' Ian Finch was saying.

Clive looked across at Kate. 'Yes, I think we are. We shall

279

have to wait till the end of the month.'

'How lovely for you, Kate, to get away. You must be longing for a break,' Carol George said.

'Yes, I am.' It was much easier to agree.

'And do give my love to that sweet Frenchman who stayed with you last year. He lived near the Redfords, didn't he? The man who printed cottons. What was his name? You brought him to our party.'

'Henri,' Kate said, very surprised, having forgotten that Carol had met him, thinking of him entirely as her own secret experience and someone only she would respond to.

'I understand he does terribly well,' Ian Finch was saying.

'His things sell very well for us,' Clive answered.

'But how can he have linked up with Mary May? Their clothes are pretty but so badly finished.' Rachel lit a cigarette. 'I'm amazed French women buy them!'

Kate tilted her head and looked up at the night sky, carelessly sequinned with stars. 'Do you wear their dresses?' he had asked her shortly before he touched her for the first time. She had said, 'No, I am too small. They make me look ridiculous.'

Much later, as Clive and Kate drove home, he asked, 'Enjoy yourself?' as he always did. There were so many habits between them Kate thought. But no habit of loving.

'Not much. Whenever Ian turns to me and says, "Kate, this will really interest you," I know I'm going to be bored!'

Clive laughed and then, in this tired darkness, alone in the car with Kate, he almost began to say it all. Almost but not quite. The words wouldn't come.

'I thought I'd go home for the weekend tomorrow. Take Karen and Melanie. Will you be all right?' Kate was saying.

'Of course. And shall we go to France, Kate? I think we should.' There was such a feeling of sadness between them, he thought. Of failure. Kate was a maze he was no longer prepared to try and find the heart of.

'Yes, I think we should,' she echoed and knew they both

expected France to frame some kind of ending.

Judith drove her car into the cobbled mews and parked in her usual space just past her own front door. It was after 6.30 but still intensely hot. London was being bleached by this summer, she thought, leaning into the back of the car to lift out her bag of groceries. Her back was damp with sweat. She got out, balancing the shopping on one hip as she searched her big shoulder bag for her keys. She found them and unlocked the narrow front door and went up the stairs.

The small flat was deliciously cool and quiet after her rushed day. For the past five months she had been with a family in Kensington, helping a gentle, pretty woman who had had her third baby the week Judith arrived. The two older children, both under four, sucked at their mother like emotional leeches, greeting her every appearance with whining demands. With Judith they were normal small children, alternately enchanting and ruthless. The job suited her well. She was almost always home by 6.30. Since Clive had come into her life she preferred to take jobs where she went in daily.

Judith unpacked her shopping and took a can of Lager from the fridge. She walked into her bedroom, peeling off her damp T-shirt and spreading herself on the bed. She closed her eyes and listened to the distant traffic. Her large breasts were divided by a diagonal line where brown skin became white. She had a small flat roof outside the kitchen where she sunbathed on free days. Judith took the triangle of tin from the can and drank. She was happy. She moved her body in anticipation of Clive and let her thoughts drift through the next four or five hours. She would have a bath and wash her hair and cook and he would come about eight and they would eat with the windows wide open and the summer evening drifting in. The ice-cold can rested for a moment on her stomach and the muscles bunched in shock. One day she would have him here permanently.

Judith ran herself a bath and washed her hair, scraping it

back from her face as she climbed out and hollowed a clear circle in the steamy mirror. Funny face but it had its uses and its appeal. She rubbed her hair with a towel, brushed it and let it hang damply down her back. It was too hot to use a drier. She put on a long cotton skirt and a T-shirt and began to chop vegetables. She believed she was gradually bringing Clive round to her way of eating but she would have to compromise with a steak for him. He would bring wine. He had taught her a lot about wine in the past year. Recently he had taken to bringing champagne, saying it was the best thing to drink in the heat, but she knew him so well now. She knew that, as Mosaic sank more and more deeply into trouble, Clive would react with greater and greater flamboyance.

He came early, just after 7.30. She heard his key and came out of the kitchen to greet him as he got to the top of the stairs, putting her hands high over his shoulders. 'I'm covered in garlic.'

'Mmmm.' He rocked her gently, his mouth in her hair, registering the feelings she always stirred in him, wanting her. 'No one should have to work in this heat, let alone pretend to care that two dozen barometers have gone astray between here and Marseilles. I need a shower and a drink.'

Judith went ahead of him to the bathroom, washing her hands, taking pants and bras from the nozzle of the shower where they were drying.

'Kate's gone home tonight . . .'

She swung round, smiling, the prospect of a weekend with him lighting her face.

'But I've got to drive to Birmingham. I should go this evening.'

'Whatever for?'

'Those ridiculous Beanies. Some marketing man from a petrol company wants to see them tomorrow.'

'Let him wait. Why should you work on a Saturday?'

'I could leave very early tomorrow morning.' He was unbuttoning his shirt. She kissed his mouth and his chest.

'What sort of drink?'

'Whisky. Lots of ice.' The water sprang from the shower and he stepped under it and made a sound of satisfaction. In the kitchen Judith heard and smiled, making two drinks and thinking that, if she were teaching Clive to eat her food, he was certainly teaching her to drink.

'Had a good day?' he was saying, above the sound of the water.

'Yes. God knows how she'll cope when I'm away. She asked me today to be sure and come back after my holiday.'

'I think you get far too involved with these people.'

'Of course I get involved. I like using my common sense and my efficiency and it's so very profitable. Besides, I like her.' She carried the glasses back to the bathroom and Clive turned off the water, lifting his face and smoothing back his hair. Judith gave him a towel. He looked massive, standing in the bath, his face and neck and arms freckled, the rest of his body white. He wound the towel round his waist and took the drink.

'Are you really taking this holiday in France, then?'

'Yes. I do need a little time on my own.'

'Why don't you wait for me? After it's all over . . .'

'I want to go to France, Clive.' She drank some of the whisky. 'Do you know, I still think about that first afternoon here. No one has ever affected me as you did then. I have never wanted a man so badly. All the waiting, I suppose.' She smiled. 'But it hasn't changed.'

'I think of it too . . .' He put his arms round her and the stillness grew between them.

'Have you booked your flight?'

'Yes. July the sixth.'

'I've made a reservation on the ferry for July the third. And I've borrowed a tent and a sleeping bag. I shall take a box of books and cassettes and two bikinis and a supply of food and be absolutely happy!'

'Bloody health food crank! Taking your own food to France!'

She hit him jokingly with her fist and they moved through to the bedroom and Clive dressed.

'All that rubbish about Charlie . . . you were joking, weren't you?'

'Perhaps.' She sat down. 'But I enjoyed thinking it all out. Like a jigsaw, piece by piece. When he vanished and they had the call asking for money they would have two choices. If they called in the police we would abandon the whole thing. If they decided to pay, and I know they would, they would either have that much money readily available in France . . .'

'How much money?'

'Fifty thousand pounds.'

'They haven't!'

'I know. So when you pointed out that Caroline's money was just sitting here and you could be here and back to Jouvard in twenty-four hours, they would agree.'

'And a customs man would open the suitcase . . .'

'You would tell them about the Bank of England's generosity under extraordinary circumstances. You would tell them you would arrange it all. But in fact there won't be anything in your suitcase except a brown paper parcel, tightly wrapped, with knots and sealing wax as the kidnapper will stipulate. And there won't be time, at Jouvard to undo it all. Who would want to? You take an empty parcel to France and Caroline's money stays here. It merely moves out of her deposit account and becomes yours.' She moved through to the kitchen and Clive followed. 'If Michael agrees to you delivering the ransom you could merely go through the motions in case they check afterwards. Destroy the parcel and take Charlie home.'

'I wish to God you'd stop talking about it,' Clive said, sitting down. 'I would never have anything to do with it. You've overlooked the fact that Charlie is Caroline's life!'

'She will get him back!'

'There would be two or three days of absolute agony for her.'

'Well?' Judith had taken *Gaspacho* soup from the fridge and was ladelling it into two bowls. 'Most people get hurt in their lives. Is she above agony? Is she to be protected at your expense?' She rested her hands on the table and the heavy gold bracelet slid down her arm.

Clive touched it and then looked into her eyes. 'Have you done this before?'

'I told you, no. But most of them have something they don't want discussed.'

'Charlie would tell them it was you.'

'Charlie doesn't speak. Caroline writes to me, pours out her worries, thinks I am an expert on children; there is nothing I don't know about her life and Michael and Charlie! Charlie says "*Maman*" and that's all!'

Clive leaned forward, closed his eyes for a moment, put his hand on to his forehead to hide his expression. He could not bear to think of Caroline hurt, even now. Perhaps twenty-eight had been too late to love for the first time? He could not bear to think of her writing to Judith . . . 'I don't want to talk about it any more. It's ridiculous!'

Judith was silent for a while. She watched Clive sprinkle chopped onion and croutons on to the soup. Eventually she said, 'What does Kate think about going to France? Is she pleased? Does she know about us?'

'She must know there is someone but I don't think she knows it is you. When I've told Kate and it's in the open I'll come here, shall I? I want to be with you . . . Kate can have Melanie. They would be happier without me. Kate's only twenty-three. She may find someone to be what she wants, although God knows what that is!'

There was an edge to.his voice which Judith had not heard before. 'She has hurt you, hasn't she?'

'I loved Caroline. Her every movement and word obsessed me and I was numb when it ended and suddenly there was Kate. Literally the same night. Needing me and amazed at my interest in her, absurdly shy and funny. Unfortunately she hatched into

285

something neither of us expected.' He paused and drank some wine. 'Now I love you. More than anyone.' He touched her hand. 'All the problems will resolve themselves in the end. We'll survive. But please don't ever mention that Charlie thing again.'

Clive left in the clean early morning and Judith leaned her elbows on the window-sill and watched him walk out of the mews. He always parked his car some distance away. The flat still smelled of his cigars. She was suddenly lonely. How much she had changed! Clive was her life now. There had been nothing like him before and she would go to any lengths to keep him and to secure their life together. She moved away from the window and went back into the bedroom and lay in the chaos of the bed. She rolled herself into a sheet. Once she had said to Clive. 'I always put myself first.' She wasn't sure that it was still true. Everything was far more complicated now. Putting one part of herself before another part. She stretched her arms, remembering how his face had changed when he spoke of Caroline. She had hated that. Judith wanted all of him, his past and his present and his future, wanted to scratch out all memories and burn his body clean of everyone but herself.

CHAPTER SEVENTEEN

Caroline stood at the sink in her big, stone-floored kitchen washing lettuce, her brown hands swirling the leaves through the water as she thought how much she loved this room, the heart of her house. The windows overlooked the courtyard. It was always cool here. She remembered Michael's voice the first afternoon. 'Better than you imagined, or worse?'

'Better,' she had answered.'Far better.'

She had enjoyed changing the house, making it beautiful. Those first months here and the time when Charlie had been a tiny baby and Michael had been with them so much more, those months had been very happy. It was necessary for her to remember happiness now, to bring it forward. She mixed garlic and breadcrumbs for the tomatoes and put a joint of veal in the oven, looking up at the big ship's clock they had brought from England. Nearly seven. She had expected them earlier but the flights were often late in the tourist season. She wanted to see Clive again. There was something left, she thought. A gentleness between them. She had wondered, frequently, what life would have been like had she married Clive. She had thought she did not love him enough, that the affection between them was nothing compared with her instinctive adoration of Michael. She remembered thinking: How incredible to feel love so strongly again.

Thirty had seemed old then. Now, at thirty-three, looking back, she cringed at her immaturity. She wanted Clive and Kate to come to Jouvard. She wanted any diversion from her unhappiness. But, she thought, I would probably do the same again. People repeat mistakes as if, having learnt one way, they cannot change. A habit of mistakes? But how can Michael be a mistake? I adore him, or the part of himself he allows me, the time he allows me. She knew she was too possessive constantly asking for attention until the words became nagging repetitions; reaching for him, trying to hold in her hands a personality that could not be held, that did not want or need holding. How long can you go on asking for demonstrations of love and being dissatisfied when they come because they had to be asked for? She hoped the strain and tension would not be too obvious to Clive and Kate.

She put her head on one side, listening, thinking she heard Charlie, but there was no repetition of the sound and Michael was upstairs and would go to him. She loved to see them together, her thin, dark husband and her beautiful little boy, communicating without words, but Michael was so rarely in the house in the daytime and Charlie needed a lot of sleep.

Michael laughed if Caroline confided her anxiety about Charlie's lack of speech. 'He thinks too much to waste time with words, Caroline.'

'Do you think he is confused because two languages are spoken here? He should use far more words, Michael.'

'Leave him alone. He's quite all right. He'll talk when he's ready.'

It was impossible to reason with Michael about anything he chose not to talk about. Any hint of a real argument and he would remove himself, leaving Caroline alone and unsatisfied. And so she wrote to Judith, long rambling letters, pouring it all out.

She put melons in the fridge to chill and washed her hands. She found herself going over past conversations with Michael in her head more and more, trying to think of another way to say it all. She had been feeling isolated and desperate for some time now. She looked at her face and dress in the oval mirror, one of Henri's long, pretty dresses. But was she too thin now? Did she seem older than her thirty-three years? She moved closer and then shrugged aside her vanity, picking up a tray of knives and forks and glasses. They would eat outside. She liked to make the first evening of any visit special and it was still special to her to

288

eat on the veranda with the night black and warm and the house behind her like a friend at her shoulder. She genuinely loved this place now.

She heard Michael and turned. He came into the kitchen looking freshly scrubbed and absurdly young, giving her a sudden feeling of weariness, of old age. She sometimes thought her awareness of the difference in their ages might be one of the reasons she gave in so much. Why couldn't she make him understand how she felt?

'They're not here yet?' He ran a hand along the back of his collar where his hair was damp.

'No. Is Charlie asleep?'

'Yes, with the whole floor covered in a marvellous pattern of books. I was careful not to disturb them.' Michael poured himself a glass of wine. 'I'm rather apprehensive about seeing Clive . . .'

'Why?' Caroline asked, surprised that he should tell her.

'Because I think things are going far worse for him than he says. It's a bad time for him to repay me money . . . but I do need it.' He watched Caroline move towards the door. He loved to watch her. She was thinner since Charlie's birth but just as beautiful. More beautiful. But distant. Lonely? He hated the coolness between them. 'Caroline . . .'

She paused, turning. 'Yes.'

'Sometimes you look so sad . . .'

'I am sad. But how can I say it all now? How can you start it now? I feel ignored and angry and . . .' She stopped as they both heard the car.

Michael went to the window, intensely relieved. 'Henri,' he said. 'I'll let him in.'

Kate and Clive were an hour and a half late taking off from Heathrow and they landed at Marseilles at five-thirty instead of four. They stayed in their seats while the first eager rush of people jostled down the narrow aisle of the aeroplane and, when

the queue thinned, Clive stood up and took Kate's denim jacket
down from the rack, stepping out and making a space for Kate
to step into. He assumed a special expression, Kate thought. As
if, an experienced traveller himself, it irritated him to watch the
anxieties of fellow travellers.

The heat was waiting for them as they went down the
unsteady steps and into the airport bus. They lurched towards
the terminal building and there were more delays. The wicker
basket Kate carried bit into her arm, leaving bracelets in the
flesh. When they had cleared customs, Clive went to the Hertz
desk.

Kate stood with the luggage and thought how very different
another country was. The light was different, the faces, the
clothes, the voices . . . she looked at Clive's wide back. He had
been so strange these past few weeks. She had hardly seen him.
He had been constantly preoccupied but had told her nothing.
He was walking towards her now, holding the car keys, still
acting his airport-weary role. Kate mentally shouted at herself,
'Oh, leave him alone!'

'It's parked outside. It's a green Renault.'

They found the car, put the luggage in and Kate thankfully
put down the basket. 'I hope they appreciate the baked beans.
They've almost amputated my arm. What an extraordinary
thing to ask us to bring. I wondered if I should have declared
them. They may be forbidden in France because of their
humble gourmet rating . . .' But Clive wasn't listening. He
handed her a map.

'If I give you this, can you find the way to the autoroute? I
should remember the last part.'

'I can try.' She looked at the different coloured road signs
and the lettering was quite unlike English . . . a whole landscape of differences. They drove for an hour and a half, finding
the way quite easily, and as they neared Jouvard Kate became
more and more uneasy, wondering why she had said she
wanted to come. It was so long since she had spent whole days

in Clive's company. What was she meant to do? Try again or admit the hopelessness? She shrank into her seat. And Henri? She wouldn't know how to be, what to say. As they turned between stone gateposts and stopped outside a lovely old stone house she wished she hadn't come.

Clive got out of the car, the double front doors opened and Michael came towards them. He was smiling.

In the tiled hall with its graceful staircase Caroline was waiting, leaning towards Clive's kiss. Kate hovered awkwardly, both hands holding the basket and saw another figure coming into the hall behind Caroline, drink in hand. She felt panic and pleasure as she recognized him. He came and stood in front of her and she saw again the face she had forgotten although she had tried so hard to remember it.

'Hello, Kate . . .'

Caroline was beside her then, bending down to kiss her cheek, gathering her towards the stairs. 'Come on up. You must be exhausted. It's so hot. Would you like a shower or a swim or a drink? Shall I bring one up?'

'The baked beans,' Kate said, holding out the basket and Caroline laughed.

'You brought them! It's the one thing Michael misses. Leave them here . . . Michael, are you bringing their cases?'

'No, I am,' Clive said and he followed them up the curving stairs.

Kate stayed upstairs to shower and change and to gather her courage. Her hands trembled. When she felt clean and cooler and had looked out of the tall windows and decided it was a beautiful house, she reluctantly started to go down. She went towards the stairs and paused as a little boy looked round a bedroom door.

'Charlie?' she said. He did not answer. Kate went towards him and he backed into the room, opening the door as he did so. 'Is this your room? May I come in?'

291

He sat on the bed. A slatted blind at the window kept out some light and the floor of the room was a complicated cross-word pattern of books, laid in paths and squares. Kate stepped between them carefully with her small feet.

'My name is Kate and I've come to stay for a few days. I've brought you a present and tomorrow, when I unpack, I'll give it to you.' He slipped his feet under the sheet, watching her with large grey eyes. Caroline's eyes. 'Shall I tuck you in?' She pushed the sheet loosely under the mattress. 'Can you go to sleep now?'

He gave her a slight smile and closed his eyes.

They were all in the garden, standing by the swimming pool, and they turned as Kate came through the wicker gate. 'I'm sorry I was so long. I met Charlie.'

'The slightest thing wakes him,' Caroline said. 'Is he in bed now?'

'Yes and he closed his eyes.' She took the glass of champagne which Michael held out to her.

'Welcome to Jouvard, Kate.'

She smiled and drank and turned at last to Henri. She saw the uncertainty in his eyes and his smile and it reassured her, made him real again.

'How are you, Kate?'

'I'm all right.'

'I'm so glad you're here. I like your hair longer. You've grown up!'

'I've grown in.' They were talking in code, she thought, wanting to touch him, just reach out and touch his hand to see how it felt.

'And Melanie?'

'She's adorable now. She is trying to walk and she says "Mummy". It horrified me at first. I didn't know who she was talking to. I don't feel like a Mummy.'

'I want to show you everything,' Henri said quietly. 'I think this year's designs are the best I've done. I've never worked so

292

hard.' He paused and then said softly: 'I've never been lonely before.'

'Is he telling you about this year's designs?' Caroline said. 'They are lovely, Kate. And he's named one for me and one for you. And put up with me sitting in the studio, distracting him . . .' Caroline's tension began to be obvious to Kate. She moved her hands so much and there was always a cigarette between her long fingers. 'Kate is a small design of lilies of the valley.'

So he remembers everything, Kate thought and met his eyes. A wave of peace touched her and it was hard not to step forward.

They ate on the veranda and the night came down over their shoulders. It was a strange evening; Clive was aggressively amusing, talking more than he had for months, as if trying to show that all Mosaic's problems had fallen from him, that there was no strain between Michael and himself. He referred frequently to Caroline, showing that he was not afraid to display the affection he felt now that their relationship was so lessened by time and circumstance. And there were heavy silences, strange among people who knew each other so well, and Michael talked about his vines with a passionate interest and Caroline watched him as he spoke, her face wearing an expression of tenderness or exasperation or closing up blankly. Once she interrupted, rather desperately. 'We had the stoves out again this year. We were up all night for four days. It was exhausting . . .' But she had been happy then. She had felt part of it all.

'What stage are you at now?' Clive asked Michael.

'Just finished spraying. Next month the grapes turn colour and we have to check our machinery and clean the vats.'

'And it still fascinates you?' Clive said.

'Yes, it does.' He looked across at Caroline. 'Too much, I suppose. It takes so much time. Especially at the harvest.' He lifted his glass. 'Caroline is thinking of going to England this year during the harvest.'

293

She stood up as he spoke as if trying to get away from the pain of the words and the failure they expressed. 'I'm going to bring coffee out here.'

Kate followed her into the house, carrying some empty plates and putting them on the kitchen table. Caroline thanked her, avoiding her eyes. 'I'm just going to see if Charlie is all right . . . you could take the coffee out if you like.'

Kate set the glass perculator on the tray of cups and saucers and walked slowly back towards the garden. Sitting beside Henri she had felt such simple happiness. Perhaps it was good to see him for a few days like this, to feel spun round and alive again?

In the garden the three men talked, the cognac relaxing them, but Henri kept his eyes on the corner of the house, watching for Kate's slight, wistful figure, wanting to have her back beside him, to watch the laughter touch her face. And yet he distrusted the simplicity of his feelings for her. Henri, above all people, knew that it was never simple and there were so many complications between himself and Kate, years and Clive and the English Channel and his own reticence, his fear of hurting Kate.

'And you have expended even more, Henri?' Clive was saying.

'Yes, I'm afraid so. I've opened a shop in Paris but the biggest success of all is the T-shirts. We knit them, making imported American yarn into cotton jersey. Mary May sell a lot of them.'

'It's good to see someone doing well,' Clive said dryly. 'I was talking to Ian Finch a couple of weeks ago. He can't even afford to make his wreck of a farmhouse habitable.'

Kate put the tray on the table and sat down and Henri thought: How does he feel for her? I would find it easier to cope with straightforward sadness if she and Clive were reconciled . . .

'Were you talking about the Finchs' house?' Caroline said as she came towards them. 'It's not such a wreck. Not when the sun shines!' They all laughed. 'You must take Kate to see it.'

'Yes, I promised Rachel we would look at it for them. I'll take you tomorrow, Kate, and get it over with.'

'And when will you come and see my place?' Henri asked. 'Tomorrow night? For dinner?'

'Yes, why not?' Caroline answered for them all. 'And on Wednesday Michael wants to drive to Aix so I thought we could all go there. It's a nice town.'

Henri left soon after eleven, saying they must all be tired, kissing Caroline and bending to touch his lips to Kate's cheek. She was afraid they would all hear her heart beating and sense the reluctance with which he drew away. 'Come early tomorrow night,' he said. 'I want to show you everything!'

'We'll leave all this,' Caroline said to Kate, waving a vague hand at the table. 'When I have people to stay, Yvette comes in more often. My untidiness appals her but luckily my cooking redeems me. She is a nice woman. A kind, good woman. She and Raoul live in a small farmhouse about five minutes' walk away. She is my baby-sitter . . . remind me to ask her to come in tomorrow, will you?' They all went inside and Caroline closed doors and turned off lights. Michael went into his office.

'And don't hurry in the morning, Kate,' Caroline said, her eyes following Michael, Clive went into the office too. She knew they would talk for hours. She followed Kate up the stairs, and went first into Charlie's room, bending and touching his forehead in some instinctive act of reassurance, as Kate did with Melanie.

Kate's bedroom was hot. She dropped her clothes over the back of a chair and went through her brief night-time ritual, washing her face and brushing her teeth and her hair. Her face had never seemed worthy of the exotic creams that were advertised. There were two single beds in the room and she got into the one farthest from the door. It was too hot to wear a nightgown. She moved her naked body restlessly under the sheet and listened to the men's voices, distant and muffled. It was so long since Clive had made love to her. Through her pregnancy and the depression afterwards she could hardly bear to be touched. She was ashamed of her coldness, very aware that the failure of her marriage was not a one-sided thing, but for Clive to approach her now would seem obscene. She rolled herself into a tight ball of panic, wondering yet again if this was to be some attempted reconciliation. Surely not. She didn't want it. She thought of how many months it was since she and Clive had made love, thought back sadly to their early months together, and wondered where that intimacy had gone? Nothing left. She knew that Henri was right, that Clive must have a mistress. One woman or several? She stared at the dark ceiling and the saddest thing of all was that the idea of Clive's unfaithfulness caused her so little pain.

Kate woke to hear a child singing outside, a strange chant without words, and for a moment she thought it was Melanie in her cot and then she opened her eyes and saw white walls instead of blue and looked across at the other empty bed. She half remembered Clive getting up earlier. She looked at her watch and it was 8.30 and she felt guilt and a left-over panic from childhood about missing it all. She dressed quickly in a cotton skirt and T-shirt and went down to the kitchen.

Caroline was laying breakfast and speaking French to a small woman who stood by the sink washing glasses.

'Hello, Kate. Did you sleep well?'

'Far too well, I think. Am I very late?'

'Of course not. The men went out some time ago. Michael wants to show Clive all the machinery. But Charlie and I haven't started yet.' She turned to the woman at the sink. 'This is Madame Gautier . . . my friend from England, Madame Holden.' Kate smiled, too self-conscious to try to speak in French.

'Yvette won't speak any English,' Caroline smiled. 'Although I am sure she understands quite a lot. Now, I usually cook something for Charlie. Breakfast is his best meal. Would

296

you like eggs and bacon or there are *croissants*.'

'I'd love a *croissant*.' Kate recognized in Caroline this morning the heavy calmness which overlaid unhappiness. There was a deliberation about her words and her movements as if her thoughts wanted to be elsewhere. Kate looked out at the shady courtyard. 'What can I do to help?'

'Could you find Charlie and tell him breakfast is ready? He usually plays on the veranda by the front of the house in the mornings. He may come with you or he may not.'

Kate found the child lying on his stomach, head on one arm, driving a lorry backwards and forwards through a small puddle which the sprinkler had left on the paving stones. The wheels made a delicate pattern of double lines. He made none of the usual sounds which small boys make when they play with cars. Kate crouched down beside him.

'Hello, Charlie. Breakfast is ready.'

He sat up, putting one arm shyly across his forehead to hide his face.

'After breakfast,' Kate said, 'shall we go to my room and find that present?'

The arm came down, very slowly, and he stood up when Kate did and brushed dust from his knees. He held out one hand to Kate and gave her four large seeds and then walked ahead of her towards the kitchen.

'Well done.' Caroline put a plate in front of the little boy. 'When the Finches stayed he refused to sit down at all. Michael says I give in too much but it's so unpleasant to have a screaming child at the table and he's so small.' She indicated a chair to Kate and put a pot of coffee and a basket of *croissants* on the table.

'What are these?' Kate asked, holding her palm flat to show the seeds.

Caroline smiled. 'You are honoured! Those are the seeds of the sun. Actually they are sunflower seeds, *les tournesols*, but somehow in the translation Charlie is convinced that they are the seeds which must be planted each night when the sun goes

297

into the ground to make a new sun the next day.'

They both smiled at Charlie but he sat quite motionless with tears in his eyes.

'What is it?' Caroline said. 'Oh . . . the mug.' And she exchanged it for a distinctively patterned one and Yvette laughed.

Kate watched with fascination as Charlie, using his knife and fork with considerable efficiency for a child who was not yet three, cut the white from the fried egg and put the pieces on the edge of the plate. Caroline poured herself a cup of coffee and sat down. She looked tired, Kate thought. Perhaps she disliked having people to stay and the story of her liking female company was just a male cliché. Kate took a *croissant*.

Michael and Clive came into the kitchen and Caroline poured them coffee and played with a *croissant*, watching her son.

'It's fascinating,' Clive was saying. 'You must come round and see it all later, Kate. And what time shall we go to the Finchs' house?'

'Whenever you like.'

Clive sat down and pulled his chair closer to the table. 'How about you, Charlie? You've grown up so much since I was here last year. Would you like to come?' Kate stared at Clive, amazed to hear him talk like this to a small child. 'Shall we take him with us, Caroline? Give you a bit of peace? Would he come?'

Caroline was surprised. Her first reaction, always, was to keep him with her but she met Michael's eyes and she knew Michael thought she sheltered the child too much. 'It's very good for him to learn to go with other people but I don't know if he will . . .'

'Of course you will, won't you, Charlie?' Michael said.

'Let's see how he feels after breakfast,' Caroline answered for him but before she had finished speaking he got down from his chair, crossed the room, and unhooked a white sun hat from a peg by the door. He put it on his head and came and stood by Kate.

298

'That's settled then.' Clive laughed.

They drove for about twenty minutes, following Michael's instructions, through St Remy and south. Kate turned frequently to look at Charlie who sat in the middle of the back seat, hands spread on either side, solemnly wearing the hat and holding the red knitted rabbit which she had given him. She was attracted to the child. His absolute silence made it necessary to study his expressions closely. His skin was honey-coloured, his small face dominated by his eyes. After a while he moved and sat directly behind Kate.

They turned off the long straight road with its deep ditches each side and margin of plane trees on to a narrow track of hard, white earth. They passed two fields of petunias, purple and deep pink, and then the small fields, each divided by tall, wind-breaking bamboo hedges, became weed-filled and neglected. 'No one farms the Finchs' bit now,' Clive said. 'They have about seven acres, I think.'

'It's very remote. Why do they want to be on their own so much?'

'God knows.' Clive's heart was beating fast as he turned the car into the space in front of the house but it was quite deserted. No sign of Judith's car. No sign of life. He was intensely relieved and then laughed at himself inwardly. She hadn't meant any of it . . . just a stupid game.

The house, Kate saw, was a large stone building with small windows. Sun blazed into the yard as she got out and pulled the seat forward to allow Charlie to climb out. She took his hand. 'Let's explore, Charlie.' They walked to the side of the house and opened a door in a high wall and found themselves in an overgrown garden. 'This could be lovely,' Kate said. And then she and Charlie went back. Clive had unlocked the front door and they stepped into a dark room. Kate went to the windows. She found that they opened inwards and she pushed at the shutters and light came in. Her fingers were marked with dusty green paint. Clive called them from the next room and they went through.

'I suppose it will be lovely one day,' Kate said doubtfully. 'Shall we look upstairs, Charlie?' He hung back.

'I've already been up. Charlie and I will go out and have a game,' Clive said and he bent and picked up a brightly coloured ball from the floor and as he did so his heart beat fast again. He bounced it on the flagged floor and told himself he was being absurd. She wouldn't come here. She had said she wouldn't . . .

Kate went warily up the stairs. Empty houses scared her. She had had so many dreams of strange houses where the floor boards moved beneath her weight. She was afraid of opening a door and finding something horrible. But she made herself go up and look. It was all part of the way she still treated herself, stifling all weakness as soon as it was recognized, pushing herself into situations she feared. She looked at the large room on the first floor. Up again to the top rooms. She looked carefully enough so that she would be able to talk to Rachel about it later when she asked and then went thankfully down towards the sun again.

Clive and Charlie were in the walled garden, bouncing the ball against the walls. The child chased it, laughing delightedly.

'I thought we might stay a bit,' Clive said over his shoulder. 'Give Caroline a morning to herself.'

Although there was so little left between them now it still gave Kate a feeling of intense regret to watch Clive play with this child in a way he so rarely did with Melanie, watching Clive's powerful figure as he moved round the garden, swinging Charlie into the air. For the first time she admitted to herself how much it mattered that Clive was disinterested in Melanie. She thought it was because of her depression, that Clive thought of the baby as the cause of it all. She had given up trying to interest him in their own child. Why then this extraordinary interest in Charlie?

'Isn't he like Caroline?' Clive said, answering Kate as if she

300

had spoken her question aloud. She went just outside the walled garden and lay on a patch of scorched grass. She closed her eyes and felt tears behind them drawn from the depths of her, from an enormous sadness and a conviction that she and Clive had entered a final stage. And then what? Alone again? Henri? The tears came from panic now. She could not go on as they were but she did not want it all broken up. She sat up, wiping her face with the sleeves of her cotton shirt, going into the garden and watching Clive and the child.

They played for another half hour and then he said, 'I need a drink and a swim, Kate. Bring the ball with you, Charlie. No one will mind.' And he locked the house and put the key back on the ledge and they went towards the car. As they passed the well Clive dropped a stone down it and Kate shivered.

'Clive . . .' she said suddenly but he was helping Charlie into the car and didn't seem to hear.

They lunched on the veranda and discussed the rest of the day. Clive wanted to go into St Remy, to the market.

'And Charlie and I usually sleep in the afternoon,' Caroline told them apologetically. 'He still needs a rest and I haven't been sleeping very well lately.' She looked up at Michael and Kate saw the strain on her face, the lack of expression on Michael's.

'I shall be tied up with Raoul most of the afternoon,' Michael said.

'That leaves you, Kate.' Clive sat with Charlie on his lap. Charlie made patterns on Clive's plate with the pieces of skin Clive had peeled from a peach. Caroline kept looking at them together.

'Well, I am absolutely happy lying in the sun,' Kate said.

'So everything is settled.' Clive moved his knees and made Charlie bounce and laugh.

Caroline and Kate stayed at the table long after the coffee was finished and the men had gone.

'Thank you for taking Charlie with you, Kate. I am so pleased he enjoyed it. I do want him to be independent, whatever Michael says. Especially as he is an only child.'

'I'm sorry about the miscarriage,' Kate said. 'Judith told me.'

'Yes, it upset me terribly. It was such a miracle to be pregnant again. Michael thinks I dwell on it far too much, that I deliberately shut myself up here with Charlie. He speaks French so well that it is hard for him to understand.' She raised her eyes to Kate's face. 'Perhaps you have realized that we are not very happy at the moment? I know it is a wonderful place to live and we have friends here and people are very kind now that they know us but it still tires me to speak French for a whole evening and I feel I miss the subtleties, the fine interpretation of words that make the difference between really knowing people and just a surface understanding. It's the way you speak to someone of another generation too often, not really expecting them to understand what you mean. So I thought, if I went to England for a while . . .' She paused and smiled apologetically. 'I'm sorry to bore you with all this. That's another thing. I feel I trap the people I have to stay here, grasping at them and talking at them.'

'Won't it pass, the feeling of being an outsider?' Kate said, thankful that Caroline's own troubles had made her quite blind to the atmosphere between Kate and Clive. Or was it so well hidden?

Caroline shrugged. 'Henri says it will. He has been such a friend. And helped so much with Charlie. Although of course he no longer practises he used to deal with children a lot. He reassured me. As Judith does when I write to her!' She laughed. 'Henri thinks, as Michael does, that it is partly my fault, that I speak for Charlie and that he never has to make himself understood.' She looked down at the child who was playing on the grass. 'Now, I must take him for a rest. You'll be all right, Kate?'

'Of course.'

Kate went upstairs with them, then changed into a bikini and found a book. At first she lay in the sun, her toes in the pool, but when she became too hot she moved into the shade. She tried to read but her mind refused to become involved in the book. It returned again and again to herself and Clive and Henri, to Michael and Caroline. The evening ahead? Her stomach bunched up in nervous anticipation. She swam, moving her slight body expertly through the water, diving again and again, and then back to the sun, offering herself up to it.

Michael came out of his office and went quietly upstairs for a handkerchief, taking one from a drawer in his dressing-room. He looked in the open bedroom door and saw Caroline and Charlie in the wide bed, the child curled against his mother in sleep, Caroline on her back, one arm flung out, hair loose, breathing deeply. Why was she so restless? Why did she talk of going to England? He knew he must try and explain to her how the thought of weeks or months without her made him feel, how much he needed her here. But he found it so difficult to make the words come. She seemed to be asking so much of him. He came close to the bed and bent and touched her hair. She and the child were shut away from him by sleep as he felt they were nearly always shut away, enclosed in the glass bubble of Caroline's possessiveness.

CHAPTER EIGHTEEN

They all gathered downstairs just before seven, even Michael who had come in only ten minutes before. Caroline went out to find Charlie and Kate followed her. He was crouched over a flower-bed at the side of the house, wearing his pyjamas, pressing sunflower seeds into the earth. He patted it flat with his small hand and Caroline picked him up and carried him into the kitchen where Yvette Gautier waited. 'I think he should go to bed now.' She kissed him. 'My garden will grow nothing but sunflowers next year! Or even this year, I suppose!'

It took them thirty minutes to drive to Henri's house and the last part of the journey was very beautiful as they climbed out of the valley, between small rocky outcrops, and the sun grew brilliant as it began to go down. They looked back towards the stark outline of Les Alpilles. They drove through a small village and out the other side to Henri's collection of grey stone buildings, turning into a paved courtyard. He was waiting for them. 'I'm glad you're on time. Come into the working part first. This has always been a cotton mill but the next door part was once a barn.' He unlocked a heavy wooden door and turned a light switch and the neon hesitated and then burst into brilliant light, showing them a room full of machines. He took them through the cutting room, the weaving and knitting room, showed them the rollers where the cotton was printed and the huge tables where some was hand-blocked; upstairs to a storeroom where rolls and rolls of cloth were stacked, the design room and the offices and, 'This is where I sit and paint pictures, Kate.' He was so proud of it all and still seemed surprised by it. 'Now, Michael, if you and Clive want to go in and get a drink, I'll show Caroline and Kate some of our clothes.'

Kate followed him into his workroom, a small room with a drawing board, paints and brushes and a peg board on the wall.

304

Henri turned and Kate looked at him and all the complicated manœuvring to keep her eyes from his was absurd. He put out his hand and touched her lips and the kiss was understood.

'I have something for you, Kate.' He held out a brown paper bag. She opened it and took out a dress made of a creamy natural cotton with a small design of lilies of the valley traced over it. Kate shook it out. It was a simple dress with a drawstring waist and long sleeves. 'I remember you telling me that Mary May clothes overpowered you. I hope this is different.'

Her face showed her delight. 'It's beautiful.'

'I should like to talk to you, Kate. Not tonight . . .'

'Tomorrow morning? They are all going to Aix. I could stay at Jouvard . . .'

'I have someone to see at eleven. I could come after that.'

Caroline came in, a skirt hanging loosely over her arm. 'This is very pretty, Henri.'

The house was cool and plain with high-ceilinged white rooms and tiled floors. Henri had a housekeeper who had laid out the meal. Hors d'œuvres, cold beef and salads, cheese and then a cherry gâteau which Henri said he had bought in the village that morning. But despite the good food and wine and the fact that they were all old friends the evening was not happy. It was full of tension and silences and they left soon after eleven.

Kate slept badly and woke early on Wednesday morning. She wanted to swim. She left the room quietly, letting herself through the trellis gate and sliding into the still swimming pool. She floated on her back and looked at the sky. Perhaps it would have been better if she had not come to France at all? Perhaps she should have waited until she and Clive were severed, until she had made a life of her own, until she had more independence? She sat on the edge of the pool and felt the heat of the morning building up, and she smelt the great field of lavender which was beside the garden.

Clive seemed almost relieved when Kate said she would rather stay at Jouvard. He tried weakly to change her mind. 'It's a lovely town, Kate.' But when her reluctance was obvious he said, 'Well, I'll come with you, Caroline. I can't have you saying those boring Holdens never go anywhere!'

'I hope you don't mind, Caroline, but I would much rather stay here,' Kate said. 'I didn't sleep very well. I should be so happy just lying in the sun and I can look after Charlie.'

'Can't we take him with us?' Clive said abruptly.

'He doesn't like the car very much and Yvette will be here. If Kate stays Yvette can leave at twelve which she prefers. Raoul takes his lunch very seriously! I expect we'll be back at twelve-thirty or one, Kate.'

Charlie was an extraordinarily peaceful child, Kate thought. She watched him playing. Occasionally he trotted inside to visit Yvette and the second time he re-appeared carrying the rabbit Kate had given him and a book. She lay on her stomach, turning the pages and telling him the story. She went through it three times but she didn't mind. She was glad to have something to keep her mind from Henri, from speculating about what would happen when he came.

At eleven Yvette brought Kate a cup of coffee. Kate was by the pool now, watching Charlie swim. He was like a tadpole in his armbands with no fear of the water, taking running jumps from the edge and bobbing up above the surface, shaking water from his face and smiling. 'He can almost swim,' Caroline said, 'but I still never leave him alone by the pool. If you go indoors for any reason, would you bring him out and shut the gate?'

The sun dried the child and when he was too hot he came into the shade beside Kate. She was surprised when Madame Gautier came out and said it was almost twelve and she was leaving. Kate watched the Frenchwoman's small, strong figure as she started across the fields. Charlie sat on the edge of the pool, kicking his heels in the water, sending up a shower of splashes and singing his chanting, wordless song.

'Charlie, I'm going to get myself a cold drink. Would you like one?'

He nodded his head vigorously. Kate went and crouched beside him, 'Charlie, will you say my name? Say Kate.'

He looked away from her and she straightened up. 'All right then, take off the armbands and come outside the pool and wait for me.' She closed the gate carefully and he ran to the sand pit. Kate put on his shirt and shorts as here, at the front corner of the house, he was in the full glare of the sun. The rabbit was tucked under his arm.

Kate went round the edge of the house and through the court-yard to the kitchen, remembering to close the door against the heat. Thinking of the fuss Charlie had made about his mug she searched for it. There seemed to be a dozen cupboards. Eventually she found it in the dishwasher and filled it with orange. She poured herself a glass of white wine from an open bottle in the fridge. The tiled floor was cold under her feet. She wondered how much longer it would be before Henri came. Perhaps the others would come back first? Perhaps he had decided not to come?

The telephone rang and she had a moment of panic but she felt she must answer it. It could be Henri. She lifted the receiver warily. 'Hello?'

There was a peal of laughter. 'It's me, Caroline. I know just how you feel. Afraid that someone will gabble at you in French!'

Kate laughed. 'I nearly didn't answer it!'

'I wouldn't touch it for months! Is everything all right?'

'Absolutely fine.'

'Michael has been ages . . . we're leaving now so we should be back about one fifteen. Clive insisted we ring you! He is a very bad influence, wanting to go into every food shop we pass. He's bought masses of *saucisson*, stuffed aubergines and cheeses and God knows what else. Enough lunch for twenty. And don't worry about Charlie. He never gets hungry! See you later!'

Caroline had had such a good morning, laughing with Clive,

307

slipping into an easy, affectionate role with him that she had almost forgotten, loving the way he instinctively made her feel although they both knew it was nothing. A little nostalgia. A little love left over. While Michael talked they wandered through the town, from shop to shop, having coffee at a pavement café, talking. She did not tell him she was unhappy. She did not want to admit it. He did not mention himself and Kate. When he said they must ring Jouvard, she took it as a touching sign of his devotion to Kate, having no idea of the nagging worry which he kept dismissing as absurd but which kept surfacing. She didn't mean any of it, he told himself. She was angry with me for taking so long to tell Kate, angry with me for Mosaic's troubles. She didn't mean it. It was so hard, sitting here with Caroline, to believe in England, in Mosaic and its death throes, in Kate and the sadness that would come. But he would say it all. Tonight or tomorrow.

Kate carried the drinks through the house, going out of the double doors that opened on to the veranda where she expected to see Charlie in the sand pit. It was very quiet. Just the distant sound of a car.

'Charlie,' she called. 'I have your orange.' She walked to the table, put the drinks down and walked the length of this side of the house. 'Charlie?' She looked over the fence at the pool but he wasn't there. Perhaps he had gone indoors to the loo? Or was he in the courtyard, playing in the shade? 'Charlie, Charlie,' she called. She walked right round the house, wondering if this was some kind of game he played and Caroline had forgotten to warn her. She went into the house, looking into every downstairs room. 'Charlie, please come out. I don't like this game. I have your drink . . .' Her voice sounded shrill. She ran up the wide stairs and began to search these rooms. With every empty, silent room she looked into, it became harder and harder to remain calm and sensible. A horrible fear, a bewilderment, was growing. Where was he? 'Charlie . . .'

She ran down again, circling the house more quickly now, looking into the outbuildings, the dark garages and storerooms, the sheds and old stables. God, the buildings were endless and all totally deserted because it was the lunch hour. 'Charlie . . .' Through Michael's office, back to the pool, just to make sure, and she stared into its empty blueness and the water was quite still. The ripples he had made with his feet had long since settled. She could not keep the fear out of her voice now. Almost a sob. 'Charlie . . . Charlie . . .'

Yvette, she thought suddenly. He has followed her home. She ran into the house, almost falling up the stairs, pulling a shirt and a denim skirt over her bikini and running down again, her heart thumping as she started across the fields towards the house Caroline had indicated the first day. There was no one in sight. Her sandals made running impossible. They had just one thong between the toes and her feet were dusty and the sharp stones hurt. Half-way she stopped and wondered if, in coming here, she had left the child entirely alone at the Château? But what else could she do? She looked at her watch. He had been gone over fifteen minutes. She went on, cursing the sandals, and it was desperately hot here in the fields, the earth shimmering between the neat rows of vines and on the path ahead of her. She reached the house and knocked, wiping sweat from her forehead.

The door opened and she looked into Yvette Gautier's surprised face.

'I'm sorry to bother you but I've lost Charlie. He's gone. *Il est perdu*. Charlie. Please come with me.'

Yvette frowned. 'Charlie?'

'Yes, he's gone.' She took the woman's arm and stood in an agony of impatience as Yvette gently disengaged herself and disappeared into the house. She re-appeared, a scarf over her head, smiling reassuringly almost as if Kate were a child herself and she talked all the way back to the Château and Kate hardly understood a word. When they reached the house Yvette walked confidently inside and called. She went from room to room, calling, and gradually her confidence faded; they went upstairs and she peered under the beds, into the linen cupboard. Down again to the wine cellar. Her concern became more and more obvious and Kate trailed helplessly after her. They circled the outside of the house and ended up inside in the hall. Yvette turned to Kate with a stream of agitated French.

They both heard the car at the same time. Kate sprang towards the front doors and saw Henri getting out of his ancient Peugeot and she ran down the steps and across the cobbles to him.

'Henri . . . Oh God, I've lost Charlie.'

'What?' He had been about to apologize for his lateness.

'He's gone. He's just vanished.' They moved up the shallow steps into the hall and Henri spoke to Yvette, then translated for Kate.

'She thinks it may be some kind of game. Perhaps he is angry with Caroline for leaving him and he will jump out when she comes back.'

'No, no, he wasn't angry. He has been absolutely happy all morning, playing outside. With me. Where can he have gone? It's forty minutes. What can I tell Caroline?' She looked past Henri at the older woman and for a moment complete understanding, needing no words, was between them. Kate felt the tears in her eyes and smeared them away, furiously, heaping abuse on herself.

'We'll look again,' Henri was saying. 'Yvette will search the house because she knows it best and you and I, Kate, will look outside and in the buildings.'

'Think slowly, think slowly.' Kate could hear Judith saying it. 'Use the thoughts to blot out the panic.' She walked outside, past all Caroline's pots of flowers, through the tall gates to the narrow road. It was empty. She walked as far as the corner in the opposite direction from which Henri would have come and as she approached the corner her brain flashed horrific pictures

310

of a child's body. But there was nothing. Just the empty narrow road, winding ahead, white with dust.

When I go back, she pretended, I will find them all laughing. Yvette and Henri, with Charlie, angry with him but laughing with relief . . . But she came into the hall and she knew by their faces that they had not found him. She began to tremble violently and Henri took her arm and led her through to-the first small sitting-room and poured brandy into a glass.

'Start at the beginning, Kate. And when is Caroline due back?'

He stood by her chair, one hand smoothing the back of her neck. The brandy burnt her throat.

'Quarter past one, half past . . .'

'Tell me what happened.'

'Just after Yvette left I was thirsty. I asked Charlie if he wanted a drink and he said yes. Well, he nodded. So I brought him out from the pool, closed the gate and I went in. I was quite a long time finding his mug and then the phone rang and it was Caroline . . .' She stopped abruptly as they heard a car. She almost dropped the glass. The engine stopped. Doors opened and slammed. Voices, footsteps, Caroline's voice.

Through the open door Caroline saw Henri and then Kate sitting down and as she came nearer, Yvette. She paused. She saw the expression of their faces. 'What is it? Henri? What's happened?'

'Charlie,' Henri said gently.

'He's gone, Caroline.' The words sounded like a whisper to Kate. 'Since twelve. Just after you rang. I've searched. We all have. I fetched Yvette and Henri came . . .'

Michael was in the room now. 'Gone?' he said. 'Do you mean wandered off ? He never does that.'

'I came,indoors to get drinks and spoke to Caroline and when I went back he had gone.'

Caroline was quite motionless. Suddenly she said, 'The pool . . .?'

311

'No, no,' they all said together, and then Kate looked up at Clive, who stood in the doorway, and his expression was extraordinary. Absolute disbelief. Kate stared at him.

The telephone rang. Automatically and grimacing with impatience, Michael picked up the receiver, 'Yes?'

A curious stiffness ran through his body so that it attracted all their attention and one by one they turned their eyes to him and watched in absolute silence. Except Clive who watched Caroline.

'Who are you?' Michael was saying. 'Who the hell are you?' He replaced the receiver gently.

'Who was it?' Caroline said.

'I don't know. It was a woman, I think. A whisper. She said, "We have your son. We will want money. We will ring later today. No police. No police or we kill him."'

It was Clive who made the first sound, his deep voice roaring out. 'I don't believe it! I just don't believe it!'

From that moment everything became quite unreal, Kate thought, as if she looked at the world through a veil. It seemed unbearably hot. Michael and Caroline made another ritual search of the house and the grounds and came back, defeated, and stared blankly at the meal Yvette had laid out on the round table, tears streaming down her cheeks. No one ate anything. Michael went into the kitchen to explain to Yvette, to impress on her that she must say nothing. Not even to Raoul . . . He came back with a pot of coffee and they sat in a stunned circle. Clive drank a second very strong whisky. He could not bear to look at Caroline's face and yet he could not keep his eyes away.

At first Caroline said nothing. She merely walked the room, backwards and forwards, twisting her hands together as if she were drying them. And then she stood in front of Michael and her face had become small and grey. 'Should we tell the police?'

'No. Absolutely not. I think it's some kind of ridiculous mistake. We're not that rich, for Christ's sake . . . But we must be

312

prepared to do as they say. They must have no possible reason to hurt him.'

'I think we should go through it again with Kate,' Henri said. He was standing beside Kate, sensing the internal panic. She felt his strength. With clear understanding, the way she sometimes realized things when she had drunk too much, she saw that it was Henri's quiet organizing presence which was preserving what little calm there was; she felt madness bubbling just below the surface in Caroline; Michael's bewildered fury; Clive's extraordinary reaction, as if he couldn't bear it. Perhaps it was true? He could not bear to see Caroline hurt. She thought: I never stood a chance, did I?

'Tell us again, Kate,' Henri was saying. 'It might help.'

'Yvette came out to tell me she was leaving . . .' As Kate repeated the sequence of events she seemed to see it all in her head. 'I can't have been more than five minutes. How did they take him? How did they know I'd do it?'

'They may have watched for days,' Henri said. 'They may have come to know Yvette's routine. If you hadn't been here this morning they could have taken him much earlier. He so often plays out there alone.'

'Why didn't he cry out?' Caroline said. 'He would have been afraid. They must have hit him. How hard do you have to hit a little boy to make him quiet, Henri?' She was rocking herself on her heels, backwards and forwards.

'Michael said it was a woman's voice,' Kate interrupted.

'That means nothing,' Michael snapped. 'An obvious attempt to mislead us . . .' He went to Caroline and took her by the arms. 'Sit down, Caroline. Please. Stop it.'

'How can I? You understand nothing of how I feel. Nothing.'

'I love him too.'

'So you say . . .' She looked up into his face and then drove her head violently into his shoulder.

'Why should they have hurt him?' Henri said firmly. 'They had only a few yards to walk to be out of sight. No one uses this

313

road at midday. They could have spent a few minutes making friends. And if he did call out, Kate wouldn't have heard from the kitchen.'

'We could test that,' Clive said suddenly. 'You could go out and call, Kate, and I'll go to the kitchen and listen.'

'But what would he call? I tried to get him to say my name and he wouldn't.'

'He would call his mother,' Clive said impatiently. 'He says *Maman*, doesn't he, Caroline?'

'Yes.'

Kate went along the veranda to the sand pit. Henri followed her. 'Do you think Michael should call the police, Henri?'

'Would you, if it were Melanie? Would I, if it were Françoise? God knows.' He took her hand and they stood for a moment.

'I'd better call.' Kate shouted, '*Maman, Maman . . .*' and then paused and called again and it was so grotesque and her husky voice was full of embarrassment.

'I heard nothing,' Clive said when they went to the kitchen. 'Try again, as loudly as you can.'

'I'll do it,' Henri said and they went back and he called, '*Maman, Maman,*' and despite the horror Kate wanted to laugh. Henri lit a cigarette. 'I'm going to drive into the town and get a sedative for Caroline. This could go on for days.'

'Please don't be long.'

'An hour. No more.' Again his hand on the side of her face, the kiss a gesture of his hand. She knew things would not stay hidden now. She knew they were all about to be shaken, rearranged, torn into new patterns. She watched him walk to his car, watched the rather abrupt movements of his body and when he had gone and she was alone she closed her eyes and registered, beneath the horror, that she loved him.

Caroline sat on Charlie's bed holding his pyjamas and feeling the terror tightening inside her all the time, like a black wire round her sanity, strangling her. Michael paced the room,

314

moving from the closed doors to the window and back again. He came and sat by her.

'Don't, Caroline.'

'Don't what?' Her voice was impatient, as if he were troublesome.

'Don't shut me out.'

She shook her head. 'I'm not . . . I'm not. I can't think. I feel as I feel. That I am going mad. You have made us like this, made Charlie and I as close as we are. You made me turn to him. I gave him everything you didn't need. I know you love him too. I'm not claiming any privilege but leave me alone.'

'Talk to me, Caroline.'

'I can't. I'm frozen.'

'I need you. Talk to me.'

'I keep imagining he is calling for me. That he is afraid. Calling and crying for me. Hurt and terrified . . .' She rocked herself forwards. 'Oh God, why did you bring me here?'

Michael shrank from her voice and the wild injustice of the attack. 'Because it's a wonderful place.'

'For you! For you it is. Therefore we must follow, Charlie and I. Clive told me about you, years ago, before I even met you. How you concentrated immense energy into one subject that interested you, distilling yourself he said. Going deeper and deeper and then abruptly losing interest. As you did with me, Michael. How long will this enthusiasm last? For nearly three years you have given your whole life to this place. You've hardly noticed Charlie and me. We have just lived here. Occasionally considered but not really important. Not as important as the things which concern you! Your intellect is greater and therefore what you consider important is what matters. My needs are trivial. My pathetic shallow need. Love, Michael. Just love! That's all!' She stopped, watching him shrink back, watching the absolute amazement on his face.

'You don't know, do you?' she went on. 'You really didn't know? I couldn't tell you. I tried. Don't look like that. It doesn't

315

mean I don't love you. I adore you. I always have. When I met you, you made me aware of everything I was missing. I loved your energy and your youth and your mind and your body but I'm afraid of your obsessions. You put me aside, long ago, and I'm lonely and jealous and sad and living with you, day after day, and yet not having you is agonizing. That's why I talked of going to England . . .'

'I had no idea you felt like this.' For the first time ever he stayed to answer her, crouching down to be level with her, putting his arms round her shoulders, his forehead touching hers. 'In the beginning I was worried about this place, and fascinated by it. Then I thought, because you had wanted a child for so long, you needed to be totally absorbed in Charlie. And then losing the baby drove you into yourself and I'm no good at understanding people, Caroline, unless they spell it out. I have no intuition. But this place would mean nothing to me without you. If you want to, we will leave tomorrow.'

'I love this place. I'm proud of it. Just let me in more.' Her eyes were closed and he held her tightly and when he drew back, took her face in his hands, touching the tears. She felt an immense relief as if a knot that had been inside for months or years had come undone. She let the tears run down her face.

They sprang apart as the telephone rang and Michael ran down the stairs to his study and switched on the tape recorder. It was just after four. Caroline came in after him, stumbling slightly. Then Kate. Michael lifted the receiver.

'Hello. This is Michael Redford.'

'We require fifty thousand pounds, four hundred and fifty thousand francs, in used notes of all sizes. Mixed currency. This must be available from the day after tomorrow. Friday. It is to be in a parcel of brown paper, strongly wrapped. Two layers, each tied with string and sealed with wax. The child is well. Listen.' There was a short burst of laughter and then the dialling tone.

'That was Charlie,' Michael lied instantly. Caroline had been listening with him.

316

'Are you sure? How can you be so sure?'

They played the recording. The whispered voice was hard to understand. 'That is his laugh,' Michael said. 'I'm sure of it.'

Clive turned away and walked to the window. Caroline's grey, tear-stained face and her eyes were unbearable. If he lived to be a hundred he thought he would never get them out of his mind. Michael was re-winding the machine. He played the cassette yet again and the message was whispered out.

'Why me, for God's sake? There must be fifty richer people in an area of twenty square kilometres. Why me?'

'I suppose,' Henri said, 'it is because you have all the outer layers of wealth and also you have a small child.'

Caroline put her hands over her face and made a muffled sound of agony and Kate looked at her, then at Clive and took his expression to mean that he still cared for her very much. Michael went to her, put his arm round her. Kate felt that something had changed between them. They were no longer separate.

'We've got to think, Caroline. We owe it to Charlie not to panic. Where the hell can I get so much money in two days?'

'There's nearly sixty thousand pounds of Caroline's money in London on deposit,' Clive said slowly, almost woodenly. He could feel Judith. Feel her pulling the strings. Hear her voice . . . 'If I telephoned today, caught the night flight to London, I could be back late tomorrow with enough money.'

'Would they let you bring it?' Caroline said.

'If I go to the Bank of England, and luckily I have a friend there who could help me, I am sure they would give permission.

'Yes,' Michael said. 'When the Adams child was so ill they were allowed to bring money out . . . I can't think of another way. If I try and raise money here it will mean involving the bank manager and the police. It could take too long. And I don't want anyone to know . . .' He could feel the desperation affecting him. He must take decisions now, before his judgement deteriorated. 'Can you telephone England now, Clive? It's just

317

after three in London. And we must book a flight . . .'

Caroline went slowly back up the stairs to Charlie's room, sitting on his bed again and still holding his pyjamas to her face, rocking herself slightly. On the table by his bed were a pile of his seeds. If he doesn't plant them tonight, she thought, and again she felt the tight wire of madness. She looked up as Henri came in. He sat by her, an arm along her shoulder, holding out a packet of cigarettes, lighting one for her.

'It will be all right, Caroline. I want you to take two of these. They are a sedative. There is no way you can make the time pass more quickly. They will not ring again until tomorrow. You can only pray and rest so that . . .'

She shook her head. 'I can't sleep. Something might be happening to him.' She shook off his arm. 'Please leave me alone, Henri.'

'Take one. Just enough to stop the panic you are feeling. You will still be able to think. You will think more clearly.'

'It won't make me sleep?'

'No.'

'All right. One. But I must not sleep, Henri. I could not bear to sleep if he is crying for me. Do you understand?' She took the pill, using water from Charlie's cup. She lay back on the bed. Small children, she thought, have no smell. There was no scent of her child. His bed, made this morning, was blank and clean. His bear and his books. As the pill took effect she began to cry but the tears brought no relief. She heard the sounds of the house, the single ring of the telephone as a call was begun or ended. She ached for her child, ached to hold him. She closed her eyes and opened them a few moments later, aware of someone in the room.

Clive crouched by the bed, taking her hand. 'Does it hurt so much?'

'As if he were dead. Worse than that. I am afraid he is calling me, crying for me. How can people do this?'

'Think of tomorrow. I'll be back with the money. We'll do as

318

they say. They will give him back. They have no reason to hurt him.'

'Do you really believe that?'

'Yes. I know you will get him back safely.'

There was such conviction in his voice that although it was absurd to do so she believed him and was comforted for a moment. 'You always come to help me. From the very beginning, that first morning in your office. I felt you would help then with the shop and everything.' Clive lowered his eyes. 'Kate said to me that she had never seen you show such interest in a child before. You feel something, don't you?' Her voice was a whisper.

'That he is your child and therefore special.'

'I know it's more than that. Taking him with you to the Finches and the way you play with him and talk to him. You know he is probably your child, don't you?'

The words seemed to repeat in his brain but he could not comprehend them. There was a long silence. 'My child?' he said at last.

'I've never been sure. At first I convinced myself he was Michael's. I wanted it to be his baby; I never would let them do a scan which would date it exactly. I pretended I was afraid. It should have been Michael's baby but Charlie was born so early. He was not at all premature.'

'Does Michael know?'

'He loves Charlie. You can see how much. He would go to any lengths for him and I've never hinted of what I feel and Michael is not at all concerned with the details of women and pregnancy. A few weeks or months here or there would mean nothing to him. I swore I would never tell either of you but now . . .'

'Why did you come with Michael? I thought it was because he gave you a child that you married him and came here. If you weren't sure . . . ?'

'I loved him,' she said simply. 'I always have from the first moment. I always will. Being pregnant gave me a reason to make up my mind, to hide all the doubts I had. The child was for me, Clive. Mine.'

Clive was very pale. He kissed her cheek and looked at his watch. 'I must go if I'm to catch the flight. I'll see you tomorrow.' He went down the stairs carefully as if he were drunk. He picked up his case. Kate stood at the door. He stopped in front of her. They made no move towards each other.

'When I get back, Kate . . .' He was so tired. Already tired. 'We must talk about things.'

'Yes. When you get back.'

Clive started the car and drove automatically, his mind in turmoil. What could he do? He should have believed her. He knew Judith well enough. She would not hurt the child. But if she was not alone in this? A large part of him said, 'Stop this terrible thing now. She must be at the Finchs' house with Charlie! She must be. Was she watching, that morning I was there?' And he thought of the joy on Caroline's face if he brought the child back. But how could he keep Judith out of it all? He thought of Mosaic as he had not done for days. Judith was right about the money. It would do so much. Without it he faced a few more months, deeper and deeper, and then what? And without Judith? He imagined her fury if he threw it all away now. And if she wasn't at the Finchs'? And if he missed the flight? And if she was involved with other, harder people?

'The child will not be hurt,' he repeated. 'Just one more day.' He drove through the narrow roads of Provence through St Remy and the brilliant evening and when he came to the place where the road divided and he must choose, Marseilles and the airport or the Finchs' house, he chose Marseilles because, above all, his own survival was what he cared for most.

Michael came slowly up the stairs and found Caroline still on Charlie's bed. It was almost dark. Caroline lay with her eyes closed but he knew she was not asleep. He lay down beside her, putting an arm under her head and the pillow, another arm over her. 'Henri has gone for a couple of hours to close up. He's taken Kate. He'll be back later.' She was silent. 'Nothing else matters, does it?'

'No.' She turned to face him. 'Nothing.'

'You know I feel the same, don't you?'

'Yes. Now I do. Whatever happens, Michael, at least I have you back again.'

'I've always been here.'

'But I felt such distance between us.'

'You caused it too. You took Charlie so close to you, wrapped yourself round him . . .'

In this desolate, dreamlike state there seemed nothing she could not say. The words came on their own. 'I suppose I've always felt guilty. Afraid . . . I was never sure . . .'

He put his hand over her mouth. 'Don't say it. He is mine.' He rocked her gently. 'Has that worried you a lot?'

'Always. I was so desperate for a child I never thought it would matter who the father was. But it does.'

'Charlie is mine.' Michael laughed. 'Look at the way he sits and thinks . . .'

'And makes those strange patterns . . .'

'And investigates things. Takes things apart!'

They both laughed, forgetting for a second, and then the horror came back.

CHAPTER NINETEEN

Kate and Henri were quite silent in the car as they drove. Occasionally he took her hand, holding it for a while against his thigh. 'I said we would go back in a few hours and stay the night, to help if we can,' Kate said at last.

Henri nodded. He drove very fast but he did not scare her. It was ten to six when he parked in the courtyard and lights blazed from all the windows. 'Come in with me,' he said and he took Kate through all the noise and the atmosphere of hard work. The day was ending. There was laughter, and gossip among the girls. They called out to Henri, teasing him, Kate guessed, and she liked the relationship she sensed between Henri and the people who worked for him. A man came forward with a bolt of cotton which had run in the steam-fixing process and they discussed the problem for a few minutes. Then Henri touched her arm and they moved up the flight of stairs to his office. He made a telephone call and Kate sat in a chair that swivelled, moving herself from side to side, sometimes shivering violently as if she were cold. Heads came round the door . . . '*Au revoir, Monsieur Bertrand . . .*'

'*Au revoir . . .*'

When the last machine stopped the silence was absolute. No more swift footsteps. They sat with the desk between them as if at an interview.

'Can you talk?' Henri said. 'Can you think? About when this is over. It must end sometime although now it seems so shattering.' He put his elbows on the desk, leaning sideways to pull cigarettes from his pocket. 'Do you want to talk about the future, Kate?'

'Yes.'

'You and Clive?'

'Nothing. Politeness, sadness. Nothing. We both came here knowing this could be an end. And this horror has strengthened our separation. We can give each nothing. And he is so affected by Caroline's misery. I had no idea he still cared so much for her . . . This afternoon when he left and he passed me in the hall, it was like talking to a stranger.'

'So? Will you come back here on your own? Stay here . . . or at Jouvard if you prefer, so that we can get to know each other? I love you already but I want to know what makes you laugh, what you like to eat, if you care about politics, if you like films. I adore the cinema! If you could contemplate life with a middle-aged ex-doctor with an anxiety complex?'

She sat forward, her smile reflecting his. 'I could come for the harvest, couldn't I? I thought of it yesterday. I could stay at Jouvard and work. I'd love to work outside. I could learn French and see how it was . . .'

'And Melanie?'

'Leave her. Just for a month.'

He got up, turning out the lamp on his desk and coming round to her. He stood behind her, feeling the sharpness of the bones in her shoulders. She put her head backwards, looking up at him and he bent to kiss her. 'Come inside for a while.'

They locked the work buildings, crossed the yard and entered Henri's house. He poured them each a glass of whisky and they went to the small garden behind the house and sat on the old swing-seat, swaying gently, shoulders touching, the seat complaining.

'How can people do things like this? How could anyone kidnap a child? They must know what terrible suffering they inflict,' Kate said.

'For money. Always for money.'

They stayed for a long time, watching the sky change colour, talking quietly although there was no one to overhear. 'Oh, you will bring a whole new set of worries with you when you come, Kate . . . You must take your time.'

'I will.' She was so tired. She closed her eyes.

'Could you eat something?' Henri said, apologetically. 'I'm rather hungry. I know I shouldn't be . . .'

'I'm hungry too!'

In the kitchen he found half a loaf, cheese and ham and a bowl of great, sweet tomatoes and they made huge sandwiches and coffee and Kate smiled, her mouth full, thinking back to David and what seemed like a previous lifetime. She was aware of a deep contentment which alternated with the misery of remembering about Charlie.

'And now,' Henri said, 'I think we should go back. They may need us.' He touched her face. 'I couldn't make love to you now with everything as it is. I'm afraid of tomorrow. I'm terrified for Caroline.'

Kate's eyes filled with tears. 'They won't kill Charlie? You don't think that? He is such a gentle little boy . . .'

Henri shook his head.

There was a constant pulse of excitement inside Judith. She had felt this way before but it had never been so intense. All Sunday she had felt it, driving down the autoroute in the early morning, stopping for lunch, arriving at the Finchs' *mas* the evening before Clive and Kate left England. She knew he would come here, out of curiosity and on the 7th, his first whole day, she drove to the coast, going over every last detail in her mind; she came back to the *mas* in the dark and knew they had been. There were footsteps on the dusty floor and the brightly coloured ball was gone.

She had woken very early this morning, before six, and lain in her sleeping bag for a long time, thinking. She made herself breakfast on the camping stove and spread all her bits and pieces around. She was here now, quite openly. Everything innocent and straightforward as it would be until she actually took the child. Even then . . . 'I found him. Wandering . . .'

It had been so easy. She drove towards Jouvard at eleven,

acting out her holiday for herself, convincing herself, parking just off the main road and wandering up the lane, hidden from the main house by the tall earth bank. So easy to step out of sight in the thick hedges. It was very hot. Anyone in the fields would leave on time. She peered through the hedge. 'You might as well know. I was desperate to catch a glimpse of Clive. We have been lovers for almost a year . . .' That wasn't needed either. She could hear Kate's voice, talking to Charlie. She watched and waited, heard Yvette Gautier come out and say she was leaving and saw the Frenchwoman start across the fields, heard Kate ask Charlie if he would like a drink, saw her bring the child out of the pool enclosure and shut the wicker gate. She watched Kate put on his shirt and shrts and saw her disappear round the side of the house. Judith moved swiftly.

'Hello, Charlie, love.' He had looked up and frowned. 'You remember me? Judy? Come and see what I've got for you . . .' Moving so swiftly, picking him up. There was stiffness in his body but he made no sound. In his memory there were traces of Judith. He held the rabbit Kate had given him. Judith talked to him all the time, carrying him down the road, putting him in the back seat of the car. 'Look in the brown bag, Charlie. It's full of presents.' She started the engine and turned out on to the bigger road. She drove towards St Remy and through the small town. So far absolutely perfect! She took him to the Finchs' *mas* and gave him three teaspoons of a harmless sedative. Judith had been putting children to sleep for years. She played the cassette through, getting it to exactly the right spot. At one-thirty she was in the telephone box on the main road.

She looked at her watch now. It was nine. Quite dark. She realized she hadn't eaten since breakfast and she cooked herself an omelette and made a salad and when she had finished she went upstairs and woke the child. She carried him down. He was drowsy. She gave him a glass of milk, a bowl of cereal and a peach. He sat on her lap and she felt affection for him. He was such a peaceful child. He leaned his head back against hers and

325

his small hand traced out the pattern on the cereal packet. He dipped his hand in and pulled out some of the small, crisp pieces. They were like his seeds. He put them in his pocket.

Judith carried him outside into the walled garden and asked if he needed to pee. He nodded and went into the far corner of the garden. And when he had finished he walked along the far wall until he found a patch of bare earth and he bent down and scraped a space with his hand and pushed his small finger into the dry soil. He made six little holes and planted three seeds which he had in his pockets and three pieces of Judith's cereal. As he straightened up she was behind him, picking him up, taking him indoors and washing his face and hands. She read him a story. He was a warm weight in her lap. When she had finished she took him upstairs and took off his shirt and shorts and lay him down. It was a hot night.

'Good night, Charlie. Sleep well.'

He smiled up at her. He remembered Judith now. She had been before. She was like his mother. He watched her get into her own sleeping bag which she had pulled across the doorway of the room. She lay for a while with her arms folded under her head, staring up at the ceiling. Charlie held on to the knitted rabbit and fell asleep.

Kate and Henri came into the hall at Jouvard just before ten, closing the front doors quietly behind them. There was a light in Michael's study but the house was quite silent. They went towards his half-open door and found him sitting at his desk, his face a mask. He looked up and rubbed his eyes.

'Is Caroline asleep?' Henri asked.

'Yes, she is. But she wakes about every hour . . .'

'Couldn't you try to sleep, Michael?' Henri stood with his hands in his pockets, his face serious, as Michael looked up at him blankly. 'All right, it was a stupid suggestion.'

'I must try and understand why, Henri.' Michael pushed back his chair and stood up. 'Why us? I feel as if my brain is on fire. Why was it so easy?'

'Because none of us had ever thought of it . . . you were totally taken by surprise!' Kate said.

'Not everything is understandable,' Henri said and Kate moved closer to him and he put an arm along her shoulders. She felt a wonderful possessiveness. No guilt, no haste, just the knowledge of the love between them, tucked away for later. Much later. Now was Michael's face and this silent, agonized house.

'Caroline thinks it is something we've done.'

Henri made an angry sound. 'Women take everything personally! The kidnappers are strangers. Cruel, greedy, perhaps desperate people. You could pass them in the street tomorrow . . . next week it will be someone's else's child, someone else's agony, unless they are caught!'

'Do you think I should involve the police, then?'

Henri was silent for a long time. 'Not now. It's too late. And I would have acted just as you have if it had been Françoise . . .'

Michael wasn't listening. He was back at his desk. 'If I think long enough and hard enough, I will realize something.'

'Do you want me to stay here? Will it help to think aloud?' Henri asked.

'No. I'd rather be alone.'

'Well, I shall be upstairs if you want me. Any room?'

'Yes.'

Kate fetched a nightgown and came with him into the smallest spare room, sleeping beside him in a broken disjointed way. Henri hardly slept at all. He held her slight body and thought of the future and he began to discount his anxieties. He had been wrong. The previous failure of both their marriages would perhaps mean they started with an advantage, both having known unhappiness. He had been wrong to be so wary. He touched her arm, put his lips against her face, but she was asleep and he did not want to wake her.

When it was almost dawn Kate woke and for some reason she

could not understand she slid quietly out of Henri's bed and went to her own room and lay for a long time watching the patterns the trees and the flyscreens made on the white wall. She felt this was not a new day but all part of yesterday, horribly elongated.

Judith woke when Charlie came pattering across to her, touching her shoulder. She saw that he wanted to get in with her and she let him do so and they stayed in her sleeping bag until it was almost nine. He lay very still. At nine they got up and she dressed herself and the child and took him downstairs. She looked outside but saw no one. She gave him cereal and a boiled egg; he didn't like drinking from the plastic mug and she told him sharply not to be stupid. When he had finished she took him into the garden for half an hour but she was nervous out there, despite the high wall, despite his silence.

In the downstairs room he wandered around and then lay on his stomach by the wooden dresser, walking his fingers into the dust beneath and making patterns. He took some of the remaining nuggets of cereal from his pocket and put them in the centre of the pattern. Judith called him. She had washed up the breakfast things and wanted to wash Charlie's face and hands and clean his teeth. It was quite automatic for her to keep any child clean. She read to him. The time dragged. Nothing to do till noon when she would telephone the third message and visit Jouvard, to make her presence known. She wanted to do that before Clive got back. She wanted no more acting than necessary. She had never doubted that once Charlie vanished Clive would follow the course she had laid out but, just to make sure, she would go to Jouvard. Just to make sure there were no police. She looked at her watch. It was eleven. Time to give Charlie something to make him sleep again. He was playing with a game she had brought with her, piling plastic counters on to squares. He was laughing, flicking them across the board with his finger. 'Charlie,' she said, thinking of the money, which should already be Clive's, of the freedom, of life entirely with Clive, having him absolutely.

'Ju-dy.'

'Yes, love,' she said, without thinking.

'Ju-dy.'

As she realized her heart lurched horribly and she became quite cold. He liked the sound. 'Ju-dy. Ju-dy,' he repeated, over and over, making a pattern of the sound. She let out her breath in one long sigh. Why now? After the months and months of urging him to speak? A surge of panic came but she stifled it quickly. One word. It meant nothing. No one else called her Judy. What did it matter?

Oh, but it did matter. She crouched, watching him play and he turned his head and smiled. 'Ju-dy.' She imagined one day, months ahead perhaps: 'Judy took me . . .'

She had always had the thought in the back of her mind that it could go wrong but she had thought of far more complex reasons. She had considered situations where she could not give him back. If it was to be her future and Clive's that was threatened, if it was to be them or the child, she knew which she would choose.

Kate stayed in her room for a long time, listening to the birds and a cockerel and once she heard Caroline cry out, as if from some terrible dream and heard swift footsteps up the stairs. She got up at nine, showered and dressed, went down to the kitchen and found Yvette, her face swollen with tears. She moved constantly, wiping already immaculate surfaces, putting coffee on the table. Henri came in, coming to Kate and kissing her. All pretence seemed unimportant under such circumstances. And there was nothing to say.

The morning crawled by. Michael said it was important that they should appear normal from the outside and Caroline wandered through her garden, rooting out small weeds, her brain shivering from one ghastly imagined climax to another.

At noon the telephone rang. Michael, who was sitting by it, snatched it up.

'You have the money?'

'By this evening I will have it.'

There was a long pause. 'Tomorrow morning you will be told where to take it and where to find the child.' There was silence. The cassette recorder repeated the brief message back to them. They stared at it as if it knew more than it said.

'Why should she speak in English?' Kate asked.

'Why not? They know we are English . . . they must know a lot about us.'

'Yes. I was thinking, about yesterday, that as the telephone bell rings in the garden they could have used a telephone call to get me inside. But Caroline saved them the trouble. But suppose she hadn't rung? Suppose I had stayed outside with him?'

'There was no second call?'

'No . . . unless they rang when I went to fetch Yvette.'

'Please stop all this detective stuff. I can't stand it! None of it helps. He is gone.' Caroline paced the room, moving in short steps. 'It can't be only a day since I have seen him.' She stopped as Henri touched her arm and held out a glass of wine to her; this slight man with his half-joking anxieties, carrying them all, reaching into Caroline and pulling her back.

'The most important thing is to keep ourselves calm and sane,' he said. He poured wine for Kate and for Michael and sat down with his own. 'Have you eaten anything today, Caroline? Have you, Michael?'

They all heard the car. Everything was frightening now, Kate thought. It was Henri who said, 'I think you had better go, Michael, to look normal.' And he went with Michael across the hall and they both saw Judith climbing from her car.

She walked across to them, smiling, coming up the wide steps. 'Hello. I'm spending my holiday here so I thought I had to call in or you'd never forgive me!' Her heart was beating fast. She was far more nervous than she had expected to be.

330

Michael's face amazed her. She had not anticipated such despair. 'How are you all?' she said but her voice faltered. 'Henri . . .'

'Come inside,' Michael said quietly. 'Something terrible has happened . . .' He led her through the hall and she steeled herself in case Clive should be here, in case it was all going wrong. But there were no police. Just Caroline and Kate and Judith looked from one face to another and admitted to herself that, although it was essential she should come here, she had also wanted to see them. To see both sides.

'I'm camping at the Finchs' house . . . They seemed pleased to have someone stay there.'

Michael stood by the door. 'Judith, Charlie has been taken!' He explained in a low voice, finding it very hard to make the words come, watching the stillness in Judith's face. She seemed able to believe what he was saying without difficulty but he had never seen her surprised.

When he finished speaking she said, 'What can I do?'

'Nothing. Just say nothing until it's over.'

'Have you involved the police?'

'No.'

'When will it be over?'

'Tomorrow.'

'I'll go then. But I'll ring you tomorrow. Tomorrow evening. And if you want any help then, I'll come.' She bent to kiss Caroline's cheek and for the first time she was afraid . . . afraid of the effect Caroline's obvious torment might have on Clive. Judith had not expected such absolute helplessness. Caroline's cheek was hot.

Kate walked with her to the car. 'None of us knows what to do. Clive has gone to London for the money. He gets back this afternoon. I don't know how we'll stand another night . . .' She took Judith's arm. 'Couldn't you stay here?'

Judith slid into the car. 'I don't think I should. I'm not really close enough to them . . .' She started the engine and Kate stood

331

back, rather surprised and rebuffed. This kind of situation was one in which Judith normally excelled, taking charge of a group of helpless people. She watched Judith drive out of the gates.

Clive was back at Jouvard at five, carrying his small suitcase into Michael's office and opening it, putting the large brown package on Michael's desk. 'I wrapped it in London, in case there was a panic here. I counted the money twice.' He found it hard to say the words. Perhaps the hardest words he had ever said as he looked at Michael's exhausted face.

'Do you think I have been wrong not to tell the police?' Michael said suddenly. 'Should I tell them now?'

'No,' Clive said. 'Not now. Not when we're so near.'

Michael was silent for some moments, his long fingers twisting in the cord of the telephone. Eventually he sat back. 'You're right. I am committed now.'

The evening was endless, each hour a lifetime, waiting for the clock to move on. It became night. Clive lay in the single bed. He was alone. Kate had collected her things and solemnly told him she was sleeping next door on her own. He knew from her eyes that they would not need much discussion. It was already understood. No pretence any more. Judith had been right then. How extraordinary she was. He felt admiration but it was mixed with revulsion. She couldn't know about Charlie, what Caroline had said. Clive rolled on to his face. Perhaps the waiting was worst of all for him, knowing he could have ended the whole thing whenever he chose.

At seven they were all downstairs, drinking black coffee and waiting. At eight-thirty the telephone rang.

'Take the parcel to the supermarket *Foure* on the road to Avignon. It is twelve kilometres before the town on the left as you approach. Take a trolley. Put the parcel in it. Cover it with tins of food and soup. Only tins. Take it outside to the car park and leave it by the long concrete wall. You must leave the supermarket by twelve. Go to the first telephone box on the left between

332

the supermarket and Avignon. It is ten kilometres. Past the Favre petrol station. Telephone your home. You will learn where the child is. If you are followed. If there are police, you will never see him again. The mother and father remain at the house.'

Michael's recorder repeated the whispering message.

'I'll take the money,' Clive said. He saw the words on Henri's lips but he said them first and as he waited his heart beat heavily in his chest. 'Let me take it,' he urged.

'Yes. And as soon as they ring here, I can go and get him,' Michael said. He went to Caroline, put both his arms round her. They stood so still they were like one person. 'It's almost over.'

'How long should I allow to drive to the supermarket? Will it be crowded before noon?' Clive was asking.

'It's Friday,' Caroline said. 'Terribly crowded. Especially then. Do you know where it is?'

'Yes, I know exactly. There is a big wine co-operative next door. I stopped there last year after I had been here . . .' Judith thought of everything. He remembered going round that supermarket with her, buying cheese and bread, buying the *Vin Ordinaire* for their picnic lunch.

'It will take an hour to drive there. Allow twenty minutes for parking and shopping . . .'

'Half an hour,' Caroline interrupted. 'At least.'

'Very well,' Michael said. 'An hour and a half in all.'

'I think I'll allow two hours, in case of traffic,' Clive said. 'I'll leave at ten.'

They stood in a row and watched him leave. He saw them in his rear view mirror and the brown package sat innocently on the back seat. And he knew exactly what he was going to do. He did not take the Avignon road. He took the road to the Finchs' *mas* because he was going to change the ending. He was going to take Charlie back himself. He needed to. He would say the child was in the telephone box. They would be far too preoccupied to question him. And later, when there was time, why should they ever question Clive? He wanted to carry Charlie home, run up the steps, the child in his arms, give him back to Caroline. He needed that. To purge himself. Because of what she had said, because of the agony he and Judith had inflicted. He needed to be that close to Caroline to justify keeping the money. His car sped through St Remy. His impatience made him sit stiffly forwards, tap his fingers on the steering wheel. He drove out of the small town. He turned into the Finchs' road and the high-grass-covered ridge brushed the bottom of the car as it bumped and lurched towards the stone house.

He swung into the yard. The door opened at once and he saw Judith and her expression was one of amazement. 'What the hell are you doing here? What's happened?'

'Nothing has happened.'

'Why have you come here?' She stood in front of the closed door as if she did not want him to go in.

'I had time. I had to see you and I want the child.'

'Why?'

'I am going to take him back with me. Burn the last recording. I shall say he was in the call box.'

'You can't. It may be out of order. You must go to the supermarket, go through the whole thing. Afterwards, when the police check . . .'

'No.'

She narrowed her eyes. 'You want to be a hero for her, don't you? She still holds you!'

'Where is Charlie?'

'You can't have him. We can't give him back.'

Clive's face was incredulous. 'What?'

'He's talking.'

'Talking?'

'He says my name, over and over again, like a parrot. I did think of things going wrong. I have considered this . . . We can't give him back, Clive. I know it seems horrible but you must think clearly. It is him or us.'

Clive shrank from her and then he pushed past her, forcing the door open. The first room was empty and he almost ran into the next and saw Charlie on the floor, wrapped in a rug. He was breathing deeply and Clive bent and picked him up and he was absurdly light, feeling as small as Melanie. Clive touched his face. His voice was husky. 'Nothing is worth that.'

'You are being ridiculous! I don't want to hurt him but I have no choice. What is he to you? Just a child? He will give us away.'

'No.'

'In a month or a year, he will tell them . . .'

'I'm taking him back. You can clear up here or finish your holiday or do what the hell you like.' There were tears in his eyes and a soreness in his throat. 'You never intended to give him back.'

'Of course I did!' she shouted. 'How could I know he would speak? I was horrified when he said my name. It's my name! Me he will implicate, not you!'

'Are these all his clothes? What else did he have?'

'The rabbit.'

'Give it to me.'

'If he wasn't her child . . .'

'He's my child!' Clive shouted. 'Mine. She told me.' He carried Charlie through to the first room and she followed, her face amazed.

'How does she know?' Her voice was utterly changed, the anger gone, she was struggling to speak normally.

'She's not absolutely sure.' Judith was close behind him and he could not bear the thought that she might touch him but Clive paused in the first room to look at her. In the shadows, Judith's face was suddenly horrific. Clive pushed at the shutters to let in more light and looked anxiously down at the child.

'Wait, please,' Judith said. 'You must go through the motions, Clive. Take the child if you must but go to the supermarket, fill the trolley. Charlie won't wake for hours. Leave him in the back of the car under a blanket . . . destroy the package on the way home. You must do it! And where is the money? In your account?'

'Yes.' He looked at her for a long time. 'So I am just as deeply involved as you are.' He went out and laid Charlie on the back seat, covering him with the light rug Judith held out. He could not touch her. He could not kiss her goodbye or even look at her. 'I'll come to your flat, next Tuesday.' He watched her turn and go slowly back into the house.

Clive looked at his watch. It was ten forty-five. He drove towards Avignon as quickly as he could and parked in the shade it was ten to twelve. He filled the trolley as instructed and then drove to the call box. Thank God it was empty! He dialled Jouvard. Michael answered almost at once.

'Yes?'

'It's Clive . . . I've got Charlie. He's quite all right. He was in the telephone box. I'm coming back with him now. He's all right.' He went home and threw the parcel in a litter bin.

Caroline held Charlie all that evening. Henri examined him and said he was drugged but quite well. He was clean and had obviously been fed and well looked after. Caroline sat on his bed, holding him and trying to believe the miracle and sometimes Michael came in and she would look up at him, her face transfigured with joy.

When Clive's car had turned in the gates they had all come running out and he had lifted Charlie and given him to Caroline. They had all embraced each other in a great spontaneous gesture of joy and relief; he looked at Caroline and it was all there again, the love, the loss, the regret, pulsing through him as if Judith had never existed. Caroline had entrusted him with the most extraordinary weapon. He could try to take the child again in a far more cruel, legal way, if he so chose, but he never would. Now Kate stood in front of him, concerned out of habit. 'Clive, you look terrible. Come in . . . come and have a drink.' She took his hand and led him in and poured him a whisky. He sat down and closed his eyes. Kate poured a drink for herself and one for Henri and brushed impatiently at the dusty green paint on her fingers and wondered why her memory stirred.

Clive opened his eyes. He saw Henri touch Kate's arm, saw Henri's hand tighten for a moment, saw the way she stood very still. 'I will go and see that Charlie is all right,' Henri said and Kate turned and watched him go.

She sat down, then, on a low stool. 'Clive, while you were gone, Jenny rang.'

'Jenny.' It was a name from the distant past. He frowned.

'Yes. About those things Bill made up from the rocking clock bodies. Those toys with the funny faces that Jenny was so sarcastic about . . .'

'The Beanies, you mean?'

'Yes. Beanies. Well, something very good has happened . . . that petrol company you took them to likes them. A marketing man rang . . . He wants to use them as a sales gimmick, to give away at the pumps after you've collected some coupons or vouchers or something. Jenny was almost incoherent. I've never heard her so happy and we could hardly let her speak because we were so afraid you would ring. But she says it will get Mosaic out of trouble!' Kate sat forward and touched Clive's arm. 'I'm so happy for you, Clive. I would have hated to leave you if Mosaic was finished.' She paused. 'You know that I don't want to live with you any more?'

Clive nodded. He closed his eyes. Michael had been right all along, he thought. Time was the most unpredictable ingredient. Extraordinary. Unreliable. Timing. More important than luck. If this had only happened a week ago. If he had not gone to the Finchs' *mas* first? But the whisky was good, beginning to enclose him like a bubble.

'Clive, you have someone, haven't you?' Kate was saying.

He opened his eyes. 'They come and go,' he said dryly. 'For some time it was Judith but not while she lived in our house.'

'Judith?' Kate sat back, silent with amazement.

'Not any more,' Clive said. He looked up as Michael came into the room.

'Henri says that Charlie is quite all right. Drugged but all right.' He poured himself a drink. 'God, I never want to live through anything like that again . . .' He sat down heavily. 'Thank you, Clive. Look, obviously I must get the police but I can't face them now and nor can Caroline. And the kidnappers are obviously long gone. I'll leave it till the morning.'

Clive nodded. 'I want to catch the first flight tomorrow morning, Clive. Jenny rang with some very good news . . . will it matter if I'm not here to talk to the police?'

Michael shook his head. 'No. You saw nothing suspicious, did you?'

'Not a damn thing. I opened the call box and there he was. I'll write it all down if you like.'

Michael nodded but he was hardly listening. He was like a man woken from a deep sleep, shaking his head, half-closing his eyes. After a few moments he stood up and went back upstairs.

Charlie woke at seven that evening, stirring gradually, sitting up and opening his eyes, registering Caroline and nestling against her. His hands were tightly clenched. Caroline held out a glass of orange for him and he drank and then wandered the room unsteadily. He came back to the bed and picked up the rabbit which Kate had bought him. 'Ju-dy,' he said and Caroline laughed delightedly.

'Is that what you call it? Judy Rabbit?'

Caroline ran a bath and undressed him and he took a handful of small brown nuggets from the pocket of his shorts and put them carefully on the table by his bed with the glass tray of sunflower seeds.

When he was bathed and fed and put into bed again Henri and Kate came in. 'I think you should leave him now, Caroline, and try to sleep yourself. And not in here. In your own room.

338

You will hear him if he wants you. You can't sleep with Charlie for the rest of your life.'

'I know, I know.' She bent and kissed him again and put her arms round Henri as she passed him and walked slowly next door to her own room.

Kate knelt over the little boy. 'I'm so glad you're home, Charlie.' He held the rabbit tightly and Kate kissed him and glanced curiously at the little nuggets on his tray of seeds, recognizing them as pieces of cereal.

'I'm going home,' Henri said quietly. 'I'll come back in the morning.'

She nodded and now that it was over the exhaustion hit her like a powerful drug and she went to the room where she had slept with Henri and was asleep a few moments after she lay down.

When Kate woke at eight the house was quite silent. She put on a bikini and went down to swim and the water was cool and wonderful, washing away some of the horror, blurring it into a bad dream. The past few days seemed quite unreal. Caroline came down in a white towelling dressing-gown, carrying Charlie. She slid on his armbands.

'Good morning, Kate. Isn't it a lovely day?' She smiled radiently watching Charlie leap into the pool. 'Michael is still in bed! That's absolutely unheard of! He's staying here all day today.' She lay down on one of the sun beds. 'And perhaps, later in the week, I shall go to see the village school. The kindergarten part. Charlie should perhaps start when he is three if all the other children do. And when he does, I was thinking how many tourists come here in the summer. Perhaps, if I did have a little shop, I would not mind Michael working so much.' She slid into the water and swam a sedate breast stroke. 'Because, whatever he says, I know he will never change . . .'

They had breakfast on the veranda and Charlie drank from his own mug and ate cornflakes and said, 'Ju-dy.'

In the open doorway Clive froze for a moment and Caroline looked up at him and smiled. There was a moment of intense closeness between them, a closeness she hadn't ever expected to feel again, something she knew she would remember with regret in the future when Michael's preoccupation kept him apart from her.

'That's what he's christened the rabbit you and Kate gave him.' Caroline smiled.

Clive's face flickered and he laughed and sat down by the child.

'This has been so terrible for us all,' Caroline was saying, 'that you must stay on and have a real holiday.'

'I wish I could,' Clive said, 'but I must go back today and find out about this new contract. It sounds too good to be true. But Kate will probably stay, won't you, Kate?' There was a most chilling courtesy between them that Caroline knew only too well. But with herself and Harry it had mutated into hatred.

'Yes. I'd like to stay until Tuesday if I could,' Kate said.

Clive left at nine-thirty. Caroline came into the hall to say goodbye to him and he kissed Charlie. He kissed Caroline too but he could not meet her eyes for more than a moment. He wondered if he would ever be able to come back here. Caroline and Charlie stood on the steps and watched him go. As Clive's car turned out of the gates the black police Citroen turned in.

Henri came at noon with flowers and champagne, instigating the celebration they all needed, giving his statement to the patient police officer who sat in Michael's office and wrote it all down. Inspector Durande, who was in charge of the investigation, was cold, despising them somewhat, Michael felt, for fearing to involve the police earlier, treating them as if they had condoned the crime.

'Come somewhere with me, Kate,' Henri said quietly after lunch as they sat and drank coffee. 'We have just three more days.'

340

'Can we go to the Finchs' *mas*?'

'Why?'

'Just a feeling.'

The house looked better this time. Kate found the key on the ledge and wondered when Judith had left? She had telephoned, the evening they got Charlie back, but Kate had been very surprised that she hadn't come to Jouvard . . . then she remembered what Clive had said and put it down to some tension between him and Judith. She still could not accept the fact that they were lovers, two people she knew so well. Why hadn't she sensed something?

'What are you thinking?' Henri asked, as Kate opened the windows and the shutters and looked down at the dusty green paint marks on her fingers.

'About Clive and Judith and why I never suspected anything.'

'I think they will suit each other very well,' Henri said.

It was so quiet, this house. She went all through it. In the top room the floor had been swept. Judith must have slept here. She looked for hiding places, hardly admitting it to herself yet. Downstairs, she looked under the wooden dresser and found the pattern of dots and the cluster of Judith's cereal.

'What are you doing?' Henri said.

She sat back on her heels, wondering how she could begin to tell him, to put her extraordinary suspicions into words? They were so weak. They would sound so pathetic . . . Would he think she was trying to implicate Judith out of rage and jealousy? But if she couldn't tell Henri, who could she tell?

'Some things about all this frighten me very much, Henri.' She indicated the strange pattern under the dresser and he crouched down and looked at it. 'Charlie does things like that,' Kate said in a small voice. 'And these nuggets are the cereal Judith practically lives on . . .'

'So? She has been staying here . . .'

'But there were some of these pieces in his pocket last night.

And on Clive's hands a dusty green colour. The paint on the shutters leaves marks like that on your hands. Yesterday, when he came back with Charlie, I went to him . . .' She shivered.

Henri stood close to her. 'I've had enough of this place. Come outside into the sun and we'll try and talk about it.'

'I can't mention it, can I, Henri? Not to the police. God, I don't want to start anything. I know it's despicable but Charlie is back, he is safe, and I have nothing but ridiculous ideas.'

Henri frowned, locking the door. 'Perhaps it would be better to say nothing yet, Kate. But wait and see . . .' In the car again, driving slowly with the warm day all round them, the light flat and white, he said, 'You are coming back, aren't you, Kate? In September?'

She looked at him. 'Do you think I should stay in London until things are resolved between Clive and myself? Until I've gathered myself together and learned to manage on my own? I'm getting better all the time . . . I'm no longer afraid of missing trains!'

'What does that mean?' He laughed.

'Just that each year helps.'

'I want you to come back for the harvest. Please. In eight weeks' time. After that you can go home and organize yourself if you want to.' He paused, lighting a cigarette awkwardly as he drove. 'I thought, as perhaps you did, that I preferred to love a woman who was not free except in small poignant spaces. Unobtainable. But it's not true, Kate.'

On Tuesday he drove her to Marseilles airport. She had promised to come back and she would. They had been interviewed by the police three times and had not mentioned Kate's secret suspicions.

On the plane Kate sat anticipating London, longing to see Melanie, wondering where Clive would be. Thinking of the future both saddened and excited her but, like Caroline three years earlier, she wanted to make herself complete on her own before she entered another permanent relationship. In the seat next to her a red-haired man watched her, smiled at her, attracted to this sun-tanned girl with the small face and bright blue eyes. He began to talk. Kate talked back and made him laugh.

Judith arrived at her flat on Sunday night, having driven almost straight through, sleeping one night at Dieppe. She found Venn in the bath and the flat like a slum. She was tired and rude and they argued violently and Venn said sulkily that she was leaving soon anyway. She was getting married.

On Monday Judith rang Mosaic and asked for Clive but he wasn't there. All Tuesday she waited. Very nervous for Judith, and he came about seven. She recognized the familiar tread on the stairs. He came in but he did not embrace her. He could not get out of his mind the picture of Judith's face when she said they could not give Charlie back.

He came and sat down. She poured him a drink. She said nothing. Her face was solemn and secretive. Clive began to talk, telling her everything that had happened when he brought Charlie back.

'And you destroyed the package?'

'Yes. And it's the rabbit who is called Judy.'

She laughed, at first shortly and then doubled over with laughter and he laughed too and she was beside him on the sofa. 'And the money?'

'Perhaps I shall try and give it back. I don't know.'

She put her hand on his knee. 'You mustn't act too suddenly, Clive. We are all still recovering.' Her touch did not make him flinch as he had expected. Rather it stirred him. Her cruelty and her determination were part of her fascination and she had, after all, done it for him. And they had succeeded, hadn't they? He touched her face, wearily. She wore her small, pleased smile. He almost asked. 'You wouldn't really have hurt the child, would you?' but he was afraid of her answer, afraid of the truth. He had to love her, whatever she was. There was no one else.

Kate was far removed as was Caroline ... Caroline? He thought again of the little boy and how different life could have been. Judith seemed to read his thoughts.

'How selfish Caroline was,' she said. 'She never considered you at all if, as she claims, Charlie could be your child!'

'She said, it was her child. She said, "It was for me!"'

Judith shrugged. She moved closer to him, putting her arms round him. 'Let's forget them all. It takes a while to adjust to success, to believe it is all finished. Let's think about the money for a while, Clive. It will be so useful ... Her wide mouth touched his.

In September at the end of the grape harvest, Rachel and Ian Finch flew to Provence to find a builder and at long last to begin work on their farmhouse. They were to spend ten days at Jouvard, discussing plans for the conversion and agreeing estimates.

'Kate only left yesterday,' Caroline said. 'She and Henri seem so happy together. She is coming back to spend Christmas, bringing Melanie this time. The separation will be legal by then, I think. It will be lovely for Charlie to have someone to play with although he talks far more now, doesn't he, Rachel?'

'Yes,' Rachel smiled. 'And have they discovered any more about the kidnapping?'

Caroline frowned. 'A lot of funny little things. They seem very determined to pursue it ... I think the Bank of England keeps pushing. Obviously they want to establish that it was a genuine kidnapping and not just an elaborate idea to get the money out of England. Inspector Durande has told Michael that there are plenty of witnesses to Clive's part in it all. He caused rather a stir in the supermarket.' She paused. 'The Inspector told Michael he thinks it strange that Clive should have made himself so obvious. Of course the airlines confirm that Clive went to London and flew back here but he still hasn't come to be interviewed. He is terribly busy, he says. I'm sure he'll come soon. In

344

fact, I think they will make him come. There is something that bothers them a lot. A woman came forward. She used the telephone box which Clive found Charlie in only minutes before Clive arrived. The box was empty then.'

The two women looked at each other, neither of them able to go on with the conversation and all the implications.

On the Finchs' last day they took a picnic to the *mas*, to explain to Caroline and Michael how it would be when it was finished. They carried the basket of food into the walled garden and spread the rug. Caroline took Charlie's hand, leading him to a corner where the blackened stems and great dried heads of some dead sunflowers stood.

'Look, Charlie . . . seeds of the sun,' Caroline said, shaking some into her hands. He stared at them blankly. He pulled at her impatiently, turning and running back towards the house, following Michael and Ian Finch in to the lower room.

'Judy?' he said. 'Ju-dy. Ju-dy. Ju-dy.'